Not as Advertised

Not as Advertised

VIOLET K. AVERY

A Note For Readers

The city of Amado and Almaden University are both fictional locations. For geographical reference purposes, Amado is located approximately forty minutes drive south-west of San Jose, California.

A note on the representation of anxiety in this book: Each person's experience with their mental health is 100% unique. The journey the female main character experiences with chronic anxiety is only meant to represent a *single* voice among millions of individuals.

Please remember that these are real symptoms, experienced by a real person and described on the page to the best of my ability. Please take this into account as you are reading.

If you would like to jump into the book spoiler-free, the contents of the book begin after this page.

If you would prefer to read the Content Warnings first, they are provided at the end of the book.

This book has been professionally edited and proofread. Every effort has been made to make it typo-free. But sometimes, despite our best efforts, typos happen. If you spot a typo, please email me at **info@ violetkavery.com**. It is the best way to ensure it gets corrected.

i used to think that
once i found happiness
the sun would shine
all of the time.
it doesn't.
some days are still dark
but with one difference:
now, there are stars.

SWRPOETRY

This book is dedicated to anyone who has ever been told they are "not enough" or "too much". Or both simultaneously.

Whoever said those things is wrong.

You are a gift.

And I'm so happy you are here.

One

ABBIE

"Abbie, I can't tell you how pleased I am that you applied for the executive assistant position."

I nodded, trying to ignore my nerves that were wound so tightly they made me nauseous but failed miserably. Linda Davis, Appeal Media's head HR manager, beamed at me as we walked toward the main elevators of our office building. But fake it till you make it was the motto of the day.

"I thought it was fabulous that you jumped on the opportunity in the all-hands meeting two weeks ago. I would have hated to see you miss this chance. Can you imagine?"

Yes, I'd imagined it. Missing this chance had been my exact plan.

I found myself in my current predicament by accident. Indie Layne, my best friend and also a colleague, and I had been sitting at the far end of the conference room during the monthly admin team meeting. I was just about to take a sip of my delicious iced coffee when Linda walked in to announce the new position. I'd pretended a sudden fascination with the lid of my cup. Avoiding eye contact was a great way to go unnoticed.

Indie had a different idea as she decided to offer me some not-so-subtle career encouragement in the form of a sharp elbow to the ribs just as I lifted my cup to take a sip. The shock nearly spilled my iced coffee all over the table. In my efforts to save it, I simultaneously scrambled to right the cup with one hand and made a "cheers" motion with the other.

Either way, Linda had interpreted my jumbled limb movements as interest. This tale of woe ends with me being voluntold into a brand-new job.

Having passed on several opportunities over the past few years, I couldn't very well tell Linda the sudden commitment to my career progress had more to do with substandard reflexes than personal ambition.

I had no choice but to show management and HR my dedication to the company. Apparently, that meant showing a desire for career progression. Even if I actually felt no inkling of ambition other than to keep my paycheck.

Flash forward to this moment, and I was about to deal with a whole set of responsibilities I didn't want.

The only thing I knew was that I wouldn't be bringing any drinks, iced or otherwise, to future meetings lest I end up tendering my resignation.

Riding the elevator to the fifth floor, I was a bundle of nerves. But quitting to avoid meeting my new boss and learning a new role? That would have been a life-destroying decision.

Although my three years at Appeal Media may not have been the most thrilling, they certainly gave me the financial security I needed. The general admin team for the smaller accounts was low stress and predictable. My days were filled with mundane tasks like filing, copying materials for meetings, multiple coffee runs, and data entry.

My job had kept me from becoming financially destitute and therefore needing to return to my mother's home in San Jose. Just the thought of having to move back there had a fresh pool of dread forming in my stomach.

When the elevator dinged to signal we'd reached our floor, Linda walked briskly toward the VP's office. I followed with the reluctance of a teenager forced to go to the mall with her parents.

Gah. The closer I got to meeting my new boss, the more the feelings of worry mounted in my stomach. Change was my mortal enemy. Well, change, and buttons on pants, equally. It used up all my mental energy when I had to adapt to new demands.

This moment was no exception. My brain had convinced me that I was doomed to fail before I even started. It was going to be a nightmare. The whole company was going to realize how inept I was, and then I'd be back in my mother's pearl-studded clutches.

My most intrusive thoughts were at it again, searing self-doubt into my consciousness.

Before I could calm down, Linda was knocking on the closed office door before us. I'd been so caught up in my nerves I hadn't registered a single face or detail about my new work area on the walk from the elevator.

"Come in," a low voice called from behind the door.

Facial features quickly rearranged to form an expression that hopefully appeared capable, I was as ready as I'd ever be to face my new boss.

As in, not ready whatsoever.

My body and mind, usually at war with each other, agreed for once. Both thought this was a big mistake.

When we entered the office, Aiden Sullivan was sitting behind his desk, head down. The only thing I'd known about him before this moment was his name. He scrolled through his phone. I realized he was on a call when another voice filled the room.

"Aiden. I wanted to let you know the status of the offer."

"Quinn, tell me you have good news."

Not being able to see his face kept me in a state of agonized suspense. Without seeing his expression, I had no idea what kind of person I was dealing with. The urge to fidget vibrated within me. Or maybe it was to run. Fleeing the scene sounded good right about now.

The parts of Mr. Sullivan I could see screamed luxury, from his dark hair styled artfully back to his crisp dress shirt, rolled at the elbow, that revealed toned forearms. The slightly informal impression his clothes gave off was contradicted by his firm tone of voice and confident posture.

"The deal is done. With the exception of whether the owners leave the furniture," said the disembodied voice on the other end of the line.

"Unnecessary. Please state the property is to be empty. Anything else?"

Whoa. I was shocked by his direct, "no fucks given" kind of tone. Mr. Sullivan sounded like a man who knew exactly what he wanted and would accept nothing less.

My stomach rolled.

The caller must have taken that as the cue that his time was up, but not before he had one last thing to say.

"Nothing. I'll take care of everything."

"Thanks, Quinn."

The call ended, and Mr. Sullivan looked up, and his chocolate-brown eyes met mine.

My stomach plummeted through all five floors of the building below. This was not happening. I couldn't believe it. It was the same man I'd clumsily flirted with at the park yesterday!

I was in the center of Amado's downtown square, working on the latest assignment for the community college photography class I'd given my monthly grocery budget to afford. Photography was my secret passion. I loved the class enough to suffer through thirty days of peanut butter sandwiches in exchange.

I was still struggling to get over my bitterness about having to work overtime for the first time in my three years at my job. I hadn't even met my new boss, but HR had called me this morning saying I absolutely "needed" to proof the new company-wide employee handbook he'd written before Monday morning.

"Hi. You left this over there." I'd been so lost in my thoughts the sound of a voice had me jolting with shock.

My head whipped to the side so quickly that some of my long hair smacked me in the face. Quickly brushing it out of my eyes, I was surprised to find myself face-to-face with a hot stranger. The rich brown of his eyes, with hints of gold around the center, drew me in. His defined cheekbones and jawline were accentuated by the five-o'clock shadow, making him look rugged and handsome even though it was early afternoon. His perfection was almost complete, except for a slight bump in his nose. Maybe he had broken it once upon a time.

Gaping like a fish was probably not the best first impression, so I'd done my best to force my sluggish brain into basic human interaction mode. I hadn't said a word or glanced at the hand he'd been holding up for too long for this moment to be anything but awkward. When I finally got my brain and body in sync, I looked down to see he was holding my lens cap. It must have fallen out of my bag as I scouted the surrounding gardens for the best shots.

"Oh. Um. Thank you!"

Brilliant. Wasn't I just the conversationalist of the year?

The rest of our interaction evaporated into mist as I shook myself out of the memory of how smitten I'd been after spending such a short time talking to him on that bench.

Now, he was standing in front of me expectantly, and I had evidently missed an essential part of this introduction process.

"I'm sorry? I was lost in thought." My cheeks heated with embarrassment at being caught not paying attention.

An indecipherable expression graced his face.

"I said, 'Good morning, Ms. Summers.'"

I stammered a rushed reply. "Uh, erm, yes! Good morning! I mean, it's uh, very nice to meet you, Mr. Sullivan." I shoved my right hand out toward him, hoping he didn't notice it was shaking.

Did I sound as idiotic to him as I did to my own ears?

His warm, dry hand enveloped mine. No nerves for this man. Only one of us was a train wreck.

Hint: that person was not named Aiden Sullivan.

With only the quickest glance over at Linda, his attention snapped back to me. But why? Was he worried that I'd bring up yesterday? God forbid, did he think I'd pick up where we left off at the park and clumsily attempt to hit on him?

Between the nerves swirling in my stomach and the shock of seeing the blindingly hot man from the park again—now my boss because the universe must be just that cruel—the last thing on my mind was anything hookup related. Meeting a stranger I was supposed to work closely with was awkward. But we'd blown straight past awkward into some sort of hurricane of social disaster.

It was official. This was going to be the shortest contract in Appeal's history. This certainly wasn't representative of my professionalism. What kind of faith could he have in my ability to do this job if I didn't have much myself?

Two

AIDEN

I closed my burning eyes and sighed. I'd been hard at work in my new office since 6:30 a.m., and I still hadn't gotten enough done to feel like I was making headway on the pile of to-dos my predecessor had left. This put me in the position of playing catch-up on my first day with the company.

I loathed being out of control, and here I was, starting my first day of the most important role of my career, frantically trying to steer a ship with no map.

One perk of my new office was the coveted "corner office" view. Apparently, I had a magnificent view of the city of Amado and its central square in the distance. Unfortunately, even a couple hours after I'd arrived, there hadn't been one moment to appreciate it.

The irony was I'd have to schedule some time to think about it later. For now, two cups of simply awful coffee and four paper cuts later, I wasn't even sure I was still breathing. I was so focused on getting everything *just right* so no one would question why I'd been hired to do this job.

Jack Blakley, Appeal Media's president and founder, was widely known in the industry as a man who ran his company like a well-oiled machine. And from what I had seen so far, this was true. Jack had taken a chance when he'd hired me. At thirty-six, I was several years younger, and thus less experienced, than most of the applicants for this job. And hiring such an important position from outside the company added even more scrutiny to my transition.

Sure, no one would question Jack to his face, but that wouldn't stop the rumor mill of office gossip present in every corporation.

The pressure was on to prove my worth as Jack's new second-in-command. I would not give anyone ammunition to use against me.

I'd never backed down from a challenge, and I would not start now. Whether it be a fistfight with a neighborhood bully harassing the younger kids or taking the top spot to keep my full-ride scholarship through college, I handled things.

Feeling the strain of the last few hours at my desk, I rolled my shoulders. The tension of the past few weeks had settled at the base of my neck, one of many reminders of what it took to succeed.

Dragging in a deep breath, I looked at the only personal item I'd allowed myself to bring into my new office: the family photo from last Christmas. That was the biggest reminder of why I'd worked so hard to get here.

Leaving my family back in LA wasn't something I'd ever planned to do. My mom, my two younger sisters, and I were a tight-knit group. Mom had done everything she could to provide for us as a single parent. Even though finances were tight, she'd worked hard to ensure we had enough to eat.

Growing up had been far from the idyllic, quaint streets of the midsized city of Amado, which sat outside my window.

After those childhood years of major financial struggle, I was now in the position to make sure my family never wanted for anything. I had a singular focus: ensuring they never had to go through the uncertainty of where they could afford to live or where their next meal was coming from ever again.

That also meant being able to send my youngest sister to the school of choice for her master's in child psychology. I also made monthly contributions to both my niece's college fund so she'd have the same freedoms when she turned eighteen and a retirement investment plan for Mom.

Everything I wanted for my family hinged on the money that came with this job. And, office gossip aside, the real imperative was proving my value to Jack Blakley was the pivotal piece in securing that career-long goal once and for all. The fear of failing had kept me up many nights since I'd accepted this job.

Expecting a call from my Realtor, I checked the time on my phone. It was close to the time HR was due to bring up my new assistant. I'd been counting on being finished with the call before she arrived.

By all accounts, I'd chosen the best person for the job. Other than three years' worth of performance reviews, which stated Abigail Summers was "reserved" and encouraged "her to set goals toward increasing her responsibility within the company," there didn't seem to be any issues with her suitability for the position.

I had no patience for employees that didn't pull their weight. I'd have to monitor how she handled the transition. She wouldn't be the first or last employee to fold under the extra stress of a new role.

With a few minutes to kill, I read over the last version of the house offer my agent had sent back to the sellers the day before. The Spanish-style detached I'd spent the past week negotiating to buy was another step to show my commitment to staying at Appeal for the long term.

As timing would have it, my phone rang just as I'd called out the knock at his office door.

I answered quickly, hopeful of getting off the call as soon as possible so that I could give my full attention to greeting my new assistant. I didn't look up. Instead, I held up a finger to indicate I needed a minute and kept it short and to the point with my agent.

I raised my head after ending the call and was greeted by two people who stood politely before me.

Barely registering Linda's presence, I nearly choked as my attention locked on the young woman from the park. What was she doing here?

I'd arrived in Amado early Friday evening to spend the weekend getting acquainted with some of Appeal's larger accounts. By Sunday afternoon, I'd been going stir-crazy in my hotel room, so I'd headed out to what they called the Square *in the center of town.*

Despite not being the type of person to people-watch, I found my attention drawn to a gorgeous young woman holding a professional-looking camera.

I couldn't help but catalog her appearance, suddenly hungry for any detail that might reveal her secrets to me. Her hair was a stunning blend of blonde and lavender that cascaded down her back in a hypnotic way. She was dressed in a T-shirt with some sort of cat-and-moon cartoon drawing on it, ripped jeans, and a pair of pink Converse my youngest sister would love. Her look screamed college student, making her way too young for my mid thirties self to be this drawn to.

As I was about to walk away from her, I saw something round fall out of her bag as she walked toward the other side of the park. Against my better judgment, I jogged over to snap up her lost item.

I was taken aback but quickly regained my composure and turned to Linda with a smile, hoping to put both at ease.

"Linda. Nice to see you again. Thank you for bringing… Ms.

Summers up." I hoped Linda didn't notice my hesitation in saying the young woman's name. I was scrambling to process my new apparent reality.

"No problem, Mr. Sullivan. Happy to help. You picked an exceptional employee as your new executive assistant. I can assure you."

"It's Aiden, please."

Slowly, I stood up from behind the desk, trying to regain my bearings. The sweet face that had kept me company last night was no longer anonymous, and the reality of her presence completely messed with my head. This shouldn't be happening.

I couldn't believe my luck when I found out she wasn't a student, but I'd spent the whole evening kicking myself for not asking for her number yesterday. I couldn't resist picturing spending more time with her, even though I didn't have the time or desire for a relationship. I had to keep my very real attraction to her under wraps, knowing she was still too young for me. I didn't want to be that guy.

The woman in front of me looked so different from her appearance at the park. Gone was the cartoon T-shirt, ripped jeans, and casual shoes. They were replaced with a plain white blouse and a fitted knee-length skirt. Her clothes did nothing to hide her curves. No matter what she was wearing, her body commanded my attention as much as her face did. A generous chest and hips made my blood heat.

At the park, her long blonde hair had flowed over her shoulders and down her back, changing into a light purple at the bottom. Now, there was only the barest hint of color, tied up at the base of her neck.

She was just as beautiful as she was yesterday, but the difference in her expression was startling. Her eyes were a stunning mix of browns and greens, and her skin had a soft pink hue.

Less than twenty-four hours ago, her eyes had sparkled when she mentioned taking a photography class, and her cheeks were flushed with what I'd hoped was mutual attraction. It was a moment I'd never forget.

She'd been so focused on looking through her camera lens when I found her sitting on a bench on the opposite side of the park.

"Hi. You left this over there." I'd spoken softly so I wouldn't startle her.

Mission failed. Her hair whipped to the side so quickly that it smacked her in the face, and I'd surprised her despite my good intentions.

I held up her lens cap, waving it lightly. My unexpected approach must have shocked her because she had just stared at me for a moment. Not that I minded. She was even more beautiful up close. I spent those precious few seconds committing her creamy skin and hazel eyes to memory.

"Oh. Um. Thank you!" She took the lens cap from my hand.

I wondered if she felt the same electric charge between us when our fingers briefly brushed.

"No problem. Are you a photography student?" I surprised myself this time by sitting down on the opposite end of the bench. Obviously, I wasn't making wise choices this afternoon.

"Not really. I'm taking a class. But it's just for fun. I have a full-time job that kinda gets in the way. Gotta pay the bills, you know?" There was a sour note to her voice when she spoke about her job.

I was curious about what she did for a living that seemed to have stolen the sparkle from her eyes and brought an expression of resignation to her face.

"Don't I know it," I said. "I moved here for a job as well. What are you taking pictures of today?"

I wanted to bring that smile back to her gorgeous lips. But before I could engage her further, a cheerful voice called, "Hey! Sorry I'm late!" from behind us.

"A friend of yours?" I asked.

"Oh, yes. Sorry. That's why I'm here. To meet my friend so she can help

me with my photography assignment."

"Ah, I see. I'll leave you to it." Her friend's interruption was the catalyst I needed to do what I should have done from the start. Leave this girl alone and not get drawn into my attraction.

Now, that chemistry we'd had felt like a curse. A specter hanging over the good fortune of my only hours-old job.

Her eyes locked onto mine with a mixture of disbelief and a clear case of nerves. A rosy hue in her cheeks hinted she might be embarrassed.

I managed a greeting and dismissal of Linda that went right over Abigail's head. I moved to shake her hand, but it took her a minute to snap out of her trance and offer me a stilted hello.

Linda's departure left a vacuum of silence behind in her wake.

"Please sit." I gestured toward one of the chairs in front of my desk. The distinct pressure inside urged me to take the chair beside her. Luckily, my brain was still in the driver's seat and insisted I maintain a safe distance. Even having the office door closed felt illicit.

"Thank you, Mr. Sullivan," she said as she sat stiffly.

With the tension ratcheted up in the room, she acted like she was about to be reprimanded in the principal's office. *Fuck, brain. Do. Not. Go. There.*

I cleared my throat and buried that image deep. Unfortunately, the magma at the center of the Earth wasn't deep enough to wipe that thought from my mind. Fighting the urge to yank on my collar for some extra oxygen, I got straight to the point.

"We should probably clear the air, right, Abigail?"

Abigail nodded, looking like she needed me to steer the conversation.

"Meeting you at the park yesterday was a nice surprise. I enjoyed your clear enthusiasm for photography. But let's start with a clean slate, okay? I don't want any misunderstandings between us, professionally speaking."

"Mr. Sullivan." I couldn't think about the pleasant cadence of her voice when she said my name. It sounded too good to my ears. "Please call me Abbie. And I totally get it. We are going to be working together."

I didn't tell *her* to call me Aiden. I left that wall of formality between us. I wouldn't be calling her Abbie anytime soon either. It was too familiar.

I nodded as if the matter was closed. If only it were that easy. The jagged edges left behind by this messed-up situation felt anything but resolved. Regardless, I needed to push forward.

"Though you haven't held a senior admin role at Appeal, I was impressed by the dedication you have displayed in your time here. I have no doubt that your exceptional work ethic is the reason you were chosen for this position, and I am confident that you will rise to the challenge of this new role."

Shit. In an effort to sound unaffected by her presence, I couldn't help but think my tone came across as overly gruff and impatient. I felt a pang of sympathy as she curled in on herself, and I couldn't help but wince at her discomfort.

A quick dip of her chin indicated her understanding once again. I felt for her that this unfortunate coincidence was daunting in a different way than it was to me. Yesterday, she revealed a more open and vulnerable side of herself. It felt a bit cruel to shove that under the rug and pretend indifference to the clear chemistry we'd experienced.

"On your desk, you will find everything you need to get set up. I've also emailed you several documents listing specific requirements for your role, a link to my calendar, and a rundown of the information I require you to report to me each morning. Those reports are due by 8:00 a.m. Every day. Without exception. Spend the day getting acquainted with these requirements. I expect your first daily update tomorrow morning."

Unable to have her in my office a moment longer, I turned my body back toward my computer in dismissal. I received another nod from my new assistant before she got up and left the room, hardly making any noise.

I couldn't help but let my head fall into my hands as soon as I heard the door close behind her.

You cannot afford to fuck this up. You can't expect everything to be smooth sailing out of the gate. One woman, who is way *too young for you, is not going to derail what you've spent the last decade and a half working for, no matter how attractive you find her. Remember the reason you're here. And it's not to get laid.*

I simply wouldn't allow myself to be distracted. I just needed to keep a running reminder at the forefront of my mind of what I was here for.

Three

ABBIE

Back at my desk, I surveyed what looked like a color-coded old-school encyclopedia full of materials, courtesy of my new boss. Despite its crazy number of pages, I couldn't drum up any suitable feelings of procrastination when my mind was still spinning from a full Dr. Jekyll/Mr. Hyde moment in Aiden's office.

How could he flip a switch like that? Where was the compelling man I'd met in the park? A wall had come down over his eyes, like he'd wiped the connection I'd felt yesterday from his memory. His stoicism and a cold kind of formality replaced what felt like real interest on his part. I was a world-renowned terrible judge of attraction from men (or I would be if I'd ever had the guts to say anything about it aloud).

I was dying to call Linda and beg her to pick someone else for this job. My hand muscles were cramped with the urge to pick up my phone.

The anxiety churning in my stomach was almost unbearable, but being dismissed like that was the final straw. I wanted nothing more than to run home and hide in bed. My books and blankets never judged me. My rescue cat, Mew, always did, but that was his imperative as self-appointed master of the universe.

I was so desperate to leave that the pain of staying seated was unbearable. My instincts were telling me to get away from the discomfort of the situation. Whatever those fear synapses in my brain were called, they were firing on all cylinders.

My bank balance was the only thing that kept me from fixing this huge mistake.

A flood of negative emotions overwhelmed me. Those thoughts now hit a lot more like "truths" than worries.

You completely imagined that connection with him yesterday.

How could you think he was attracted to you?

Flirting? Don't be naïve.

That debacle of a meeting was completely embarrassing.

So much for your "fake it till you make it" motto.

The barrage of self-doubt held me completely paralyzed. I was supposed to start reading this tome of an EA manual, curated specifically for my role, and I couldn't even open the cover.

I hated this. I let my head drop forward in defeat. For the millionth time in my life, I lamented the need to constantly fight my brain just to be able to do things that seemed normal for everyone else.

Unable to stay here any longer, I aimed another glance at Aiden's office to make sure his door was still closed and texted Indie.

Abbie

Listen, I will forgive you for making me grow as a human being if you get coffee with me right NOW.

Indie

I'll just remind you once again that all I

did was give you a *literal* nudge in the right direction. That said, to what do I owe this unexpectedly generous offer? (I accept, by the way).

Abbie

I can't even type out the dumpster fire that happened this morning. But I need you to tell me that I can get through it.

Indie

Of course you will get through it. You always do, remember? And if not, I'll hire a hitman to solve your problem.

Abbie

Violence is not the answer. See you in five.

Indie

You're right. It probably isn't. Then again, while I was tutoring on Friday, I heard some kid at the community center say it was "the solution." On my way.

Abbie

Thank you. PS: I'm not sure that's a reliable source of advice.

A quick elevator ride later had me waiting in line to buy our caffeine injections, aka Barista Dean's epic café mochas. I felt a pair of arms circle me from behind. Indie's warm vanilla scent wafted into my nose, and a small smile formed on my lips for the first time that day.

Indie would have some sage advice to help me get through this morning's crisis. And even if Indie didn't have anything useful to say, she'd always have some juicy office gossip so I could forget myself for a little while.

"Sooooo, tell me, what's the emergency, Abs? I thought being way up on the fifth floor was going to be awesome, even if you were holding out on being mad at me like a champ."

Indie came around to face me as the line inched forward (Dean's masterpieces could not be rushed). Covering my face with my hands, I tried to gather the right words to explain what I was feeling. I dropped my voice to a whisper, hovering somewhere just above a dog's hearing range.

"Oh my god, Indie. It's such a disaster. I didn't tell you because I was hung up on being annoyed, but yesterday, when Emery met me at the park, I was talking to this really hot guy."

I peeked through my fingers at her, expecting the interrogation to begin immediately since I never brought up guys.

"What? This is serious business. I can't believe you let a silly little thing like me ruining your perfect bubble of predictability on the admin support team get in the way of hearing the news about a hot guy. It's been a literal ice age since you went out with someone." Indie tried putting on her best innocent, wide-eyed pout. The effect was lessened, however, by the cheeky expression that broke out over her face.

I dropped my arms back to my sides. Indie's signature snark was too irresistible to keep up any pretense of being annoyed. It wasn't her fault I turned being clumsy into an art form.

"Please refrain from calling any news outlets. It was like a five-minute conversation. This is not a national news story."

"It's close," Indie said with a wink. "Let's deal with the immediate crisis that brought us to our second coffee before noon. Then you can tell me the good stuff."

Knowing that there were too many ears capable of eavesdropping on what I was about to say, I hesitated. The thought of someone else in the company finding out about my personal hell was too much for me.

"I will. It's just… Let's get our drinks first and get out of the crowd." I got more uncomfortable by the second, hating the idea of drawing any attention to myself.

Nothing to see here, folks.

So that was what we did. After paying Dean for his works of art, we found a tree several steps away from the Appeal building to lean against. Even though it'd been less than ten minutes, Indie was anxious for me to spill all the details.

"Okay. You need to talk now. I am not designed for this level of patience."

Completely untrue, but I let that slide. She may want gossip like she worked as a paparazzi for a living, but there wasn't anyone else I knew as fiercely willing to hold out for what she wanted than Indie.

I couldn't help the pained expression that took over my features. The words I had to say tasted sour in my mouth.

"Fine. So you're lucky. You don't have to wait on the 'good stuff' about the guy from yesterday because my new boss *is* the guy from yesterday!"

Indie's expression had me tempted to pull out my phone to capture her in a rare moment of speechlessness. She opened her mouth once, twice, before she was able to form words.

I had to admit feeling a little smug that I'd shocked my friend, who was the epitome of calm. Too bad the disaster was mine.

"Damn, Abs. Aiden Sullivan is incredibly hot. Like, supernaturally so. I was going to ask you to sneak a mirror into his office to see if he had a reflection. And you talked to him out of nowhere yesterday?"

"My god. You looked up his picture already?"

"Seriously, who do you think took his photo for his ID badge?"

Indie said. Easy for her to focus on his looks as someone who hadn't experienced the whiplash of yesterday vs. today's Mr. Sullivan. "He's got a hot daddy look about him. So bossy."

My face heated to the approximate temperature of the sun's surface. "Do not ever call him that again. I need a brain bleach now. All I know is he couldn't get me out of his office fast enough this morning. And I'm going to be working directly under him."

"Babe, I wouldn't mind being under him at alllllll." Indie waggled her eyebrows and winked at me.

"Shit. You're doing this on purpose!" I wanted to hide my face again but managed to stop myself. Indie's response was a smile and a shrug.

Scandalized, I looked around to see if anyone had overheard her. Everyone nearby seemed to be absorbed by their phones or were chatting with other people, but I couldn't help feeling embarrassed. When I looked back at my friend, Indie's expression was completely unconcerned, not caring what people thought. I felt as though we were having this conversation via a megaphone.

"Indie! You are not helping," I muttered. "I have to look this man in the eye every day. And you can't go around saying stuff like that in the office."

"Whatever you say, Abs. But for a man that handsome, I'd break a few hundred rules. But enough wishful thinking for me. What really happened?"

I'd never admit out loud that Indie's outrageous comments were just what I needed. My muscles were already relaxing, tense from stress and nerves. The riot of anxiety in my stomach had gone from crisis mode to higher-than-usual discomfort. The shock of Indie's unrepentant opinion was an effective distraction.

"It wasn't like I did anything. I was working on a photography assignment for that class I'm taking for fun. Next thing I know, he sits down on the bench next to me and hands me my lens cap."

This was the part of the story where Emery, the third member of our trio, melted into a puddle of swoon when I told her what she had interrupted at the park. Indie was more mercenary than that. She never stopped until she had all the details.

"So he was definitely interested," Indie said while she lifted her hand like a stop sign. "Don't start. He was interested. It's a fact. We're not going down the 'he was just being nice' rabbit hole because if he wasn't, he wouldn't have sat down. Period. Go on."

"He gave me my lens cap and started asking me questions about my photography."

Indie gave me a look that said, "See? Interested!" before I could continue. "Then this morning, Linda and I walked into the VP's office, and it's the hot stranger from yesterday! I basically blacked out for the introductions before realizing he was talking to me. I looked like an idiot in front of him."

Indie rested a comforting hand on my shoulder, giving it a small squeeze in sympathy before letting it fall back by her side.

"Yeah, that totally sucks. So he was a jerk to you?" The idea had Indie frowning. She had major mama bear instincts and would call out anyone who hurt her friends.

Shaking my head, I tried to explain the sinking feeling I got the longer he spoke to me.

"Not a jerk, per se. But it was like talking to a totally different person. He said we had to put yesterday aside, and that was it. It wasn't so much what he said as how he said it. Like he was irritated or inconvenienced or insinuating it was my fault somehow that we were in this situation, even though he was the one who approached me. It was just jarring that he might think I would act unprofessionally."

Indie pressed her lips together in thought. For all her cheekiness, she was a deep thinker who was careful about what she said when it mattered. I could tell Indie didn't want to upset me further, no doubt thinking about the anxiety spiral I was going down. But she wasn't going to lie to me to make me feel better.

Realizing I'd chewed the edge off my thumbnail while I waited for her response, I had to consciously pull my hand away from my mouth. Instead, I gripped the fabric of my skirt at my side.

"Okay. I can see how it feels really awkward now," Indie said slowly. "What do you want to do?"

"I want to go back upstairs, type up my resignation letter, and drop it off at Linda's office so I never have to see Mr. Sullivan again."

I gave her my best pleading, hopeful look so she might agree with my totally irresponsible plan of running away from this situation.

"Cool. So unemployment is the answer. I guess you can stay with me for a while. But what happens when you run out of money?" Her tone was patient and calm. She nodded for me to keep going, encouraging me to purge my worries. Sometimes, no matter how little sense it made, it helped to just get the words out.

This was not Indie's first rodeo with my anxiety. I had a bit of savings. But between rent and other living expenses, plus paying back my student loans, there was a reason I'd held on so tightly to my job at Appeal.

It might seem hard for someone who'd had a family they could count on, but I would never live at home again. The toxicity of living with my mother's emotional manipulation until I was eighteen had taken so much "normal" away from me. Constantly being told I was too sensitive, never being able to meet her ever-changing expectations, being denied the right to feel my own feelings was too much for me to bear ever again.

I had to do everything in my power to avoid a situation where I put myself back under my mother's passive-aggressive thumb. Where she could grind me into dust with every look of disapproval, sigh of disappointment, micro-aggressive and blatant denial of me as a person. All because I couldn't become another version of herself she'd always wanted to mold me into.

Even knowing where Indie was going with this, I couldn't stop myself as I spewed out my worst nightmare version of this scenario.

"That's easy. I overstay my welcome at your place and ruin our friendship forever. Then I have to go home to San Jose to live with my mother and stepfather. I'll be under my mother's influence again, which means that I'll have to give up Mew because she's allergic. I'll go back to having my life picked apart daily because I'm a disappointment as a daughter. Arthur will give me some job in his company to keep me busy as she forces me to date a series of horrible men until I just don't care about anything anymore other than pleasing her."

It wasn't like I would implode my entire life or anything. Clearly, nor was I dramatic in the slightest.

But that was the thing about anxiety. My brain could know something was true, but my soul and body couldn't feel it. It was terrifying.

"Well, that sounds about perfect, doesn't it? It'll be like the last seven years of your life didn't happen. So should I make up the couch for you tonight?"

I had to laugh. Indie was so committed to letting me catastrophize out loud. It was hard to fathom how she kept a straight face at this point. I loved how normal her cheekiness made me feel.

Most of the time, I had to work hard to keep my anxiety hidden from others. But not with Indie and Emery, and that was such a gift.

"No. That's okay," I muttered.

"Wait. What are you going to do, then?" Indie said. Her smile was feline, and her eyes were alight with humor. She tilted her head to the side as if she was genuinely mystified about what my answer would be.

"I'm going to go back into that *stupid* building and figure out how to do this *stupid* new job."

Petulance bled through my tone because I hated acting reasonable when my emotions were so mixed up. It was not as if I was an adult or something.

"Good idea. It's one of my many missions in life to keep us from falling back into our parents' clutches." Indie had her own family issues that she dealt with.

Indie put her arm around my shoulders and gently guided me back into the front of the building. Giving Indie a limp wave as she returned to reception, I headed to the elevators.

Uncertainty made its reappearance in my stomach the whole ride up to the fifth floor. My only consolation was that I'd been dismissed from Aiden's presence until tomorrow. I would try my damnedest to lose myself in the company of the EA manual nearly the size of *The Iliad* for the rest of the day.

Four

ABBIE

The expression "a comedy of errors" could describe my new role as an executive assistant. The problem being there was nothing funny about it.

It was all errors.

The first few days of working for Aiden were a steep learning curve, mostly because he seemed to be a machine. I couldn't help thinking of him as Aiden, even if I only ever called him Mr. Sullivan.

His ultra-organized work habits meant that I knew what was expected of me at any given time (if I didn't, I could reference the compendium of all knowledge, my trusty sidekick—the EA manual). Predictability was allegedly to be my sweet spot, but even knowing what was coming wasn't stopping me from making new mistakes and then scrambling to fix them before Aiden noticed. But there was no solace in being able to predict that I would screw up my next task, day after day.

Even a week later, I didn't feel any closer to being able to meet his demands, despite them being written down in nearly fifteen-minute increments. I hadn't even managed to prepare an adequate cup of coffee yet.

I was unsure as to why I expected anything different at this point. It was day seven of working for Aiden, and I stood in his office and waited for the latest coffee critique, hopeful that I'd finally gotten it right.

He eyed me over the rim of the cup as he sipped. My nerves were on fire from anticipating his reaction and struggling not to drop my gaze.

"Hmm, too much milk today. And there's some sort of burnt undertone. Are you sure you cleaned it properly yesterday?" He got these little crinkles in the skin next to his eyes when he half squeezed them shut in displeasure.

More than once, I'd considered asking him to show me how to make his coffee, but that seemed to be the rock bottom I wasn't willing to hit yet. He might drive me to it one of these mornings.

I had also wondered if this was some sort of high-level corporate initiation ritual. And one day, Aiden would just laugh and say, "Ha! Well done. Welcome to the club!" while suddenly transforming back into the man who smiled warmly at me in the park that day. Wishful thinking on my part.

My opinion of Aiden's personality had not improved over the past seven working days either. The fact that I still knew how many days had passed since I started this new position meant time was passing slowly.

It wasn't like counting down to Christmas or a tropical vacation. It was tallying up the days I'd survived without getting fired.

Gah. Personal growth was for perfectly tailored, aesthetically pleasing Instagram posts. Out here in the wilds of real life, it was all bumps and bruises.

And I had enough of those for a trip to the ER at this point.

Though I had spent my first week mostly isolated in my desk

bubble, the few interactions I'd seen Aiden have with other employees showed that no one else seemed as intimidated by him as I was.

Every morning, after his disappointing coffee and my stilted daily update, he made the rounds of the floor. He made sure to be available if anyone had questions or needed a quick approval of a concept. On the other hand, it felt like he was checking up on my ability to condense the reports I received from each team on their status, which made me nervous.

I could not figure him out.

Today, however, was the first senior all-hands department meeting. I had been excused from my morning routine to ensure the meeting room was ready.

It would be my first real opportunity to see how the rest of the staff reacted to Aiden. I only wished Indie had been required to attend so I'd have an objective perspective to rely on. *Sigh*. I was on my own.

The main benefit of being first at the meeting was my chance to sit in a completely impractical seat at an awkward angle to the room. I hazarded my best guess at where Aiden would want to sit and then picked the opposite side of the large conference table.

With my seat claimed, all I had to do was wait for everyone else to file in. As people took their seats, there was a lot less chatter than I was used to from other meetings. The junior teams' meetings downstairs were full of chatter and not-so-whispered gossip.

I had no idea if this was normal with the most senior teams. I suspected everyone was just nervous about the new boss.

Aiden came into the room a full five minutes early. I didn't glance up from my notebook to see his expression at my seating choice.

He won't even care where you sit, my inner voice chimed in. *He has way more important things to think about than what you're doing with your day.*

When the last chair was filled at 9:59 a.m., Aiden cleared his throat and stood. No one spoke. The nervous anticipation in the room had my pulse thudding my ears.

Grateful that my only role here was to take the minutes, I noted the time in my notebook. I was just as interested as anyone in the room, maybe more because of how our interactions had gone, about what Aiden was going to be like as a leader.

The group was not kept in suspense.

"Good morning. Thank you, everyone, for being on time. I've met most of you informally over the past couple of days. But for those of you who don't know me, my name is Aiden Sullivan, and I've been brought on as the new VP of marketing. I know many of you have been promoted into new roles, and we are all in quite an adjustment period. I want you to know that everyone in this room has been selected personally by me, based on your history here at Appeal, as well as your annual performance reviews."

He was magnetic in how confidently he spoke. His deep voice resonated throughout the room, making me shiver with its low timbre.

Glancing around to see if he had the same effect on anyone else in the room, I saw a few members of the various teams looking at him appraisingly. Even as clueless as I was in the dating world, I saw that more than a few women and men found him attractive.

It went beyond his looks, though. There was no denying how appealing he was in his effortless ability to command everyone's attention.

A wave of discomfort flowed through me. Why should I care if other people found him appealing? He was objectively hot. I was his EA, nothing more. It shouldn't bother me. Even if I could admit that I hadn't fully shaken my physical attraction to him, regardless of his exacting standards, that made me question my competence for this job.

Mentally shaking myself, I forced my attention back to the task at hand. Phillip Kane, the senior head of accounting, was laying out the current financials and future projections for Aiden. He nodded along as Phillip spoke about department budgets. Phillip's assistant, Anne Sun, made notes and then passed documents to him as he spoke. Aiden looked like this was all old news to him, so I took a quick look around the room again.

As Phillip presented some pretty hardline department budgets, I noted how the various heads were taking the news. Sheryl Mann from print media was pissed, her lips tight and losing color. Likely, she had been expecting more, but even I knew Appeal was deep-diving into digital ads these days. Ethan Wilde, head of the digital arts team, looked confident and unsurprised—he must have figured Phillip, who was conservative by nature, would try to impress the new boss with his fiscal due diligence. Jean Pascal, one of the main copy editors, was totally disinterested in the update, maybe because he knew their budget was protected.

Phillip had nearly wrapped up his portion of the meeting when Aiden asked him about advertising subsidies for nonprofits. Phillip waved that away as if it were irrelevant. Traditionally, Appeal chased mid- to larger-sized corporate contracts, which were guaranteed income streams.

"Uh, well, Aiden, Appeal hasn't ventured very far into investigating what state and federal grants are available to the NGOs at this point, but…"

Aiden cut him off. Shuffling through his papers, he pulled out a list.

"Interesting, Phillip, because it says here in last quarter's financial rundown that we'd made four different proposals to nonprofits to increase their public presence. Not only that, but we're forecasting a 15 percent uptick in revenue in this area for the current fiscal year due to the extra goodwill exposure provided in subsidizing these nonprofit's campaigns. That is nothing short of remarkable. How are they not more of a budget focus?"

Phillip's eyes widened. Anne discreetly passed a note over to Phillip. Looking down, he tried to recover from the situation.

"Oh yes, that's right, I did have a micro team investigating the nonprofit section, mostly for tax benefits, you see. It's very unlikely to be a viable path to pursue…"

Anne's eyes closed, and she took a small breath, which did not go unnoticed by Aiden.

"Ms. Sun, it seems like you might have something to add. Please do." His tone left no room for argument as Phillip floundered.

"Mr. Sullivan, there's nothing for her to add, as an assistant…"

Aiden wasn't having it. Ignoring Phillip, he focused solely on Anne.

"Anne, please share any additional information you have on this topic."

Others around the table shifted nervously.

Anne cleared her throat. "Well, Mr. Sullivan…"

"Aiden, please."

"Right, Aiden. Well, you see, Grace and I"—she nodded to another member of the accounting team—"saw that many of the larger corporations had allocated more funds to partnering up with nonprofits. We wanted to see if there were true partnerships being formed or if it was only lip service to please the public."

Anne launched into an eloquent and succinct explanation of how Appeal could offer several plans to help nonprofits to incentivize corporate partnerships and promote industry change while simultaneously building Appeal's own brand.

I saw a few mouths open and shut around the table. From my experience filling in for other assistants a few times in the smaller account team meetings, it was unusual for someone other than the heads of departments to speak at meetings. And here was Anne, making a full pitch.

When she finished, Aiden's eyes warmed with something like admiration. He congratulated her on her ingenious efforts. It was the first time I'd seen his expression as anything other than ruthlessly calm since that first afternoon at the park. The emotion in his eyes made him even more unfairly devastating to look at. A pang of regret struck me since fate had decided I'd never had the chance to know the Aiden Sullivan I'd met that Sunday afternoon.

Anne took the praise humbly like the rock star she apparently was while also emphasizing how Grace was equally deserving of any credit.

I shifted in my seat uncomfortably. Over the past several days, I'd forced my inconvenient attraction to him deep into the back of my mind. Surviving Aiden was necessary, and I couldn't do that if I allowed myself any real feelings for him.

He was complimenting Anne openly in front of the entire floor. His reaction to Anne's clearly excellent work had me sinking lower in my chair. Here she was, getting positive feedback when I couldn't even get a cup of coffee right. I could admit to feeling a bit jealous of the praise.

I also didn't want my opinion of Aiden to change. Cutting through the hierarchical bullshit of corporate culture gave him too many "good guy" points.

I needed him to stay firmly in the dislike column, despite how gorgeous he was. The less I liked him, the less I had to juggle emotionally. I wasn't equipped to handle an unrequited crush and to be resilient enough to make it through this period where I made all kinds of professional mistakes.

That kind of pressure was too overwhelming and made me want to shut down mentally. Sometimes, when things felt like too much to deal with, my feelings trended toward numbness rather than the discomfort of feeling so many things at once.

Of course, because I had unusually bad luck, Aiden chose that moment to glance from Anne over to me, that lingering warmth still in his eyes. Locked in his stare, I couldn't look away. His eyes narrowed just slightly, and something intense sharpened his gaze. But he blinked and smoothed his face into his usual stern expression. His focus might have only been trained on me for a microsecond, but it had my stomach clenching and my body frozen in a mess of emotions.

"Abigail, can you please add an NGO forecast review to my Friday schedule?"

I nodded woodenly, trying to relax my shoulders, which had risen toward my ears under his scrutiny. Had I done something that annoyed him for that warmth to change into a look of something else? Now I was worried I'd made mistakes in my summary of Anne and Grace's report. Everything Anne had just said tracked with my work. I couldn't figure out what had put that look on his face.

The rest of the meeting ran smoothly, despite the excitement of the beginning. No one else wanted to get on his shit list. And Aiden seemed to respect everyone's time as much as he did his own—which was rare in my experience with management. Nope, nope, nope. I wasn't going to like him.

As people started leaving, Aiden moved quietly over to Phillip and pulled him to the side. Trying to make myself as unobtrusive as possible while tidying the table, I strained to hear what he had to say to Phillip. Apparently, Indie's nosiness was contagious.

"Listen, Phillip, I'm not a man to look to for second chances. I want to be clear with you. I'm not at all interested in how things 'have worked in the past,' nor am I concerned with who good ideas come from. I am someone who expects his senior employees to put their own egos aside and give credit where credit is due. Regardless of your personal ambitions, I expect that evidence-based leads will be pursued and reported. You've got one more shot to show me you can adapt, otherwise, I'll be pushing Jack to offer early retirement. You get me?"

"Yes, sir." Phillip was doing his best to appear in control, but he was clearly angry, and they both knew it.

It was awkward to be in the room while they talked, but the nosey part of me secretly loved it. I hated when someone's hard work had been overlooked or dismissed.

To his credit, Aiden didn't gloat but offered Phillip a firm handshake and walked him to the door.

As Phillip headed out of the doorway, I fought a smile at Phillip's retreating figure. There was no denying that I'd enjoyed his dressing-down. I didn't care if that made me petty.

Recycling the last lot of leftover papers from the table and tossing a few rogue coffee cups in the compost bin, I gathered up my laptop and notebook to head back to my desk to type up the official minutes.

When I looked up from the table, I saw Aiden leaning against the doorframe. Confused as to why he wasn't already back in his lair, surprise tracked its way through my body when he didn't move aside to let me exit.

"Abigail, a moment. Show me your minutes from the meeting."

I clutched my notebook closer to my chest. My notes were not for his consumption. They were a cross between meeting minutes and a high schooler–style gossip. I couldn't even remember what I'd doodled in the margins. Just the thought of all my comments on everyone's reactions had me embarrassed and off-balance.

"Um, Mr. Sullivan. My initial minutes are very rough. Almost illegible, honestly. I'd rather take them back to my desk and forward you a typed copy within the hour."

"I didn't ask you what you preferred. I said to hand them over. Now, please." He narrowed his eyes. Damn, those displeased eye crinkles were back.

Shit. He had a stern professor vibe going. Fighting the urge to squirm, I handed over my notebook quickly, hoping he wouldn't see my arm trembling.

I was absolutely not attracted to this alpha-hole attitude thing.

Lies. I totally was. Why did he have this effect on me?

And why couldn't I put his behavior just now in the asshole boss column?

Careful not to grab it anywhere near where I held it, he took the notebook and flipped through the pages until he got to today's meeting. He scanned the minutes, not saying anything. His eyebrows arched a few times as he read through my writing.

Nerves kept my body rigid as he read, fighting the urge to fidget while I waited for him to find whatever he was looking for. He could rattle me, but I didn't have to let him know it.

Finally, after an eternity, which might have been two minutes, he handed the notebook back with a completely neutral expression.

"Very interesting. Once you're back at your desk, type up the minutes and send them to me for formal approval before sending them out to the team. Then, you will give me your handwritten notes for my reference. This goes for all future meetings as well, understood?"

"But Mr. Sullivan, I really think that the typed minutes will be much more..." My mouth clamped shut with his interruption.

"Abigail, I'll stop you there. I'll let you know what I need, and I require your handwritten copy. Remind me whose assistant you are?"

"Yours, sir." There was nothing else to say. I had no idea why he wanted them, but this wasn't the hill I was going to die on.

There was a hill made of coffee beans for that.

My words had his jaw tightening and eyes darkening before he shook whatever emotion he was feeling away. What had I done now? He hadn't left me any opportunity to disagree.

I edged toward the opposite side of the doorway, hoping he would get the hint and release me. No such luck.

"Tell me one more thing. What was so amusing to you during the meeting?"

His eyes never left mine as he surprised me with the question, like a naughty student caught cheating on a test. Oh god, what was with him today? I had no experience being called out like this. His penetrating gaze left no room to lie.

"It was great to see Phillip put in his place. A couple times at lunch, I've heard his team gossip about him pushing his own agenda. Anne did great work, and he was wrong to ignore that."

I slapped a hand over my mouth. I had blurted out my thoughts without filtering them first. It wasn't my place to criticize a senior team member. Yikes. What was it about this man that allowed him to get under my skin so easily?

Trying to recover, I ducked my head and tried to move past him, but he took up even more of the doorway. Unless I wanted to brush against him, I had no clear path to exit the room.

He leaned down to catch my gaze. Looking away, I was not keen to listen to the dressing-down that was coming. I had been out of line, and we both knew it.

"Abigail."

Ugh. He insisted on calling me by my full name, despite me telling him to call me Abbie. Even though I'd been irritated at first that he'd ignored my request, the authority in his tone made my stomach erupt in butterflies. His commanding aura was annoyingly hot.

One word. My name said in his deep tone of voice was all it took to have my cheeks heating furiously. Embarrassment and arousal swirled inside me.

"I'm so sorry. I shouldn't have said that." I couldn't hold eye contact with him any longer.

"You're correct, Abigail. You shouldn't have."

My shoulders slumped. I felt deflated because he wasn't going to let it slide. Why had he asked me if he didn't want to hear what I had to say? Unless he wanted me to get myself into trouble so he had something negative to use against me?

"However, in this case, you are right about Phillip. I can't stand it when an employee takes credit when it doesn't belong to them. Keep yourself out of the office gossip, though. Your involvement in that kind of thing will only hurt you in the long run. It's clear you're going places—don't let anything get in the way of that. That is, if we can get the coffee situation sorted out."

I thought I saw him wink before immediately schooling his expression.

Before I could reply, he turned on his heel and walked back toward his office. I stood there, stunned for a moment. For the second time in as many hours, he had surprised me by the way he reacted to a situation.

Had he actually made a joke?

How could he go from avoidant overlord to supportive boss in just a morning? What was going on with Aiden Sullivan?

Five

AIDEN

She was going to kill me. There was no other outcome for this situation. I could not be in the same room with Abigail Summers for more than ten minutes without getting worked up.

As the days passed, I realized her effect on my body and mind was not lessening. I'd fought to separate myself from her as much as possible, only in close proximity to her during the morning briefings and in essential meetings, determined to harden myself against how much I wanted her.

Oh, you're hard all right. I shut that inappropriate thought down quickly.

Perhaps if I had only been attracted to her on a physical level, the situation might have been manageable.

But while her beauty captured my interest, her genuine goodness held it. A day didn't go by where I didn't see an example of Abigail going above and beyond what the average person might do. I knew she was struggling with some areas of the job, but she showed her determination by sticking with a task until she figured it out.

More than once, I'd wanted to come to her rescue. To spare her the discomfort or disappointment of making a mistake or having to redo something. But before I figured out a way to help her without making it seem like I was micromanaging her, she'd searched out her own solution by asking another team member for clarification or through more trial and error.

She had impressed me with her work ethic, not through perfection but with effort. And that was usually difficult to do.

Then, to make matters worse, I kept finding out new things I enjoyed about her. Even just the other morning, she'd surprised me with the spine she showed when she called out Phillip's behavior after the meeting. Though she came across as introverted, she had moments where she was much more expressive.

My problem was that my willpower was built on reservations I'd had before learning more about her. I was her boss, first and foremost. I needed to make the right decision and stay away from her for both our sakes.

The ethical issue aside, I had been certain the age difference between us was a major obstacle just by itself. She was only a few years into her career, only just starting to see some real progression and potential for growth. Abigail was in her midtwenties, and I was ashamed that one of my first actions after meeting her in my office was to check her HR file for her age. She should be out having fun and experiencing life.

Right. Because you like the idea of her out at bars and clubs exploring her options so much, huh?

I'd had to suppress that thought one too many times these past few days. I knew I was in trouble when I started to feel protective of her and not a little envious of all those hypothetical men out there who weren't too old for her and her boss, to boot.

Rather than honing my success within Appeal, I was lecturing myself daily to stay away from my employee. I was on dangerous ground here.

My phone rang, tearing my thoughts from my assistant.

The video call on my screen contained all I cared about in the world. It was Sunday evening, and my sisters, niece, and brother-in-law were at my mom's for our weekly family dinner. My chest ached every time I had to miss one of these nights.

Even with their busy schedules, my sisters, Isabel and Claire, always made time for family. When Isabel had married Andreas and had my niece, our tight-knit circle had grown.

"Aiden! Are you in the *office*? It's Sunday!" My mom's scolding voice was just as effective over video call as it was in person.

"Hi, Mom. Nice to see you too. How are things?" Knowing any rationale I had for being in the office on a weekend evening wasn't going to fly with my mom, I skipped any explanation.

"Don't even pretend you think I'm not happy to see your beautiful face after two weeks of 'everything's fine' text messages. You can't distract me."

Just as quickly as I'd landed in the hot seat, I was yanked out of it again. Tiny fingers grabbed the phone off Mom's kitchen table, and I was treated to a disoriented blur of hallways until my adorable niece's face filled the screen.

"Hi, Uncle Aiden! I stole the phone from Grandma!" My niece, Adrienne, or Rennie as the family called her, grinned proudly.

"Good one, Rennie." I shouldn't be encouraging cheeky behavior; I knew my sister Isabel would not approve. But the perks of being the "fun uncle" was that this was the one area where I could choose my level of responsibility.

"Guess what, Uncle Aiden?" She bared her teeth in a "see" type smile. I could almost make out her molars with her efforts. Such a toothy grin would make wild hyenas proud.

Rennie was a mirror image of Isabel and me because of our resemblance to our mom. She was tall for her age, with dark chocolate-colored hair and rich brown eyes. The only evidence of my brother-in-law, Andreas, was the warm golden undertone to her skin.

Noting an extra gap in her teeth, I feigned anticipation. "What, Rennie?"

"I lost another toof! And the toof fairy left me four dollars in my toof pillow." She pulled the phone right up to her mouth to make it obvious to her poor, bad-at-guessing uncle, so I could see the new gap in all its gory glory.

"Wow! I never would have guessed that! What are you going to buy with your money? Did you put it in the piggy bank I gave you for Christmas?"

Having already picked up a few of Claire's facial expressions through osmosis—maybe there were a few disadvantages to living in each other's pockets all these years—Rennie rolled her eyes in expert sixteen-year-old fashion.

"Uncle Aidennnnnnn! I'm gonna buy somefin' wif it." Her "th" sounds were now truly lost to the Island of Misfit Teeth, the sound of her little voice scolded me across the line.

"Oh, of course. What was I thinking? You can start your retirement fund at seven. Six is much too early. What are you going to get? Please tell me Auntie Claire isn't taking you shopping."

Claire could talk a saint into mischief. She and Rennie were an even match in their love of all things silly. I could see Claire paying the difference in whatever Rennie wanted and them bringing home a live alligator or goat to live on Isabel and Andreas's balcony.

"How did you know? I sent her a voice message on Mom's phone dis week, and she said she'd take me to the mall after school tomorrow! I wanted to buy a huge bag of lollipops like it was Halloween in May, but Mom said no." Her little lip popped out to pout.

Her disappointment was a wrecking ball to my chest. There was nothing I wanted more than Rennie to have everything she wanted. Unfortunately, her Type I diabetes prevented her from indulging in the glucose free-for-all she wished for.

"Aw, I'm sorry. What about a stuffie or something? I bet Auntie Claire would help you buy one if it's more than four dollars." Great, now I'd be an accessory to the new alligator or goat. But I couldn't stand to see her disappointed.

"Yeah, maybe. I could probably get a new Pokémon or somefin'." A tiny smile appeared on Rennie's mouth.

"Rennie! Time to share the phone," Isabel called from my mom's kitchen.

"Okay, Mommy. Bye, Uncle Aiden!" Rennie waved quickly before essentially tossing the phone to Isabel. Talking to first graders on video was not for the faint of stomach.

"Go finish your dinner, sweetheart. Daddy can help you cut up your chicken." Isabel smoothed back Rennie's dark brown hair lovingly.

His niece muttered something about "dumb chicken" on the way back to the table.

My heart thumped at the love I could see in Isabel's eyes. Rennie had wrapped the whole family around her finger the moment she was born six years ago.

"Hi, Aiden." Isabel's voice was many decibels quieter than her daughter's. "Did she tell you that her big bad mommy said no to lollipop-looza?" The guilt in her tone was clear.

"Hey, Isabel. You don't have a choice, though, right? I can't even imagine what that kind of thing would do to Rennie's numbers." Isabel and Andreas's lives had revolved around Rennie's diabetes since she was diagnosed at ten months old.

"Yeah. But it still sucks. She's such a good kid. I want to be able to say yes to her more."

I couldn't fully understand my sister and brother-in-law's challenges because I wasn't a parent. But I wished I could do more for them.

You can do even less for them now that you're hours away from LA. The guilt over moving still rode me hard.

"Rennie is a *great* kid. And that's all you and Andreas, Isabel. Remember that. Mom and Claire will tell you the same." I could see my reassurance didn't quite penetrate Isabel's maternal guilt, so I tried for a smile instead. "Admittedly, Rennie's genetics are excellent. I like to think that her sparkling personality is because of her brilliant Sullivan genes. I mean, just look at how well her uncle turned out."

That made Isabel snicker. "Right, Aiden. Obviously, Rennie won the same genetic lottery you did. What do your new employees think of *your* sparkling personality?"

Ah, shit. I'd thought I'd be able to keep the focus off myself with the chaos of Sunday dinner. I didn't want to let on that I was feeling the weight of the pressure at Appeal.

"It'll be six months before the end of the year performance reviews come out. I'm sure I'll hear how they've never had a better boss." I kept my voice light to hide the unsettled feeling that rose within me. The thought of everything I had to accomplish to prove myself before then made my blood pressure rise.

"I'm sure." Sarcasm bled through Isabel's voice. "You're not a taskmaster or anything. Most easygoing guy I know." Her fondness for me as the hard-done-by sister warmed her tone.

"You know it." I wanted to get off the topic of Appeal. There were too many questions I didn't have answers to. I couldn't let Claire join Isabel in a two-on-one interrogation. I hardly ever won those conversations.

"Did Mom tell you about my new house? I had the Realtor do a video walk-through for her last week."

Isabel shook her head. Juggling long shifts at the hospital with family life, she had a lot on her plate as a nurse.

I bypassed the talk about work and settled back in my office chair. I was excited to describe the two-story, four-bedroom house I would close on the next day.

"You'll be the first family member to own walls that aren't attached to someone else's. That's a big deal, Aiden." Her voice rang with pride.

Sharing the news with my family gave me mixed feelings. The money I'd earned didn't automatically feel deserving of a house all for myself when my mom and siblings were paying such high rent in LA. The success I'd had in my career paled in comparison to the albatross of poverty of my entire childhood. Although I had a steady income, I still felt the weight of not having enough.

Every day felt like one bad decision away from the life I'd left behind. And I didn't want that for any of them, especially Rennie.

"You know, I still want to help you out on the rent for a bigger place. Maybe you could swing an extra day off each week." I couldn't stop myself from making the offer.

"And *you know* that I told you Andreas and I are managing fine, Aiden. Our finances are not your responsibility." Exasperation bled through her tone. "I appreciate you. Now, I want to see you take care of yourself for once."

I let the subject drop, knowing I wouldn't get anywhere with

Isabel. I moved back to a safer topic.

"It's still a bit surreal to think of being a homeowner. It's a lot of white right now. I also have about ten pieces of furniture, so it's going to feel pretty strange with all that space. Amado's market was more accessible, and I wanted to have room for everyone to visit."

"Once I tell Rennie that she'll have her own bedroom at your place, I'll never hear the end of it."

The thought of my family filling in the blank spaces of my new house warmed me. Maybe it would start to feel like home after I'd lived in it for a while.

Before I'd sold my condo back in LA, it had just been a place to sleep and keep my clothes. I'd been managing the luxury brands team at my last firm, so I'd had little time outside of work. Most of my time off was spent with my family or at the gym.

Settling down hadn't been on my radar, despite turning thirty-six this year. The closest I got to a relationship was no-strings-attached hookups with like-minded women over the years. There was no one pining for me back home.

I glanced at the time. It was just after 7:30 p.m. I still had at least four hours of work ahead of me. If I wanted to catch at least five hours of sleep, I needed to get back to my reports.

"Listen, can you pass me over to Claire for a minute? I am about to head home and don't want to lose you in the parking garage."

I fucking hated lying and tried not to make a habit of it, especially with my family. But there were just some things that they wouldn't understand. The hours I had to put in at work was one of those things.

Moving to a new city had one upside, my family wouldn't know I was pulling long hours. It wasn't as if they could just drop by as Claire often did when she'd been out for a late night near my condo in LA.

"Okay. Love you, Aiden. Take care of yourself, please." Isabel's soft smile was warm with affection.

"You too, Iz. And by the way, that's my line."

My youngest sister, Claire, grabbed the phone before I could be sure that Isabel had heard me.

She was tall like Isabel and me, but she looked most like her father and my stepfather, Patrick Sullivan. She had his auburn hair and pale Irish skin. Freckles covered her nose and cheekbones and dusted both her shoulders and arms.

He'd been part of our life for four brief years but he'd been the father I never had. I'd been ten when my mother brought Patrick into our lives and fourteen when we'd lost him to a drunk driver. His warmth and positivity gave us a sense of completeness as a family. Though only Claire had been born with his name, we'd all chosen to take it when my mother married him.

When we'd lost him, we'd all been torn apart in different ways. I'd wanted to fill his absence by taking care of everything while Mom worked and tried to provide for three kids on her own for the second time in a decade.

Claire had only one or two memories of her father, which had made me feel responsible for making up for Patrick's absence. I worried most about Claire, feeling wronged on her behalf.

"Aiden. Aiden. Aiden. What could you possibly need to say that you haven't said in the ninety-seven text messages you've sent me since you moved?"

I resisted the impulse to give her an eye roll so dramatic it would have made Rennie proud. Claire loved making all aspects of her life as riveting as an HBO drama.

"I hardly think one text message every other day has added up to ninety-seven in just under two weeks, Claire." My voice took on the father-figure inflection that I inevitably fell into with Claire.

Nine years between us had me thinking of her as a perma-teenager, despite her being in the final year of her master's.

"Potato. Potahto. The fact that you know how often you text me shows you want to text me every day and stop yourself."

"Not untrue," I admitted. I did have a hard time not checking up on her to make sure she was okay. Old habits were hard to break. "I just wanted to make sure everything went okay with your tuition payment for the summer."

"Geez, Aiden. I told you in the reply to text number seventy-three that I spent all of it on cocaine and online gambling." Her reply had me releasing an audible sigh.

Pinching the bridge of my nose between my fingers, I fought to release the tension building in my body. The headache that had been threatening to appear all day was creeping into my skull. Was it because Claire was a literal pain in the neck? Maybe.

"Claire. Be serious for four seconds and just tell me, please."

She must've heard something in my tone that had her sobering. She practically whispered, "Yeah, Aid. I did, and thank you again. You know you don't have to do this for me."

"I do, and I want to. Though I need to get going. Can you give Mom my love? Love you, little sister."

"Love you, big brother." She disconnected the call.

I reached blindly into the desk drawer for some ibuprofen. I swallowed two capsules with the eight-hour-old bottle of warm water on my desk. The room temperature, stale flavor had me grimacing.

Allowing myself one moment to tip my head back against the headrest of my chair, I closed my eyes to gain control of my stress levels. There was so much to do before I could call it a day. Several teams were starting new campaigns that coming week, and I had to approve their proposal designs before tomorrow.

Willing away the pain in my head, I opened my eyes and brought my focus back to the document in front of me.

It was better that my family didn't know that I wasn't going home. What they didn't know, they didn't have to worry about. I preferred to do the worrying on their behalf.

Six

ABBIE

*I*f Aiden was surprised to be going on a business trip just over a month into our new working relationship, he certainly didn't show it when he'd casually announced we'd be heading to LA the previous week. It had meant many hours of frantic bookings and scheduling for me.

Two days later, we were leaving for five days.

After the whirlwind of the past few weeks, I hadn't even considered a trip. But Appeal had an opportunity to meet a group of philanthropists that Aiden had been pursuing to be the first to take part in the new NGO initiative.

If I thought working outside his office door was hard, the next five days were going to be torture. I was still awkward as hell during every morning report.

I'd had no idea that idly looking through the photos I'd taken on my camera in the breakroom last week could land me an all-inclusive trip to LA. With my boss. Where I'd get to see exactly none of the sights.

This was all Ethan's fault. I developed a friendly working relationship with him as the head of the graphics design team on our floor. Had I not indulged his curiosity about the photos I was working on for my community college course, I could have saved myself from being sent to LA with Aiden. Ethan convinced Aiden that I should also document the trip for the company's social media platforms in addition to my EA duties.

"These are good, Abbie. Have you ever considered pursuing a graphic design position?" Ethan asked.

Next thing I knew, I'd been assigned the extra task of social media photographer. Those moments basking in Ethan's comments about my photos during lunch hour were overshadowed now by my unease about the trip.

Aiden had somehow not only single-handedly convinced the CEO to give Anne and Grace their own department to pursue nonprofit accounts more aggressively, but he believed in it enough to pursue opportunities on their behalf to generate more contacts.

I found myself once again reluctantly impressed. He was risking his reputation on an untried venture so soon after assuming his new position.

That's why, despite my conviction not to like him, spending five days close to Aiden was a very, very bad idea. I didn't want to discover any more of his good points. I could barely manage my attraction in the controlled environment of the office. But outside the office felt like a different story.

My entire nervous system was on fire with an anxious type of adrenaline while waiting for him at our gate at the San Jose Airport.

I'd just checked that my anxiety medication was still in my bag for the third time this morning. Ending up in another city and needing a rush trip to an urgent care was not on the itinerary I'd meticulously planned. Taking my meds consistently not only kept my mood stable but also prevented wicked withdrawal symptoms. Sure, I forgot to take it sometimes. But my body was quick to remind me of that forgetfulness. Two days without meds was tolerable, but by the third day, I'd be suffering from a monster headache and terrible nausea.

Reassured that it hadn't fallen out of my purse since I arrived at the airport, I looked up to see Aiden coming toward me. He was reading something on his phone, allowing me a precious few seconds to observe him without him knowing.

To my utter humiliation, he was wearing his usual perfect designer suit. My mouth gaped open. *What the absolute fuck!*

I second, third, and fourth guessed my wardrobe choice as he walked toward the gate. Feeling a bit weird about wearing something so similar to the day we'd met in the park, I'd dressed in another one of my favorite anime shirts and jeans. I was the epitome of a casual, maybe borderline starving college student chic. Today's shirt had an adorable illustration of the Pokémon Mew, my cat's namesake.

He had told me specifically in an uncharacteristically informal text earlier this morning to dress casually as there was no sense in being uncomfortable on the plane. Apparently, I should have thought twice about taking him at his word. What was going on? We weren't due to meet the first set of prospective clients until early the next morning. Before I'd booked our plane tickets, Aiden had told me he wanted to arrive before dinner the day before our meetings started so that he could spend the evening reviewing details for client discussions.

As was always my luck, I didn't have a chance to get my features under control before he spotted me.

His stride didn't change as he approached. This man even made walking an art form. He strode confidently through the throng of people, never taking his eyes off me.

I straightened my spine as a strange sort of buzz filled my bloodstream. He was so magnetically attractive I momentarily forgot my annoyance about the wardrobe setup.

Finally, when he was a few steps away, I realized he was not actually in his usual office suit. Was that a tweed sports jacket? Were those elbow patches?

Shit, he had that sexy professor look going on that I had absolutely *not* fantasized about during idle moments at my desk. One, two, or ten fantasies didn't count at all. That pesky arousal I felt in his presence just added to my unsettled state.

Was it possible he thought a tweed jacket was casual? I had no idea with this man.

In an attempt to school my facial expression and thus salvage a scrap of my pride, I flattened my lips into a line.

"Good morning. Did you have trouble getting here this morning?" He sounded calm and in control, as usual.

He wanted to talk about my ride to the airport? Oh no. I was going to find out what was going on here.

I was pissed enough that I would head out of security and back to the check-in counter to beg for my bag back if I had to. I was not getting blindsided into looking unprofessional on my very first business trip.

"Aiden, I don't want to overstep. But I'm concerned that our schedule for the day may have changed without my knowledge?"

If he was put off because I'd completely ignored his greeting with a swift topic change, he didn't show it. His eyebrows lowered slightly, frowny-eye crinkles appearing.

"No. Not to my knowledge. After all, you are in charge of the itinerary for this trip, are you not?"

Oh, so the condescending part of our day had begun. Annoyed, I struggled to choose my next words.

"Okay then. I'm curious. Why did you specifically tell me to dress casually, and then you show up like…?"

I gestured to all of him-—from his impeccably styled hair to his crisply pressed pants and matching dress shoes, he was the epitome of perfection.

Catching on to what I was talking about, he took a slow perusal of my outfit. So slowly, in fact, that he had my cheeks heating by the time his gaze returned to mine.

Damn it! My body betrayed me again with a rush of arousal.

His eyes darkened, and an amused smirk appeared on his lips. He glanced down at my T-shirt once more, where the enormous image of the pink kitten-like Pokémon was printed.

"You look perfect," he murmured so quietly I wasn't sure I'd heard him incorrectly.

Butterflies erupted in my stomach.

"There is no agenda going on here, Abbie. As I said in my text, there is no sense in you being uncomfortable while we travel."

I held his stare, searching for the truth. His words sounded genuine, and my shoulders relaxed slightly from where they had been approaching my ears. Surely, he had to be aware of how completely mismatched we looked?

"But then why…?"

Here I was, gesturing again. My awkwardness increased as I waved a hand toward him like I was directing traffic. Was I doomed to speak only one coherent sentence per conversation with him?

"My comfort is not the point here."

Unsatisfied with that strange answer, I was at a loss for words. Why should his comfort be less important than mine?

Not willing to go any further down this road, I admitted defeat and pointed to the empty seats a few steps away. He nodded, and we sat down. The awkward tension shadowed us everywhere.

He went back to scrolling through his phone. Our conversation was apparently over for now. That suited me fine. I always seemed to find new and exciting ways to embarrass myself in front of him.

It was only after we had sat down that I realized the implications of narrow airport waiting area seats. Aiden was a tall man who was obviously in incredible shape. I knew from his schedule that he worked out like a machine, at god-awful early hours, seven days a week.

He always physically dominated the room, no matter what situation he was in. But it wasn't until this moment, with the soft skin of my jean-clad hip pressed against the rock-hard muscle of his thigh, that I felt just how overpowering his body was. It didn't matter that there were multiple layers of clothing between us.

The only time I had ever been this close to him was on that very first day in his office, when I'd stood in front of him like some idiotic high schooler who couldn't form proper sentences.

Most of the time, I kept the entirety of his desk between us, or better yet, an entire conference table built for twenty.

I could feel the heat of his body through his carefully tailored suit pants. Was he running a fever? Was I? How was it that all of a sudden, the point of contact between our bodies felt like the surface of the sun?

Maybe this whole power battle was going on in my head only, but I would be damned if I let Aiden know he rattled me in any way this many weeks into working together.

Feigning the need for something in my carry-on, I bent from the waist and pulled my wallet out of my bag. This movement allowed me to shift my lower body away from where it was touching his.

Taking a deep breath to keep the blush from reaching my cheeks again, I pretended to check that my boarding pass was exactly where I knew it would be.

Sitting back in my seat, I realized, to my horror, that he had moved his huge arm onto the armrest, and now the side of my breast was pressed against another set of deliciously hard muscles.

My little plan had only brought an even more intimate part of my body in contact with his. His upper body was radiating heat, and my torso felt like it was on fire. I was mortified that I couldn't control my reaction to this man.

I looked over at him to gauge his reaction to our close proximity. He looked infuriatingly unaffected. Every cell in my body was lit up from the contact, and he could have been sitting next to a concrete pole for all the effect this seemed to have on him.

I resisted the urge to hide in the restroom until our flight was ready to board and decided to stick it out. If it didn't bother him, I'd do everything I could to show it didn't bother me either.

Moving the arm that wasn't next to him, I pulled up the book I was reading on the Kindle app on my phone. An escape into a fictional character's life sounded just right about now.

Rereading one of my favorite books kept me moderately distracted from the current standoff between my arousal and Aiden's goddamn drool-worthy muscles. Consequently, I had mostly tuned the airline employee's voice out until I heard our names over the loudspeaker.

"Would passengers Sullivan and Summers please proceed to the gate? Passengers Summers and Sullivan. Please report to the desk and speak to the gate agent."

I sighed and locked my phone, not wanting to leave the sanctuary of the fictional world where I'd been able to ignore my seat partner.

Following Aiden, I gathered my purse and carry-on and strode toward the desk.

I hoped we weren't going to be bumped off this flight. I felt a headache forming in my temples at just the thought of rescheduling flights, hotel rooms, and not to mention no less than five meetings in the next thirty-six hours.

Reaching the desk, Aiden took control of the situation. For once, he seemed to know that his typical stern demeanor wasn't going to win us any favors. He offered the airline employee a polite smile that didn't reach his eyes, but it was a vast improvement over the controlled neutral expression I was used to seeing him wear.

"Our last names are Summers and Sullivan. Is there a problem with our flight?"

I felt the woman struggle as he aimed his devastatingly swoon-worthy face at the poor woman. That first look packed a punch. I could still remember my shock and pleasure at seeing him sitting next to me that day at the park.

The employee squared her shoulders, no doubt expecting a guy this good-looking to be a jerk.

The truth was, I didn't know how he was going to react if there was a problem.

I'd seen him take down the head of accounting in that first team meeting, but that guy was a douche-canoe. This airline employee was only the messenger. If there was going to be a problem for us to deal with, it definitely wasn't going to be this employee's fault.

The introvert inside me braced for a storm. I hated even being near conflict, let alone in the middle of it. Still, no matter how uncomfortable I was, if Aiden became too demanding, I'd make myself intervene. I hoped I would, anyway.

Clearing her throat, the employee tore her gaze away from his face and gave me a quick glance. I couldn't even blame her. I'd want to spend these moments with all my attention focused on him too.

"Mr. Sullivan, Ms. Summers. I'm afraid that we've had a last-minute plane change. I know you were both booked in first class, but the new plane is much smaller and only has economy seats available. On behalf of the airline, I would like to offer our sincerest apologies. Most of the other first-class passengers opted to take a flight later this afternoon. Or I'd be happy to recommend alternate transportation options?"

The employee bit her lip when she was finished speaking, no doubt nervous about Aiden's reaction.

"I see." He looked briefly at the name tag on her chest, but his gaze didn't linger there. "Well, Melinda, nothing to be done. If you can keep us on this flight, seated together, that'd be great."

Now, Melinda did give me more than a cursory glance. It must have been like looking in a mirror, perhaps wondering if I deserved any credit for him being so accommodating.

Little did she know I had absolutely no sway with Aiden Sullivan.

First, he didn't look like the type of man who would take this kind of inconvenience in stride. Second, I knew he wasn't this easygoing. For god's sake, he had practically given me a manifesto on my executive assistant duties!

He looked back down at his phone as it buzzed with a notification.

Melinda efficiently clicked away at her keyboard to get us on the flight and printed out our new boarding passes.

Taking both in my hand since Aiden was now typing out a text on his phone, I said thank you on our behalf, and we headed back to our seats.

Not wanting a repeat situation of the close quarters we'd been sitting in before, I made a point of sitting at the end of the row and putting my carry-on in the seat between us.

Aiden, having finished whatever he was doing on his phone while following my general direction, came up next to me. He glanced at my bag before taking the seat opposite.

I was sure I saw one side of his mouth curve briefly in amusement. But as quickly as it had appeared, it disappeared again, replaced by his normal infuriatingly calm expression.

Did he know I was twitchy from our bodies touching for so long? Worse yet, had he knowingly kept his body close to mine? Was he just trying to make me nervous or throw me off my game?

Well, he'd succeeded. He had me off kilter. Each moment we spent alone succeeded in dismantling my defenses.

Seven

AIDEN

The rest of the flight to LA went smoothly. I smiled as I looked at my lovely seatmate, asleep on my shoulder. Normally, I would be concerned about adding wrinkles to my suit, but I couldn't bring myself to care as I enjoyed the warmth of Abigail's body pressed against me. With each breath, the coconut scent of her shampoo had been tempting me for the last hour.

She must have been exhausted to fall asleep so quickly after takeoff. I hadn't had the heart to wake her.

Just as the plane approached the runway for landing, the change in pressure must have woken her because she suddenly jerked her head off my shoulder.

"Oh my god, Mr. Sullivan. I'm so sorry! This is so embarrassing. Look at your jacket!" Abigail quickly covered her face with her hands.

I glanced down at my shoulder to see that there were several large creases in the fabric. She peeked through her fingers and whispered, "Oh no! Did I drool? Just kill me now," before hiding her eyes again.

Aware that it was a bad idea to touch her but unable to stop myself from attempting to comfort her, I pressed my right hand lightly to one of her elbows.

"Abigail. It's fine. Don't even worry about it. It's just a jacket. If I was worried about it, I would have woken you, okay?" I kept my voice low and soothing, hoping she could let this go.

I could understand her embarrassment. But she was acting like she might get fired over this. I didn't want her to worry.

"Okay, sir. Thank you." She let her hands fall into her lap as she nodded.

"How about you call me Aiden, hmm? Since I have your drool on my shoulder, it only makes sense to dispense with the formalities, don't you think?" I couldn't keep the teasing tone out of my voice. The more I thought about how horrified her reaction had been, the funnier it became.

"Oh nooo." She groaned, looking for signs of said drool. "Fine, I'll call you Aiden if you agree to call me Abbie, deal?"

She held out her hand like we were making a formal agreement. I took her hand, squeezing it gently before releasing it again. All my good intentions would crumble if I touched her for any length of time.

"Deal." I smiled.

We made our way to the airport exit about an hour behind schedule, due to the plane change delay.

Pleased to see our driver from the car service waiting for us near the exit, I gave our altered driving directions to a café near our hotel.

Abigail—*Abbie*—had gone quiet after the embarrassment over her nap on the plane, despite my reassurances. I felt her gaze on my face, knowing that I had changed the plans without consulting her.

The plan had been to go to the hotel first to prep for tomorrow's meetings. Once there, I'd planned to duck out for an hour or so to meet my sister.

With our later arrival time, I needed to head straight to the café. Being away from my mom and sisters for the past month and a half had felt much longer. Claire had a busy week with some convention she was attending before digging back into her thesis research for the rest of the summer. I refused to miss my chance for a visit to make sure she was fine in my absence.

"Abbie, I'm sorry for the change of plans. I'm supposed to meet my sister before the dinner hour."

She looked surprised. "Your sister?"

It was out of character for me to bring up anything personal since our first day working together. I'd gone overboard to keep the boundary between us wholly professional. I never discussed my family at work, though I had caught her glancing at the family photo on my desk a time or two.

"I had hoped to drop you off first. But now we're running late. Would you mind if we did the reverse instead? Our driver can drop me at the café and then take you to the hotel?"

A light came back into her eyes for the first time after her embarrassment over falling asleep on my shoulder. All of a sudden, she looked like she'd just been told an inside joke that I didn't understand.

"Ohhh. It's no problem. There's no point in me going back to the hotel. I'm sure I have work I can do. You won't even notice I'm there." The gleam in her eyes revealed she was enjoying this, the order of things having changed to put her in control of our plans.

So charmed by the mischievous look on her face, like a kid about to get a sneak peek at her Christmas presents, I didn't have the heart to tell her no.

There was zero chance I'd be able to concentrate on my sister with Abbie there. Let alone ignore her completely.

God, it wasn't even the end of day one of this trip, and I was already breaking my own rules about keeping this trip all business. I could do this. I made it through the first month without incident. It was just five days, after all.

The car pulled up to the "adorable French café" Claire had raved about in her message to me.

Scrutinizing the exterior, its crosshatch gold design and a small pink café cart, I could see why Claire had picked it. It was just the sort of place we'd only been able to dream about growing up. Claire loved her sweets, whether it was a free lollipop from the doctor after a shot as a child or now, as an adult, a twelve-dollar slice of expertly made French cake.

"Oh my gosh!" Abbie's excited squeak came from the seat opposite me.

Turning my head, I saw she was looking at the little restaurant like a kid who'd been taken to Disneyland as a surprise. Her adorable expression outshone the appearance of the café in my mind.

"Have you been here before?" I asked. Her apparent enthusiasm had me wishing I could take credit for the restaurant choice. It made me uneasy to instinctively want to be the one who was responsible for her smiles.

"No, but I know they have locations in cities around the world. My mother never brought me to LA when I was younger, so I've never had the chance. She worked so much after my dad died, and then after she married my stepfather, she had other priorities. This kind of stuff wouldn't be on her radar."

It was a direct hit to my gut to hear her mention the loss of her father in such a casual way. My father had left right after Isabel was born, leaving me no memory of a man who'd only been in my life for two years.

I wondered if she had any bond with her stepfather, like the one I'd had with Patrick. It didn't sound like it.

I couldn't ask, despite just how much I wanted to know. We were treading on dangerous territory already, with my bringing her along to this little family reunion.

Her attention returned to the front of the café, where the front window displayed the small sets of white tables and chairs inside, not noticing that I had exited the car and moved around to her side.

Opening her door, I held out my hand to help her out of the car. We'd only had a few occasions where we needed to be out of the office together in the past couple of weeks. Each time I offered her my hand, she was surprised by the gesture.

I hated how much I liked that I had the ability to give her these little moments of pleasure. I collected snapshots of times our skin touched over the weeks. Small brushes past each other in meeting rooms, when I held doors for her or, like now, a quick clasp of her hand while helping her out of the car.

Shutting the car door, I tapped the roof to signal "goodbye" to our driver for the time being and then followed Abbie into the shop. She stopped just inside, not knowing what Claire looked like, and stepped aside to let me survey the patrons sitting in the shop.

Claire had not arrived yet. I saw a stylized booth near the back of the shop that would likely be the most comfortable, and quietest, place to sit.

Now that I was faced with the idea of sending Abbie to her own table—to what? Stare at her phone for an hour? It felt wrong to exclude her.

It wasn't as if Claire would reveal anything terribly private about me. I hoped, anyway. Claire was the wild card of the family.

I turned to face Abbie and found her marveling at all the desserts behind the glass case at the center of the store.

I couldn't care less about sweets, but I enjoyed the way she had a literal kid-in-a-candy-shop kind of excitement in her eyes. I pulled a black card from my wallet.

"Abbie, why don't you find out what they recommend at the counter while I grab that table with the green bench at the back?" I handed over the card for her to pay. "You should sit with us. It would be rude to ask you to sit on your own."

"Oh. Nooo. That's okay. There's a couple tables up front that are open. I don't want to intrude." She shook her head. Abbie was unfailingly polite. I could imagine she thought she might be intruding.

Without realizing what I was doing, I put my hand on top of hers, which was still suspended in the air. She held my card aloft as if she expected me to take it back. Abbie's mouth snapped shut.

"Seriously. It's fine. I'd like you to sit with us. You'll like Claire and vice versa. She's the free spirit of the family. I only hope she keeps the embarrassing stories to a minimum. You know how siblings can be."

"Not really. I'm an only child. But I have an idea." An uncertain smile lingered on her face. Did she think I didn't want her there?

"Please. I want you to. Order whatever they suggest, okay?" I said, squeezing her hand once before letting my hand drop.

"Okay." She dipped her chin in agreement.

I motioned for her to go ahead to the counter before I walked to the back of the store to claim our table.

There were several people ahead of Abbie in line, so I settled into one side of a booth to review my emails. I'd barely opened my inbox before I heard a familiar voice.

"Aiden!"

Raising my gaze to the front of the café, I saw my sister coming toward me. I waved as I cataloged any potential changes in Claire in the weeks I'd been gone. She appeared as healthy and happy as when I'd left her.

Many years as a student had gifted her a low-key style of cutoff shorts and a tank top with some sort of lightweight scarf around her neck to protect her skin from the early summer sun. Her eyes sparkled with excitement the closer she got to reaching me.

It wasn't until I stood from the bench that I realized there was a hulking, dark-haired shadow trailing her dutifully. Heath, Claire's best friend since third grade, had come along as well. Claire hadn't mentioned Heath coming, but after this many years, I should have expected it. I gave Heath a sharp head nod "hello" and received one in kind.

Focusing back on Claire, I opened my arms, and she stepped forward and wrapped hers around me in a tight hug. God, I had missed her. It was good to see for myself that she was fine and taking care of herself. It was one thing to hear her say she was doing well. It was another to see it with my own eyes.

I would never admit it aloud, but Claire held such a tender part of my heart. I'd never get over feeling overprotective of her.

"It's good to see you, Aiden. I've missed you!"

Letting Claire go with reluctance, the three of us sat down in the booth.

We were a tight-knit group, unused to the distance of even the few hours between LA and Amado. I was accustomed to Sunday meals at my mom's or Isabel's home, not brief visits in cafés full of strangers.

My chest pinched at the thought of only seeing them a few times a year. I had to remind myself that I left LA for the financial security that Appeal would provide.

With Claire sitting across from me, the sacrifice of missing them seemed even bigger. At the same time, the need to have the financial means to protect my family sat heavily in my chest. I would feel like I failed them if I moved back to LA into a job that paid less, just to be close to them again. The separation was the cost I had to pay. At least they still had each other.

Abbie returned to the table, pulling me from my thoughts. Her arms were empty.

"Hi. Um, yeah. So I may have gone a bit overboard with the order." She lifted her hands in a helpless gesture. "One of the staff will deliver everything when it's ready."

Claire's face registered confusion, followed by keen interest, as she directed her gaze over to me. I hoped she would rein in her mischievous tendencies for this short visit, but I feared it was unlikely.

I stood to make the introductions, watching a blush creep up Abbie's cheeks as she took in Claire and Heath.

"Abbie, this is my sister Claire, and Heath, her best friend since forever. Claire and Heath, Abbie is my executive assistant at Appeal."

I watched Claire give Abbie a huge, warm smile as I signaled for Abbie to sit. Heath, to his credit, stood up to shake Abbie's hand before she sat down.

"Nice to meet you." Heath was the quiet calm to Claire's chaos.

"So nice to meet you both as well." Abbie gave them a warm smile.

Once we were all settled back into our seats, Claire did not wait to dive into her usual shenanigans.

"So, Abbie. Tell me. What's it like working for my big brother? I bet he's a super-annoying boss. He was always on my case to clean up my room as a kid. I mean, what fourteen-year-old boy gives a crap about his little sister's room?"

"Umm…" The way her eyes widened with shock, Abbie could have been mistaken for a human version of one of those cartoon characters. I couldn't figure out if she was shocked at Claire's apparent playfulness or worried Claire's question was a serious one and she'd been put on the spot to attempt a truthful answer.

"Seriously, Claire? Leave my poor assistant alone. No one should be subjected to your pot-stirrer ways without prior notice," I admonished.

Turning to Abbie, I hoped my smile was reassuring.

"Ignore her. She just says things to rile me up."

"Aiden! You malign my virtuous character. I'm actually curious about what it's like to work for you. *Poor* Abbie has probably been dying for someone to vent to since you started." Claire looked imploringly at Abbie, her expression so saccharine Abbie laughed, her shoulders relaxing.

Claire had that effect on people. She had the ability to make strangers feel like family.

Even Heath, who'd yet to crack a smile, was no match for Claire's irresistible ridiculousness. His mouth curved with fondness as he watched her.

Attempting to school her expression, Abbie propped her chin on her hands, as though she was about to reveal some major secret. She hesitated briefly before seeming to relax in response to Claire's encouraging smile.

"Okay, so get this. Your brother," she said as she glanced at me, "is an impossible coffee snob. We have been working together for weeks, and I have yet to make a single cup of coffee to his satisfaction."

Abbie's lips pressed together as if she couldn't believe she'd been tricked into hopping on the "rile up Aiden train," but the hint of humor in her eyes said she didn't completely regret her contribution.

It was all Claire needed to jump all over me. "My god, bruh." She wrinkled her nose at the endearment. "Forget I said that. All my undergrads are saying it, but it sounds ridiculous when I do. Anyway, what kind of tyrant are you playing over there at Appeal that you can't make your own goddamn coffee?"

Not sure how I felt about my sister and assistant ganging up on me at the same time, I held up my hands in surrender.

"I don't think I'm that particular about the coffee at all, Ms. Summers." I hadn't been complaining or anything. I'd simply made a couple of select comments about changing the coffee brand or whether the milk seemed off.

A choked laugh escaped from Abbie's mouth. "If you say so." The words came out slightly breathless from her laughter, her expression skeptical. "It really is quite the blow to my ego, knowing I can't even get coffee right." Her smile dimmed slightly.

Had I really been that demanding and not noticed it?

Before I could say anything to reassure her, Claire, who'd been watching us intently, jumped in to steer the conversation in a new direction.

"Aiden, what have you put this poor woman through these last weeks? Abbie, seriously, you must be an angel. Where are you hiding the wings? I'm going to give you some super-embarrassing stories about my brother that you can use against him anytime he acts like an entitled jerk, okay?"

That seemed to shake Abbie out of whatever feeling had taken the light out of her eyes. Her smile appeared genuine again when she answered Claire.

"Sounds good. I'm all ears."

Knowing my participation wasn't needed, I sat back with my arms crossed across my chest, content for once to simply observe. My chest warmed, even with Claire airing my dirty laundry and Abbie listening with rapt attention.

The waitstaff had arrived shortly after Claire started to regale Abbie with the tales of our childhood mishaps. Abbie had not been exaggerating when she said she'd ordered what had been recommended.

Even over an hour later, the tabletop was covered in empty plates, water glasses, and coffee cups. The decadence of the food looked to have defeated the other three at the table. Even Heath, who had gamely eaten anything that Claire didn't really enjoy, appeared slightly nauseous from too much dessert.

I had stuck to coffee, *delicious* French coffee. I should order whatever they served here for the office. In bulk.

I'd zoned out briefly when Claire and Abbie started talking about some book series they had in common, so I was startled when Claire announced they had to go.

"What, already?" I hadn't felt this calm since leaving LA. The next five days of high-stakes meetings couldn't rival this slice of contentment surrounded by sugar-addled companions.

"Aidennnn. Heath and I are going to Anime Expo, remember? I took a week off from my very pressing research schedule to gorge myself on popular culture."

Having no recollection of what she'd no doubt explained over video call in the past few weeks, I had filed her plans as a "convention" and moved on.

"Really! Wow. I've always wanted to go to FanimeCon in San

Jose but wasn't allowed. My mother always thought it was a waste of time. Then, it was just too expensive after college. You two are going to have a great time." Abbie perked up at the change in topic.

Clearly, Abbie knew what Claire was so excited about. Her admission about her mother made my chest ache, thinking about a teenage Abbie being disappointed to miss out on something she clearly loved.

"Aww. Too bad you can't make it work while you're here. Maybe next time." Claire offered Abbie a small smile.

We stood to make our goodbyes. I gathered Claire into my arms and held tightly. I recognized she was an adult now, but it didn't stop my big brother instincts from roaring to life when I thought of her out in the chaos of the city without me.

"Be safe, okay? This convention thing sounds crazy busy. Love you," I whispered in her ear.

Predictably, she groaned theatrically at my overprotective comments. "Geez, okay. I know, I know. I will." Claire squeezed me tighter for a moment before echoing my "love you" quietly back to me.

To everyone's surprise, Claire wrapped her arms around Abbie next, murmuring in her ear. Abbie's cheeks flushed as she nodded to whatever Claire had said.

I offered Heath a firm handshake accompanied by a stare that said, "You watch over her, okay?" His responding nod acknowledged he understood my meaning.

I was aware of Abbie watching me again as I stared at Claire and Heath's retreating back as they left the store. I wondered how much she had learned about me during this short meeting.

I'd felt a wall had come down between us, thanks to wrecking-ball Claire. The carefully drawn lines of professionalism I'd clung to so desperately these past weeks felt blurred.

In the span of an innocuous coffee date, the landscape between us had shifted with the small truths about our respective childhoods coming to light.

"Shall we head back to the hotel?" I asked.

"Yes. Sure." She, too, looked more than a little unsure of how to behave now. There was consolation that I wasn't alone in this new confusion, but it also meant that she felt something on her side, making this problem even more real.

We made our way out of the café and saw our driver waiting for us. Pleased that we wouldn't have to stand on the curb making awkward small talk, I ushered Abbie into the back seat.

Once we were back on the road to our hotel, Abbie turned toward me with a smile.

"Your sister is amazing. Thanks for inviting me."

I knew Claire was likable in general, but it warmed something in me that Abbie genuinely seemed to like her.

In true big brother fashion, I rolled my eyes in a required put-upon gesture.

"I'm glad you enjoyed hearing all about my teenage humiliations. I'm going to need to swear you to secrecy, Abbie," I grumbled but didn't hide the amusement in my tone.

"Your secrets are safe with me," she swore as solemnly as she could while trying not to laugh.

A natural bridge between who we were to each other before entering the café and the knowledge we held about each other now could not be found. There wasn't a way for me to address it, anyway. And I found I didn't want to rip away this small sense of intimacy that hung tenuously between us.

I knew I'd have to find a way to shift things back to wholly professional before long. We weren't even in the position to be friends.

Certainly, nothing I felt toward Abbie was in the realm of friendship.

I needed time to think. For that, I had to get Abbie safely to her room at the hotel and use the remaining hours of the day to get my head on straight.

Given enough time and space, I could think clearly again. If Abbie also felt the shift between us as something significant, we'd be in trouble.

I had no problems denying myself things I wanted. My childhood and teenage years were a story of hard decisions and going without. But I realized more and more that saying "no" to Abbie Summers was a test I wasn't sure I would pass.

Eight

ABBIE

I snoozed my alarm no less than three times the morning after arriving in LA, unable to pry my eyes open and face my nerves about the coming day.

My first full day of this business trip, and even though I had technically set the itinerary, I had no idea how I was going to handle meeting endless streams of strangers.

This morning, Aiden and I were scheduled to check out a nonprofit called BrownBag that provided kids and their families in LA with additional food resources through a neighborhood pantry system. The program received donations via the local food bank, which were then packaged into meal staples by volunteers. BrownBag's social media shared the current state of food bank usage: approximately eighty-three million Americans currently experienced food insecurity (and nine million were children).

That's where Appeal came in. Nonprofits across the country could benefit from partnerships with corporations. Grace and Anna had designed a pitch that could be tailored to each prospective corporation to encourage increasing their company's charitable donations. It modeled growth for both the nonprofit and the corporations through targeted advertising to various demographics.

Basically, as I understood it, it meant getting the nonprofits more money as a result of the corporations earning more goodwill points with existing and new customers.

I rushed to get ready after the alarm snoozed, scanning the room to make sure I had everything I needed for the day.

Satisfied I did, I made for the hotel room door. My phone buzzed with a text from Aiden as I reached for the handle.

Aiden

Good morning, Abbie. I'm going to have to meet you at the BrownBag office. There's a call with the Board that Jack needs me for. The car is waiting for you when you are ready.

Abbie

No problem. Do you need anything else from me? Just heading down for breakfast.

Please have already eaten. Please. Please. It was too early to make stunted small talk, especially because I felt a little unsettled after spending time with him and his sister.

Aiden

No, thank you. I grabbed something early after the gym.

Abbie

Sounds good. See you there.

Aiden

Abbie, also sending something to your

**email for your review at breakfast. No
rush, just a heads up.**

Seeing those three dots appear and disappear a few times, I waited to see if he would elaborate. But ultimately, no other messages came through.

In no hurry to begin my workday before that first glorious sip of caffeine, I didn't check my inbox. Making my way to the little bistro in the lobby, I ordered breakfast and spent a couple of minutes people-watching before the staff member delivered my coffee.

After a sip and a deep breath, I opened my inbox for the latest task he'd sent.

Oddly, and totally unlike Aiden's usual organized manner, the email didn't have a subject line. That in itself was pretty weird. I bet every email he had ever received was in a highly specific folder and archived perfectly. After all, per page fifteen in my EA instructions, I'd created no less than thirty folders in his brand-new Appeal inbox on my second day on the job.

And the email itself had no content other than the words "*For you*" and an attachment.

When I opened the file, my breath caught. I was glad I had set my coffee down before reading the email, or I would have spit it out in shock.

He'd bought me a ticket to Anime Expo. No, make that, tickets. Two tickets, in fact. Not only that, but he had purchased access for all four days and tickets to every single paid event. Except for today, the majority of our meetings didn't take place until after 2:00 p.m. each day, meaning I could attend almost all the different events.

I glanced around the breakfast nook, feeling dazed by the surprise and pleasure of the gift.

Why would he do that? Had I really geeked out so much yesterday afternoon? I couldn't remember saying more than one sentence about how much fun Claire and Heath would have.

I had dreamed of attending an anime con but had never had the funds for tickets, hotels, and everything else during these last five years of supporting myself. Before that, I'd been at my mother's mercy. It had been particularly crushing when I'd been a teen and the way my mother had lectured me about what a waste one of these conventions would be, her tone rife with disapproval still rang in my ears. To a sixteen-year-old in the height of my fandom obsessions, it had been a major blow.

My eyes misted at the thought of that stinging rejection. Why did my mother always have to invade my thoughts when something amazing happened? Why couldn't I just hold the joy of the moment without those shadow memories popping up?

I had to consciously remind myself that my mother wasn't here and didn't get a say. Her values were not my values.

The roller coaster of emotions I felt was compounded by Aiden being the one to give me something I'd always wanted. I couldn't afford to lower my defenses around him. I'd only end up hurt.

He'd only done this to be nice. Or as some kind of thank-you for me being flexible about going to the café with him yesterday. It would be stupid to read anything more into it than that.

My next thought betrayed my resolve to keep him at a distance. If I asked him, would he go with me? Maybe before he'd sent this email, I would have been fine to go on my own, but now, I didn't want to go with anyone but him.

Nine

AIDEN

We seemed to be on a roll. The meeting at BrownBag had gone spectacularly well. There was no doubt in my mind that the nonprofit was a perfect prototype for our new project. If Appeal could get a couple of big-name corporations on board, awareness and donations could skyrocket.

I'd watched Abbie giggle with the other volunteers as they sorted the nonperishable food items and struggled to keep a smile off my face. I was supposed to be laser focused on hearing all the ways its founder was determined to make it grow. Abbie had constantly switched between helping and photographing, swinging her camera bag behind her back when she sorted food.

The founder, Sonia Martinez, was one of those people who was simply a force of nature. Doing so much without government funding was a Herculean task.

With the strategy of placing the pickup pantry stations in centralized neighborhood locations that families were already frequenting, the program saved parents and kids alike from feeling a sense of hesitation in receiving the help. It also kept the kids from gaining any unwanted attention at school.

I thought back to all those mornings when I'd had to cobble together some sort of lunch for my sisters to take to school so no one would notice we were really struggling. Most of the time, I'd forgo breakfast and lunch myself to send enough food for them to not go hungry all day.

I'd ended up relying on the kindness of the business owner or manager from whatever restaurant or business where I managed to score a part-time job to have some leftover food at the end of the night or in the breakroom. I thought about how me and my mom could have caught our breath if BrownBag had been around back then.

Those memories made BrownBag tug extra hard on my heartstrings.

Just as quickly as it had arrived, the high in my mood plummeted to where I'd had to feign a need to go to the restroom just to get my emotions under control again. Seeing the reality of how much help was still needed everywhere brought back all those vulnerable moments of not having enough money for food and not *being* enough to change it for my family. Looking in the restroom's mirror, I didn't see the thirty-six-year-old Aiden making 190K a year. I saw fifteen-year-old Aiden. Thin, tired, and trying to get another year out of secondhand clothes I was rapidly growing out of.

Shaking myself back to the present, I checked my watch and realized the morning had flown by. It was time to head to our next meeting.

Back out in the sorting area, I signaled to Abbie that it was time to get back to the hotel. I shook the founder's hand goodbye.

"You've got a great assistant there, Aiden," she said.

"Thank you, Sonia. She is one of a kind."

She smiled at me with the indulgence of a woman twenty years my senior.

"Make sure she knows it too. What I wouldn't give for an employee who triple-checks appointments, remembers every single person's name, and does it with grace. Don't let yourself get so caught up in the 'work' that you forget the big picture."

Her expression hinted that this was more than professional advice. Was my fascination with Abbie that apparent? I sure as shit hoped not.

"Noted, Sonia. Thank you."

Thankfully, Abbie had been working her way through saying goodbye to each volunteer and had missed this little exchange.

She rushed over with a big smile on her face just as I finished texting our driver that we were ready to go.

She sparkled with the pleasure she had gotten out of helping.

"Oh my god! They are so amazing! I'm not even sure I can feel my hands after stuffing four hundred bags with peanut-free granola bars. How do they do this every day?"

She looked back over her shoulder and waved to Sonia once more. Sonia gave Abbie the same indulgent smile she'd given me, as though we were two children who had made her proud in the school play.

"Sonia is sooo cool." She said this with such hero worship in her voice that I struggled to keep a laugh contained. I admired her ability to let her guard down and share her enthusiasm. People often underestimated how brave a person had to be to share their joy with another.

I tucked her sweetness away into what was becoming an Abbie-shaped box near where my heart would be if it were fully functional. I struggled to admit to myself how much I enjoyed being the person who got to witness her happiness.

Once we were settled in the car, I pulled out my phone to check my inbox for the flood of emails that had come in while we'd been at BrownBag. Abbie cleared her throat, and I turned to see her sitting across from me with a half grimace on her face.

I waited to see what she wanted to say.

"I just wanted to say thank you very much for the tickets to Anime Expo. It was totally unexpected and unnecessary, but I am too excited to pretend I'm not thrilled by the chance to go."

"Not to mention," I said with a roll of my eyes, "they are final sale."

She laughed. "Yes, that too."

"It's my pleasure. Claire was ecstatic to scold me about not giving you credit for the outstanding job you've done so far. I know I have been remiss in saying so, but you have done an exemplary job in a period of a lot of change."

Abbie looked stunned. Recovering as best she could, she stammered out another thank-you.

"I was just wondering, though. I know it's a bit awkward to mention…" she began.

That lovely shade of pink had spilled over her cheeks.

"Um. I, um, was going to say. I know you are probably way too busy and want to use our off-hours to catch up on work, but I was wondering if you might be able to come with me to the expo?"

Before I could reply, she rushed on.

"It's not a big deal if you don't want to. Or think it's inappropriate… God, it probably is, right? I know it's probably way too silly or geeky for you. It's just that I feel a bit uncomfortable going into such a busy place on my own, you know? Typically, Indie or our friend Emery would go to something like this with me. And you know, we're in a new city where I don't know anyone. So…"

A surge of protectiveness ran through me. That was the reason I'd bought two tickets in the first place. I'd planned to broach the subject of going with her so she wouldn't feel uncomfortable in the crowds. We'd just been so busy all week that this was our first moment alone.

There was no way I wanted her walking into a situation where she felt too overwhelmed by all the crowds to enjoy herself.

"Of course, no problem. I did buy two tickets, after all. But I didn't want to presume you'd want my company."

She looked like she wanted to ramble some more about inconveniencing me, so I cut her off.

"We're coworkers. There's nothing wrong with attending a public event together."

Her blush darkened as she bit her lip self-consciously. I wanted to pull that lip out from between her teeth and bite it myself. My fist rested on the seat next to me between my thigh and the door, clenched with fierce restraint not to reach out to her.

"Thank you. I appreciate it." She offered me a shy, soft smile.

"Seriously, Abbie. Speaking out when you are uncomfortable is a really tough thing. I hope my sisters do the same. There's nothing to be worried about here."

She turned to the window and then back to me once more when I cleared my throat, the tension of the conversation slowly easing out of her body.

Hoping to lighten the mood, I gestured to my suit.

"Here's the problem. I only have suits packed for this trip. From what I saw on the website, to say I will stick out like a sore thumb is an understatement."

She laughed. I was irrationally pleased that I was the one to amuse her.

"Don't worry, Aiden. I've got you."

Yes, she did. If only she knew how much.

Ten

ABBIE

I adjusted my new wig in the hotel room mirror. I was channeling my inner Jessie from Team Rocket, a triad of *Pokémon* villains. Jessie, James, and Meowth were my favorite part of watching twenty-five-year-old reruns of the original *Pokémon*, not to mention every generation since. They'd been trying to steal Pikachu for that long. Twenty-five years was a lot of attempts to fail every time. It could make anyone feel good about their ambitions in comparison.

With the wig on, I was technically ready to go. I pulled on the hem of the cropped white T-shirt, second-guessing the length now that I saw my reflection. Thank goodness for shopping services that delivered.

I'd modified my character's outfit to something adjacent to my comfort zone. Jessie's Team Rocket uniform consisted of a white cropped T-shirt with a small slit up the middle, showing hints of an even shorter red top underneath. This was all complemented by a short, matching white skirt with knee-high boots. I'd also ordered an iron-on capital *R* to complete the look.

I'd felt too self-conscious to wear just a sports bra under the crop top, so I'd cut a red tank top instead, still wearing my bra to keep my boobs under control. There was no willy-nilly bra decision with D cups. My girls needed serious support.

There was about an inch and a half of midriff showing between the bottom of the shirt and the higher waist of the skirt. I had to get out of this room before I let my anxiety talk me into changing my clothes and just saying, "Let's forget about this whole thing."

That was the thing with feeling so anxious. If my anxiety levels reached overload level, I just wanted to completely back out of whatever was making me nervous. Over the years, I'd given up on a lot of chances for potential new experiences because I'd let that shadow of anxiety convince me to stay in my safe zone.

But not today, I vowed. I was going to grant sixteen-year-old Abbie's greatest wish, damn it.

Even though my brain had me feeling like there was a spotlight shining on the soft skin of my belly. And that the way it rounded slightly had me wanting to rip everything off and texting Aiden I was sick.

The skin on your stomach has never seen the light of day. Why did you ever think today would be the day to start?

At the moment, time was going to win over nerves. A glance at the clock told me I didn't have time to change.

Shit. I'd just have to be brave. Ew.

Ensuring my room door was locked, I made my way to the elevator with shaky limbs. My body was a soda can that had been shaken too hard, all sorts of feelings bashing against each other, trying to escape.

My mind reminded me again that dressing up was a bad idea. Just because Aiden hadn't seemed put off by his sister's enthusiasm didn't mean he wouldn't think I was being unprofessional by trying to "be his friend" or something.

I felt the cool whoosh of the air-conditioning and pressed my palm to the exposed skin of my stomach once more. I concentrated on pushing aside my inner critic as I watched the floor numbers decrease on the digital screen.

The elevator dinged to signal when I had reached the main level. When the doors opened, I caught sight of Aiden waiting by the front door of the lobby, in the same suit from our breakfast meeting with a climate change nonprofit.

Clutching my tote bag a little tighter, I felt the squish of the item I had inside. These next few moments were either going to be a disaster or highly amusing. I was hoping the Aiden that I'd seen interacting with his sister was the one waiting for me just now.

"Aiden," I called his name when I'd closed the distance between us.

He was so engrossed in whatever message or email he was writing on his phone that he hadn't heard me approach.

His gaze lifted from the screen to my face, eyes widening with surprise. His mouth was kind of hanging open like he was about to say something, but the shock had made him forget.

"Hi," I tried again.

He recovered right away. He was good at that. No matter what situation was thrown at him, he was a hard person to rattle.

"Abbie. Fuck… Shit! I mean, sorry… It's just your hair." He pointed at his own head. "It totally threw me for a second there. I hardly recognized you."

Aiden Sullivan was flustered. For anyone else, I would be embarrassed on his behalf. But something about the combination of my overthinking this whole thing and hearing him speak in a way I knew he never allowed himself to at work made a laugh bubble up inside me.

He waited for my response, but all that came out was a cackle. Once the dam broke, there was no stopping my giggling.

"Your… your face just now. And you said *fuck*… Oh my god, I can't breathe…"

My laughter had me doubling over, the tote bag pressed against my stomach to avoid dropping it.

"I'm glad you find me so hilarious. Shall we go?"

Looking up at the amused smile on his face from my hunched over position sent me off on another round of giggles. I tried to brush away the tears that escaped my eyes while not messing up my eyeliner.

Aiden, recognizing he was fighting a losing battle, applied featherlight pressure to one of my shoulders to move me out of the doorway.

Even the lightest touch of his hand on my shoulder had a buzzing sensation competing with the laughter I'd been trying to tamp down. The heat of his hand transferred through my thin T-shirt, lighting me up from the inside. God, what would that hand feel like if my skin was bare?

No. No. Not going there. Get yourself under control.

He watched me try to compose myself. It took several deep breaths and some awkward hiccup-choking noises before I was able to fully calm down.

My dignity had obviously left the building without me, but the laughter had released the vise grip of tension and insecurity that had consumed me minutes earlier. A definite upside to a bit of embarrassment.

"I'm sorry, I'm sorry. That was super unprofessional. I don't know what came over me."

He gave me a wry grin, and I felt my shoulders drop that he wasn't going to hold my meltdown against me.

"Well, what a start to the afternoon. I wish Claire was here to see the impressive work on your costume. Even having no idea what you are dressed as, you are certainly a convincing character."

My insides melted under his praise. Aiden wasn't one for fake platitudes.

"I'm a character from *Pokémon*. And speaking of *Pokémon*, this is for you."

I pulled the medium-sized stuffed cat plushie out of my bag and held it out toward him. He stared at it for a second before taking it from my hand.

"What… I mean… Why are you giving me a cat?"

It was my turn to offer him a grin. "I told you that you didn't need anything but your suit. Well, except for this cat. It's a surprise. I promise to show you a picture of the character before we leave for our meeting tonight. I just want to see if people guess it."

He held my stare for a moment before shrugging.

"I suppose I don't have time for a crash course in anime in the next five minutes either. Fair enough." He tucked the cat under his arm and gestured to the main entrance of the hotel. "Your chariot awaits."

Eleven

AIDEN

"Giovanni! What's up, man?"

Clearly, Abbie knew what she was doing when she'd creatively figured out how to turn me into the supervillain boss of a *Pokémon* criminal organization. He had a cat-inspired Pokémon called Persian that lounged on his lap while he made his nefarious plans. From what I'd understood from a hastily performed Google search while she was in the washroom, Giovanni, the character she'd selected for me, was also Jessie's boss.

That made me smile. Clever girl.

The young couple raised their hands for a high five, and I reluctantly did the same.

I didn't need to look over at Abbie to know she struggled to keep from laughing. I gently pressed the side of my arm into her shoulder, silently acknowledging my resignation to the chaotic attention that was thrown my way every few minutes.

Sadly, for my pride, they weren't the first or even fifth group of anime fans to call out my costume in this land of cartoon chaos.

Two other groups had actually asked for selfies. Abbie had said I didn't need to smile, so there was no pressure.

Supervillains weren't known for their warm and fuzzy personalities. Another point for my sweet assistant.

At least she hadn't said, "Just act naturally." Then I'd have known she meant to send me a message. As it was, she seemed amused by all the attention I clearly didn't want.

For her, I could accept being the butt of a joke.

She had attempted to explain it to me on the way over, but as far as I was concerned, Team Rocket sounded like they needed new leadership and some intensive performance reviews if they hadn't managed to catch Pikachu in twenty-five years of trying. Talk about a lack of return on investment.

I smiled thinking that while Rennie did in fact like *Pokémon*, she was still young enough just to like the different animal-type creatures rather than the whole universe Abbie seemed to want to live in.

Realizing I'd been pressing into her a little too long, I took a half step to the side. It was unnerving how natural it felt to have our bodies in contact.

Jesus Christ. Now was not the time to think about how tempting she looked in her costume. I'd been watching her carefully over the past month, and whether she wore casual clothes or business attire, she often kept herself as covered as possible.

While I felt pleased for her that she was comfortable enough to step out of her comfort zone to truly embrace the spirit of the con, she was wreaking havoc on my ability to keep my hands off her.

The combination of her sweetness and how goddamn sexy she looked was lethal. Her appeal was multiplied by the fact she seemed unaware of it. She was just acting naturally. I'd grown so disillusioned by the artifice of LA that Abbie's genuine nature was intoxicating. My caveman side wanted to whisk her away so that no one else got a peek at the pale, supple skin of her stomach. I'd had to stop myself multiple times from brushing my hand against her middle "accidentally."

"I'm in heaven. Everything is so impressive." Abbie couldn't turn in enough directions to capture all the sights at once.

"Yep" was the only comment I could manage.

The huge auditorium was bursting with people in all sorts of character garb. I could see how a "fun" kind of person would enjoy this. Being fun was not listed on my resume of skills. God, when was the last time I'd had time for fun? Did I even know what I enjoyed doing anymore?

Abbie looked up at me from my side. "Really? You sound so convincing. Please try to contain your excitement." The glint in her eyes went from cheeky to uncertain. "Are you sure you don't mind?"

A little kick in my chest warned me that her earnest concern meant she thought I didn't want to be there. There was some truth to the idea I'd have preferred going to a dentist appointment to this elaborately costumed kaleidoscope of madness, but seeing her this unguarded and happy for the first time felt monumental to me. I wouldn't have missed it.

Seeing her happy was fun for me, I realized.

"I'm fine, Abigail. Trust me. If I didn't want to be here, I wouldn't be. Simple as that."

Tucking my toy cat further into my arm, I turned toward Abbie. Hoping to move to an area where fewer people would look at me, I was keen to get this show on the road.

"So, where are we going first?"

She was busy looking at the map of all the different areas of the arena and hadn't heard me.

That hot-as-fuck Team Rocket uniform captured my attention again. When she'd stepped out of the elevator, it felt like I had been struck by lightning. All my nerve endings lit on fire, and I'd stood there frozen and speechless. And each time I'd allowed myself to look at her today, my reaction hadn't lessened in intensity.

As she continued to study the map, a fellow attendee sent an appreciative glance at Abbie. I settled for a warning glare. When the other guy lifted his gaze off her body and saw my face, he startled but then gave me a *Whoops, sorry, man* kind of shrug.

Though I couldn't claim Abbie as my own, I took an unhinged amount of pleasure in being the man by her side. For today, I could indulge in the fantasy that she was mine to care for.

Returning my attention to Abbie when I realized she hadn't replied to my earlier question, I tried again. "Abbie?"

I allowed my hand to gently clasp the smooth skin of her elbow. I rubbed my thumb across her forearm, realizing how completely inappropriate I was being but not able to stop the motion once I got my hands on her skin.

Fuck. She felt amazing. Warm and soft. I wanted to touch her all over.

At the contact of my skin on hers, she whipped her attention from the map up to my face, cheeks turning a gorgeous shade of pink.

And still, I didn't drop my hand. I let my thumb make a couple more passes against the top of her forearm before slowly dragging my hand away from her elbow. Each of my fingertips grazed her skin at an excruciatingly decadent pace.

Her tongue came out to swipe between her lips. Fuck, she was as affected by this as I was. I needed to get a grip before I got hard in the middle of muppet-mayhem here. What the hell was I thinking?

"What? I'm sorry?" She looked at me with a dazed expression.

"I said, where are we going first?" My voice came out in a rasp. So much for hiding my arousal from her.

Abbie closed her eyes for an extra second, perhaps trying to wipe the last couple of minutes from her mind. Lord knows I was currently tunneling deep inside for a fucking shred of common sense.

"Huh? Oh, right. This is *so* exciting! It's hard to decide. Just look at everyone. They all look incredible."

The return of her enthusiasm cooled my heated blood enough for me to clear some of the fog of my desire.

"Yes. The setup is impressive. But I asked what you wanted to see first?"

"Oh, right! I realllllly want to see the vendor stalls because they'll have so much hard-to-find stuff. But there's also Artist Alley. How cool would it be to get an autograph from an uber-talented manga artist?"

As her voice rose in excitement with each syllable, my chuckle broke free. She was adorable. Her endearing nature brought back my need to see her happy, helping me to shelve my baser needs for the moment. Thank fuck.

"Whoa. Okay, look, you have four days, remember? Just pick something, and then we'll go to the first ticketed event."

"Okay, vendor hall first! I really want to see all the neat stuff. Plus, there'll be tons of manga there that's hard to get in bookstores or online, and I know it's going to take me forever to choose."

Drawing in a deep breath, she nodded to our left with one more glance at the map. "Okay. Then let's head this way…"

Her palpable excitement had her moving quickly through the crowd.

It took serious concentration to weave my way through the crowd and keep my eye on Abbie at the same time.

According to the map, the route Abbie followed to get to Artist

Alley was more convoluted than necessary. We just "happened" to walk through way too many vendor aisles and the Maid Café before we reached our first stop.

I was unused to free time and struggled to stand still as Abbie contentedly browsed the tables filled with piles and piles of books.

The urge to pull out my phone to check work emails was strong. Being idle made my skin itch. Not wanting to think about why I couldn't just settle my mind, I randomly picked up and flipped through books at the table where I stood a couple of stalls away from her.

I'd always prided myself on my intelligence, whether street smarts or business acumen, but it took me longer than it should have to realize manga books read right to left. I randomly picked up and put down books, giving Abbie space to look around without feeling like I was standing over her shoulder.

It must have been the third or fourth table of my unfocused browsing when I fanned through the pages of yet another title, and my eyes noted what was on the page.

The heat built at the back of my neck when I realized the images I was looking at were suddenly a lot less family-friendly. I angled the book slightly to the side to get a better look at the couple engaged in some pretty hot sex, if I was being honest. How did they…? Nope, I didn't need any more material for my Abbie fantasies. My mind was depraved enough on its own.

My gaze whipped up to the stand employee, who just smiled at me benignly, before I snapped the book shut again.

There wasn't a prudish bone in my body. But I felt shocked to find intimately detailed sex scenes just feet from some more well-known series I could vaguely remember being a movie or show on one of the streaming services.

Still not wanting to rush Abbie, I hesitantly picked up another book. I almost didn't open it, but I couldn't imagine they'd all be like the last.

Wait... Were those tentacles? How were they... Why would someone want... I was in over my head.

A snort-giggle came from my left. I looked up to see Abbie clutching a book to her chest as she nearly choked on her laughter. She obviously knew I was in the Adult Rated section and could see the shock on my face.

"What the hell am I looking at?" I mouthed to her. I widened my eyes purposefully, which only made her laugh harder.

Making sure my trusty sidekick, the stuffed cat, was still secure under my arm, I held up the cover of the book to show her. It had a completely nondescript cover with two characters on the front.

Oh, wait. Maybe there was a hint of a sea creature in the bottom corner once I looked more closely.

"Tentacle porn?" I mouthed again. I couldn't believe I was shaping my lips to form these words, even without sounds.

I hoped I wasn't flushed. Something about silently referring to X-rated illustrations to my assistant had me feeling like an inexperienced teenager, not a man in his mid-thirties. But Abbie seemed to bring out all kinds of feelings long buried inside me.

Another snort-choke was my answer. I decided she would just have to deal with a shopping companion for the rest of this section of the vendors. My poor, addled brain obviously wasn't safe without supervision.

I just wouldn't pick up anything else. I'd offer to hold her shopping bags instead. That sounded like a safe choice.

Once again, I'd found myself the reason for her laughter, and I could see myself getting addicted. Abbie had a way of shrinking the world to the two of us.

Even with ten feet between us, hundreds of people around, and a cacophony of noise so loud I couldn't hear my own thoughts, she had a way of drawing me in and making me forget anything else but her.

Twelve

ABBIE

By day three, my head spun with fatigue.

Before our dinner meeting, I spent my free time under the covers of my hotel room bed. Meeting Claire, Heath, and the nonprofit volunteers in the last two days was great, but peopling for long periods just wiped me out. This had been the third day of meetings, plus going to the convention this afternoon.

I liked people, mostly. Well, some people, at least, but only in small, controlled doses. Preferably in ones or twos.

Almost everything we'd done so far in LA had involved larger groups. Food bank employees and BrownBag volunteers' faces filled my camera's memory card. Hopefully, I had taken some good shots to represent the program. With all that we had been doing, I hadn't even sat down to go through the photos yet.

Tonight was going to be a medium-sized nightmare with about eight people at the table. If I was going to be expected to smile and nod convincingly at this dinner tonight (please, God, let everyone ignore me and focus on Mr. VP of Marketing), then a recharge of my batteries had been an absolute must.

I gave myself exactly sixty minutes to get cozy and rest. A quick power nap was first, followed by spending the rest of the time reading in bed. It was glorious, and I didn't want to leave when my alarm signaled it was time to get ready.

As I headed for the bathroom, I gave the sleek black dress hanging in the wardrobe some serious side-eye. The dress was one of Indie's bright ideas. Indie had sworn up and down that it looked amazing on me but was still professional. Or professionally adjacent, anyway.

I mostly shunned dress clothes. Too many torturous episodes of shopping with my mother throughout my childhood and teenage years had put me off fancy clothes. My mother's lavish parties left me shuddering with memories of the itchiest fabrics known to humankind and unflattering designs that emphasized all the parts of my body I felt the worst about. That was why I owned basically the same dress shirt and skirt combination in several neutral colors for work and called it a day on fashion.

Now, take me shopping for pop culture T-shirts, and that was my idea of a good time. Unfortunately, *Hello Kitty* or *Pokémon* wasn't dinner-appropriate attire unless the restaurant I was visiting had a kids' menu.

Knowing the kind of things needed on business trips, Indie had taken me shopping the week prior. I recalled only giving myself the briefest glance in the dressing room mirror when Indie had all but shoved me into this new dress. She declared I needed at least one cocktail dress in my wardrobe. Spending too much of her life at some country club function or lavishly decorated ballroom, I trusted her to steer me in the right direction. I remained unconvinced but with no other options at this point.

Nothing short of a T-shirt and leggings was going to fix the current churn in my stomach at this point. My own sense of what I looked like varied from neutral to insecure, depending on my mood. I felt drained, making me vulnerable to negative thoughts I fought hard to overcome.

Meeting new people and being "seen" or judged on my appearance made my anxiety skyrocket after a reasonably pleasant afternoon. There was a big difference between the safe space of meeting Aiden's sister, who could make even the most introverted person feel welcome, and a table full of wealthy investors expecting me to act in a certain way.

My phone rang as I glanced back at the dress, now more dubiously than ever. My fashion consultant devil was video calling me. Indie's call made me laugh out loud as she popped up on the screen.

"Hey! I'm Ash Ketchum from Pallet Town, and this is my partner Pika-Mew!"

Indie had taken my *Pokémon* baseball cap and flipped her dark hair forward to give herself the exaggerated anime male character bangs. She was holding Mew up in the frame too. Indie had somehow forced Mew into a Pikachu pet costume I'd never seen before. He looked incredibly adorable and utterly miserable.

Behind Indie, I could see my bookshelves stuffed with half romance books and half manga series. Emery was sitting next to my prized collections, sketching. Seeing my adorable rescue kitty on the screen, my worry over Mew restarted. Even though I was 100 percent sure he was in good hands with Indie and Emery looking after him, I still felt worried. That's how my anxiety worked. Rational thoughts be damned.

"Hey, Em." At the sound of her name, Emery looked up, obviously deep into her work, and gave me an absent away-with-the-muses-type wave.

A pang of longing for home hit me. I'd rather be home with my cat and books than in a strange hotel room getting dressed up.

"Oh, hi, buddy. What is she doing to you, huh?" I cooed. Mew looked more disgruntled than usual, his little face squished inside a hood with heavy-looking ears.

"Ind, not that you both don't look amazing, but what the heck are you doing?"

Indie gave me one of her signature mischievous grins.

Emery, tuned into the conversation for the moment, called out, "Don't worry! I've taken lots of pictures. What she's not showing you are the scratches on her arms from wrestling your little kraken into that costume. Mew definitely got his revenge already."

"Babe, you said one of us had to come over and check on Mew each day. Did you know one of those anime con things is happening in LA this week? You should see if you can get tickets one night. But just in case you can't, I figured the least Mew and I could do was give you the best check-in possible. And Emery was keeping herself locked in her studio, so I dragged her over too."

My chest warmed at the thoughtfulness of the gesture. Most people just saw Indie as a force of nature, but under her confident nature was a tender heart. She simultaneously took care of Mew and Emery at the same time.

"Aw, girl, you are the best. Here's the thing. Aiden kind of…" Rushing my next words in one breath, I said, "*Hekindofalreadybought metwoticketsandwewenttogetherthisafternoon.*"

"I have my ways, babe. My neighbor dressed her pug up as Pikachu last year, and she gave it to me after they were done with it. I've been saving it for just the right moment, and that smile on your face was worth it." Indie beamed proudly. Mew was definitely not loving his first foray into cosplay and let out a sound that was something between a loud meow and a bellow.

Indie had been so excited about her costume find that she'd missed the second part of my sentence.

Emery, however, was not holding a furious dressed-up cat and parsed my statement with no difficulty.

"He *bought* you tickets! And you *went* together! Like a *date?*" Emery's voice alternated in volume as she processed each piece of information.

"Wait, *what?*" Indie had caught up after setting Mew on the couch beside her. He remained a pissed-off lump of yellow. "Daddy Aiden bought you tickets to Anime Expo? Mister Cracks-A-Smile-At-Everyone-But-Abbie?"

Emery's eyes widened as she mouthed the words "Daddy Aiden." Maybe it was the first time she'd heard Indie say that. Wishful thinking could hope it would be the last, but it was highly unlikely. Indie loved riling us up.

I groaned. "Em, it was definitely *not* a date. And Indie, please have pity on me and stoppppp with the nickname already! Not my thing!"

Indie just smiled. Rolling my eyes, I should have known by now that I wasn't going to change Indie. Nor would I really want to. No one told her what to do.

That afternoon had not been a date, just two coworkers going to an event, as he'd said. Nothing romantic about it. Although, it had been such a kind gesture for him to get those tickets. I never would have considered buying a ticket for myself, being too conscious of my tight monthly expenses.

And Aiden wasn't really that intense. Okay, maybe he was, but after seeing his softer side with his sister, I was having trouble holding on to my reservations about him.

He also played along with your cosplay idea, don't forget. And never complained once about following you around as you browsed endless booths.

Damn, he'd been cute with his pretend Persian Pokémon under his arm.

"Anime Expo is amazing! It's just like I pictured it to be. Aiden even carried around a stuffed cat I got at a gift shop. It's actually been pretty okay so far…"

Indie made her signature expression, raising one of her perfectly shaped dark eyebrows at me. Whenever she did this, she looked like an assassin in a spy movie. I knew Indie wasn't going to let it go unless I elaborated.

"Our flight got all mixed up the first morning, and he was completely cool about it to the airline employee. Not a single grumble or complaint. And if that wasn't enough, he took me along on an unscheduled visit with his sister and her best friend, who was totally interested in Claire, by the way. I'm pretty sure I'm the only one at the table who understood that. And there were these amazing French pastries at the café where we went, and he said to order whatever, and I got so many and…"

"Whoa, whoa, whoa. Go back to the part about meeting his sister. You're telling me he actually invited you to meet her? Mr. I-Haven't-Revealed-A-Personality-Trait-That-Proves-I'm-Not-A-Robot took you to meet his sister?"

"Indieeeee… He's not that bad. I told you before. He's not a robot. Just closed off. His sister was amazing. She talked more than any person I've ever met before. She's so warm and open and kind. Maybe it was a brother/sister thing. She hugged me when we said goodbye. Me! A stranger who just works with her brother."

"Whoa. That's kind of a big deal in sibling territory, babe," Emery chimed in. "I would never let my brothers near anyone I was dating until the day before the wedding. Meeting the family is serious stuff. He must think really highly of you."

I didn't have the time or the inclination to think about what it meant that Aiden had let me tag along to meet Claire.

Indie hummed in response. "It's that trustworthy face you have. It tricks people into involving you in all sorts of situations they'd never consider otherwise."

I ignored Indie's musings for the moment.

"I wonder how they can be so different? What happened to him that made him so unapproachable?" I asked.

Indie shrugged, causing her to jostle Mew, who had been frozen in his prison of misery for the entire conversation. At Indie's movement, he turned his head to give her a death stare.

With a laugh, Indie booped his nose. "Okay, dude. We'll get you all fixed up now."

She looked back at me on the screen, missing the feline mastermind beside her plotting her painful doom.

"I don't know, babe. We're both only children. I have no idea how this sibling thing works. Emery gets it."

She was right. Emery was one of four kids in her family. She was the youngest and the only girl. And even though she always said her house had been insane (and stunk like boys) growing up, I'd been 100 percent jealous of her family life.

I would have given a kidney and half my liver for even one sibling growing up. Someone who could have shared and understood what it was like to grow up the way I did. Another person who could have reassured me that all the things that happened to me really did happen the way I experienced them.

"Good point. Em, is this a sibling thing?" I asked. "You have the most functional family out of the three of us."

"Not that the bar is very high!" Indie called from her new position behind the couch.

Emery had centered herself in front of the camera, her sketchbook now closed beside her.

"Brothers are the worst. All they do is think of pranks to play on me when I go home. The twins are twenty-eight and still act like preteens. Especially since I'm the youngest. With Theo away playing in the NHL, I'm the only one left to annoy. I am the picture of innocence while they torture me with their existence."

I wasn't sure if that really answered my question. But I could see how brothers and sisters could really get on each other's nerves. Maybe it was more personality dependent. Indie would have loved the shit-stirrer role in a family if she'd been dealt different cards. I would probably be the unsuspecting victim of all the pranks, too stuck in my own head all the time to notice.

I shrugged. "Thanks, Em. I kind of get it. Maybe you have to experience it first-hand to really understand."

"They drive me crazy, but I do love them. Most of the time, anyway." Despite her prior words, Emery's smile always warmed when talking about her three brothers. It was the same smile Claire and Aiden gave each other after the teasing portion of the conversation had calmed down. There was a "knowing" there.

"I gotta go, okay? Make sure Mew is still in one piece. The dinner meeting starts in an hour."

Indie's head appeared from behind the couch, her hair slightly mussed. "No worries. I brought him a bag of obscenely expensive treats to make up for my antics. He'll be fine. Text us tomorrow to let us know his reaction to seeing you all dressed up. DA's going to melt into a puddle at your feet. I only wish I was there to see my fairy godmother magic at work." Indie sighed.

"I'm sure he'll be nothing but professional, like always. There'll be nothing to tell."

"Whatever you say, babe. Ciao ciao!" Indie called while Emery waved and ended the call.

Thirteen

AIDEN

That evening, as Abbie opened the door, I had to grab the doorframe to keep my hands from reaching for her.

My gaze involuntarily ran over her delectable body. Her dress was simply incredible. The black satin hugged her curves in an obscene way. It was deceptively simple, nothing flashy about it. It didn't hold a candle to the stunning woman beneath.

I overlooked one important point in telling Abbie to book an upscale restaurant for this dinner. Seeing her in a cocktail dress might just kill me.

Trying to pull myself together, I realized I'd been staring for too long. She worried her bottom lip between her teeth, seemingly apprehensive about my reaction.

I had no idea how a woman could be so sexy to bring me to my knees while simultaneously being so adorable that I wanted to gather her up in my arms and never let her go.

"Abbie, you look beautiful." *Let's forget dinner, and I'll devour that gorgeous body of yours instead.*

My voice sounded rough with the effort of masking the desire I was trying to keep hidden. I cleared my throat and stepped back, allowing her into the hall.

"Thank you. You look beautiful as well. Uhh, I mean, it's a beautiful suit, and you wear it well."

She blushed, and I decided to put her out of her misery, even though I wanted to tease her. That was not the kind of relationship we had.

But you could, that fucking devil on my shoulder whispered. Where was the damn angel telling me to smarten up?

"The car is waiting downstairs. Do you have a wrap or something in case you get cold?"

Translation: Was there something we could use to cover up all that gorgeous skin and those incredible curves? I wanted to whisk her away to a dark cave and never let anyone lay eyes on her again.

Would it be too much to insist she wear my suit jacket so that no other man could see her like this?

Probably.

She looked at me curiously. "It's, um, July in LA. I think I'll be okay."

Right. Of course she would. Damnit.

I offered my arm, and we made our way out of the hotel and into the back of the town car. I may or may not have held her hand captive between my bicep and tucked in tightly to the side of my body. Apparently, so deep was my craving for her that I was hoarding every press of skin possible. Fuck this suit jacket and dress shirt from keeping my skin from hers.

I couldn't stop staring. She looked so stunning in the pink light of dusk.

I didn't attempt to make small talk with her on the way to the restaurant because I feared what would come out of my mouth. My mental shields were lowered from our afternoon together, and my desire for her made me feel out of control.

You are too incredible for words, and I need to put my hands and mouth on you right now.

Let's forget this dinner and go back to my room so I can kiss you for hours. Then you will be mine, officially.

That last thought caught me up short. I had never imagined myself in a committed relationship. I had enough experience taking care of my sisters in my teenage years that I had never had the desire to settle down with a family of my own. It was enough to be financially prepared to support the family I already had. Even though things seemed stable at the moment, life could change in a heartbeat. I needed to remain vigilant in my priorities.

I couldn't shake the need to get closer to Abbie.

Thank god the drive wouldn't take more than forty-five minutes. The traffic gods must have taken pity on my poor brain.

The car stopped in front of the restaurant, its entrance looking like a hidden door surrounded by foliage. It was both charming and mysterious at first glance. I could see immediately why Abbie would choose it. It was appealing, not pretentious, just like her.

We left the car, walked through a nondescript black door, and entered a cozy library with booths and tables along the bookshelves.

I watched Abbie take it all in with a smile.

As we approached the hostess area, Abbie looked up at me from under her eyelashes. "I'm so glad this restaurant looks this good. The food is supposed to be amazing. Hopefully, everyone will be impressed."

She looked relieved. We had wanted to impress these potential clients without going overboard. Appeal didn't need to hide behind smoke and mirrors. Our work spoke for itself.

Feeling the need to reassure her in ways I hadn't previously, before introducing her to Claire, I praised her efforts.

"It looks perfect to me. You've done well here, Abbie."

Abigail's body jolted with my compliment. Had I truly been so stingy with any positive feedback that these simple words would shock her?

A sense of heaviness settled over me. I hadn't been fair to her, had I? I'd been so busy making inroads with the other teams I'd neglected to show appreciation to the person who helped me most in my job. She worked her ass off every day and met all my expectations. I determined I needed to do more to reassure her that she was a valued team member.

The hostess led us into the central dining area, and I was surprised that the ceiling was open air. The dark beams of the rafters were accented with all sorts of glowing lanterns hanging over the tables. But the real centerpiece was a huge live tree in the middle of the dining room, covered in thousands of twinkle lights. It continued that hidden fairyland feel.

I wished that it was just going to be the two of us tonight so I could savor the sight of Abigail in that exquisite dress throughout dinner. I wanted to spend the evening feeding her all sorts of delicacies before whisking her back to my hotel room. The idea of sharing her attention with five strangers was completely unappealing. Admitting my own primal tendencies when it came to her, I'd rather have a private dinner with her than a bunch of rich pricks staring at her. I loathed them already, and I hadn't even met them yet.

Observing her in team meetings, I knew she hated group attention. Protectiveness surged through me at the idea of her discomfort.

As her boss, I knew learning to deal with uncomfortable situations would help her in the long run. It sucked being the one responsible for bringing her into the lion's den. We were in the big leagues with these philanthropists.

We were first to the table, and I made sure to take the chair immediately beside Abbie. There were four men and one woman coming tonight, and I would be damned sure to escort the woman to the seat next to Abbie if I could have my way.

No sooner had the waitstaff poured our waters when the hostess brought the rest of our party to the table. After shaking hands with everyone, I quickly ushered Agatha Carmichael, the main client we were trying to impress, into the seat next to Abbie's with an exaggerated bow.

Of all the philanthropists I had been in contact with so far, Ms. Carmichael was my favorite. At eighty-four, she had more energy than most people half her age, and she wasn't afraid to call anyone on their bullshit. When I had personally invited her to this meeting, her response was to agree only if "the food was good, and the company was even better." A half smile formed on my face as I remembered promising her that there wouldn't be any "boring, soulless suits" at this dinner table.

The other four potential investors included a tech prodigy who had made his first million at fifteen, a former special ops military who'd inherited an obscene amount of money and was now funding veteran programs throughout the country, a former Wall Street trader who had left the boardroom for a surfboard, and finally, a British lord who had given up his ancestral title and moved to LA to work for a climate-change think tank.

As impressive as all these people were, my teeth clenched at the appreciative and covetous attention a couple of them directed at Abbie. Even while we made small talk (that was until Ms. Carmichael declared she was about to fall asleep before the appetizers arrived if I didn't "get on" with the pitch already), all I could see were the gazes skimming over every inch of Abbie's exposed skin.

Fortunately, she didn't seem to notice their attention. She kept giving me subtle glances every few minutes.

I eyed the men across the table, wishing I could put my arm around her chair to warn them she was off-limits. My pulse pounded in my temples. I sipped my ice-cold water to regain a semblance of control. The last thing I needed to do was act like a possessive asshole in front of a group of people who were worth a billion dollars combined. Especially considering I had exactly zero rights to feel the way I did.

I couldn't help myself. I shifted in my chair to press my thigh against Abbie's while directing my attention to one of the potential investors.

Glancing over at Abbie, I saw she was watching me in return. Maybe she thought I was concerned about the pitch, thinking I was trying to get her attention.

I wanted her full attention, and it wasn't about business. Unaware of the direction of my thoughts, she gave me a small smile of encouragement and reached over to quickly squeeze my wrist.

The surface of my skin burned where she had touched me. I wanted to put my opposite hand on top of hers and keep it there.

Her awareness of the smallest shift in my emotions was another one of her superpowers. Even though she couldn't exactly tell what I was thinking, she wanted to reassure me. It was intoxicating to be the center of her focus.

She soothed my agitation by empathizing with me in a stressful situation and providing quiet support. Especially when she was practically broadcasting her own nerves to the entire restaurant with the stiffness in the way she held her body and clenched her napkin in her lap with her other hand.

Looking around at everyone else at the table, I decided I needed to get through this night as quickly as possible. I wanted this pitch over with so I could take her back to the hotel and away from these clearly interested men.

Pressing my thigh more firmly into hers, I didn't deny myself this small amount of contact, however inappropriate.

I jumped into the heart of the pitch, keen to get out of here.

"So, Ms. Carmichael and gentlemen, let's get down to business…"

Fourteen

ABBIE

I still couldn't figure out why he kept his leg pressed against me throughout dinner. Whatever he had been trying to communicate, he'd succeeded only in making me dizzy with wanting him.

The warm feeling of his body against mine still lingered on the skin. The delicate satin of my dress was no barrier against the pressure from the rock-hard muscles of his thigh.

More than once, it had caused me to wonder what it would feel like to climb into his lap. I'd had to take a few deep breaths to keep myself from blushing throughout dinner after the illicit thought made my core throb.

You are out of control. You cannot act on these feelings.

For once, my inner voice was right, and I couldn't feel bad about it. There was a part of me that liked the illicitness of those thoughts.

I prayed he'd chalk up whatever he saw on my face to nerves.

By all accounts, it had been a successful evening. I had never seen Aiden turn on such charm in the office. Ms. Carmichael had smiled at him like she wanted to adopt and eat him at the same time. She was smitten and made it obvious to the rest of the table. It had been very endearing to watch.

The men seemed equally convinced by every word that Aiden spoke. Throughout dinner, he managed to keep them both entertained and interested in our proposition. They'd left with a handshake promise from each philanthropist that they'd donate to several up-and-coming non-profits as Appeal signed new agreements.

It was just another item to add to the growing list of amazing qualities that Aiden seemed to possess. My cheeks heated at the thought of how each new part of him that I discovered only made me more attracted to him.

This was becoming a big problem.

It couldn't have gone any better. Despite the evening turning out well, Aiden sat next to me with a stoic expression on his face.

After wishing our driver a quiet good-night, we rode the elevator to our adjoining rooms.

Somehow, the tension between us ratcheted up during the ride. As the elevator doors opened, I walked briskly to my room, keen to get away from this feeling. Butterflies were going crazy in my stomach, and I couldn't even pinpoint why.

Was he upset that I'd largely kept quiet during dinner? Did he expect me to take a more active role in the discussions? As we reached the door, I bit my lip and spun around to say good night, but Aiden was closer than I expected.

Startled, my voice quaked with an embarrassing squeak.

"Umm, right, so… Good night, Aiden."

I turned back to my door with a shaking hand to get the key card into the freaking slot so I could escape his potent presence. My whole system was out of whack because of him.

His large hand suddenly covered mine, and his right side pressed against me. His proximity did not help my nerves. I pulled in a choppy breath.

With his palm pressed down on my hand and fingers wrapped around mine, we managed to get the key card into the lock. The little green light was like a beacon calling my name.

"Good night, Abbie. You looked stunning tonight."

His voice rasped right next to my ear. The rush of his breath against my skin. A shiver racked my body. My center lit up with the power of an electrical storm.

Just as quickly as his hand appeared, it was gone again. I gave him what I hoped looked like a sane smile before sliding into my room.

Once inside, I tried to calm the rapid beating of my heart. I took a few deep breaths and tried to make sense of what had just happened.

His whispered compliment had taken me completely by surprise. If there was one thing I knew about Aiden, it was that he conducted himself with the utmost professionalism, without exception.

Why would he break that rule just to say those words to me?

I flopped onto the bed, creasing the satin of my fancy dress without a care. Placing my palm over her heart, I felt it pound in a way it shouldn't after only a few words. Because of my attraction to him, he held such power over me. I knew I was in trouble if I let myself fall for him.

I would have to find a way to bring things back in line tomorrow. There was no other option other than to pretend that the moment hadn't happened and keep as much distance between us as possible. It was going to be tough for the final days of the trip, but I had overcome harder moments than this.

Fifteen

AIDEN

Seated on the bed back in my room, I stared at the inner door that separated my room from Abbie's. Stone-cold sober, I couldn't blame alcohol for the utterly irresponsible things I wanted to do at that moment. I wasn't sure if two locked doors were enough to keep me away from her.

Something broke my restraint tonight. I didn't know if it was the interested glances two of the men at our table kept throwing Abbie's way. It could have been how, only hours away from Amado, LA felt like a different version of the world, one where I could take Abbie to dinner and not worry about the consequences.

Or it might just have been that damn dress that snapped my control that had been weakening ever since she fell asleep on my shoulder on the plane. Had that only been three days ago? It felt like I'd been reining myself in for a lifetime already.

I picked up my phone to text her an apology for the way I had behaved just now. I never put my hands on a woman uninvited. I respected Abbie too much to behave so unprofessionally, and I needed to own up to that. I texted her before I could stop myself.

Aiden

I need you to keep the joined door between our rooms locked.

Goddamn it. My fingers had a mind of their own. She didn't make me wait for a reply.

Abbie

What? Why?

Aiden

Because I might unlock my side and I need you to be the responsible one here and not answer if I knock. You looked too beautiful to resist tonight.

HR manuals worldwide were screaming in horror. I was sure Linda's office back at Appeal had spontaneously burst into flames. I thought of Abbie's breath catching when my hand made contact with hers at her door. And the tiny shiver that ran through her body when I'd whispered in her ear. The scene played itself over and over in my mind until I was going insane.

Abbie

What if I don't want to keep it locked?

Aiden

Keep it locked, Abbie. Please.

Throwing my phone onto the comforter, I pushed myself up and forced my body to move into the bathroom. I'd take a shower and lecture myself on all the ways I'd already screwed up tonight.

I made it to midnight before I unlocked my side of the door.

I'd lain in the dark for an hour, staring up at the ceiling. The room was dimly lit by the city lights of LA.

Abbie had not replied to my last text. As soon as I'd gotten out of the shower, I hadn't been able to resist picking up my phone. I had only allowed myself to check it one time before shutting it off for the night. There would be no sleep for me if I left it on.

Despite knowing I'd made the stupidest mistake since my early teenage years, when I'd let impulse rule my life, the connecting door called to me. I knew I had to check her door. Just once.

My footsteps were soundless as I closed the short distance between the bed and the door.

The scrape of the dead bolt boomed through the silence of my room. I struggled to turn the doorknob, which felt like it weighed a thousand pounds.

What if her door was locked? I'd have a shitstorm of unknown proportions on my hands.

But fuck, if it was unlocked…?

It was the second thought, with the doorknob still gripped tightly in my hand, that connected my brain and body and allowed me to turn the knob.

With a deep breath, I pulled the door open slowly and felt my throat close in shock. Abbie's door was open on her side. There was one inch of gap letting the warm light from what must have been one of her room lamps spill through the crack.

Before I could stop myself, I rapped my knuckles gently on her door, causing it to push open further. I couldn't see her, but I saw a partial view of the disheveled bed linens.

God, was she in bed? Had she waited up for me, and then I'd spent so long restraining myself that she'd fallen asleep?

A quiet "Aiden?" pulled me from my thoughts. Her sweet voice had me nudging the door open until I could see her.

The sight of her was a blow to the solar plexus. She sat against the bed's headboard. Her long hair, released from her preferred work style of a low knot, flowed around her shoulders. Abbie still wore that sinuous black dress from earlier, now with many more creases from being pressed against the bed by her body. One slim strap had slipped off her tantalizing smooth shoulder, resting lazily on her bicep.

"Jesus Christ" was my only greeting. All other words had failed me at the slightly debauched vision she made.

"Hi." She rested her arms on her knees, seemingly oblivious to the torture the glimpses of the pale skin of her plush thighs were inflicting on me.

When I still didn't say anything, her lower lips wobbled just slightly in uncertainty. "Aiden?" she tried again.

The soft sound of my name on her lips spurred me into action. I crossed the distance between our adjoined doorway to the side of the bed she sat on.

"Can I look at you?" I held out my hand for hers. Placing her much smaller hand in mine, I helped her to a standing position so I could look at her freely in a way I hadn't allowed myself before.

"I don't know what we are doing here, Abbie. But I've never wanted anything more than this night with you. Can we have that?"

We were about to break every rule that should stand between us. And now, here with her, I couldn't have given a fuck about stopping.

My gaze consumed all the little details of how she looked in that damn dress. The rumpled satin still slid sinuously over her curves. I could see the outline of her hard nipples through the delicate fabric. Christ, had she taken off her bra? Was she completely bare under that dress?

Confusion marred her pretty features for a moment, and she said, "Just tonight?" She brought her hand up to the bottom of her hair to twirl a section of those soft lavender waves around her finger as she waited for my reply.

"I want to forget about everything outside of you and I tonight. We can worry about being responsible tomorrow. Can I touch you tonight?"

I had been caressing her hand the whole time we'd been standing by her bed, staring at each other. The electric current running through my body sizzled in my hands and fingers with the urge to feel all of her lovely body under me.

"Yes." She smiled, a little bit of her usual reserve returning after her uncharacteristic openness to unlocking the door between us.

"Anything you don't like, I stop. Okay? I'm going to go crazy with every second of touching you. I want you to feel the same."

A quick nod of her understanding, and I was in motion. Gently bringing the hand I held back to her side, I grasped both her wrists and gave them a gentle squeeze. I glided my hands along the silky skin of her arms to her shoulders. When one palm came in contact with that naughty little strap, I toyed with it between my fingertips, tugging it softly so the top of one of her breasts was bared to me.

My other hand reached the opposite strap, and I slipped my fingers underneath it. "May I?" I pulled it downward to indicate my intention.

A blush had risen to the surface of her pale skin under my unwavering attention. She nodded once more. My already hard cock grew painfully harder at the thought of the rosy-pink arousal blooming on her skin.

After dragging the second strap to match the first, my focus lasered in on her firm, plump nipples pushing against the satin of the dress. I couldn't believe I was about to see all of her. I wanted to rip the dress down and bare her completely, but I decided to remove it slowly instead.

I wanted Abbie to feel every inch of her skin as I revealed it for my consumption. I held the neckline of the dress somewhat taut so she could experience the graze of the satin across her skin.

I began my task, never taking my eyes from where the descending fabric's edge made contact with her skin. I firmly, but measuredly, pulled the neckline of her dress down until half of her generous breasts were visible. God, I wanted my hands and mouth on them immediately. I wanted to suck and bite and suffocate myself in her skin.

The picture she made was much more illicit by the way her dress was held suspended by the fullness of the bottom of her breasts, pushing those hard nipples against the satin. It looked as if one swift tug could send the dress down to her waist.

"I need to kiss you." I waited for her to meet my stare, needing to know that she wanted this as much as I did.

She had allowed me to take charge since I'd entered her room, hopefully content to enjoy my attention. But in answer to my statement, she stood up on her tiptoes and wrapped her arms as far as she could around my ribs, angling her mouth for me to reach. The straps of her dress held her captive in how much of me she could reach without tearing them. She gripped my T-shirt tightly with her fingers to bring me closer.

Breaching the distance between us, I surprised myself with my own softness in the almost sweet first press of my lips to hers. Only a whisper of our lips brushing together wrenched a deep groan from my chest. "My god, Abbie."

The hunger I'd managed to suppress came out full force as I pressed my mouth more fully to hers. I wanted more, deeper, harder. I wanted to lick into every corner of her mouth and suck her pleasure from her lips.

I capitalized on the small gasp she let out when I gave her lower lip a sharp nip with my teeth. My arms moved to the soft skin of her back. I pressed my hard cock into her soft stomach as I remembered walking behind her earlier in the evening, watching the dip of her spine and the flesh of her hips play peekaboo beneath the black satin.

Lost in the kiss, I sucked her lower lip into my mouth hard enough that I drew the first raspy moan from her throat. My tongue tangled with hers, surging forward to fuck her mouth the way I wanted to fuck her body with my cock.

We pressed into each other, getting as close as possible. I never wanted this to stop. But I'd kept this long-held fantasy at bay all these weeks, but now, it raced to the forefront of my mind, and I couldn't ignore it.

I tore my mouth from hers, leaning down to press our foreheads together. I refused to move any further away than the parting of our lips, wanting not a millimeter of space between us.

Drawing one hand from her back, I slid it over the roundness of her hip and to the front of her body while I pressed my other hand against her hot core. Fuck, I couldn't tell if she was wearing any panties, but I wanted to find out right then.

"Every goddamn day in my office, I think about tasting this delicious pussy." I punctuated my words by sliding my middle finger to the cleft of her lower lips and pushing the satin between them.

Shit, no panties. The answering heat and wetness as I gently stuffed the fine fabric between her folds had me salivating.

"Every time you stand in front of my desk giving one of your very thorough reports, I want to pull you across it and spread your legs for my tongue. Can I do that?" I enunciated the words against her lips—each word its own caress with my mouth.

I leaned back slightly to nod at the small functional desk that mirrored the one I had in my room. I wanted to sit in that too-small chair and pretend we were back at Appeal with the whole fifth floor outside the door.

"Yesss." Abbie drew out the word like she was drunk. It gratified me that she, too, hadn't had anything to drink with dinner, even though I had thought nothing of it at the time. But in this moment, it meant that the pleasure in her voice was all due to the potency of our desire for each other.

Briefly letting go of her body, I guided her over to the little desk. I took a seat in the utterly uncomfortable chair and slid it back to allow Abbie to lean against the desk. Instead of sitting up on it like I expected, I saw she was worrying her hands together.

Bringing the chair closer with my feet so that my knees pressed against hers, I sought to reassure her if she'd changed her mind. Hell, I'd settle just for holding her in my arms tonight, surrounded by her warm coconut scent.

"Sweetheart, we don't have to do this." I kept my tone gentle and calm, hoping to put her at ease.

She didn't look at me as she said, "No. I think I want to. I mean, I do want to." Before I could say anything, she continued. "It's just that I've never… you know, been able…"

"To come from oral sex before?" I couldn't tell if it made it better or worse for her if I voiced the words on her behalf, but I hated the idea of being uncomfortable. "But do you like it?"

Now she looked at me, a bit of pleading in her eyes. "I think I would like it with *you*. But before, I'm not sure. Maybe I was thinking too much? What if I can't?" She was still whispering.

I moved in closer to press my mouth against the curve of her belly. I adored all the peaks and valleys of her body; her innate femininity and softness made me the moth to her flame. I thought maybe it would be easier for her to tell me what she wanted if she didn't have to look me in the eye.

Pressing kisses to the area near her belly button, I reveled in the heat of my mouth dampening the fabric of her dress, leaving any part of me against her skin that she could feel.

I lowered my voice and asked, "Do you want to try?"

Sixteen

ABBIE

"*Do you want to try?*" he asked. Despite the heat simmering between us, he still sounded calm and confident. Aiden looked up at me, appearing truly content to wait for me to gather my thoughts.

Using his hands to stroke the skin of my inner thighs, his touch sparked pinpricks of pleasure in its wake.

I wasn't sure if I'd enjoy it, but all of Aiden's touches felt different from any I'd felt before. Maybe oral would feel different too?

"If you don't like it, we'll stop," he said as if he'd read my mind. "I could spend all night devouring these."

Sliding his hands from my thighs and up my body until he reached the neckline of my dress, he brought the top down until it settled at my waist. Aiden brought himself closer to me and took a nipple into his mouth, sucking hard, his hands returning to cup my breasts. At my exhalation of surprise, he began licking its sensitive underside, alternating between slow, deliberate swipes of his tongue and quicker flicks against its peak.

My pelvic muscles tightened and released with his teasing motions.

I was sure I'd never felt this aroused. He wouldn't think less of me if I couldn't orgasm from oral sex as he truly seemed to derive so much pleasure from my responses.

"Yes, Aiden. I want to."

To my surprise, he didn't immediately switch gears from my chest. He continued his ministrations with his mouth until the nipple he was focused on felt hot and achy. However, he didn't ignore the other nipple, occasionally tugging it with his forefinger and thumb while the rest of his hand cupped my breast.

At some point, I moved my hands to hold the sides of his head. They were currently buried in his thick, dark hair. Tightening my fingers slightly on the strands, he took the cue and pulled off my tender bud.

His full lips were slightly swollen from drawing the pleasure from my skin. His hungry gaze took in the redness left by his lips and the scruff of his five-o'clock shadow.

He brought his hands down to my thighs once more, leaning back to take in the picture I made. I could only imagine what I looked like from his point of view, with my dress pooled at my waist and my sensitive skin marked with his ministrations.

I edged myself back up and onto the desk, completely turned on by the idea that I'd been on his mind while he was locked away in his office. It was dizzying to imagine him sitting behind his desk, looking imposing and in control of everything while getting hard thinking of doing this to me.

Now, we were about to live his fantasy. God, it was overwhelming in the best way.

Aiden rolled the chair and guided my legs so that they rested on the outside of his thighs, causing my dress to hike up with the motion. He took advantage of the movement to slide his hands to the inside of my thighs, his thumbs pushing my dress up until my core was bare to him.

"Fuck, Abbie. No panties." It sounded like he had to force the words out. His gaze was lasered in on my folds, causing me to release a burst of wetness.

Aiden let one hand move down to the bottom of my pussy, catching some of my arousal as it dripped down through my folds.

"Jesus. You are so wet for me. I can't wait to taste you."

Despite his filthy words, he didn't seem in a hurry to stop the movements of his fingers, having added a second, which were currently smoothing my own wetness between the lips of my labia. The wet sound of his fingers running through my cleft seemed to echo in the silence of my room, though the sound was likely amplified by the way my attention remained riveted by his every movement.

He seemed to deliberately avoid making contact with my clit or pushing his fingers inside me to give me any relief.

Just as I would have sworn on my official EA manual that my clit was literally throbbing so hard he could see it, his fingers withdrew, causing me to gasp in disappointment.

"Shhh, baby. I'm going to take care of you."

The confidence of his tone had my muscles loosening. Right or wrong, I loved the way he took command of a situation, letting me sink into the sensations rather than having to worry about what I was doing.

Aiden leaned down and took a deep inhale, pressing his face into my mound. I felt the cool air of his inhale and the hot release of his exhale against my most tender flesh, nose bumping my clit. My center clenched with the jolt of pressure. It was so perfectly indecent that I had to bite my lip to prevent whatever sound was bubbling up in my throat.

"Aiden." My voice cracked as I said his name. I didn't even know exactly what I was asking for at this moment, but I knew I needed more of him.

Hearing me call him by his name seemed to strike to something primal within him because he turned absolutely feral at my request. He put his entire mouth on me and started attacking my pussy like he was trying to consume me and fuck me with his mouth at the same time. He pushed his tongue inside me, and it felt like he was replicating the passionate kisses he had given my lips moments before. He thrust his tongue as deeply inside me as he could, growling while he sucked my pussy lips into his mouth. I gripped the edge of the desk to keep myself upright. I was edging closer and closer to a release of pressure I could feel building deep within.

He gripped my thighs, holding them apart to keep my core wide open to him. Zeroing in on my clit. He started kissing it, sucking and licking. He kept his mouth on that tiny piece of flesh and increased his pressure and speed as I rolled my pelvis as much as his grip would allow. Letting go of one of my thighs, he brought two fingers to my pussy and pushed them inside me. He pressed upward against my walls, somehow intensifying the pressure building from my core.

I had a quick flash of concern that I might not be able to come before a deep contraction of my inner muscles signaled he had found my G-spot with his fingers. My gaze snapped back to his. I fought against closing my eyes so badly because I wanted to show him how much this moment meant to me, even if this was our only night together.

His absolute focus on my reaction and the relentlessness of his mouth made everything else disappear. He latched on to my clit one more time and growled. The vibration of his mouth and the suction combined pushed me over the edge. I was coming in waves, and he never let up the pressure on my clit, riding each spasm with his mouth against me.

As my orgasm slowed, he continued giving me featherlight kisses against my overly sensitive core. He gave my mound a final sweet kiss before leaning back in his chair. I could see the shine of my wetness on his nose, mouth, and chin. He was covered in evidence of my arousal. He licked both of his lips devilishly, as if he knew exactly what I was thinking.

"You are addictive."

I tucked my hair covering the sides of my face, lost for words. Aiden wasn't having any of that, though. He put his hand under my chin and brought his face close to mine. I blushed when I realized I could smell the musk of myself on him.

"Baby, watching you lose control was absolutely amazing. No need to feel shy or embarrassed anymore. I loved every second, okay?"

"Okay," I managed.

He stood for a better angle to wrap his arms around me and kissed me tenderly. The sweet kiss turned scorching hot in seconds.

Aiden pulled back an inch. "See what I mean? Delicious." Referring to our shared taste of my pleasure.

With him standing, I felt how hard he was against my stomach. I wanted him to feel as good as I did. But when I started to reach between us, he stopped my hand.

"You don't have to." He spoke against my mouth. "Tonight was just for you. It was incredible to share this with you. I don't need anything else."

I opened my mouth to argue, but he silenced me with his fingers. I playfully bit his fingertips. His hand recoiled with mock outrage, making me laugh.

It was something special to see Aiden Sullivan being silly. I wanted to burn this moment into my brain to revisit over and over. He'd always been too gorgeous for words, but right now, he was sweet.

After spending a minute or so gently rubbing my thighs as my breathing came back down to normal, Aiden gently pulled my dress over my knees.

"Can I stay here tonight?" After what we'd just shared, he watched me intently, as if I would tell him no. Still, I appreciated him asking, just in case I wanted some space. It was heartwarming that he didn't want to leave.

"Yes, please."

He helped me off the desk before moving to the still-made side of the bed and sliding in. Sneaking into the washroom, I grabbed my pajama shirt and shorts, whipped off my dress, changed, and brushed my teeth.

Coming back out into the bedroom, I found him lying on his side, waiting for me. Aiden pulled back the covers in invitation, and I slid beneath them. He wrapped me up tight in the sheet and duvet. God, I loved to be tucked in. It emphasized his attentiveness, and I couldn't get enough.

He gathered me in his arms. I didn't know if I could sleep like that, but I was damn sure going to try.

"We can talk tomorrow, okay?" Aiden whispered into my hair.

"Okay," I replied quietly.

So much had changed. My mind was spinning. I couldn't think right now, though. I was going to melt into Aiden and face reality in the morning.

Seventeen

AIDEN

My internal clock woke me at 4:48 a.m. from the best sleep I'd had since changing jobs. The night before came back to me as I realized I was pressed up against Abbie's back, my arm slung low on her hip. Her long hair spread out behind her, tickling my shoulder and chest with its softness.

Knowing I should get up versus getting out of bed were two different things. I couldn't remember the last time I'd considered sleeping in. Going to the gym before work had been my routine since I started my first job out of college. Thirty minutes on the treadmill every morning helped clear my head and get me focused for the day ahead. It was the only time I pushed business to the back of my mind.

This morning, my body wanted to stay in bed with Abbie. No one with an ounce of sense would leave the haven of tropical scent and warm skin created by the gorgeous woman beside me.

But we had said one night, and I didn't want to make her uncomfortable. It might be easier for her if I left now while she was still sleeping. She could have some time to herself before our final day of meetings to process last night for what it was.

Could I really do that? Just go? This wasn't a one-night stand, and Abbie was much more important to me than that.

Resolved to stick with the routine that hadn't failed me yet, I shifted out of bed and eyed the open door between our rooms. It felt wrong to leave, but things would be too complicated if I stayed.

My steps were soundless as I moved to her side of the bed. I didn't feel right simply leaving a note, but I didn't want to wake her fully after so few hours of rest.

"Abbie?" I whispered. "Abbie?"

"Hmm?" Her eyes remained closed. "Aiden?" Her words were slurred with sleep.

"I'm going to the gym now. We can talk at breakfast, okay?"

"Oh. Okay. Sure." Abbie managed to squint in my direction, some awareness seeping into her voice. "Do you…?" Her voice drifted off. I couldn't tell if she'd fallen back to sleep or changed her mind about saying something.

I was ashamed that I hoped it was the first option.

Leaning down to give her a brief kiss on the cheek, I moved toward our adjoining doorway.

I couldn't resist a look at the desk where she'd taken her pleasure hours earlier. Flashes of our intimate encounter threatened to overwhelm my thoughts. And send me right back into her bed.

Once her door was closed, I did the same to the door on my side, locking the dead bolt with a gentle click.

I leaned back against the door, scrubbing my hands over my face. I thought I'd feel relieved after we spent time together. But if anything, my need for Abbie increased having seen her experience pleasure.

Hell, I hadn't even gotten off, and it was the best sex I could remember in forever. I cringed at the idea of going back to the office and pretending like the intimacy between us had never happened. The draw I felt toward her was stronger than ever before.

Shedding my T-shirt and boxers, I quickly rummaged through my suitcase for my workout clothes, then put on my running shoes.

I used the hotel's gym to burn off the adrenaline of finally having Abbie in my arms. Maybe I could push myself hard enough to outrun these dangerous feelings.

After a grueling workout, endless emails, and a shower, a few hours later, I found myself sitting in the hotel restaurant waiting for Abbie.

Since leaving her bed, she had been all I could think about. The initial thrill was still running through me, but the reality of our situation had added a layer of unease that I couldn't shake.

I was in the midst of chastising myself for putting her in this position when I looked up to find her sliding into the seat in front of me.

A shy smile graced her lovely face. Her eyes held a mix of uncertainty and excitement, like our first day at Anime Expo. Goddamn, I liked being the sole reason for any of her happiness.

Abbie's voice was quiet and wavered slightly. "Hi."

"Good morning." Her presence made my face light up with a warm smile. "Were you able to sleep in a bit?"

We didn't have a meeting until 10:00 a.m. that morning. It would be our last one of the trip. We would have the remainder of the day for Anime Expo and fly back to San Jose the following morning. Once I'd bought the convention tickets, I urged Abbie to see if she could change our return flights to allow her more time. Her bright smile at the time had been my reward.

I felt nothing compared to sitting across from her, remembering all the little moments that now hummed between us. I couldn't deny the connection; it was stronger than ever.

"Yeah, um, I did. Did you go to the gym?" Her gaze flicked down to her lap, then back up to me. Had I done the wrong thing by leaving so early? Without knowing what she was thinking, I couldn't be sure if it would make it easier for either of us in the aftermath of our choices.

"I did. I can't seem to sleep past 5:00 a.m. now, and I didn't want to wake you by being restless." I hoped that explanation would show her that she wasn't the reason I left. I'd needed to get my head on straight, and I'd failed at that. The urge to stay close to her was just as strong as when I'd woken up.

"Ah, I see. No problem. I get it," she agreed too quickly for my comfort.

I wanted a clear picture of what we were dealing with. I couldn't wait any longer. I needed to know what she was thinking.

"Abbie. Are you okay after last night? You don't regret anything this morning?" I had to know where we stood, even if it made her feel awkward.

"No, Aiden. I don't regret anything." Her voice came out stronger than when she sat down. "Do you?" The question was accompanied by two spots of pink that appeared on her cheeks.

"Definitely not." My voice was calm and sure. I wanted to reach across the table and take her hands in mine to offer her some reassurance. But the line on how much comfort I could, or should, offer her was totally unclear to me at this point.

Regardless of what we decided in the next few minutes, I vowed to behave as professionally as before, which meant keeping my hands to myself during the business day. But that didn't mean I wasn't going to test the waters to see if she would want a repeat of our nighttime activities.

"You know." I cleared my throat. "We did say one night, but technically, it's still the same day. It's our last hours in LA. How would you feel about another evening together?" I left the question vague so she wouldn't feel like I was pressuring her for more than we'd already done. Hell, I'd be satisfied just to sleep with her again if that's all she wanted.

The color in her cheeks intensified. "I… uh… yes. I would like that," she finally managed.

"Good. We can order room service when we get back and just relax. It's been a big week. Are you feeling okay about things going back to the office on Monday?"

Hoping that she would understand my meaning, I wanted to make sure we were on the same page before we were back in Amado and working side by side again. There was no way for us to be in a relationship with each other. It would be career suicide for us both if word got around the office.

That I was her boss was enough of a problem on its own, but factor in our difference in ages—I was steadfastly ignoring that Abbie was a year *younger* than Claire—and I might as well tender my resignation on the spot.

Even knowing the potential consequences, I just couldn't deny myself one last taste of her. I'd done everything right for years. Hopefully, we could savor our moments together for what they were and then move on like mature adults. I knew I could trust Abbie's discretion.

I had faith it would turn out okay. It wasn't as if I was in love with her. We were two consenting adults making our own informed choices.

Making the responsible decision after last night was more difficult than ever before. A pang of disappointment in my chest surprised me with the realization that I wished I *could* pursue her once we were home again.

"I'll be fine, Aiden. No need to worry about me. I understand what this is and what it isn't." Her answer was more direct than I expected.

She gave me a secret smile. A smile drawn from our intimate knowledge of each other and what was yet to come.

Later tonight, hopefully, both of us would.

Eighteen

ABBIE

I was glad I'd taken detailed notes during our last client meeting of the trip. I'd been so busy thinking about the night ahead of us that I'd retained nothing business related.

I'd even considered telling Aiden we could skip (blasphemy!) the final afternoon of Anime Expo, but I'd come to my senses after remembering there were a few exhibitors I had wanted to revisit, as well as making sure I attended the remaining paid events. I didn't want to waste my gift from Aiden, even if I was anticipating a different kind of fun instead.

As it was, we'd gotten back to the hotel earlier than expected, and he'd left me at my door with a heated look that promised all sorts of post-dinner debauchery.

We'd separated long enough for me to have a shower and put on some fresh clothes. As enticing as last night's dress had been, I didn't want to spend the evening in my restrictive work shirt and skirt.

If my *Hello Kitty* T-shirt and pajama bottoms turned Aiden off, it would be better to know now. Not that it would matter after tonight, of course. But I didn't think he was shallow enough to be put off by cartoon characters. Heck, he was almost proficient in identifying a couple of starter Pokémon after four days at the convention.

That thought gave me pause. What if he was anime'd out? Well, it was too late to change now, not when I'd heard that firm knock against the inner door between our rooms.

I hadn't left it unlocked tonight because I would have lost my mind if he had walked in on me in the shower. We weren't *that* comfortable with each other. Plus, getting the crap scared out of you with a surprise shower visitor definitely said "horror movie" rather than "hot off-limits hookup with your boss."

It still felt surreal to me that I was doing this. I was about fifty-fifty on whether this whole thing was a lust/stressed-induced dream after being alone with Aiden for so many days. But it was happening, and I was going to approach it with the same abandon I had the night before.

I never got to be carefree and let go of my responsibilities. Aiden's discretion was trustworthy since he had as much to lose as I did.

Unlocking the dead bolt, I let Aiden in. He appeared in the doorway wearing a black T-shirt and thin gray pajama bottoms. God, I couldn't look at his pants for too long, or I might burst into flames. They were indecently enticing.

I could practically see the full outline of his… Nope!

I looked up to see that he'd caught me staring at his "assets." His bright expression suggested he was highly amused.

"Hi." My tone was rife with embarrassment.

"Hi." In contrast, his voice showed his confidence.

I remained frozen with my hand on the door, trying to recover my senses until he arched a brow at me.

"Can I come in?" The humor in his tone had the opposite effect on the inner calm I was scrambling to achieve.

"Oh! Yes, sorry. I'm not sure what's going on with me tonight." So much for seducing him with my charm.

Not that I had any idea about the seduction part. I hoped to avoid making a fool of myself, especially since I was so attracted to him. His handsome face vaporized half my vocabulary on a regular day.

I moved back as he entered my room and sat casually on the end of the bed.

After shutting the door, I seemed to glitch again, not knowing if I should sit beside him or invite him further onto the bed. Should we order dinner first? Should I get the room service menu?

"Hey, Abbie. Come sit down. There's no pressure here." He held out his hand to me.

Accepting that I was doomed to spend most of the evening embarrassed, I closed the distance between us, letting him guide me down to the bed.

He kept my hand in his as he seemed to want to settle my nerves.

"Look, nothing has to happen tonight. Let's just have dinner and relax, okay? It's been a busy week."

Rather than pretend I felt a calm that I didn't feel, I gave him a small smile.

"Good. Have you looked at the room service menu at all?"

"I haven't. Let me grab it."

Eager for something to do, I rummaged through the desk drawer for the hotel's information binder. Bringing it back to the bed, I felt more comfortable than before taking a seat beside him. Resuming my spot, he let his arm come around my waist and hold my hip lightly as he shifted over to see the menu pages more clearly.

I could smell the clean scent of his skin after his shower. Now that some of my powers of observation had returned to me, I could see his hair was still slightly damp and curled up at the ends.

After deciding what to order, he moved to the head of the bed to use the phone to call down to reception. I crawled up the bed to lean back against the multitude of pillows in front of the headboard and scooted under the comforter, feeling immediately better with the extra fabric surrounding me.

Aiden hung up the phone and turned back to me, taking my lead and pulling back the covers to get under himself.

"They said it was going to be about forty-five minutes for our order."

"That's fine. I'm not super hungry yet anyway." The nervous energy running through my system had zapped my appetite.

He shifted closer so that our sides were touching from hip to shoulder and lifted his arm to wrap it back around me. I leaned forward to let him, then settled back into the warmth of his body with my head now on his shoulder.

Aiden took a deep breath, his body reclining further into the pillows.

"God, what a week. I think we did well, though. One signed deal and more to come."

"I'm glad. I liked Anime Expo best."

"I bet you did. You got to have four afternoons seeing me out of my comfort zone." He squeezed my side playfully.

"That's true. It's only fair. The tables have to turn sometime."

He pressed his cheek to the top of my head. "It hasn't been so bad, though, has it? Being an executive assistant?"

"Well, once I stopped giving the wrong reports to the wrong departments and figured out the scheduling software so I didn't accidentally invite everyone to all the meetings, it's been okay."

Aiden chuckled at my frank assessment of the minor disasters during my first few weeks on the job.

"There's a learning curve for everything," he offered generously.

"Right… Another step up in the corporate world. I'm on my way."

"Do you want to be? Moving up the ladder, that is?"

I pulled away a little so I could look into his eyes. He'd been a better than expected listener this trip, I considered how honest to be.

"You don't have to tell me." He must have seen the hesitation on my face. "That said, you can tell me, and it will stay between us. Just like this whole twenty-four hours. We're taking a step out of reality."

I tried to smile in response. It had felt so good in his arms I'd forgotten this was a stolen moment in time. That everything would go back to the way it was tomorrow morning. A little bit of sadness dampened the lightness of my mood.

"Not really," I admitted quietly, not looking into his eyes anymore but instead at the way his T-shirt stretched across his well-toned chest. Turning toward him, I put my hand over his heart, soothed by the steady beat. What was the harm? I was decent at my job now. It wasn't like he was going to demote me.

"Why not?" His tone didn't show any surprise or disappointment, just the same deep well of calm he seemed to have endless access to.

Unconsciously smoothing out the wrinkles in his shirt, running my hand over the spot on his chest repeatedly, I struggled to verbalize my secret wish.

"Remember how we met that day at the park?" I felt like that moment was years ago rather than a few months. "I'd rather be taking photos for a living, but I wasn't brave enough to go to school for it."

My chest caved in with the panic of admitting where my true passions lay, followed by a deep well of relief that was unexpected. This was big for me. I'd never uttered those words out loud to anyone other than Indie and Emery.

The world didn't end because I told Aiden that I'd rather be doing something else. I'd shocked myself by having the ability to let out one of my most tender pain points. My regrets were a reminder that I'd let my mom fearmonger me into a career path I hadn't even wanted because it was what she considered practical.

I chanced a peek at his face through my lashes, not ready to see if he thought that my idea was stupid reflected in his face. But his face was clear of judgment. Aiden wore the same attentive and interested expression he'd adopted during our time alone on this trip.

"Why not? I've seen the photos you've been sending Ethan in graphics for the company's social media account. It's clear you have talent. I don't have the technical background to explain why, but I know images that can be sold, and you've achieved that."

I couldn't speak for a moment as the rush of emotion built behind my eyes at his praise. I'd always played off my interest as a hobby or something "fun" to pass the time. Blinking to keep the overwhelming emotions at bay, I struggled to find the words to reply to him.

"Thank you. I'm bad at taking compliments. But I appreciate you saying that." It was an understatement that I wasn't good at accepting praise. More like I avoided situations where my efforts were recognized, preferring to stay out of the limelight. Compliments made me feel like a fraud, like I'd fooled the person into believing something about me that wasn't true.

But somehow, coming from Aiden, the statement that he liked my photos felt genuine in a way I couldn't doubt. Maybe it was because he was such a direct person who didn't pull his punches. Aiden never offered flattery or praise that was undue.

I tucked his words into a little corner of my heart. I knew it wasn't a good idea to let him affect me this much, but next time the world felt dark for me, I hoped to be able to pull out this moment to remind myself that someone else believed in me.

"Well, it's true. I hope you take it to heart. If that's your area of interest, you should look at applying to the temporary position that's coming up when one of Ethan's team goes on leave next month."

Now I was surprised. "What?"

"There's no reason you shouldn't take advantage of an opportunity to learn more about something you're interested in. Maybe it's half a step down in terms of the admin role you have now, but I think you'd enjoy it. Ethan runs a good team."

"But what about my role?" I wondered now if he was looking for a reason to get rid of me. Was I doing a shitty job, and he was just trying to let me down easy? That thought made me a little ill.

"Hey, now listen." He pulled me in tighter to his body and reached up with his other hand to cover mine where I realized I was now gripping his T-shirt. His hand enveloped my whole fist in warmth. "You've got a good handle on your job now. Don't doubt yourself. I'm shooting myself in the foot by telling you that you should talk to Ethan about that role. I'm going to end up with someone inept from the admin pool to cover you."

His deep sigh made me giggle. "Well, there is your trusty manual. Whoever might take over for me temporarily could learn to live and breathe it."

He pinched my side lightly, making me squeak. "Brat. I'll have you know it took weeks of overtime to put that together." His tone took an imperious edge. I knew him well enough by now that he was putting on the affronted voice.

"I have no doubt," I said with a mocking solemness, batting my eyelashes exaggeratingly. "That thing is the equivalent of anyone else's life's work. You should be very proud of it."

"Somehow, I doubt you mean that as a compliment the same way I did when you mentioned your photos," he replied dryly. "But seeing as I have something else to discuss with you before our food gets here, I'll let your insubordination go for now."

I grinned. Playful Aiden was fun to experience. "What else did you want to talk about?"

"This." He moved his hand to my chin and tilted it up as he leaned down to kiss me—a light brush of his lips over mine.

"Mmm. I agree," I whispered the words against his mouth.

"I thought you would." He pressed his lips more fully into mine, deepening the kiss.

I shifted my body further toward him to be able to feel as much of his body against me as I could manage from this angle. Letting my hand move the rest of the way across his chest to his shoulder, I gripped the firm muscles under my hand tightly.

A nip at my lips had me opening my mouth, allowing his tongue to press forward and slide sinuously together with mine. The contact had a low sound rumbling from his throat. Aiden let go of my chin to bring his hand down to my other hip and used his strength to help me climb into his lap.

"Much better," I whispered before resuming the kiss. I felt his arousal hard against my center. Wrapping my arms around his neck to keep my balance, I gave in to the urge to shift my body against him, pressing us together through the thin layers of our clothing. His hands moved down to my butt cheeks and grabbed a firm handful in each. I stopped mid-motion for a second, thinking he didn't want me to move, but he squeezed my flesh in response. He pushed me into him, signaling my freedom to wiggle impatiently against him all I wanted.

Despite the movement of my lower half, he didn't let up on his conquest of my mouth, randomly altering kisses from slow and smooth to hard and deep.

I loved that he didn't rush to do anything else. He seemed happy to make out like teenagers—something I hadn't gotten to do when I was actually a teen. His hands occasionally tightened on my cheeks forcefully before caressing them again.

Time ceased to exist for me at that moment. I had no idea how much time we spent exploring each other's mouths and bodies over our clothes until a light knock on the door showed our dinner had arrived.

I pulled back in a daze. Aiden looked like he had come out of a similar trance.

"Uh, do you mind getting the door? I would, but... I need a minute." His gaze dropped to where I was pressed against his hardness, which was absolutely indecent in those pants.

My eyes widened, and he laughed. "Yep. Of course."

I climbed off his lap clumsily, feeling a bit light-headed from all the giddiness running through my system. Throwing on a sweatshirt, I went to answer the door.

Nineteen

AIDEN

My mind woke before my body would cooperate. Slowly, my senses came back to me, and I realized my face was nuzzled into something soft. A wonderful sense of déjà vu settled over me. Just like yesterday morning, I had woken to Abbie's warmth next to me, my face pressed into her hair, and my hard cock was nestled against her ass.

I slowly leaned up and saw the clock read just after midnight. We must have fallen asleep after dinner while watching a movie. The TV's home screen cast a glow over her room.

I didn't want to wake her and break the spell of this moment. She was just mine in this tiny pocket of space and time. I wanted her badly, but it wasn't even sexual. I felt a small shift in her body and looked down to see her eyes open.

"Hello. What time is it?" Her voice was scratchy with sleep.

"Hi. How are you feeling?" Even though I should, I wasn't letting her go yet. I wanted to hold on to our little world a little longer. I wondered if I had woken her or vice versa.

A soft sigh was her reply as she pressed her face into my neck. I suppressed a groan. Didn't she know how insane my body was for her?

She rocked herself back against my cock, so yes, she knew exactly what she was doing. I slid my hand around her front and rested it on her stomach to stop her movements.

"Maybe we should just get some sleep, hmm?" Clearly, we'd been wiped out if we were falling asleep before 9:00 p.m.

She resumed rubbing her ass against me in answer. My hard length pressed deeper into her backside through the flimsy barrier of our pajamas.

"I don't want to sleep." Abbie surprised me by rolling over and pressing the fronts of our bodies together.

Resting my head back on the pillow, I watched her.

"What do you want, then?" My voice rasped with desire.

"This." She closed the distance between our mouths, and her tongue took a tiny taste of my lower lip.

That little movement snapped the thin hold on my feral need for her. I rolled her over so I could be on top and angled my pelvis into the cradle of her hips, rocking my hard length against her, much harder than her earlier tentative movements.

Fuck it. I was through denying myself and her. We promised to spend the rest of the day together, and I was finally giving in to our mutual desire.

This was no hesitation in the way I sucked at her lips and bit her bottom one. I capitalized on her shocked whimper to push my way into her mouth. I rubbed and flicked my tongue against hers, mimicking fucking her with my tongue. Showing her everything I wanted to do to her delicious body. This was not the slow seduction of the previous night. We were a torrent of lips and tongues and teeth.

I pressed harder against her center, angling my thrusts until I heard her gasp when I applied friction to her sweet spot.

I bracketed her body with my arms and leaned up on my elbows to look down at her flushed face. I wanted to make her as delirious as she made me. Abbie rewarded me with a sultry look that reflected my own level of desire.

Lowering myself back down to get closer to my prize, I couldn't get enough of her skin. There were too many soft spots to suck and bite along her neck. I worked my tongue as low as the collar of her infuriating T-shirt would allow.

I needed more of her.

"Baby, you feel so good. I want to see all of you."

Abbie murmured, "Yes," against my mouth.

Balancing on one arm, I pushed a hand between us and dragged her pajama shirt upward, revealing the creamy skin of her belly, pausing when the shirt caught on the bottom of her full breasts. I could see her nipples were rock hard against the taut fabric. I thanked the universe she wasn't wearing a bra.

I thought of all the days in my office when I'd been tempted by her graceful, perfect neck. Now, the scruff on my face had marred its perfection, leaving it rosy in patches, a temporary mark that called to something primitive inside me.

She arched her back in invitation, and her shirt slipped an inch so I could see the silky bottom of her tits. I nipped the skin on the underside of a breast before pulling her shirt up to her neck. My memory from the night before paled in comparison to the real thing. They were more than a handful and a shade paler than the skin of her face and arms. I cupped a breast in each hand and gently squeezed. The softness of her skin was unlike anything I had ever felt. I needed more time to fully worship her the way I wanted to. I could spend hours loving on her two mounds alone, but I needed to see her come for me again before we had to leave this temporary haven we'd built.

Squeezing her again, she let out a desperate "Please" and ground her pussy down over my cock.

"Please what, baby?"

"I want more."

She was going to spell it out for me. I wanted to hear all the words tumbling from her lips, free of inhibition. Her consent meant everything to me.

Pushing her tits together with my hands, I bent my head to lick the deep valley of plush skin I had created. I teased the skin of each breast, giving quick flicks of my tongue just above each of her rosy areola. Knowing my teasing was only stoking her need further, I rubbed my stubble across her tender skin and was gratified when she whined for more.

I just smiled as I watched her face scrunch in frustration.

"More" was all she could manage.

I gripped her tits in both hands again. Squeezing tighter than before, just enough pressure to sharpen the sensations she was feeling, no pain.

"Do you know what I want to do to these tits?" I said conversationally, as if she wasn't twisting and pushing back against me. She replied with a quiet moan. I'd held my tongue the night before, but if this was the last time I was going to have her under my hands, then she was going to *know* just what she did to me.

"I want to lick and suck and bite them until they are covered in my marks so that there is no doubt that they belong to me. When you go about your day at work, and I have to see you talk to other men, each little bruise will twinge with the reminder that I own you. Just like you own me."

In the low light of the room, I could see her cheeks pink with the directness of my words.

"I don't look at other men, Aiden. Not the way I look at you."

"Oh, sweetheart, I like knowing you are as desperate for me as I am for you. Since you are such a good girl, I'll give you a little reward."

I returned my attention to her breasts, moving my fingers to her nipples and giving them a gentle pinch. Her breath hitched, and her hips bucked with the mild sting. Holding her gaze, I lowered my head slowly to her right breast and sucked the warm pink skin surrounding her nipple. Her back arched, encouraging me to take more of her flesh into my mouth, but I wouldn't allow myself to be rushed. Abbie was a delicacy meant to be savored. My second circle around her nipple was to give her little nips with my teeth. I was pleased when I saw the marks I had made.

Taking pity on her for a moment, I engulfed her nipple with my mouth again and sucked with long, strong pulls. She keened at the pressure, and the undulation of her hips showed me how much she liked that. I repeated the motion until I looked into her eyes and saw a glazed expression.

"Do you know what I fantasize about, sweetheart?" Not giving her time to answer, I gave her nipple another suck, following with several quick lashes of my tongue.

"I'm sucking on these glorious nipples, so ripe and hard for me. I want to make you mine in every way. I want to mark your skin and pussy with my come. Every time I touch you, I feel an out-of-control need that I've never felt before."

"Aiden…" She sucked in a choked breath. The black of her pupils had almost swallowed the rings of hazel. Combined with her short intakes of breath, I could see how overwhelmed by desire she was.

Still, I kept talking to give her mind a moment to catch up to her body's sensations, just to make sure she wanted to move forward.

"I'd suck on these sweet little nipples so often they'll be so tender you can't stand it anymore. They'll be so sensitive that I'll be able to make you come with a few flicks of my tongue. Would you like that?"

I switched over to her left breast and alternated between firm bites and soothing sweeps of my tongue, marking her sweet mound of flesh at random.

"Yes." The *s* elongated in a whisper.

Her words brought a hard grin to my face. I wanted her actively imagining this fantasy with me so that we could forget we only had tonight and answer only to our desires.

I rolled us to our sides and slid down beside her so that my face was lying next to her breasts. I saw how swollen her nipple was from my ministrations, a ripe summer cherry just waiting to burst in my mouth. Groaning, I pulled as much of her flesh into my mouth as I could and settled back into a rhythm of deep pulls, followed by short licks. Just when she seemed to anticipate my next move, I switched my movements again, changing to soft kisses and gentle licks and back again.

She started rubbing her pelvis against my stomach.

Sliding my left hand between her thighs and under her shorts, I cupped her hot center. Sucking and licking her breast while I spread her juices all over my hand, I could feel her pussy clenching down. I pushed two fingers inside her and moaned around her nipple at the sound her wetness made. My fingers reached toward her front wall for the little ridge of her G-spot while I rubbed her clit hard with the heel of my hand.

She whimpered, clearly overloaded with sensations, and I pulled out my fingers to add a third. I pushed them gently back into her, mimicking the rhythm I wanted to fuck her with.

I needed to watch her go over the edge, to memorize the blush of her skin, the unevenness of her breaths, and the pleading in her eyes. She made me a feral king, beating my chest with victory at my conquest.

"I want you to come on my hand and fingers, and then I'm going to watch you lick your juices off me."

I redoubled my efforts with my fingers in her channel and my palm against her clit. Her eyes squeezed shut as she plunged into the pleasure of her orgasm. Her pussy pulsed so fiercely it became a battle to keep my fingers pumping in and out of her, wanting to wring every last drop of climax from her. She came in a flurry of "Oh fuck" and whispers of my name. I reveled in her moisture coating my hand. It was incredible.

As she came back to herself, she looked into my eyes with a soft, fond expression. It took my breath away, the way she could take me from animal to intimacy in seconds.

Seeing her so wrecked with pleasure had me grinning at her. She was beautiful with her chest heaving, her hair a mess from her pillow, and her skin swollen and marked from my mouth. I moved back up so our faces were level. She greeted me with a kiss, tangling her tongue with mine.

She pushed herself up to a sitting position.

"Aiden, it's my turn."

A rumble sounded in my chest at the idea of finally having her mouth on me. Tonight, I wouldn't deny either of us.

"Yes, sweetheart, it is. And I have just what you need to help that mouth slide all over me."

I held up my hand, still covered in her pleasure.

Twenty

ABBIE

My gaze moved between Aiden's hand and his face. The temperature in the room ratcheted up with his filthy words.

Looking at him kneeling on the bed with a smile Lucifer himself would envy, I was at his mercy.

Lowering his hand and tugging his pajama pants just below his cock, he gave it a few slow strokes, making it shiny with my come. Jesus. His sexual confidence was so incredibly seductive.

Aiden had made me come spectacularly twice now without regard for his own pleasure. I wanted to please him too.

His dark eyes were almost pitch-black in the shadowed room. His broad shoulders expanded with his deep breaths.

I pushed myself to sit next to him so I could see his face clearly. I needed him to tell me how to make him feel good. "Please tell me how to make it good for you."

"Are you sure you want to get on your knees for me?" His gaze was hungry and focused.

I loved how he even made asking for my consent sound sexy.

"Yes."

"Fucking right. You are unbelievably sexy. Anything you do is going to feel amazing."

I scrambled off the bed, eager to please him, and knelt on the hard floor, waiting for his instructions.

He slowly climbed off the bed and stood in front of me.

"Take them off." He slid a finger into the waistband of those gray pajama pants. His hard length waited for my mouth. This part of him, of course, was perfectly proportionate to the rest of his body.

I shivered as his words washed over me. I could see why he'd enjoyed going down on me so much. There was something amazing about being deliberate and conscious of giving him pleasure versus a lust-induced frenzy.

He kept eye contact as he pulled his T-shirt over his head, dropping it beside him.

I obeyed and pulled the fabric down from his waist, stepping out of them when they reached the floor.

He grasped his cock at its thick base. The hand with my come on it. Little sets of fireworks shot through my blood. Jesus, he didn't even need words to communicate his debauched ideas.

With a firm grip, he leisurely stroked his cock all the way to the tip, swiping the bead of precome. Now, he was using our combined juices to jack himself off.

After a few more pulls, he stopped. His length was now even harder than before. He took his hand off his cock and brought two fingers against my mouth. His other hand reached behind my head and gathered my hair in a ponytail. Sliding his hand down to the ends of my hair, he wrapped it around his fist. Wrapping my hair around his hand, two, three, four times, he gave it the gentlest tug forward and pushed his fingers between my lips.

"Open for me."

My lips parted excitedly for him. I laved his fingers with my tongue. Sucking his fingers a little deeper, I stroked them with my tongue to show him what I wanted to do to his cock.

He pulled his fingers from my mouth with a growled "Good girl" for me. Gripping himself by the base once more, he brought his tip up against my lips and tapped them lightly. More precome stuck to my bottom lip. I quickly flicked out my tongue to lap it up, my eyes closing.

"I want to see your eyes, Abbie. Can you open them?" I blinked them open to return my gaze to him. His smile was all teeth, a wolf that had found his dinner. It wasn't a pleased smile—it was a hungry one. I squirmed under his gaze, feeling turned on again despite just having come down from my climax.

"There you are. You're going to make me feel so good."

Opening my lips, he pushed the tip of his cock between them. I immediately started sucking him with as much pressure as I could, licking the underside with long, hard strokes. He used my hair to gently but firmly hold me in place while he slowly pushed toward the back of my mouth. He stopped just before he hit my throat, pulling back so that I was mouthing his tip once more.

"Goddamn, sweetheart, your mouth is a thousand times hotter than I've been dreaming about all these weeks."

I tried to communicate how much I wanted this by never taking my eyes off his. His cock grazed the back of my throat, so I concentrated on breathing as best I could through my nose. With the way he was looking at me, I knew even if I messed this up, he wouldn't hold it against me. It made it a lot easier to let my mind relax and concentrate on his reactions.

He paused for mere seconds before he pulled back, letting me gasp for a few breaths of air before plunging forward again.

His gaze was fiery, and his jaw clenched as he watched his cock move in and out of my mouth. I could feel the strength of his body chasing his release. I loved that I had this power over him.

"Fuck yes. Like that. Just thinking about this moment will keep me hard all day."

With a few more strong thrusts, he stalled his movements. My lips were tender from the stretch of his cock, but I sucked as deeply as I could, determined to show him I was all in. Spurts of come lashed my tongue. I sealed my lips around him, trying to not let any of his release escape.

"My god! You're going to make me an addict."

He slowly slipped his cock out of my mouth. I gave him a few more firm licks with my tongue before one last flick into the little slit at the head. My movements had him grunting, overly sensitive. His cock fell from my lips as he let go of my hair.

Aiden reached down and helped me up, pulling me into his arms. My muscles were tight from holding the position for so long, but I felt high with adrenaline.

He gathered me to him, pressing our bodies together and kissing me deeply. I loved the heat of his naked skin against mine. Guiding us onto the bed, he arranged our limbs so we were wrapped around each other. The haze of pleasure abated a bit as I watched his eyes for a hint of what he was thinking. He gazed back at me with such pure affection that it took my breath away. I didn't have a clue what he might say next.

"Abbie, you are incredible." I blushed as he rubbed his thumb over my cheek.

I hazily wondered if someone could pass out from pleasure. The state of euphoria brought on by the orgasm Aiden had just wrought from my body had me feeling boneless. It was like he had known all these magical ways to light up the sensations I was feeling and coupled it with the most shockingly filthy talk he could think of. How could he appear so proper and then have such a depth for depravity?

While the contrast in his words initially shocked me, my body responded to the visions he described. I'd never imagined I would appreciate dirty talk, but it seemed Aiden could do no wrong when it came to me. Take that, book boyfriends!

I knew this dance we'd been doing this week was not the start of a relationship. He was not, and couldn't be, my boyfriend. Being so drawn to him had me jumping in with both feet, for once just forgetting all the consequences. The combination of his protectiveness, how attuned to my reactions he was, and his fierce need for me was deadly.

There was no switch to turn my feelings off.

But I reasoned that those were problems for tomorrow's Abbie. Instead, I pressed my face into his neck and savored the scent that was pure Aiden. The warm smell of his skin was too good to pass up.

If I allowed myself to think for even a moment, I'd have to admit I wanted it all with Aiden. A real relationship. I wanted to savor hundreds of mornings just like this one, our sated bodies entwined.

But I wasn't going to let these last few moments be ruined by thoughts of what I couldn't have.

Liar. You'd take any part of him you could have. Anything to hang on to what you've just found in his arms.

Twenty-One

AIDEN

Monday morning saw me hanging by a thread to my convictions. We'd agreed before leaving LA to take the weekend to cool off from the heated moments on our trip. Other than a couple of texts assuring me that she was okay, we hadn't had any contact.

I'd thought of nothing else other than her warm laugh and soft skin under my lips for the past two days.

How had I kept my hands off her all these weeks? I needed to regain my ironclad control. And I needed to do it quickly. Abbie was due in my office in less than five minutes.

I mentally ran through all the reasons this thing with Abbie couldn't work. I was her boss, and any kind of intimate relationship would be ethically wrong. I was in a position of power, and even if she and I knew that there was nothing untoward happening in the way we got together, it would be awful if others at work were to find out about us.

We'd also signed conduct clauses in our contracts, and even if they were on the generic side, I didn't imagine us enacting filthy fantasies in my office and every room of my house could be considered proper conduct.

Our age difference was a significant barrier. At twenty-five, she was just beginning her career and finding her place in the world. I was set in my ways while she should be out having fun with her friends on the weekend. How could it work?

Oh yeah? You going to feel good about her letting some other idiot touch and taste her like you did in LA?

Jesus Christ. Those thoughts had me literally seeing red. No, I didn't want her to go and meet anyone else. I wanted her all to myself.

Of course, Abbie knocked on my door while I was trying to get my Neanderthal brain to calm the fuck down.

"Come in," I practically growled.

Abbie swiftly made her way into my office, her arms full of reports.

"Close the door," I ordered. She looked back at me uncertainly. Prior to our trip, the last thing I would have ever done was allow myself to be alone in a closed room with Abbie.

I knew I was acting out of character. But goddamnit, if these next few minutes were the only time I was going to have Abbie to myself all day, then I was going to hoard every one of them away from prying eyes.

"Um. Okay," she whispered as she shut the door almost silently.

Abbie returned to her spot, standing in front of my desk. I allowed myself to take her in. She was dressed in her typical work outfit of a white-collared shirt and a dark-colored pencil skirt. Today's skirt was navy, and it clung to every curve of her hips and thighs. Her shirt was unbuttoned just enough to give me a glimpse of her collarbone and the soft skin of her neck.

I realized I could still see some of the tiny marks from my mouth on her pale skin. I had to grip the arms of my chair so as not to stalk over there and ravage her again.

The animal side of me liked that there was still evidence on her skin of what we had done in LA.

My gaze traveled up from her neck to her face, where her cheeks had pinkened during my silent inspection. She stood there, waiting for me to speak, while I ogled her.

Fuck. I was off to a rough start if I intended to keep my hands off her from now on.

"Whenever you're ready, Abbie. I'm sure we have a lot to go over."

She also seemed to be lost in a haze of distraction. It took her a moment to compose herself, but her cheeks only continued to deepen in color. She briefly shifted the files into one arm so she could smooth down her skirt over one hip, subtly adjusting her legs so that I could see her knees rub together.

Was she thinking about my mouth on her delicious pussy? God, I could have spent hours making her come over and over until she couldn't stand it. Every sweep and flick of my tongue against her folds and clit had only stoked my need for her.

Was she wet now, standing in front of me? Would I find her hot and wet for me if I lifted that skirt? I needed to stop these wild thoughts. I was fucking hard under my desk. I dared not move my hand to press against my hard cock. She'd see how little control I had right now.

"Um. Right. Okay, I'll start with the feedback we got from our client dinner…" Abbie's voice was a little strained as she muddled through the first of several updates.

Resigning myself to not being able to concentrate on anything other than every salacious thing I wanted to do to her in my bed, I decided to just enjoy having her all to myself in this moment.

I could read the reports for myself later. For now, I'd just torture myself with having her in my arms mere days ago. I was an addict going through withdrawals of her feel and taste.

For all the willpower I thought I'd previously possessed, I made it one business day before crossing the line with Abbie in my office.

I couldn't stop myself, not even when I had her pinned against my desk at 6:00 p.m. on a Monday evening when she came to tell me she was leaving. I was about to obliterate our common sense with a kiss.

"Are you sure?" Abbie whispered. She peered into my eyes, searching for uncertainty.

She should have been looking for insanity instead because it was utterly insane to kiss my employee in my office with a few stragglers working late to catch up before the morning. Not to mention, the office cleaning staff would come through within the hour.

"Yes." I leaned down to put my hands on my desk on either side of her body. "Is that okay?"

Abbie nodded, biting her bottom lip with a hint of shyness. Considering we'd seen all of each other already, I found it terribly endearing that she was still finding her feet when it came to me.

She could snap her fingers and have me on my knees. Happily.

She was too damn sexy for words. The moment she figured out how much power she held over me, I was doomed. I'd never get anything done again.

Closing the distance between our mouths, I took her lips in an aggressive kiss. I thrust my tongue along her closed ones to get her to open to me. A cross between a rumble and a groan emanated from my chest, the lust and want I'd held in all day escaping my body.

My reservations from this morning were already lost to the passion between us.

I moved my hands from the desk to her hips, giving her curves a firm squeeze under her tight skirt. God, it was a fantasy come true for me to put my hands on her in her prim work attire. I wanted to make a mess of her: her hair loose from its bun, her shirt wrinkled with buttons askew, and that goddamn skirt hiked to her hips.

Before I could indulge myself in making good on my fantasies, Abbie pulled back, already breathing heavily from our kissing.

"Aiden, we shouldn't do this here. We said." Her gaze darted between my eyes and my mouth.

I rested my forehead against hers, closing my eyes. If I kept looking at her, I was going to convince her to let me take her right here on my damn desk. That would really put us both in danger.

"Shit. I'm sorry. You're right." There was resistance in each of my fingers as I pried them from the fabric of her skirt and the soft flesh below.

Taking that first step back from her was harder than it should have been for a man as disciplined as I prided myself on being. It shook me a little how fast my defenses had crumbled.

"Let's sit." I gestured toward the chairs in front of my desk. Unlike the first day we'd met in the office, when I'd forced myself to stay in my chair on the opposite side, I chose the chair next to hers, guiding her to a seated position by taking her hand.

I couldn't make myself sever that last bit of skin-to-skin contact, so I sat leaning toward her so I didn't have to let go of her hand.

"What are we going to do?" She'd surprised me by being the first to speak. Abbie's expression was open and guileless as she clung to my hand. It warmed me that she didn't want to let go of me either.

Huffing out a breath, I tried to think reasonably about our situation.

"Honestly, I don't know." It was foreign for me to be so out of my depth on anything. I was the type of man who only put himself in circumstances where I could control the outcome. Or, if not in my control, I had a reason to believe the end result would be in my favor.

It occurred to me that I hadn't asked her about the outcome of her chat with Ethan. She'd said she would talk to him about filling the leave for his team's admin.

"Did you have a chance to talk to Ethan today? What did he think?" It certainly seemed like something she would enjoy more than what she was currently doing. I felt regret that she'd spent her degree and years since college doing something she didn't feel any passion for.

Abbie deserved to do something she loved.

If she was surprised by the quick subject change, she didn't show it.

"Yeah, I did." She looked down at our joined hands before meeting my eyes again. "Ethan was confused as to why I would ask when I'm working for you, especially because it's kind of a step down. But once I told him you had encouraged me to try it out, he was fine. I can pull together a portfolio of photos for him to have a look at. So, I'll be heading home to have a nervous breakdown about that shortly. He wants it by Friday."

"Well, good. I'm glad he's giving you the opportunity. I'm sure you'll get it, and I can tell you it won't be because you're currently working for me. Ethan isn't the least bit intimidated by my position. He and Avi are the best design and copy team in the company, and he knows it. So he'll only give you the trial period on the team if he sees you have the potential required to succeed."

Some of the tension in Abbie's shoulders seemed to lessen with my comment. Had she been worried that I was going to use my influence to get her a position she wasn't qualified for? As much as

I found myself addicted to Abbie's presence, I'd never manipulate anyone using my power within the company. Besides being unethical, if she wasn't a good fit for the job, she'd suffer in the end anyway, and I didn't want to set her up to fail.

"Okay. That makes me feel better." Her smile wobbled a little. "I don't like the idea of getting anything I don't earn. It feels yucky."

"Yucky? Very professional, Ms. Summers." I had to laugh at her word choice.

"Right." Abbie eyed me in return. "Because we're so worried about professionalism right now?"

She opened her eyes wider and lifted both her eyebrows in an expression I thought was maybe her version of a sarcastic question but couldn't quite pull off. I resisted the urge to laugh again.

There was no getting away from this thing between us.

"No. You're right," I said, my tone more serious than her teasing one. "We need to worry about this."

She remained quiet, seeming to have no cheeky reply to the seriousness of my tone.

I brought my other hand to where our hands were joined, now encapsulating her much smaller hand between both of mine.

"I want to keep seeing you, Abbie," I admitted. It loosened something inside me that had been previously strung perilously tight to say the words aloud.

"I want that too." She gave me a bright smile.

Before she could say anything else, I cut in to make sure she understood what I could offer her.

"I want to be clear about the terms of us continuing this." I didn't have the right definition for what we'd done so far. "One-night stand" was wrong. This wasn't a fling either. I felt more for Abbie than for any casual hookup agreement I'd ever had with a woman before.

It was incredibly intoxicating. And horrendously inconvenient.

"By 'terms,' do you by any chance have a handy manual for this situation?" She was laughing at me. The little shit. She was never going to let my admin binder go, was she?

"Brat." I smiled before sobering again. "As much as it makes me sound like an asshole to say it, if we want to keep seeing each other, no one can know. It would destroy us both if it got out now."

The humor drained from her expression at my words. She let her gaze slip from mine without saying anything. At least she let me continue to hold her hand.

I didn't want to force the next part, but I owed it to her to be as honest as possible before she agreed to any further risk.

"Even without the company complication, I'm not at the place in my life to offer any woman a proper relationship right now, Abbie. It has nothing to do with you. I just have too much on the line to allow myself the distraction of thinking beyond the present."

"I understand." Her gaze returned to mine when she spoke. She'd been staring into space while I spoke.

"I don't want to assume anything about what you want. But I can't afford any confusion. All I can promise is that we can spend time together, and no one can find out about it."

Now she pulled her hand from where it was sandwiched between mine. Giving my hands a quick pat, she brought her fingers to her mouth to worry her bottom lip. I fell under the spell of watching her pinch the flesh reddened from my kisses between her index finger and thumb. I wanted to pull her hand away and nip that spot instead.

Clearly pausing to think about what she wanted to say, I waited as patiently as I could. I knew what I was offering her wasn't fair, but I didn't know what she'd decide.

"Can I think about it?"

Maybe I had been more confident that she would agree because I found myself surprised, but not upset, that she would ask for time to consider her options.

She was right to take her time. Even if we called this casual, the consequences, if anyone found out, would be anything but.

"Of course." I couldn't stop the hint of formality that slipped into my voice. There was a small part of me that stung with her response, making me aware that I wasn't as invulnerable to hurt where Abbie was concerned.

"It's…" she began.

I stood, offering her my hand. She took it and rose, so we stood together.

"Seriously. You have nothing to explain. It will be good for both of us to cool down a little bit."

Abbie stepped forward and put her arms around my waist. I realized that I had never held her just to give her a hug before. I wrapped my arms around her in return, letting out a deep breath.

"No matter what. We'll be okay," I forced out.

Abbie didn't say anything in answer to my weak attempt at reassurance. I couldn't guarantee we would be okay regardless of what she decided.

I also felt more concerned than ever that I wouldn't be able to put this "thing" with Abbie behind me the way I had done with all the brief relationships I'd had in the past.

I hoped like hell she got that temporary position with the graphics group. Maybe a little bit of distance and the distraction of training another EA might be enough to lessen the pressure I felt in my chest at the thought of giving Abbie up for good.

"I hope so." Her voice was so low that if I hadn't felt her movement against my chest, I would have assumed I'd imagined her words.

And even though I should stop hugging her so we could both go home for the day, I couldn't bring myself to release her from my arms. *Just a couple more minutes. Then, I'll be ready to let go.*

Twenty-Two

ABBIE

I was due to deliver my photos to Ethan so he could look them over. The morning had been entirely unproductive, not that I could afford to be distracted with a week's worth of emails and reports to summarize for Aiden.

A quick look back at his office door confirmed it was still closed. I couldn't tell if he was just respecting my space or avoiding me.

I snapped my portfolio shut after second- and third-guessing the selection of photos that I'd put together the night before. It had gotten to where I needed to just show it to Ethan and be done with it. I no longer felt good about any of them, having gone over and over the visual presentation order too many times.

The rational answer was that he was just busy. Unfortunately, my logic sometimes didn't stand up too well against my worry.

There wasn't any question that I wanted to say yes to Aiden. I'd discovered the other side to him—a softness he kept hidden that tempered his everyday intensity— during our time in LA. But insecurity had made me hesitate.

Aiden didn't know I struggled with managing my mental health. It was simpler to ignore my reality when it was just five days away together. Even though there had been a lot of pressure with the various client meetings, Aiden had borne the brunt of that stress.

Attending Anime Expo had allowed us both to relax without the prying eyes of the other Appeal employees.

I had already been feeling overly sad about our trip coming to an end. That happened to me every time I'd enjoyed myself while on a vacation; the adrenaline crash left my emotions low and unsteady.

The wobbly feeling had caused me to doubt my instincts.

The lingering uncertainty in my mind and body was a barrier against believing that Ethan was going to give me a real shot on his team. Sure, he'd used my photos from the business trip on the company's social media, but a few snapshots and assisting with the first pitch deck Appeal would deliver to BrownBag were not on the same scale. This would be a trial by fire for the nonprofit market with little room for error.

What kind of chance would Ethan be willing to take under those circumstances?

The portfolio in my arms felt heavy as I walked across the floor from my desk to the congregated workstations of Ethan's team.

Luckily, Ethan spotted me as I neared his workspace, so I didn't feel like I was disturbing him. His smile was welcoming, and his posture remained relaxed in his chair. It was definitely a world away from Aiden's intense drive, but I knew for a fact that Ethan ran the most senior team in the company, so his style must work for him.

"Abbie. Hey." Ethan motioned to the chair next to his desk for me to sit down.

Under any circumstance other than this one, I liked Ethan's company. He seemed to read people well and was good at making me feel comfortable enough to chitchat when our lunches coincided in the break area. He was also good at sitting in silence if he sensed I wasn't up to talking. Ethan didn't fill the space with words just for the sake of hearing his own voice.

It was strange how nerves could change my comfort level so quickly. I didn't know how to act, even though he had never been anything but kind to me.

"Thanks again for agreeing to look at my stuff." I waved shakily in the general direction of my photos.

"It's no problem. You did great work in LA. The fact that you had a proper camera made a big difference. The photos turned out so much better than just a lot of shots taken on a phone." He dropped his voice. "Plus, the fact that I don't have to do an external posting for this saves me a ton of time. Let's hope this is workable for both of us."

"I hope so too."

He opened my binder and remained quiet as he slowly turned the pages. This was not my idea of a good time. I wasn't positive, but an entire geological age might have passed before he looked up at me again.

"How many photography classes have you taken so far?" Well, directness was a trait he had in common with Aiden.

"Um, I just finished my second one. It's really okay if you want to say no, Ethan. I promise." I twisted my fingers in my lap as I spoke.

I couldn't help but jump the gun to the worst-case scenario. It was easier to keep my expectations at rock bottom rather than get my hopes up. Why did I even think I could do this?

Hold on. Deep breath. You are not going to fall apart. You want this chance. Just try it.

I was counting myself out of the race before he even gave me any feedback.

"Hey, hey. Just wait. There are some interesting images here. It's hard to see a personal style when you've been mostly taking pictures prescriptively for a class. When I spoke to Aiden yesterday, he said this might be a better fit for you than the EA position."

"What?" My stomach clenched with nerves.

Ethan's lifted in his hands in a don't-shoot-the-messenger gesture. "He didn't say you were doing a bad job over there. If anything, it's the opposite. I've only worked with him less than two months, and I could tell from that first meeting that he was hard to impress, yet you've done it."

"Okay. Thank you. That means a lot that you would say that. It wasn't smooth sailing in the beginning." I made an effort to relax some of the tension in my muscles.

"I'm not just saying it to make you feel better. I believe he is impressed with you. What I can't figure out is why he would encourage you to change teams, even temporarily, when you've obviously become an asset to him?" He looked at me curiously.

"Are you asking me?" I raised my eyebrows in surprise. How was I supposed to answer him? It wasn't like I could share the heartfelt conversations I'd had with Aiden while in *my bed during our business trip!*

Ethan nodded, seemingly content to wait for me to answer this mystery for him.

"Uh, he doesn't seem like the type of boss to stop someone from trying something new?"

"That's true." He nodded in agreement. "It's just surprising. That's all. Leave this with me, and I'll go through it with Avi. We won't keep you waiting for an answer."

Ethan seemed to enjoy bouncing ideas off Avi, almost like he was an assistant department head.

"Okay, thank you so much. I totally understand whatever direction you guys choose to go. But I would really be excited to have this opportunity."

There you go. You showed some enthusiasm instead of just blind terror. Gold star for you!

Getting up from the chair, I left Ethan to get back to his work, feeling a little bit like I was leaving a piece of myself behind in that binder on his desk.

I was starting to see what Aiden had meant about the difficulties in being involved with someone at work, especially when the relationship couldn't be public knowledge. If Ethan had been a different person, he could have pushed harder for an answer from me. I was just lucky he seemed happy enough to accept my thoughts.

A boulder took up residence in my stomach. This situation with Aiden could make things difficult at work very quickly. And I wasn't even factoring in how vulnerable my heart was in this whole situation.

It should have stopped me from saying yes to him. I should focus on the potential pitfalls likely before us, but my mind wouldn't let me forget how supportive Aiden had sounded when I talked about my photography in that hotel room. Other than Indie and Emery, I'd never experienced someone in my life believing in me and making me want to aim for more for myself. I felt special and cared for, a deep hole inside me filling in just a little.

Ethan's comment just now reinforced how different Aiden was from so many other bosses, truly putting my ambitions ahead of another period of inconvenience while he adjusted to a temporary EA.

I felt heady knowing he supported me. It emphasized how much I'd been lacking in support as I grew up. The only thing I ever achieved in my mother's eyes was being top-notch at disappointing her.

Who was I kidding? I didn't have it in me to resist him. Next time

I could get him alone, I'd tell him yes.

I hoped to make that moment happen soon.

The trip to LA had me missing my weekly girls' night with Indie and Emery. Other than a few text messages about the basics of arriving home and being tired, I'd been too nervous to put anything about Aiden in writing.

Despite being a college town, Amado was not just a city full of bars with a party scene. I appreciated the calmer, quieter choices of the many independent cafés and restaurants. Since it was my turn to pick the venue, I'd chosen a cat café where the owners fostered rescue cats until they could get adopted. It was halfway between Appeal and Almaden University, so I'd decided to walk to give myself time to think.

Distracted by my meeting with Ethan, I hadn't thought about what I was going to actually share with my friends. I knew Aiden insisted that everything between us be kept private, but I didn't want to be alone in thinking through the consequences of pursuing a romantic relationship with him.

He might be able to compartmentalize his emotions that way, but I wasn't built like that. If one part of my life was out of balance, all the other parts were affected. I didn't want to shoulder all this pressure on my own. Indie and Emery would never disclose what I shared with them to anyone else.

Before Aiden came into my life, they were the only safe space I could count on.

When I arrived at the front door of the café, I couldn't help but smile at the cat trees behind the windows, each with a dozing cat or two enjoying the late-day sun.

Leaving the office a little later than usual meant that Indie and Emery had already beaten me there. I could see them through the café's glass door as I pulled it open and went inside.

Making my way to the table, I saw Emery's sunny smile, joined by Indie's disgruntled expression.

As I sat down, Indie kept up her ruse. "Why do I want cat hair in my coffee again?" She slid me the third cup of coffee that was already on the table.

"It gives it extra flavor." Emery laughed. "Hey, Abs."

"Hey. Sorry I'm late."

We both knew Indie was just making a fuss for the sake of it. While not a sucker for animals the way that we were, Indie did like them deep down.

"I'm just saying, Mew is going to know what a traitor you are when you come home and he smells all this on you." She waved her hands in a sweeping motion to encompass our surroundings. "I'm glad he won't be smelling any of his feline competition on me."

I smiled. "Thank you both for checking on him. Especially for feeding him every day, Indie."

"You're lucky I stopped her at one outfit," Emery replied.

"Listen, just because I downloaded a few patterns off Etsy does not mean I was planning to dress him up all week." Indie sniffed.

Indie totally would have had an outfit per day for him if I'd had more notice of the trip.

"By the way," Indie continued, "I taught him my excellent taste in TV shows. He now needs you to stream his nightly episode of *The Bachelorette*. He didn't care for *The Bachelor*, so we gave up on that right away. Too much cattiness." She gave us an exaggerated wink.

That had both Emery and me giggling. Indie had a secret love of reality TV shows where contestants continuously made bad decisions.

"But enough about Mew. Tell us about the trip. I can't believe Aiden got you tickets to Anime Expo and then went with you. How did you manage that?" Emery's gaze radiated curiosity.

"He has a thing for her, that's how," Indie jumped in before I could form an answer.

"Who wouldn't? But maybe he did it as a thank-you for all her hard work." Emery shrugged off Indie's assumption, more inclined to believe the best in people. I loved that she didn't assume everyone had a motive for their actions. Emery did things to be kind, so she often thought the people around her were doing the same thing.

"Well, er…" I started.

"Oh my god!" Emery's eyes widened in shock. "She's right?"

Taking my stilted attempt to form words as evidence, Emery turned to Indie, her expression in direct contrast to Indie's smug smile.

"What can I say? I just had a feeling. I love being right." As her reward, a cat jumped up and sat in Indie's lap. Rolling her eyes, she patted it lovingly. It was cute to see Indie melt a little bit.

"Tell us what happened." Emery was not going to be distracted by anything, feline or otherwise.

"I don't know. We met with his sister and her friend, who were also going to the con. Then later in the evening, I just had these tickets in my inbox. It was so nice of him."

"But that's not all, right?" Indie said knowingly.

Emery turned to Indie once more. "How do you know that?"

"See the embarrassed blush coming up on her face? It takes more than playing a little bit of public dress-up to put that look on someone."

"Excuse me, it's called cosplay, which you already know. But you are right." I decided not to keep them in suspense after Indie had called me out so directly. "We, uh, kind of hooked up." I brought my hands up and buried my face in them.

"Oh my *god*!" Emery's screech of excitement scared the cat right off Indie's lap.

Indie looked down at the fur her new friend had left behind and sighed.

"Em, you keep saying that. I'm so proud of you, Abs. Look at you being all spontaneous. Keep going," Indie encouraged.

Parting my fingers, I gauged my friends' reaction to the news. It was no surprise that they were both watching me carefully. Their expressions remained open and attentive but clearly ready for the juicy details. I brought my hands down to the table again, holding on to my coffee cup for something to fuss with.

"Well, it was just supposed to be one night," I said, not comfortable getting into specifics in public. "But that one turned into two. And now he asked me to keep seeing each other, but no one at work can know."

To her credit, Emery's first reaction wasn't an opinion. "What do you want to do?"

"I haven't been able to think of anything else since he asked me. I know I *shouldn't* say yes, but I really want to."

"Why shouldn't you say yes? It's your life. You can do what you want," Indie argued.

"I just don't want it to be a disaster. He could end it. There are so many potential complications with work. We signed conduct clauses in our contracts, Indie. It's not specifically spelled out, but I can't imagine an intimate relationship with one's boss is considered aboveboard by any company."

"It's true. And it's not just him that has all the say either. You get to decide whether it's working for you too." Emery nodded. "But if it did, couldn't you figure out something with the work situation?" She always looked for the silver lining.

"Yeah…" I conceded. "I guess we could? It's hard to think too far ahead. I'm not sure it's even going to work out in the short term."

"What are you most worried about here?" Indie said.

I dropped my voice. Despite the café being relatively empty, I was hypersensitive to talking about anything private in public. "Everything to do with struggling with my mood sometimes."

Saying the words aloud made me feel insecure. Even though Indie and Emery had been with me in high school when my earliest mood changes started, I still felt like my constant anxiety was something about me that other people wouldn't like. They had never been anything but supportive, Indie being the one who encouraged me to see my doctor when my mood first got too low to cope with, but I couldn't help feeling *less* in some way.

I didn't want to have this vulnerability that others around me didn't seem to have. Logically, I knew that lots of people did experience mental health challenges, but for someone else finding out, my fear of rejection outweighed all my positive feelings.

"I don't think you have to tell him anything right away. No one would expect you to share something so personal without being sure you could trust your partner first. You could just take it day by day," Indie suggested.

"I think I'm going to need to do that. Right now, we're just getting to know each other, and I'm not ready to tell him that."

"Then don't. You decide when. And we can be here as sounding boards if you need us." Emery's support eased my nerves further.

"Okay. That makes sense and makes me feel a bit better." I had control over what I shared with Aiden and when I shared it.

"Abs, I know you see your anxiety and low moods as this major personal flaw, but they aren't. We've both said this before, but people go through all sorts of stuff, and anyone who would judge you for being strong and coping the best you can doesn't deserve to be in your life." Indie reached across the table to squeeze my hand. "Plus, if he turns out to be a jerk, I'll kick his ass."

"Thank you for saying that." I couldn't fully make myself feel the truth of Indie's words, but I appreciated her support and tried to believe Indie as much as I could.

"Now. I have a feeling that we're not going to get any good details while we're here. How about we go to my apartment, and you can really tell us what happened in LA?" Emery's expression turned imploring. "Nothing this good has happened to any of us in ages. I want to know everything."

"Yeah, fine. Let's go." I laughed.

I was lucky to have friends I could lean on. I would decide on the way just "how" detailed I was willing to get.

Twenty-Three

AIDEN

*E*than had offered Abbie the temporary position on his team. She'd been working for the digital arts team for two weeks, and we'd barely had a chance to check in with each other. I was drowning in work, with new client inquiries coming in so frequently that I was considering hiring more employees.

My new EA, Miles, was the only thing going smoothly for me. I knew even that was due to Abbie's careful recommendation of who she knew in the company would do the best job.

Before Miles started, Abbie recommended a change to a particular EA duty.

"I just have one suggestion for you with Miles if you want things to go smoothly."

"What's that?" I asked.

"Maybe make your own coffee? Or send him down to Dean's cart at the very least. No one needs that kind of stress on their shoulders."

I smiled, recalling the moment she handed over the infamous admin manual. She had faked being out of breath as she returned it to me, not so subtly reminding me it might be a tad too detailed.

In the present, I was seated in my office, talking myself out of going to Abbie's new desk for no reason other than to see her. It was harder than I thought, giving her the space to think about my request. The combination of our incompatible schedules had left me in a miserable kind of limbo.

I tried to be aware that the ball was firmly in her court on this one. I'd told her I wanted to continue our relationship and knew that the circumstances were less than ideal. She had to be the one to come to me, even as it pained me to wait for her answer.

My phone rang, with the CEO's extension showing on its display. "Hi, Jack."

"Aiden. Listen, I wouldn't normally ask this of you, especially after all the catch-up you've had to do after your trip. But there's a fundraiser in San Jose that I was meant to attend. Lots of big corporate companies will be there. Something with the family has come up. I need you to go in my place."

"Sure. No problem." It wasn't as if I had anything planned for the weekend other than overtime and thinking about Abbie.

"You're a lifesaver. There are two tickets. Take whoever you think makes the most sense from the team. I'll have my admin deliver them to you by day's end."

"Thanks, Jack."

After ending the call, I suddenly felt a lot more optimistic about the day ahead. I picked up my phone and texted Abbie. No one needed to be privy to our conversation outside my office.

Aiden

Good morning. Can you please come into my office?

There was no response, but I heard a soft knock on my door a couple of moments later.

"Come in," I called.

Abbie opened the door and stood in the threshold, hesitating. I knew things were uncertain between us, but I thought the fundraiser sounded like the perfect opportunity to tip the scales in my favor by spending more time together.

"Hi. Don't you have a conference call in like five minutes?" She made no move to enter the room. I hated to think that we were back to the early days of our working relationship, where she tiptoed around me. I much preferred the more open, funny woman I'd spent time with in LA.

"Yes, but it can wait if necessary. Please shut the door behind you and have a seat." I tried to keep the formal tone I assumed for work out of my voice.

"Oh, okay." Shutting the door quietly, Abbie walked over and sat in one of my guest chairs. I stood and rounded my desk to sit in the seat next to her.

I'd realized the day Miles started working for me that I missed her being just outside my office. I'd grown accustomed to working side by side and taken it for granted. Spending free hours with her, like we had in LA, had only accentuated that feeling of missing her presence.

I wouldn't go so far as admitting I'd rather be back walking around a convention carrying a stuffed cat toy. But it was close.

I had made sure to carefully pack it for the trip home. The damn thing was sitting on a chair in my bedroom. It was the first and last thing I looked at each day.

Abbie Summers was embedded deep in my skin.

"Has your week been okay? I've barely seen you." While she was still incredibly beautiful, her pale skin looked a bit darker under her eyes. I didn't like to see her tired, especially knowing she'd been taking home work every night this week, if the emails at 10:00 p.m. were any indication.

"Yeah. It's been fine. There's just a lot to finish up, reports-wise. All the month-end stuff should have gone out last week. But it's fine." She also sounded a bit tired, but maybe it was just the adjustment period for her new role.

Don't even think about asking Ethan. That would absolutely overstep your place as the boss.

I didn't love hearing her say "fine" twice in a sentence. I had been working fourteen-hour days all week myself, but I didn't want to set any kind of precedent for my staff.

"Listen. I know we haven't had a chance to talk." She opened her mouth to say something, but I barreled on before she could interrupt me. "And you should absolutely take all the time you need. But Jack just called me about a fundraiser tomorrow night that he needs me to attend in his stead. I would like you to go with me. Will you come?"

"Oh. Sure. I will." Abbie's cheeks pinkened with her reply. I wondered if she was feeling shy or embarrassed by my attention. Moments like these were why I wanted to spend more time with her. Getting to know Abbie better was now a major priority for me.

"Fantastic. From a business standpoint, you are the most logical person to go with me, having a grasp on all our biggest projects." I smiled at her. "Personally, there is no one else I'd rather spend the evening with. Just to enjoy each other's company, nothing else."

I wanted a lot more than just her company but didn't want to push her. She had just as much to lose in this arrangement as I did.

"And if I want more than just your company?" Her blush deepened, turning her cheeky words into a mix of seduction and adorableness.

"Then you'll have it," I assured her.

"Is it a date, then?" Abbie whispered.

"It's a date. I'll pick you up at 6:00 p.m."

Her lips pressed together as she struggled to keep her smile to herself. Her bold words unlocked the door I'd kept tightly closed for weeks. I wanted this workday to end so I could anticipate all the possibilities tomorrow night.

After the longest twenty-four-plus hours of my life, I was finally on my way to pick up Abbie from her apartment. I'd briefly been concerned about the way it might appear if someone saw me outside her building. Just as quickly, I'd dismissed the thought.

Although San Jose offered a better chance at anonymity, the reassurance of several hundred thousand people living there meant it would be a rare coincidence to encounter someone from work.

I further rationalized that it was perfectly acceptable for me to pick her up to attend a work function. Until Monday, she was still my assistant. Traveling to San Jose separately wouldn't have occurred to me in any other circumstances.

I felt assured until I saw her exit the front doors of the low-rise apartment building wearing the same dress from our client dinner in LA. That dress held too many delicious memories for me to keep any thoughts of work in my mind.

As she opened the car door, I watched the black satin slide sinuously over her curves as she got into the passenger seat.

"Holy fuck. That dress." The fabric pressed against her body was too distracting for me to worry about my crass greeting. "I remember quite a few more wrinkles in it during that night in LA." The dress in question didn't burst into flames despite the fire in my gaze.

"Hello to you too." She laughed. "I had it dry-cleaned."

"Damn. Are you trying to distract me tonight? Because by wearing that dress, you've just guaranteed I won't be leaving your side for a single second."

"Well, considering this is the only dress I have that's fancy enough for any kind of function, I guess I just got lucky that you like it so much." She winked.

I watched her buckle her seat belt, the satin pulling tighter against her breasts as the strap restrained her body.

Once she was settled, I pulled out into the Saturday evening traffic. We had about forty minutes until we reached the convention center where the fundraiser was being held.

I needed to get her talking. Otherwise, I was going to spend the whole drive obsessing about how she looked in that dress and wondering what she was wearing underneath it. I needed to get myself under control—I still had a job to do tonight, and I couldn't be so far off my game that I'd fail Jack's purpose for sending me. I also didn't want to spend the next five hours aroused beyond belief.

"Sweetheart, I need you to distract me. You look too damn good." I reached across the console to offer her my hand. Just because I had to behave myself didn't mean that I was going to forgo touching her while I had the opportunity.

That brought a laugh out of Abbie. "Aiden, come on. Be serious."

"I'm dead serious." My mind worked overtime to think of the least sexy thing I could think of. "Quick, give me a list of all the Pokémon you know."

She laughed again at my ridiculousness. "Before I bore you to death, then, let me say that I am saying yes to us. We can take it one day at a time."

"You just made my night, sweetheart. You'll never get rid of me now." A part of me I didn't know was out of sync clicked into place hearing her agree to seeing each other. "Now, the list. It was so calming in LA to listen to you go on and on and on about a fake world full of things I don't understand."

"Was it really on and on *and on?*" She sounded skeptical about just how enthusiastic she had been about Anime Con.

I chanced a brief look over at her. Her eyes narrowed as if I had defamed her character while she struggled to keep her lips from smiling.

"I cannot tell a lie. There were definitely a lot of facts." I couldn't hold back my chuckle at her cutely affronted features. "But seriously, I love that you love it so much. I enjoy listening to you."

She angled her body toward my side of the car and dove in. Clearly, full-body engagement was needed for a topic as important as Pokémon.

"Okay, you asked for it. Every kid can get a Pokémon when they turn ten if they want to. Depending on where they live, the Pokémon options change. So for Kanto, where Ash Ketchum lives, Charmander, Squirtle, or Bulbasaur are the options. In Hoenn…"

As I drove toward the highway, I let the smooth cadence of her voice wash over me. She was irresistible when she got going about one of her favorite things.

Twenty-Four

ABBIE

It had been several months since I'd made a trip back to San Jose. Other than the quick drive getting to and from the airport for the LA trip, I didn't have any reason to travel to the city where I grew up until Thanksgiving. I was only required at three mandatory dinners a year at my mother's house in Almaden Valley: Easter, Thanksgiving, and Christmas.

Thankfully, we would be a fair distance away from the house where I'd spent my teenage years, as the convention center we were heading to was in the heart of downtown San Jose.

I tried not to think about how big this event was going to be, knowing it was taking place at one of the main event venues in the city. The idea of being stuck in a room full of strangers and having to make conversation wasn't my idea of a good time, to put it mildly.

Nerves aside, I couldn't refuse the chance to go on a date with Aiden. I wanted us to have as many moments together as possible.

We'd arrived shortly after the cocktail hour began, and so far, I had been dutifully following Aiden as he scoped out the room. I'd been introduced to a few fellow advertising executives that Aiden knew from other events like this in his previous company and promptly forgotten their names because of my mounting nerves.

He looked at me now as they walked away from another industry executive and his wife, not retaining either of their names because of nerves.

"You doing okay?" he asked quietly.

"Yep." I did a poor job of masking the tightness in my voice.

"Why doesn't that convince me?" He chuckled. "Aren't so many pretentious people in one place a balm to the soul after a hard week of work?"

I shifted my gaze from the sea of faces surrounding them to Aiden's dark brown eyes. The mirth in his expression allowed some of the tension to flow out of me. It was a relief that he didn't mind my nerves in these types of situations. I wasn't going to start liking big crowds anytime soon.

"I'm glad it's not just me. Why don't they take the five-thousand-dollar-per-plate tickets and donate that money to—" I checked the program in my hand to remember the name of the charity. "—the Bay Marine Reconstruction Project instead?"

"Maybe they give the sea lions the leftovers? They'd surely enjoy the caviar," Aiden suggested unhelpfully, still amused.

"Aiden, seriously. It's such a waste. Now I know why Indie always rages when her parents force her to one of these things."

He tucked my hand into the crook of his arm. I relished the reassuring warmth that radiated through his suit.

"Seriously, if you don't laugh, you'll cry if you think about it too hard." Aiden sobered. "I don't envy the number of these Jack has to attend every year. I'll gladly play second fiddle at Appeal for a long time if it means avoiding nights like this."

I watched his expression change from shrewd while he looked at the crowd to warm as his stare returned to meet mine. "My choice of companion, however, is unparalleled."

Even though I outwardly rolled my eyes, his compliment sunk into some of the empty spaces inside me. It was moments like this one that had me accepting his invitation to come tonight. I could deal with any situation with Aiden by my side.

"Can we go to our table, maybe?" Six strangers for the duration of the evening sounded a hell of a lot better than the untold number out here milling around.

"Sure." He must have read some discomfort on my face because he agreed right away. I knew he should have mingled longer, making contacts. But I could feel guilty about that later. For now, I trusted he would tell me if he needed more time.

And I was comfortable enough with Aiden that I could ask for what I needed, which was almost unheard of for me.

He led me through the large double-door entryway to the main ballroom. The high-end decor could have doubled for a celebrity wedding or an exclusive concert venue for Beyoncé. I definitely wasn't the target market for this type of excess. Aesthetically, it was beautiful, but it was all so overwhelming. It was all I could do to read the table numbers as we passed through the room.

"Here we go." Aiden pulled out my chair for me and then sat himself.

Conveniently, the close quarters of the table meant that Aiden's thigh was pressed against mine under the table. I shifted so that my arm lay in the divot where our legs touched, the fingers of my hand resting on his leg. Since we were at a business event, I needed to keep my hands to myself, but I needed just a little bit of comfort to get through the rest of the night.

In return, Aiden rested his own arm on his thigh, letting the tips of our fingers touch teasingly.

If I could just take a minute to calm my jagged nerves, I might be able to tell Aiden I was ready to talk to more people.

That thought was interrupted by a voice calling my name.

"Abigail?"

Oh no.

It hadn't occurred to me that my mother and Arthur would be here tonight. I'd been so focused on spending time with Aiden I hadn't made the connection between tonight's dinner and all the high-profile events my mother and stepfather attended regularly.

Nausea worked its way through my stomach and into my throat, making it hard to swallow. It was actually work not to let the bile creep up my throat.

The last thing I wanted was to be under my mother's scrutiny in Aiden's presence, let alone make introductions.

Bowing to social niceties, we stood to greet them.

"Hi, Mom." I turned to face my mother. "Hi, Arthur." I gave my stepfather, who stood dutifully beside my mother, a minimally enthusiastic wave.

Unlike my mother, Arthur had always been kind to me, if very reserved. He preferred to stay out of our mother-daughter relationship, so even after more than a decade living in his home, we were still basically strangers.

"When will that wash out?" My mother gestured to my lilac-colored hair, currently down around my shoulders. The gloves were off already, I realized.

"Excuse me, I don't think we've met. I'm Aiden Sullivan, VP of Appeal Media. Mr. and Ms....?"

My mother's critical stare morphed into a plastic expression of politeness, not having noticed Aiden standing near me, so distracting was the sin of my dyed hair she hadn't even noticed him yet. That's how much she disliked me dying my hair in fun colors.

"Caroline Maartan, Abigail's mother." My mother extended her hand to shake Aiden's daintily.

"Arthur Maartan, Abigail's stepfather. Nice to meet you. I was expecting to see Jack tonight." Arthur looked at Aiden with interest. Arthur was more than just my stepfather. He was the CEO of one of the largest telecommunications companies on the West Coast. He obviously knew the players in the advertising game, both big and small, if he knew Jack Blakley.

"Right. Nice to meet you both. Jack had a conflict. I was happy to attend in his place. Abbie is my assistant."

"What a small world," my mother commented. "Is this your table? We'll join you. I'm sure we'll have no trouble making the change."

"Oh, we couldn't inconvenience you both that way." Aiden's stare was laser focused on me as I watched this nightmare unfold. But I was frozen and couldn't give him a reaction.

"Nonsense." My mother waved away his protests.

Arthur looked around and raised a single finger. As if summoned by magic, a server appeared next to him, and they exchanged a few words. It never ceased to amaze me how much the mountains of money behind Arthur's name could accomplish with a simple gesture. With a nod, the server was gone again to do his bidding.

I would take back every bad thought about this event having too many strangers if I could rewind the last two minutes and escape this moment. The last thing I wanted was Aiden around my mother for any period of time. He would discover just how awful she was, and it would be humiliating. As much as I wanted to know him better, this was one thing I would keep him in the dark about. It was awful that he was seeing this part of my life after we'd just gotten together. Who would want to stick around after meeting her?

When the server returned to switch out the nameplates on the table, Aiden checked in with me.

"You okay?" I could hear the concern in his whispered tone.

"Yep. Don't worry about it." I didn't want him to feel responsible for bringing me to hell on earth with place settings for eight.

"Let's sit and you can tell me what you think of Appeal so far?" My mother directed her question to Aiden as we took our seats again.

Much to my dismay, my mother chose the seat next to me. Was it too much to ask to sit beside Arthur all evening? He would just ignore me, as was the established dynamic that worked for both of us.

Aiden pressed his thigh against mine once again, this time as a gesture of comfort or solidarity, I guessed. I didn't dare let my arms drop from where they rested lightly on the table.

I struggled to keep my expression neutral as I turned in Aiden's direction to listen to him answer my mother's question.

"It's a change from the multinational firm I was working for in LA. I like the collaborative approach to client relationships. My former firm kept me in one type of market."

Arthur nodded politely, but my mother was after more information.

"I can see how a 'boutique' firm would have the time to afford lots of attention to clients," my mother said "boutique" the way someone might say "gonorrhea," complete with her nose wrinkling with thinly veiled disdain.

Aiden's lips tightened briefly. I was mortified that we were going to have to endure this for the entire dinner. Was my mother going to continue to needle Aiden?

"We sure do," he confirmed my mother's statement as if it had been a compliment instead of an insult.

Thankfully, one organizer took to the stage at the front of the room and announced dinner would begin. I hoped the inevitable obligatory speeches would prevent conversation as a temporary reprieve.

I turned my body slightly to face the front of the room, and that meant pulling my leg away from Aiden's warmth. Unfortunately, it also put me in the perfect spot to hear my mother's low pitch.

"What are you even wearing? Did I teach you nothing about how to dress for occasions like these? You look like you're ready for a nightclub. You need to wear dresses with more structure. It's hardly flattering to wear a dress that clings to all those problem areas," my mother admonished in a hissed whisper.

Acutely aware of the rest of the table and the strangers surrounding us, I didn't want to be rude while everyone else seemed to be attentively listening to the first speaker.

"It's okay, Mom. No one will notice. I'm just here to support Aiden in meeting new clients. They needed someone who knew the basics of all the ongoing campaigns, and that's me, I guess."

"Well, you're hardly invisible with that hair. Are you fourteen still? Why do you insist on making yourself stand out like that when you know Arthur is well-known in all business circles?"

My first thought was that I hadn't been allowed to dye my hair while I was living in Arthur's house. Even though it was years ago, the repressive environment of my mother's control lived inside me still. It only took being in her presence again to set all those painful synapses on fire again, sending me right back into those same emotions.

I couldn't figure out why, if she hated my hair so much, she'd put a spotlight on it by choosing to switch tables.

There was something to be said for a multicourse meal because whatever my mother planned to say next was interrupted by the waitstaff serving the first course. It also gave me a chance to return my attention to Aiden rather than be in the direct line of fire.

I knew the extravagance of the whole event meant that the food was probably gourmet, but it tasted like ash in my mouth. My stomach had shut down the moment I saw my mother.

"You okay?" Aiden leaned over to whisper in my ear.

I was so frozen inside that I couldn't access the pleasure I felt earlier in Aiden's presence.

"Yep. I'm fine." I had to hold it together for a few more hours. It was nothing I hadn't done before. Hell, I'd done it for years at a time.

The problem with living away from home was that my tolerance for my mother's cutting criticism and passive-aggressiveness meant that it hit me harder when I was back in her orbit. Every comment and microexpression was layered with years of disappointment and disapproval of me as a person. Each of my mother's words blew catastrophic holes in my self-worth.

Out of the corner of my eye, I noticed Aiden staring at me intently. I was not going to give him anything to work with at this table. I was a computer in shutdown mode, and there would be no rebooting myself until I could get out of this situation.

It took all I had to hang on until then.

Twenty-Five

AIDEN

I was seething underneath the calm facade I'd projected to the others at the table. I wanted to get Abbie out of that ballroom immediately. Anyone with a single brain cell could see that she was uncomfortable, though she'd tried valiantly to hide it.

I'd spent enough time with her both in and out of work to know some of her tells. Abbie's shoulders were creeping slowly toward her ears, and the warm hand she'd placed briefly on my leg had turned clammy and cool.

Despite her initial tendency to be quiet in new situations, once Abbie warmed up to someone, she was open, adorably excitable and funny. Like she had with Claire or when she forgot to be self-conscious about loving Anime Expo so much and she let herself enjoy it. But less than ten minutes into this encounter with her mother and stepfather had her withering away before my eyes.

There wasn't a goddamn thing I could do about it without looking like a total ass in front of the precise group of people Jack had sent me here to interact with. The last thing I wanted to do was put

Abbie's comfort on the back burner for a group of strangers though.

I waited until Caroline Maartan was engaged in conversation with another couple across the table before leaning in to murmur in Abbie's ear.

"Are you okay?" I didn't know why I'd asked that. The answer was no. I knew she wasn't okay. But I had to say something to let her know I saw she was struggling. I hoped she could hear the worry in my tone. I didn't want her to think I was ignoring her discomfort.

Her reply was a small, sharp nod and a tightening of her lips until they were nearly bloodless.

I chastised myself for being such an idiot. Of course she wasn't going to do anything to screw up this business networking opportunity for me. She knew how hard I'd worked with all the overtime I pulled on a weekly basis. Abbie was too good of a person to get in the way of that.

Even knowing the answer to my next question, I still asked because there was a minuscule chance that she might agree.

"I'm good to leave. Do you want to?" I carefully phrased my question to let her know it was her choice and more about what she wanted at that moment than what the company needed.

Fuck it. I would call Jack from the restroom and fake food poisoning if I had to in order to get her out of this. I realized how special she was to me that I was willing to risk pissing off Jack to put her first. For the life of me, I couldn't find the will to care about anything outside of doing everything in my power to make her feel better.

And that meant getting her away from her witch of a mother.

My question was met with a quick head shake as she continued to stare at her second-course salad that she had yet to take a bite of.

Holding back a sigh—or maybe a frustrated growl, I wasn't sure at this point—I resigned myself to the fact that I couldn't be her knight in shining armor and whisk her away from the miserable woman she was sitting beside.

Fuck if I didn't feel like as much of a social hostage as Abbie was at this moment. It made me feel like a coward, like I was letting her down.

It was an awful feeling.

One thing I could do was try to keep her mother's focus off Abbie for the remainder of the meal. When I saw Caroline had turned toward her daughter again, I jumped in to distract her from whatever vile comment she was about to make.

"Mrs. Maartan, have you and Mr. Maartan been patrons of this charity before this year? I have to admit, being new to the Bay Area, I'm just getting familiar with all the organizations. I'm sure you have a wealth of knowledge on all the worthiest causes." The bullshit that fell from my lips was forgotten the moment I uttered the words. But I needed to keep these two busy.

I could not have cared about anything less than her response, but I knew people like Caroline Maartan. For whatever reason, her entire life was one big performance, and there was nothing someone with her personality liked more than to brag about how wonderful she was.

"Oh Aiden, it's Caroline, please. Considering Abbie works for you and all. I can hardly blame you for your lack of knowledge about all the important charities we support. It's not as if Jack makes much of an effort to prioritize his company's philanthropic endeavors," she simpered.

Caroline Maartan's passive-aggressive game was on point. Maybe she practiced subtly insulting people at home in the mirror. I hadn't been insulted so thoroughly since high school. The only difference between Abbie's mother and the rich high school kids who used to pick fights with me because I was a scholarship student was that those teenage boys didn't hide behind veiled politeness when they belittled me to my face.

She'd droned on about the various charity events her husband had "generously donated" that year, giving Abbie a reprieve to escape the table for the restroom.

I'd wanted to follow her immediately but didn't want to draw any more attention to Abbie or raise suspicion about the appropriateness of our relationship, so I forced myself to stay seated. I made an excuse to check on "my assistant" after five more minutes of pretending to listen to her self-aggrandizing chatter.

After I took my leave from the table, I went straight to the entrance of the room to find Abbie. It didn't take much looking to find her in a little alcove outside the restroom area. She was leaning back against the wall with her eyes closed.

Not wanting to scare her, I called out to her just loudly enough for her to hear me as I approached.

"Hey."

Her eyes shot open. So much for not startling her, but her body relaxed when she realized it was me. I closed the distance between us, wanting to gather her up into my arms, but resigned myself to a professional distance.

"I'm so sorry about tonight. It was supposed to be about making contacts for work, and it's turned into another episode of the Caroline Maartan show." Abbie's eyes looked weary and sad.

Checking behind me to make sure no one was nearby, I put my hands on her bare arms, gently rubbing them up and down.

"Hey, hey. Nothing about tonight is your fault. You don't need to be sorry. I hate that we're stuck at the table with them. Not for me—for you. I want to tell her to fuck off so badly, but Jack would murder me. And there's the small problem of her being the mother of the woman I'm seeing. What kind of first impression would that be? 'Fuck off' is absolutely a post-third date with her daughter kind of thing." I went for humor, grasping for something to bring her back to me from wherever the protective place she had gone to in her mind.

The absurdity of my statement had the desired effect of returning some of the light in her eyes that Caroline had dampened.

"Definitely post-third date." The tiniest curve appeared on the corner of her lips.

"Do you want to leave? I don't feel right about subjecting you to more of this fiasco of a table. I'll make some excuse to Jack."

"No. We can't." Abbie shook her head. "It would look terrible. Plus, I'm used to it. It's been this way my whole life. If I just keep my head down and stay quiet, she'll get so caught up in talking to the other guests she'll forget about me. I'll be fine. I'm just embarrassed."

I didn't believe for one second she was fine. I knew there was a lot more hurt she was trying to hide from me so that we could get through the evening.

"You have nothing to be embarrassed about. Whatever she's doing in there"—I gestured back into the ballroom—"has nothing to do with you. You're just an innocent bystander here. That woman is operating in an entirely different reality to ours. I hope you can see that."

"Yep." She looked down; her tone wasn't convincing. We'd have to work on the trust between us. I wanted her to be able to tell me the truth.

"I'm going to head back in before they miss me. You take as much time as you need. We'll go as soon as we can."

I wished I could walk her back in there myself to show her mother that Abbie was far from needing anything from her. But as far as everyone knew, I was just her boss, and that was definitely not my place.

Abbie returned to the table, plastic smile in place, remaining quiet. I participated in the table discussions and networked as Jack had sent me to do. By the time we were about to make our escape, I had more than a few business cards in my pocket.

On the drive home, I worried about her as she withdrew further into herself. The silence in the car was deafening. I tried to talk to her a couple of times, but she had shut her eyes, claiming she was tired.

When we returned to Amado, I dropped her off at her place. Without speaking, both of us knew this night was not the right moment to move our relationship forward. Since she wouldn't talk to me, I wanted to give her space to work through whatever she was going through.

I put my hand on her thigh, smoothing the fabric of her dress. I hoped to both soothe and reassure her that tonight had not changed anything for me. I still wanted all of her.

"Hey. I know it's easier said than done, but nothing that was said tonight was about you, okay? Text or call me if you want to talk. Anytime. I'm here for you. Please, baby." I'd resorted to pleading with her.

"Thank you. I know you are," she whispered, blinking rapidly against her tear-filled eyes. "It'll be okay. I just need some time."

This wasn't the answer I wanted as she got out of the car, not waiting for me to get out and open her door. I understood that she likely wanted to put this evening behind her as fast as possible, but I was still disappointed that we seemed to have moved backward in our connection.

I'd give her tomorrow to decompress. On Monday, I would try again to get her to open up to me.

Despite my best intentions, the start of the week meant I had to hit the ground running, and I was so wrapped up in my never-ending workload that I didn't realize Abbie had taken a sick day until I was ready to leave. It was supposed to be her first day with Ethan's team. It was completely out of character for Abbie to shirk her responsibilities like this.

I texted her on my way home, hoping that she might let me stop by. I'd started to worry that something was really wrong.

Aiden

> **Hi. I heard you took a sick day. You feeling OK? Can I bring you anything you need?**

Her reply didn't come until after I was at home, eating a rewarmed dinner that my housekeeper left for me at the beginning of every workweek.

Abbie

> **Hi. Sorry for the wait. I am just not feeling well. Just trying to rest. I don't need anything but thank you for asking.**

I wished she would lean on me. Not sure if she had really caught a bug and was just resting up, I didn't feel right insisting on seeing her when she had every right to take a sick day if she needed it. I'd see for myself the next day at work.

My tune changed midday Tuesday when Ethan requested a meeting over the slim thirty minutes I tried to eke out for my lunch hour. I'd immediately said yes, ready to forgo eating because I knew Ethan was coming to talk about Abbie.

Just after twelve, a knock on my door signaled Ethan's arrival. I wanted to believe Ethan was coming to me out of concern because

I was going to have a hard time reining in my temper if Ethan was here to complain about Abbie's work quality. Especially since she'd been transitioning to her temporary role while still shouldering the bulk of my admin duties and bringing Miles up to speed.

"Come in."

Ethan's head appeared when the door opened, hesitating to come into my office.

"You sure? I know it's your lunch hour. I wouldn't bother you if I didn't think it's important."

"It's fine. I believe you. Come in and have a seat." I waved him away from the door and waited while he took a seat.

"So I'm going to cut to the chase. I'm worried about Abbie." Ethan's tone was serious but not critical.

"Go on," I encouraged, trying to keep my cool.

"Well, there's been some signs over the past week where she wasn't feeling her best. Our team is pretty great and makes an effort to go out for dinner once a week. Since she was offered the position and while shadowing some of the team, we've invited her twice. Abbie declined both times. Which is fine. We don't pressure her."

I nodded. The timeline made sense if Abbie was a little off. She'd asked for time while she decided whether she wanted to pursue a relationship with me. Maybe that pressure had taken more of a toll on her than I had realized.

"Between you and me, I have some experience with someone suffering from mental illness in my personal life, so I'm always kind of on the lookout now. Abbie never wants to bother anyone with any problem, always taking it on herself. I know she's had a lot of learning to do on our team, and it must bother her, but she won't let herself be a burden to anyone. And what's got me most worried is that she's now on her second sick day. I gave her a call this morning just to check on her. She didn't sound sick but sounded really fatigued. I could be totally wrong, but it set my warning bells off. I couldn't live with myself if I didn't let you know since you're technically still her boss."

Ethan sat back in his chair and watched my expression carefully for my reaction.

"I will keep this confidential. It's no one's business, of course. I care about Abbie as a person too, and I don't want her to struggle if there's some way I can help. As soon as she's back in the office, I will talk to her. Off the record. If she needs some support, I'll make sure she gets it, okay?" What I didn't say was that I'd do everything personally to make sure she knew she wasn't alone.

"Sometimes for someone who struggles with their mood, it's enough to know they have someone in their corner. Everyone is different. But I'm going to do what I can to keep reassuring her that I am on her side here in the office," Ethan said.

"You're a good leader, Ethan. We're all lucky you're part of the team. This is what separates the truly successful from the people only in it for the money. Seriously, thank you for coming to me."

Ethan gave me another careful once-over, as if verifying my sincerity. In another situation, this level of scrutiny would be humorous coming from one of his employees. Whatever he saw seemed to satisfy him for the moment. It warmed me to know that Abbie had more people than she knew who cared about her.

With a nod, Ethan left my office. I promised myself that the second Abbie was back in the office, we were going to talk. She was an adult who could manage her own life, but I wanted her to know that I would be there for her if she needed me.

I wasn't above cornering her in the office if she was determined to keep her distance from me outside of it.

Twenty-Six

ABBIE

After taking two sick days in a row for the first time since I'd started at Appeal, Wednesday had me back at work, feeling steady enough to start with my new team full-time. First thing this morning, I'd opened my email to a meeting invite from Aiden. I hadn't thought of anything else since. If pressed, I wouldn't be able to remember what I'd said to Ethan and Avi this morning. I had been too distracted by the impending conversation with Aiden.

I felt every bit of gravity in my feet as I walked toward Aiden's closed office door. Pausing with my hand raised to knock, I took a deep breath and asked the universe to be on my side today.

After the softest knock in the history of doors, he called out a low "come in." My nerves took me back to the first day we met, and it helped me to remember that no matter how these next thirty minutes went, they were not going to be anywhere near as bad as meeting him in his office for the first time.

Gingerly opening the door, I stepped into his office to find Aiden's attention laser focused on me. His eyes were bright and warm. His mouth was turned up slightly in each corner, so minute that if someone hadn't watched him as obsessively as I had over the past weeks, he would look all business.

How did he manage to be so composed when I felt like a balloon about to burst?

I didn't know what to do with my hands. My awkwardness reared its head because of my racing thoughts. I gave a jerky wave hello. Great. This meeting was off to an excellent start.

"Abbie, please come in and sit down."

I shut the door behind me and took tentative steps toward one of the office chairs in front of his desk. Aiden stood to come around the front of his desk, taking a seat opposite me in the other chair. That made me feel better. His casual seat choice eased some of my nerves.

Nothing had felt right to me since the fundraiser. My mood had plummeted after seeing my mother. I'd already felt a bit off with the challenge of another new role and trying to decide about what to do about Aiden.

It had felt wrong to put Aiden off under the guise of "not feeling well," especially after telling him I wanted to move forward in our relationship.

His expression had morphed into concern the longer he looked at me. He knew something was wrong, but not what. I wasn't sure I had the energy to tell him. I wanted him to ask the questions, so I wouldn't have to offer any more than necessary.

"You've been keeping me at arm's length for days, sweetheart. I'm worried. So is Ethan. He came to see me yesterday."

Pressing my fingernails into the palms of my hands, I thought about where to start. I didn't want him thinking that I couldn't do the job I'd actively pursued, and I definitely didn't want to go back to my old role now that I'd had the smallest taste of the creative side of the business.

"Aiden, I will tell you what's been going on with me. But first, I need you to promise me that everything I say in this office will be kept strictly confidential. I am going to tell you these things not as my boss, so nothing I say can get back to HR or be shared with the team. I don't want it to change how you think of me."

Never having been this direct with Aiden before, I saw the impact of my words hit him. He'd gone from leaning forward with his elbows on his knees to sitting straight and grasping the arms of the chair with his hands.

"You need to tell me right now if someone has hurt you. If someone put their hands on you or said something to you that made you feel scared, I'll make them wish they'd never been born."

I could see how my withdrawal might make him wary that something had happened to me. I'd done my best to hide the depth of what I was feeling on the way home from San Jose on Saturday night. It wouldn't be out of the realm of possibility for him to assume something worse had happened to me in the interim.

His protective side had me instantly reaching out to pull one of his hands with both of mine.

"No, Aiden. Nothing like that at all. No one has bothered me in any way. The team is great." I attempted a smile, but my heart wasn't in it. It was harder to lie to someone I trusted.

Giving his hand a quick squeeze to reassure him, I pressed him to assure my privacy.

"I'm going to explain. But please promise you won't tell anyone first."

"If no one is bothering you, then yes. Everything you say in this office will just be between us. I promise."

Seeing the intensity of his honesty reflected in his gaze, I decided

I believed him. He had never acted in a way that showed I couldn't trust him.

Unable to hold eye contact while I confessed my secrets, I considered what to say. Rationally, I knew I shouldn't feel bad about it, but there was always the ever-present fear that he would see me as "less" or "flawed" the way some people who misunderstood mental illness could.

"So I guess the reason Ethan said I haven't been myself lately was probably because I've been going through something personally."

To his credit, he waited for me to speak instead of jumping in with a lot of questions. God, why was this so hard to force out? Gripping onto his hand to reassure myself now, I continued.

"So, when there's a lot of stress, I get anxious. The fundraiser was a lot. When we saw my mother, I was horrified and embarrassed. My whole system got overloaded, and I didn't want to be there. She said some critical things to me, and even though I know she's not right, I can't stop it from making me feel really bad. Her criticisms go round and round my brain until it's hard not to believe them. So I had to take two days off just to take care of myself. I know I've been off a bit before this week because of what was going on with us, so Ethan must have noticed that. Today is the first day I feel almost back to my normal self."

Chancing a quick look at his face, I saw him struggling to keep his expression neutral. I could see worry in his eyes, but this time, he nodded for me to keep going. I looked back down at our joined hands.

"Aiden, I have chronic anxiety. Not the kind of worry that someone might have where they are concerned about something for a little while and it goes away. I get so anxious that it affects my ability to communicate with people and socialize. Even though I take medication every day to help me manage it, sometimes, life just has more stress than I can handle. Then I get too overwhelmed to cope."

Needing to see his reaction, I lifted my head fully. He let go of my hands to swipe his fingers through his hair and opened and closed his mouth a couple of times. I could see that he was trying to figure out what to say. At least he didn't look angry or disappointed, but it would remain to be seen if he still wanted anything to do with me romantically after this.

"I can tell that was really hard for you to say…" he began.

Oh no, the brush-off is coming… Shit! I pushed my chair back. Maybe I wasn't ready to hear him reject me after all. I had to get out of his office.

My panic must have shown on my face because he grabbed both my hands to prevent me from moving.

"No, sweetheart. Wait. I'm not done. I calmed down and listened just now. I need you to listen to me too, okay?" The look he gave me said he meant business.

"As I was saying, it couldn't have been easy for you to share that, especially because I'm your boss. So thank you for trusting me that we will keep this information between us. I need you close to me. I don't feel like I can have this conversation with you over there."

He got up and walked to the office door and turned the lock before coming back to his seat. Once he was sitting again, he took my hands and guided me into his lap. I was as graceful as a newborn giraffe, so I landed on him in a pile of limbs. He quickly took hold of my hips and righted me so that I was sitting on one of his hard thighs (he clearly never missed leg day). Wrapping his arm around my waist, he leaned forward to put his nose in my hair and took a deep breath.

"That's much better," he said while he cuddled me closer to him.

He was right. Being this close to him helped me relax my tense muscles. The churning in my stomach abated slightly as I let myself lean back into him. His hand at my waist started making slow strokes on my hip.

"I know why you wouldn't want to say anything. Having been in the corporate world for so many years, I've seen the way employers sometimes deal with mental illness, and it can be unfair. Being a younger person in the company must have also made this more of a risk to you. Thank you for being so brave."

I didn't have the words to tell him how powerful it was to be called brave when worry had insidiously stripped away so many of the good things I could believe about myself. I held his gaze, hoping my expression could say what my lips could not.

"As hard as it is for me to admit, sweetheart, I don't know much about what it's like to feel how you feel on a daily basis. But it doesn't scare me or make me think less of you. I lived with three women growing up and welcomed a fourth into the family, so I like to think I've seen a lot of female emotions. But this is going to be all new to me. You'll have to have patience with me."

I was floored by his sense of calm. Not only that, but he wasn't giving me the brush-off either. He could have easily gone back on what he said about seeing each other and gone with the "it's against the rules, and I've thought about it" excuse. But he didn't. Maybe I shouldn't have been surprised. Aiden had never done a predictable thing since I'd known him, other than his choice of lunch.

"Okay, um, I'm not really sure what else to say right now. I wasn't expecting you to want to continue whatever it is between us after I told you…" I spoke into his throat as I buried my face in his warm skin, muffling my words.

"Abigail, let me clear up two things right away. First, 'whatever this is' is a relationship. An exclusive one. You are mine. And I am yours. Since you've taken such a risk, I'll be honest in return. I don't know the first thing about being someone's boyfriend, nor have I ever wanted to. But with you, I'd like to try. The hitch in the plan is that we must keep it to ourselves. Do you still want to?"

Taking a deep breath of his scent, I thought about giving up moments like this. Quiet moments where we were just holding each other, talking. The safety I felt in his arms was no small thing. No one had ever made me feel as comfortable in my skin as Aiden. I'd already decided that having this time with him, however long it lasted, was a risk I was willing to take. I would not change my mind now.

"Aiden, I want to make this work however we can."

Leaning my head back, I saw his lips part in a huge grin. He grabbed me to pull me closer, as if he was trying to merge us into a single being. He didn't give me a moment to catch my breath before his mouth was on mine, devouring my lips with his teeth and tongue.

Just as intensely as he began, he stopped our kissing as it started to get heated.

"Abbie, wait. We need to stop. If we're doing this, we're going to be smart and not draw attention to ourselves. We've slipped twice now."

With that, I licked the shell of his ear and smiled back at him. His pupils dilated with lust, and it was liberating to feel a bit of a thrill after running the gamut of emotions lately.

"Oh, pretty girl, you have no idea who you are playing with here. But you are going to find out soon. Will you stay at my house tonight? I also want you to know that I can wait until you are absolutely sure you're feeling okay."

A rush of excitement ran through me as I thought about spending the whole night with him.

"No, I don't want to wait." I would love to see the place that Aiden called home. If I waited for everything to be perfect with my mood, I would never do anything in life.

"Good girl. We can have dinner and just relax. No pressure. But for now, we have the rest of the workday to get through. I'll be looking forward to it all day." He pressed his lips briefly against mine once more, as if sealing our plans with a kiss.

I reluctantly pulled myself out of his arms and headed back to the door. Unlocking it, I looked back at him, feeling much lighter than when I'd walked in. This was really happening.

"I'll text you my address." He smiled.

"See you tonight."

Opening the door, I quietly closed it behind me. I tried to appear normal and not to look completely overwhelmed. This time in the best way possible.

He'd accepted my anxiety. Well, he'd accepted it in theory, anyway. I'd have to wait and see what he thought of the real thing. I told myself again that I could trust him. We'd spend more time together, and then I would share more if he wanted to know. I prayed with every fiber of my being that this was not too good to be true.

As the end of the workday drew closer, my phone lit up with a text from Aiden that included his address.

Aiden

Looking forward to tonight. Dress comfortably, casual attire only.

Abbie

Understood, sir.

Aiden

Be careful with the sir, Ms. Summers. Very cheeky.

Abbie

See you later on ;)

I considered what to wear that night. If I was going to be anticipating taking the next steps in intimacy with Aiden, I was going to be comfortable. He was going to get a crash course in all things Abbie today. Mental health *and* anime shirts.

209

Twenty-Seven

ABBIE

In the back of the Uber, I scrolled through my phone without really seeing anything on the screen. I was too preoccupied with staying over at Aiden's house for the first time, especially with it being our first real chunk of time since the trip to LA.

My stomach still felt uneasy every time I remembered how easily this thing I had going with Aiden could unravel. It made me want to hold on to him tighter, but I couldn't see a way to do that publicly yet. Or maybe ever.

I was so gone for him that I was willing to keep our relationship secret longer than I should. I felt more accepted and comfortable with Aiden. What we had together was a stratosphere apart from the few lukewarm, slightly awkward relationships I'd experienced during my college years.

As the car slowed, I looked up to see we had arrived. Aiden's house looked like it had been plucked from an architectural magazine. Somehow, he'd got his hands on a larger lot that embraced the U-shaped Mediterranean-style house. Larger trees and shrubbery gave him some distance from his neighbors on both sides. He'd found himself a private oasis in the city.

The darker beige color of the large stones that made up the exterior were shadowed in the evening light, making the atmosphere slightly gothic with the pitch of the roof and the wrought-iron framing the windows. I loved it.

This was a world away from my small studio in the center of the city, surrounded by the constant noise of people moving about the streets.

The driver pulled up to the front door, and I grabbed my overnight bag as I offered my thanks for the ride. By the time I was about to reach for the door handle, Aiden was there, opening it and helping me out of the car.

Had he been waiting for me by the door? My heart warmed with the idea that he might be as eager for this night to begin as I was.

"Hi." His simple greeting was accompanied by a sweet kiss to my lips.

"Hi," I echoed when we broke apart. "Your house is amazing."

"Thank you. It's still a bit surreal to have all this space to myself, but I'm getting used to it." Ever the gentleman, he reached for my bag and offered me his other hand. "Let me take you on a tour before we eat. But first, tell me who is on your shirt today?"

"It's Hello Kitty. Another Japanese cartoon character."

"I like it. It looks a lot like the one you were wearing on the day we met."

"Wow. You remember that?" I was truly surprised. "You're close. That one was Sailor Moon, but both have a cat character."

"I remember everything about that afternoon." He squeezed my hand. It was my turn to observe him. Looking at Aiden in the low light of dusk, he was wearing a white button-up shirt rolled at the elbows. Had I ever seen his forearms in the light of day before? I knew the feel of his hard muscles around me, but those forearms deserved their own calendar.

Realizing I'd been staring at his arms and chest for entirely too long, I looked down to see he was wearing a pair of worn jeans for the first time since we'd met. I couldn't wait for him to turn around so I could see how they hugged his firm ass.

He allowed my silent ogling with an indulgent smile.

"Have you looked your fill, sweetheart?" This came out with a small chuckle.

"Hey!" I swatted his arm with my free hand. "It's not my fault you come out looking like all of that?"

I gestured to his whole body. He pulled me to his side, sliding the arm that was holding my hand around my waist. He dropped his nose into my hair and took a deep breath.

So much for catching that view of his ass. I sighed in disappointment.

"I love the way you smell. I can't wait to get you inside, where I won't have to share you with anyone. Let's go."

We walked into the house, entering the main foyer. The walls were a light color to highlight the warm wood accents along the ceiling, with matching floorboards. He set my bag down near the base of the stairs.

"This is really nice, Aiden."

"Let me show you the kitchen, then, so we can get our evening started."

He led me from the foyer into a wide-open room with windows all along the wall. There were trees that surrounded his yard on this side. Looking out into what must be the side yard, I couldn't see any sign of the neighbor's property. The sense of privacy made me feel like we were in our own little world.

Through a large arch in the far wall, what I could see of the kitchen itself was completely modern, with clean lines and stainless steel appliances.

Making our way through the living area and the arch separating the rooms, Aiden moved with practiced ease over to whatever was simmering on the stove.

"You cook too?" This was too much to handle. Was this man bad at anything?

"My sisters and I learned to cook for ourselves pretty early. But we only learned the basics, so I have about five meals that I know how to make."

"Are we eating chicken and steamed vegetables?" I teased. I'd never seen a sweet pass between Aiden's lips.

"Brat. I'll have you know that we're having pasta. I figured I couldn't go wrong with that. Now, go sit down."

Pleased that we were eating in the kitchen rather than what I was sure to be a fancy dining room for twelve, I made my way over to the table, sitting at one of the two place settings. He had put us side by side, which I loved.

"Would you like a drink? Wine?" he asked while dishing up the pasta.

"No, thank you. Just water, please. I tend not to drink very often. It doesn't really mix well with my medication."

I stopped myself when I realized that I'd brought up my anxiety. I froze, suddenly unsure of what to say next. Not wanting to turn him off, I didn't know how much he really wanted to hear about it. And he probably wouldn't want to hear about it on our first proper night alone. I couldn't imagine him finding anxiety sexy.

Feeling insecure, I let my eyes wander to the backyard. The floor-to-ceiling windows continued in this room. Anything to avoid looking in his direction right now. I wasn't ready to process his reaction.

"Sweetheart, look at me. You aren't going to scare me away by talking about it. I don't want you hiding things from me that matter, okay?"

My gaze returned to his at the gentle reassurance in his voice.

"Okay," I agreed quickly. The trouble was believing he meant what he was saying.

What if he says he is okay with it but then you get really upset or overwhelmed and he changes his mind? Do you think he really wants to deal with you in that state?

Pushing my inner voice down, I made the conscious decision to take him at his word until he showed me any sign it was really a problem.

Placing a plate of chicken and vegetable pasta in front of each of me, he sat down beside me.

"I see we aren't too far from the chicken and vegetable lunch routine. I'm going to miss the lovely employee at your favorite delivery restaurant. She doesn't even need to hear my voice to know what I'm ordering for you," I teased.

I looked at him from beneath my lashes, trying to keep my lips from curving upward. In retaliation, he gave my waist a quick pinch, causing me to yelp in surprise.

"Hey now, snarky girl. I'll have you know there's cream sauce in here too. Need to make sure I cater to those decadent tastes of yours." Mirth danced in his eyes.

"Just because I ordered the entire menu of that dessert café in LA, you think you know my tastes?" I challenged him.

"I think I know a couple of your tastes." His tone was thick with innuendo. But thankfully, he didn't take that line of thought any further for now.

Digging into our pasta, we fell into light conversation. By some tacit agreement, we chatted about the easy stuff while we ate: how I felt about transitioning over temporarily to the digital arts team, how Anne and Grace had transitioned from accounting into full-time nonprofit campaigns, how boring his lunches were without me having to come in and out of his office with questions.

I stood to carry my plate to the sink, but Aiden grabbed them both and insisted I sit and let him take care of everything. It was such a luxury to have someone focused on just me for once. Returning to the table, he took my hand and led me back into the living room, where an overstuffed couch awaited us. He flicked a remote to turn on a cozy fireplace.

He sat right beside me, the whole side of his body touching mine from shoulders to thighs. I loved how he wanted to be as close to me as I did to him. Tucking one leg underneath me, I turned in my spot to face him, bracing myself for whatever questions he might have.

This would be our first opportunity with the time and space to talk about what I had shared with him.

While we'd eaten, dusk had fallen. Aiden looked out at those shadowed trees in his backyard for a moment before returning his gaze to mine, then gathered my hands into his.

"I can see that talking about your mental health worries you when you have to bring it up. But I need you to know that I want to be here for you. You're going to have to help me know what that looks like exactly. I'm definitely going to make mistakes, so I need to apologize in advance."

I had not expected such an open response from him. I had zero experience, other than Indie and Emery, with telling people about my anxiety and receiving a supportive reaction.

To be fair, I'd kept everything to myself for almost a decade.

Other than my doctor, I'd only told my mother about it back in high school. My mother had dismissed me as being "too sensitive." That had resulted in me having to constantly mask my feelings ever since. I didn't want others to see my mental health as a weakness or some deficiency.

"Um. Thank you. I'm not actually sure what to say. This is new territory for me. I just wanted to make sure you knew before we started this for real." I gestured between us.

"It means a lot that you would trust me, especially since we work together. I would never betray your confidence. I hope you know that. Still, it took a lot of courage to say something to me."

I searched his face for any hint that he was being insincere. But he looked back at me with kindness and attentiveness. He seemed to really mean what he said.

Before I could reply, he added, "I also want you to know that you didn't have to tell me before we continued exploring our relationship. You have nothing to be ashamed of. My feelings for you wouldn't have changed by telling me a month from now. That said, I am so happy that you told me because I want to be here for you."

I hardly felt brave at the moment. I was still working on accepting his calm reaction. I was always braced for the rejection of not being good enough. The world could be cruel about mental illness. It made me want to open up about my reality to anyone.

"Is it okay if we talk about something else now?" I didn't want to say anything more. Getting bogged down in worry before we even began was not a headspace I wanted to entertain.

I felt as steady as I could with the nerves about staying over at Aiden's house for the first time and all the implications that came with that. I wanted to enjoy this time with him.

"Sure. I just need to say it again so you hear me. Nothing has changed for me since this morning, okay?" He leaned closer and brought his mouth to my ear. "I still want you. So badly. Would you prefer not to talk at all?"

I shivered with the pleasure those words brought to my body. It was a huge weight off my shoulders to know that I hadn't thrown everything off track by being honest.

"Yes, please," I whispered.

"So polite," he teased with a wink.

Before standing to return to the kitchen briefly, he brushed his lips light against mine, a promise that there was more to come.

Something sparked inside me, wanting to surprise him.

"Aiden, where is the washroom, please?" I called through the archway separating the rooms.

"Down the hall on the opposite side of the front door," he directed from the kitchen.

Standing, I made my way across the dim hallway at the front of his house. I located the bathroom and searched the counter for what I needed.

Because it was Aiden's house, everything was in perfect order. I found what I was looking for. I closed my eyes and took a deep breath before enacting my impulse.

He was either going to love my little spur-of-the-moment idea or laugh at it. Either way, I felt safe enough to take the risk.

Twenty-Eight

AIDEN

The anticipation of being intimate with Abbie without interruption had too much energy running through my system. Not wanting to spend much time cleaning up, I quickly rinsed our dinner dishes, leaving them in the sink for the morning. I walked back into the living room, more than ready to whisk her upstairs.

When I didn't see her on the couch, I felt concerned. Was she having second thoughts? Was she not feeling well?

Walking down the hall to the powder room door, I knocked softly.

"Abbie, everything okay?"

There was no response from the other side of the door. Knocking again, I looked down at the bottom of the door and noticed that there was no light coming from underneath. Taking a chance, I checked the knob and found it unlocked. When I opened it and flicked the light on, the small room was empty. What the hell was going on?

I glanced at the mirror over the sink. The little sneak had left me a note written with the bar of soap by the sink: "You're it!"

The surge of desire caused by those two words had me grinning.

The tension I'd been holding faded away with the understanding she was all in.

Game on. Ready or not, here I come.

Making my way to the stairs, I debated my course of action. The upper hallway was divided by the staircase, with guest bedrooms on one side and the primary bedroom and my office on the other. The light in one of the guest bathrooms cast a moderate glow into the upper level, but the rooms themselves were dark.

I reached the top of the stairs, considering my next move. Announcing my presence would rush this, and I wanted to savor each moment ahead of them. She had upped the ante on the situation by about 10,000 percent, so I would return the favor by keeping her in a bit of suspense.

My mind was still trying to catch up to this little turn of events. She'd upended my slow plan of seduction for the evening. I'd thought we'd spend the evening on the couch. Maybe watch a movie where I'd stare at her more than the screen. But she had turned my plan on its head.

Stepping as lightly as I could into the dark hallway, I avoided the loose floorboard a few feet from the top of the stairs. I'd stepped on it often enough to know the squeak would echo through the quiet hallway. She knew I was coming, but I wasn't going to go easy on her. There were a few advantages to this being my literal home turf. She may have started this game of cat and mouse, but I was going to finish it my way.

With her. In my bed. Underneath me.

I spared a quick glance at the guest bath. There was a little bit of light coming from the windows, but I didn't think she would hide in the first room she came across. My height gave me an advantage in that I could see over the rim of the large soaker tub. Nope, not there.

My blood was boiling in my veins. Once more, I had to fight against the urge to rush this.

Making my way into the first two guest rooms, I listened for any sign of Abbie's breathing or the rustling of fabric.

I imagined with each moment that passed that she was getting more restless and less comfortable, relishing the rising anticipation.

Pulling my phone from my back pocket, I shone the light into the room. There was no evidence of a disturbance, but I checked the closet just in case. Nothing.

Moving more quickly but still as quietly as possible, I gave a cursory glance to the second guest room. The soft white bedding of the two double beds stood out like beacons in the room. But no Abbie in there either.

Stalking back into the hallway, the two remaining doorways on the opposite side of the upstairs level faced me. On the left was the master suite, and although hot, the fantasy of finding Abbie in my bed seemed a little too daring for our first night together.

Goddamn. I hoped she'd be up for a repeat of this little adventure.

Door number two was my home office. It looked the same as the day the movers had put the new furniture in it. I'd considered working from home some days. But my desk remained undisturbed, as I'd never chosen to spend one day outside Abbie's orbit if I had the choice.

Aiming my flashlight at the floor a few feet in front of me, I scanned what I could see of the room. Nothing seemed out of place in this room either, making me doubt my bet that she was in here. I rounded the desk and was just about to check underneath when I heard the sharp intake of breath coming from underneath it.

Gotcha, sweetheart.

Turning off my flashlight, I took a couple of steps away from the desk before darting back to pull out the chair and diving below the desktop to grab her ankle. Abbie let out a cross between a shriek and a squeal. I reached for her other ankle and pulled her out from underneath the desk and straddled her hips.

Reaching up, I pinned her arms in place.

Leaning down, I relished the heaving of her chest from the surprise of my movements. Pressing my forehead to hers for a moment, I tried to claw back some control into my body. I was afraid if I moved, I'd fuck her right here on the floor.

Her enticing scent filled my lungs as I ran my nose up her neck to her ear. Neither of us had uttered a single word yet. Pressing my lips to her ear, I whispered, "Caught you."

"Yeah, but who won the game?" Abbie tossed out cheekily, still slightly breathless from my surprise attack.

"I guess we're about to find out, sweetheart."

Hoping I had the wherewithal to walk the fine line between arousal and adrenaline, I stood, pulling her up along with me, and then lifted her over my shoulder. Carrying her into the hall toward my bedroom, fireman-style, I enjoyed her surprised intake of breath at suddenly being upside down.

Entering my bedroom, I tossed her onto the bed and heard the air leave her lungs when her body hit the mattress.

"Stay," I ordered with lust lacing my voice. One game of chase was enough for the night.

I couldn't see her with the lights out, and that wouldn't do. I flipped on my bedside table lamp, the room illuminated with a soft golden light.

I turned back to assess how Abbie was feeling. She lay back on her elbows, watching me carefully.

Moving back to the bed, I used her legs to pull her gently to the bottom. She let herself fall onto her back with the motion.

The amount of trust she was giving me made me lock my knees so that I didn't just devour her all at once. She was magnificent.

I carefully laid my body over hers and brought my face down until I could focus on her eyes only.

"Abbie, you okay?"

As if my words reminded her to move, she restlessly rubbed her pelvis against mine, bringing her arms up to wrap around my neck. I groaned and pressed my full weight on her lower body to hold her in place.

"I need you to tell me this is what you want." I could wait if she changed her mind. As mind-blowing as the evening had been already, I wanted nothing more than her complete comfort and ease.

"Yes. I want it."

"You can change your mind anytime. There is no pressure here."

"Honestly, I'm good." Her voice remained steady.

With her permission granted, I ground my hardness into the softness of her body to show her how much I wanted her. Her pupils were wide with lust and excitement.

I crushed my lips to hers and reached one hand behind her head to tangle my fingers in her hair. I moved her head into place so I could fuck her mouth with my tongue. Soon, I was going to taste every inch of her body. All that beautiful skin that had been hidden from my greedy eyes for weeks and weeks.

We'd only had stolen moments in LA. Both of us were in too much sensory overload to be able to appreciate all the facets of our intimacy. I wanted to commit her body to memory.

Her lips were plush, and I bit down lightly on the bottom one and tugged on it. I could kiss her forever, but I couldn't deny the soul-deep need to have every part of her. To be the one who helped her find out how to lose herself to pleasure.

Moving my hand down to her waist while nipping down her chin and throat, I was quick to remove her cute little shirt and bra, sorely tempted to spend hours torturing her full tits as they were released from their confines. After leaning back on my knees, I wasted no time in getting to work on her ass-hugging jeans. I'd waited too long to have the freedom to rip them off her.

I had thought my need for her was under my control, but I'd been wrong. Nothing short of her own wishes would stop me now. There was a distinct rawness with Abbie that I'd never felt with anyone else.

Tossing her jeans somewhere behind me, I ran my hands up the insides of her legs until I reached the uppermost part of her thighs. I guided her legs apart and stretched her muscles by wedging myself between them.

Leaning back down, I ran my nose up the valley where her thigh met her hip. Her sweet scent was so much stronger there.

I followed my initial sweep with a hard press of my tongue from the top of her hip to where her panties met the hottest, wettest part of her.

An unexpected chuckle broke from me when I came face-to-face with the little cartoon drawing on her panties. I loved that she felt comfortable enough to show me the adorable side of herself, even knowing what was likely to happen when she came here tonight.

I pushed my tongue beneath the gusset of her panties, giving one of her lips a quick lick, and was rewarded with a yelp from Abbie.

She'd been so good so far to let me just explore her. I lifted my head to check in to make sure the pressure was right and not uncomfortable for her.

"These are very misleading panties. We both know that you are no innocent young lady."

Her face was still flushed with need, so I knew I was on the right track down here.

Getting back to my new happy place, I repeated my ministrations on her other hip, feeling her shift in anticipation of what was next.

Bracing myself on my elbows, I reached up to yank her panties down her legs. They joined the discarded clothing on the floor. Mouthing deep kisses all over her pelvis, I pushed my tongue against her skin with the same pressure I had used to invade her mouth.

Using both hands, I parted her pussy. She was just as beautifully pink as I remembered. The difference being I could see her clearly, all laid out for me. She was the ripest forbidden fruit.

I dove in like the madman I was for her, focusing all the pressure of my tongue on that tight little bud at the top of her slit. I didn't want to allow her head to get in the way of her pleasure.

I hummed as I lapped at her with increasing speed. She began to push back against my mouth, taking her own pleasure against my tongue.

Sliding two fingers into her wet heat, I quickly added a third to stretch her limits. I loved the sensation of wetness dripping down my chin, a combination of her juices and my saliva. Determined to make her come, I guided my fingers to her G-spot, needing to push her over the edge before I sunk my cock inside her.

Her breathing sped up, and her pussy started contracting against my mouth and around my fingers. The level of possession I felt inside me was growing. The thought of anyone else touching her now that she was mine had me growling unintentionally, adding sensation to the motions of my tongue and fingers. As she approached her peak, I doubled down on the pressure and flicks of my tongue and my fingers against her G-spot.

As much as I wanted to watch her face when she came, I wanted her to fully experience the pleasure more. There would be lots of times for me to watch her in the future. For now, she was going to be putty in my hands after her orgasm.

Her breath hitched, and then her muscles bore down against my mouth. I felt her channel squeeze and release around my fingers. She keened out her orgasm with an exclamation of my name, and it was a siren's call to my cock.

After making sure I'd wrung out every drop of her pleasure, I stood to briefly rid myself of my clothes and pulled the condom from the front pocket of my jeans.

She lay back with her chest heaving as she came down from her high while never shifting her gaze from mine.

Did she have any idea how sexy she looked? Her skin was flushed and hot from her orgasm. Her hair was spread out all around her head, like a mermaid in the sea of my bed.

Rolling the condom onto my impossibly hard cock, I crawled on top of her, pulling her knees up so they were pressed against my hips.

I looked into her eyes, taking one last moment of calm before the storm I planned to unleash on her body.

"You ready?"

"Yes." Her orgasm had brought a huskiness to her voice that was unbearably sexy.

I kissed her deeply as I reached underneath the pillows at the head of the bed. With one more surprise in store for her, I planned to give her as much pleasure as she could handle tonight.

Twenty-Nine

ABBIE

I couldn't believe I'd actually gone through with hiding from him. I'd felt every second of those minutes spent waiting for him. Each breath felt like it echoed through the room, reverberating back to me in the mostly enclosed space against the side of his desk.

By the time he'd found me, my heart was beating out of my chest. With a combination of nerves and anticipation, I'd second-guessed myself, hoping that he would find my actions playful and spontaneous. Even though I heard him come into the room, my heart had stuttered with surprise when he pulled me out from under the desk without a word. He was clever, letting me think he didn't see me backed into the corner below the desktop.

I should have known better than to underestimate Aiden and his ability to excel at anything he tried. He'd beaten me at my own game.

But I couldn't help but feel like the winner as I lay below him sated after the most powerful orgasm I could remember. Every time he put his hands on me, he tucked away all my little tells and used them to increase my pleasure. He kept me firmly tethered in my body so that my anxious brain couldn't take away from the moment.

Both of us were breathing hard after his crushing kisses, our skin damp with a sheen of excitement.

He held my gaze as he brought his length up to my hot, wet center. This felt like more than sex. I wanted him to take what he wanted from me, knowing he would give it back tenfold.

It did something to me to be wanted with this level of ferocity.

Without warning, he moved his hips forward and filled me with one powerful stroke, punching the breath from my lungs.

"Fuck yes, baby."

His girth held me captive as my body tried to accommodate his size. With the briefest pause to let me adjust, he started moving. He pushed in deeply before pulling out almost to his tip and then snapping his hips again.

I was overwhelmed by sensations in a good way, still sensitive from my climax.

His scent was all around me. Aiden's powerful arms held me wrapped up as he moved my body with his.

"Abbie, you feel unbelievable. I can't… It's like nothing…" He panted out his thoughts as though he, too, was feeling too much at once.

"I know. Me too," I barely managed a whisper.

"You feel. So. Fucking. Good." He punctuated each word by slamming his hips forward. Each stroke was harder than the one before.

I gripped his shoulders and tried to meet his movements with the limited space between our bodies.

Suddenly, he pushed himself upward from his elbows so that he was on his knees, his torso upright. He brought my legs up so they rested flat against his chest. He continued his powerful thrusts, grinding against my center between each one.

"Now, you are going to come for me again." His voice was husky with lust and exertion. In the warm light of the room, I could see every detail of his toned body working toward our mutual pleasure. Had there ever been a man sexier than Aiden Sullivan at this moment? I didn't think so.

I clenched around him in reaction to his words. Even with the hum of pleasure simmering in my body from his movements, another orgasm seemed out of reach. He nipped the first ankle he had just kissed to bring my attention back to him.

"No thinking. You will come." I could get drunk on his confidence alone.

Just then, I heard a faint vibration start up. I jerked my gaze to the hand not holding up my legs. He held a small rose-gold vibrator with an air-suction head. Those were goooood. Aiden was nothing if not resourceful, always prepared like a debauched Boy Scout. He had clearly done some research or was just naturally an expert in all things Abbie pleasure related. I was stunned into silence. Aiden bringing a toy into bed had never occurred to me.

Aiden took my breath away with his consideration. The vibrator took the pressure off me and let me sink deeply into the moment.

He upped the vibrations and pressed the head along my skin. I felt the air pull lightly against his movements as he dragged it closer to my slit. The cool pulses of air against my clit combined with the way his cock spread the vibrations inside was incredible.

He slowed his thrusts slightly, but not their intensity, as he kept the toy pressed against the top of my opening. My inner walls clenched around his thickness in reaction to the powerful vibrations and suction motion.

Having him inside me and knowing he could feel every ripple of my flesh as he stretched me was decadent.

"That's right. I want to feel you lose it around me before I fill this condom. Goddamn it, Abbie, I'm not going to last."

With those words, he renewed his hard thrusts, the vibrator pushing against my clit with each movement of his hips. In turn, his thrusting turned unhinged in pursuit, losing some of his earlier finesse.

His cock transferred the vibrations of the toy to throughout my core. I felt an urge to bear down against a sensation almost like a tickle with a simultaneous deep pull inside me.

I started breathing more quickly in shock. No way was I going to say aloud what my body felt like doing.

"Let it happen, baby. Come for me."

Unable to stop myself, my muscles clamped down on him, and I felt a major pull deep inside my muscles as they clenched, followed by a torrent of hot liquid between us. I keened a nonsensical sound as my system flooded with pleasure.

The sound of his hips wetly slapping against me prolonged my pleasure. My come dripped down, coating both our skin, trickling between my cheeks and onto the sheet below us.

"Fuck, yes, baby. That's it."

Before I could process what had just happened, Aiden pressed into me deeply and held. He came with a deep noise from his throat while continuing to push into me as if he could fuse our skin together.

"Fuck, baby. That was so fucking sexy. You're incredible."

The best I could offer was a semi-coherent "Mmm" sound. Nothing like that had ever happened to me before, leaving me both satiated and shocked.

Postorgasm, Aiden began pressing soft, lingering kisses into my neck and shoulder as our breathing returned to normal.

Best cardio ever. This was a type of exercise I could endorse.

He rested some of his weight on me. But wanting more of him, I pulled him down with my arms wrapped around him. I loved the feeling of him overwhelming me with his size.

Reaching between us, he pulled out gently. My oversensitized sex felt every bit of the friction of that slide, causing me to unintentionally clench around him.

The combination of the powerful tension between us minutes ago and the lingering awareness that I had squirted during sex for the first time had me holding in an inappropriately timed giggle.

Nothing said serious and sexy like potentially laughing right after sex.

"Abbie…" he groaned, and I felt him shift his hips.

The sound of his voice, like he thought I was trying to torture him in some way on purpose, had my laugh breaking free. My body shook with the effort to hold it in.

I buried my nose in his neck as I rambled an apology.

"I'm sorry! I'm sorry! It's not funny. It's just that I've never… and then you made that noise, and it's all so…"

Great. Just great, Abbie. Way to go from vixen to madwoman all in one evening.

Finally getting myself under a bit of control, the stark silence left behind had shyness bubbling up inside me.

"Shh, baby. It's fine. I understand. So you've never squirted before, hmm? God, that's hot."

He said "squirted" so casually while I was still having trouble thinking about it. I envied his ease with his sexuality. He just continued to make shushing noises until he felt my breathing slow down.

With one last nip on my shoulder blade, he squeezed me extra tight before pulling a roll-and-grab maneuver, taking his weight off me while simultaneously keeping our bodies as pressed together as possible.

Knowing I had nothing to be embarrassed about, I tried to push my intrusive thoughts to the side. We were finally here together and had expressed ourselves physically and emotionally. I was determined to savor these moments with him.

Movement to my side revealed him subtly removing the condom, followed by a kiss to my forehead before he swung out of bed. He pulled up the covers and tucked them around me, and walked into the bathroom.

It warmed me that he was so thoughtful to think about my comfort before taking care of the practicalities. I snuggled deeper into what must have been the pillow that Aiden slept on because it smelled just like him. I shut my eyes and took in a deep breath of all things Aiden.

I heard the water running briefly and then opened my eyes to see him come out of the bathroom with a cloth in his hand.

His complete ease with his body, his hard muscles, and innate sexuality made me want to check that my mouth was closed and I wasn't drooling. God, if I had a body like that, I'd never put any clothes on.

Though that would make things complicated at the office. Not to mention all the traffic accidents he could cause on the way to work.

Like he knew exactly where my mind had gone, he gave me a knowing smirk.

"Like what you see?"

I sure did. But I would never stop blushing when he kept calling me out like that.

"You know you're sexy, Aiden. I'm just appreciating all your discipline and feeling a little sad for you that you've missed out on so many sweets."

His eyes sparked with heat, as if he was ready to devour me all over again.

Hmm. He likes hearing me openly talking about my desire for him.

"Sweetheart, having to keep my hands off you all those months was temptation enough. As far as I'm concerned, nothing else was ever on the menu."

He got into bed and wrapped his arms around me, whispering in my ear. "Rest for a bit, baby. I am far from done with you tonight."

I smiled into his pillow as I thought about spending future nights just like this. Quite possibly, he was going to kill me with orgasms. But what a way to go.

Waking up in Aiden's bed was like waking up from a deep sleep where the dream felt like it actually happened. It took me a moment to figure out if I was conscious or lost in my wildest fantasy.

Hesitant to open my eyes and find that last night had all been an elaborate creation of my overactive imagination, I took stock of my surroundings via my other senses. I was warmer than usual. I could feel heat radiating toward me from my left, like I was sitting side-on to a fireplace.

The air had the distinct scent of skin and sweat. Like that amazing smell of sun-kissed skin from the outdoors. Only now, there was the warm scent that was Aiden mixed with my coconut shampoo. The result was an addicting feeling of a tropical paradise. We would make a fortune if we could bottle it.

Feeling the acute stiffness in my muscles from last evening's activities, I blushed when I thought of how insatiable Aiden had been, waking me to make love to me again in the middle of the night. There were no other words to describe it. The unhurried pace, paired with his hand working my clit almost the entire time, had pulled another throbbing orgasm from me.

The tenderness between my legs intensified when my inner muscles clenched with my thoughts.

I felt the prickliness of my blush spread to the roots of my hair and spread over my cheeks and chest as I thought of the sounds I had made last night. Aiden had a way of disarming my inner critic and freeing a part of me that I didn't know I had.

The strongest confirmation that I truly wasn't dreaming was the rough voice emanating from the man beside me.

"Baby, what are you thinking about over there? It must be something hot because you're flushing that gorgeous pink color again."

Aiden was awake and apparently watching me jump through the mental Olympics of waking up. It should have made me feel self-conscious knowing he was watching me sleep. But it just felt sexy because, well, my brain and body agreed that everything he did was sexy.

I turned my head on the pillow toward the sound of his voice, opening my eyes approximately one millimeter, because if this was a hallucination, I never wanted to be sane again.

"Abbie…"

His deep voice took on that hint of amusement I only heard when he was talking to me.

Opening my eyes further, I brought my hand up to his chest and placed it over his heart. The steady beat reassured me. He wasn't freaking out or regretting us. Thank God.

"Hi." I gave him a shy smile, tempted to squeeze my eyes shut.

"Oh, don't hide from me now. We've just gotten started."

His smile broadened in a way I had never seen before. Was this Aiden Sullivan happy?

There was a shine in his eyes that definitely wasn't a trick of the early morning sunlight. I was seeing him truly relaxed for the first time in all the months that I had known him.

I rubbed my hand back and forth over his heart, loving the warm, firm muscles of his chest under my palm.

"I'm not hiding. I'm just making sure I'm not dreaming." I slapped a hand over my mouth. "Forget I said that! I have no filter with you."

He outright laughed as he wrapped his arms around me and pulled me to his chest.

"God, you are absolutely adorable."

"Just what a woman wants to hear the morning after," I grumbled.

He took my chin in his hand and tilted it upward so I was looking into his eyes.

"You are adorable, Abbie. You are also brilliant, kind, loyal, and gorgeous, both inside and out. I like all parts of you. I never want you to filter your thoughts with me."

The pink of my cheeks heated to what I was sure was bright red at this point. I might just spontaneously combust at this point.

"Ah, you don't have to be embarrassed. You are all those things, even though I know you might have a hard time believing them. Don't worry, I won't tire of telling you."

He seemed determined to run me through the gamut of emotions before breakfast. Now, I felt the telltale sting of tears behind my eyes. I blinked a couple of times to clear them, but one traitorous drop fell down my cheek. He caught it with his thumb and gently brushed it from my skin.

"This can work, Abbie. I know we don't have everything figured out yet, and we will talk about that later. But I'm willing to do whatever it takes to be with you."

His eyes radiated a certainty that I had caught glimpses of in other moments between us. For the first time, I didn't see any doubts or fears clouding their depths. It took my breath away.

"Me too, Aiden. I've wanted this with you for longer than I would admit to myself. That's why I was afraid that I was dreaming."

He looked back at me like I had told him he'd won the lottery. It was nearly impossible for me to imagine how I could give him anything near what he was giving me, but I was desperately going to try.

Grabbing his phone off his bedside table, he pulled up a food delivery app and ordered us the longest list of breakfast items I could imagine. Perhaps he was ordering the whole menu.

"Are there more people coming to breakfast that I don't know about?" I giggled a little at his stern face and poked him in the stomach. Ouch. Those abs were lethal. Totally jealous.

"I know my sweetheart likes her sweets, so I don't want you to have to choose. I want to spoil you. We have a couple of hours before we need to get to work. With enough sweetness, you won't protest when I insist we spend the coming weekend naked."

A devious grin took over his expression, and I sucked in a breath, knowing he was dead serious.

Letting so many inhibitions go last night felt safe in the shadows and darkness. But with the morning sun determined to blaze in around the edges of his blackout curtains, I wasn't sure how I felt about even getting out of this bed to pee (which was becoming more urgent by the second), let alone parade around his very expensive house bare for two days.

Biting my lip with hesitation, I tried to think of the best way to say, "Um, I need to slow down a little here," without ruining any of the desire swimming in his eyes.

The churn in my stomach came back with force.

I tried to reason with myself that Aiden wouldn't care if I said I wanted to put some comfy clothes on. This fledgling relationship was not going to be knocked off course by a T-shirt. I reminded myself that he got a kick out of my collection of anime T-shirts. And did I really want to start this relationship, now that we had finally gotten here, by pretending to be someone I wasn't?

Ever attuned to the emotions I tried to keep off my face, Aiden gave me an out.

"Abbie, that was just teasing. Not a demand. I want you here in my arms more than anything. But I want you to let yourself fully be here with me as much as you can this weekend."

Scrutinizing his beautiful face to make sure he really meant those words, I blew out a breath (not anywhere in his direction, though, because hello, morning breath).

"I feel childish saying that I'm not ready for that after last night," I whispered. "I'm just not ready to be that free in the light of day. Especially when you are all that."

I gestured to all of him, as I seemed to do. There wasn't a place on his body that wasn't perfect. It was a pain point that I was going to have to work. He'd shown me how much he enjoyed my body just as it was last night. I'd need to work on believing him.

Choosing not to push me, he gathered me into his arms tightly and pressed my face into his neck. He just seemed to know when things got too intense for me, and I couldn't express how much relief I felt about not having to make eye contact and discuss my insecurities at the same time.

"Hey, it's not all or nothing here. Whatever rule book you think you need to follow in your head, throw it away. I'm thirty-six fucking years old, and this is the first relationship I've ever had that has meant anything to me. We're going to make choices that work best for us. Okay?"

I pressed a kiss to his jaw, liking the scratchy stubble that had grown there overnight. I wondered if I could convince him not to shave all weekend. He'd look so sexy… *Girl! Focus!*

"Okay," I forced out, wishing I could bring back the inner siren that I'd channeled last night.

He took a deep breath and pressed his lips to my forehead. I felt how relaxed his body was next to mine. It was almost as if we were sinking into our own personal cocoon. It was totally foreign to be able to have my feelings out there without falling into some sort of anxiety spiral.

Was he a magician?

He just held me until my breathing was slow and steady again.

"Just one sec," he said.

Untangling our limbs, he briefly got out of bed and headed to his dresser. Coming back to the bed, he handed me one of his well-worn T-shirts to wear so I could sit up comfortably. This was a compromise I could get behind. I could absolutely forgo underwear while wearing one of his shirts. His kindness made me feeling a little like a lunatic with how hard I swooned.

"We'll figure it out together, okay?"

"Together," I said, my voice coming out stronger than before.

This was going to be so damn good.

Thirty

AIDEN

After our first night together, I couldn't get Abbie back to my house quickly enough. That first night gave way to our first weekend together.

Though our physical chemistry was unlike anything I had ever experienced, I found my favorite moments were the quieter ones.

Then, I'd finally gotten the movie night I'd had planned the following weekend at Abbie's apartment. Wary of her place being so centrally located, I didn't stay the entire weekend at the risk of being seen by someone from Appeal. We had both felt the tension and spent our weekends exclusively at my place, with Abbie's cat, Mew, in tow.

After a few petulant meows, Mew had been sauntering around my house like he owned the place ever since. Each time Abbie brought him in his cat carrier, he dove out of it as soon as she opened the door. Mew had claimed the most expensive piece of furniture I owned, the custom-made black velvet armchair in my bedroom.

I was now ordering lint rollers off Amazon in bulk to battle the white cat hair that had invaded every corner of my home. Even during the week when Mew was at Abbie's apartment, I had to spend an extra ten minutes rolling cat fur off my clothes.

Despite how in sync we were, I had started to feel bad that all we did was stay in. I felt like I was cheating Abbie out of the experiences of a real relationship, despite her insistence to the contrary.

By the fourth weekend of us officially being together, I'd devised a plan to take her out to dinner. I wanted to show her that she meant more to me than someone I was trying to keep a secret.

If I was put under oath, I would absolutely deny scanning through the employee files to figure out the safest area outside Amado to take her. I didn't want to risk seeing anyone from the office.

I thought our best chance for anonymity would be to head to Palo Alto for an evening. After attending several client meetings there, the city felt busy enough to offer us some cover.

Despite my girlfriend practically vibrating in the seat next to me on the hour-long drive to our destination, I still felt good about my choice.

Moving my right hand from the steering wheel over to put my hand on Abbie's thigh, I enjoyed the warmth of her leg through her jeans. I hoped she would take the hint to intertwine our fingers. Currently, her fingers were twisting and untwisting in her lap as she stewed.

"Hey. It's going to be okay." I fully believed that everything would turn out fine.

"Are you sure? I honestly don't need to go anywhere. I'm happy spending time at your place. Mew is even starting to expect the weekend trip to your house."

"I'm glad he's warming up to me. At this rate, we'll be best friends in two to three... years." I glanced at her quickly, giving her a wink. "I know you don't need to go anywhere. But I want to take you out. To show you the only reason we're keeping it between us is because of work and nothing more."

The thing I'd learned about Abbie's anxiety was that sometimes her body communicated it so strongly that it was almost a physical beacon, showing me how wound up she was. Her apprehension was a tidal wave sweeping from one side of the car to the other. I didn't want her to get so completely swept away by her worry that she would be beyond enjoying herself tonight.

"Listen, there are tons of reasons why we might have run into each other in the city. You have your camera with you, and I'm in Palo Alto monthly for work. Can we just try to enjoy it?" I squeezed her thigh gently with reassurance.

Something in my tone must have gotten through to her because she untwisted her hands from the Gordian knot she was making. She slid her left hand underneath mine to link our fingers together, giving my hand a little squeeze in return.

"Yep. I'm sorry. I can do that. I just don't want anything to go wrong for you."

"You have no reason to be sorry. Anyone would be nervous. But if we're going to keep doing this, we're going to have to be okay with taking some small risks so we have a little slice of normal."

I could tell she wasn't totally convinced, but she seemed more relaxed than before.

The silence that fell between us for the last portion of the drive was comfortable, neither of us feeling the need to fill the space. I appreciated these quiet moments with her too, giving her space to mull things over.

I chose a casual restaurant away from the college campus. Since we'd done the fancy dining thing in LA with clients, I wanted to take her somewhere quieter where she would feel comfortable.

The little Italian bistro I found had about twenty tables and had the air of a quaint, family-run establishment where the food was more important than the decor.

Once we were tucked away in the back corner, I laid my hand on the table and was pleased when she reached across to hold my hand.

"Hi," I said, as if we hadn't spent the last hour together.

"Hi." She smiled.

"So. Do you come here often?" I knew I was being ridiculous, but I wanted to do everything I could to help her enjoy herself.

"You know what? Believe it or not, this is my first time here." Abbie played along.

The waiter came over to take our drink orders and told them the specials. I tried to pay attention to what the young man was saying, but my gaze kept returning to Abbie's sweet face as she listened attentively to whatever was being relayed to us.

"What do you think?"

"Hmm? Sorry, about what?" I'd been caught out.

"I said we would share the raw octopus appetizer." She smiled, blinking innocently.

"Uh."

She managed to keep a serious expression while I scrambled for something to say, but that only lasted as long as it took for the grossed-out look to appear on my face. When she laughed at my expression, I gratefully realized she was joking.

"You really enjoyed that, huh?" I asked.

"Your face..." Laughing again, she covered her mouth with her free hand to muffle the sound.

"Well, it's not my fault that I'm distracted by sitting at a table with the most beautiful woman in the city."

The mirth in her gaze turned to delight at my compliment.

"Very smooth, Mr. Sullivan. You're dangerous when you're

charming. You should come with a warning label."

The waiter returned to take our orders (we did not order raw octopus). Having not looked at the menu because I'd been staring at Abbie, I ordered the same thing she did: chicken primavera. I wondered if she ordered that for my benefit, knowing I hadn't even glanced at the menu.

It didn't take long for our food to arrive. I was happy that Abbie seemed to have let go of the worries she'd felt in the car. I regretted having to let go of her hand so we could both eat.

"Let's pretend we don't work together. People on dates talk about their jobs. Tell me how Miles is doing," Abbie said after a few bites of her meal.

"Surprisingly well, actually. You know, unlike my last assistant, he hasn't complained once about the thoroughness of the training materials I supplied him with."

"To your face, anyway," she said under her breath.

"And," I continued as if I hadn't heard her, "my last assistant, who was somewhat of a brat, would be pleased to hear that I haven't burdened him with the task of making coffee for me. I wouldn't want my 'impossible to please' coffee requirements to come up in my first performance review with Jack at year end."

"Sounds like your last assistant was a saint to put up with all that coffee nonsense. Have you checked on her well-being after going through such trials?" Her tone was laced with false concern.

"From what I've heard, she's doing really well in her new temporary department."

Abbie hadn't given me very much detail about her role in digital arts. I'd hoped she'd let him in on how she was feeling about it. Letting the silence hang between us for a moment, I was rewarded when she finally shared more than a "It's going fine" comment.

"Well." She looked down at her food briefly. "The team is great. And the work is interesting. But with no experience with Photoshop other than through the very basics in my photography courses, I'm way behind the rest of the team's abilities. Not to mention having zero knowledge of digital drawing software."

The disappointment she felt in herself radiated across the table. I hated she was struggling to feel like she could add value to the team.

"What has Ethan assigned you to help with?"

"I've been mostly working on copy." She sighed. "And doing a little bit of preliminary layout work for graphics since that's more basic."

"Did you expect to be good at it right away?" I was curious why she was being particularly hard on herself.

"Kind of?" Abbie set her fork down to put her face in her hands. "No matter how much I practice at home in the evenings, I'm moving at a snail's pace."

"Hey. Look at me."

She brought her hands back down to her lap, looking at me with a baleful expression.

"Remember that everyone on that team has three or four years of college courses behind them. Not to mention their professional experience. There's no way to bridge a gap like that in four weeks. I know you want to do the best you can, but you already are doing that. Can you give yourself a bit of a break?" I kept my tone gentle.

"Yeah. I can try."

"Do you remember why you wanted to take the temporary assignment in the first place?" I knew she remembered but wanted her to remind herself by saying out loud.

"Because I wanted to see if I was interested in doing more with my photography."

"Okay. So can you maybe treat it like an experiment for the next two months? Just learn what you can by watching the team and see if you'd like to do that in the future. "

"Yeah. It's just hard."

As much of a fixer as I was by nature, I knew this was something I couldn't fix for her. I couldn't ease the way for her or make any decisions for her. The only thing I could do was support her while she figured it out.

More and more, I was realizing I wanted to be the person she came to when she was feeling like this. I knew she had her two best friends, but I wanted her to know that I was firmly in her corner too.

"It is. And you're totally right to feel that way. Career shit is hard. It doesn't come easy to any of us."

"Really? It's even hard for the youngest VP in Appeal's history?" Some of the sadness left her voice when she teased me.

"Absolutely. There is nothing easy about this job. Leaving LA was really hard at first. And I'm still working too many hours of overtime, according to my mom's weekly reminder."

"Of course. I shouldn't have joked about it. You love your family so much." She tried to apologize, but I waved it away.

"No, don't worry. I just wanted to say that we all have to make tough choices and sacrifices for what we want. I found someone extra special when I moved to Amado, though."

"There's that lethal charm again. Wield it sparingly, or you're going to have to scoop me up to get me out of this restaurant. I'll be in a permanent state of swoon." She put the back of her hand to her forehead for emphasis.

"Noted. I didn't realize the strength of my powers before now. With great power comes great responsibility and all that."

"Let's not go that far. You're movie-star handsome, but you're not Spider-Man."

I was happy to hear the playfulness return to her voice. I didn't mind being the butt of the joke for her sake.

"I don't know… I think I'd look pretty good in Lycra." I winked at her.

"You'd be positively indecent in Lycra. I'd like to keep that view for myself. Thank you very much." She crossed her arms in mock disapproval.

"Oh. I see now. My Abbie is jealous, hmm? I like it." Truthfully, I loved it. It made me irrationally happy to hear the possessiveness in her tone. God knows it took everything I had not to glare at every man who looked at her in the office.

"*Your Abbie* is going to use the restroom while you ponder your future calling to fight crime with charm alone."

She rose from her seat, catching the attention of our waiter, who came to direct her to the restroom's location.

I took a moment to finish my meal. We'd spent so much absorbed in our conversation that I'd forgotten to keep eating. I was ready to take her home for the next part of our date, hoping she'd be willing to skip the sweets at the restaurant for something more decadent at my place.

I was occupied looking at my plate, so I didn't notice anyone coming toward me until I heard the voice right beside me.

"Aiden?"

Bringing my slightly started gaze to the person now standing beside our table, my brain came back online, realizing that Ethan stood there.

"Shit. Ethan? Uh, what are you doing here?"

What was Ethan doing here, of all places? I knew from a couple of casual conversations in the break area that Ethan lived smack in the middle of Amado, appreciating that he didn't need a car to get around.

Ethan regarded him strangely. "This is my uncle's restaurant. My parents always send me here to grab food to bring home with me after I visit them."

God, I needed to get rid of Ethan before Abbie came back. This was a disaster in the making. I realized I'd taken too long to formulate a response when I heard Ethan's tone change and Abbie's sharp intake of breath.

"Abbie. Uh. Hey. Sorry to interrupt your dinner. I was just heading out. See you Monday." With that, Ethan walked away from the table toward the front of the restaurant.

Needing to do damage control, I looked at Abbie and spoke as calmly as I could muster.

"Don't worry. It's going to be fine. Ask for the check. I'm going to go talk to him quickly. I'll be right back." I pulled out my wallet and handed her my card, knowing that she was probably freaking out.

I had another fire to put out first before I could help her, though. Walking briskly to the front door of the restaurant, I exited the building into the warm August night air. Checking both ways on the sidewalk, I saw Ethan about two shops away and headed in his direction.

"Ethan!" I called.

The other man came to a stop and turned around, a look of concern on his face. Thankful for all my days at the gym, I jogged quickly to catch up with him.

"Listen, Ethan. It's not what you think…" Aiden began.

"So you're not seeing Abbie, then? Shit. Is that why she applied to my team?" Ethan looked increasingly worried by the minute.

"Okay, yes. We are seeing each other. It's serious. I haven't had a chance to figure out how to approach Jack about it yet. And no, Abbie definitely applied to your team of her own volition." It was hard for me to wait while Ethan collected his thoughts.

"Shit, man. This is bad. You know that, right? You could blow up your career. And hers! What are you going to do?" Ethan scrubbed his hands over his face, clearly dismayed at all the ways this could blow up.

"I need time to make a plan. And we both need time to make sure this works for both of us."

"I'm not going to tell anyone about this. It's not my business. As far as I'm concerned, I never saw you here. But that's only a temporary fix. You need to decide what you really want here. If you're not in this for the long haul, you need to break it off with her before it becomes impossible for you to work together. If it isn't already." Ethan's expression said he was dead serious.

"I know. I'm trying. I don't want to hurt her. I care about her."

"Well, you need to decide how much you care about her. Sooner than later. It's only a matter of time before someone notices something between you two at work, and then the shit will hit the fan."

I nodded, knowing what Ethan said to be true. My gut plummeted at the thought of things going south at work or having to give up Abbie.

"I'm a vault. Now, go back to your girl. Be careful, okay?" Ethan gave me a friendly slap on the shoulder before he turned to leave.

"Thanks, man." I waved goodbye as we went in opposite directions.

Once I was back inside the restaurant, I saw Abbie ready with her bag around her shoulder, looking ready to go. We didn't speak as I tipped and signed the receipt.

It wasn't until we were back inside the parking garage, getting into the car, that I broke the silence.

"It's going to be okay," I tried to reassure her.

Wrapping her arms around herself, she looked back at me with red-rimmed eyes. I could see tears forming as she tried to blink them back.

"How can you say that?" she whispered.

"Ethan doesn't care that we're together. He promised me that he would keep this confidential. From what I've seen over the past months, he's a good person. I believe him. He's not going to tell anyone. He's okay. And we're okay." My tone held a hint of the desperation that I felt now that there was a chance of her walking away.

Abbie closed her eyes for a moment, taking some deep breaths. When she opened them again, her expression still looked worried, but she released her arms and laid her arm across the console, offering me her hand.

It meant so much to me that she would reach out first, as she often waited for me to set the tone when it came to affection. A tightness in my chest released when I grasped her hand.

"What do you want to do? If you need some space, I can drive you home?" I left it as a question because I did not want her to be alone tonight. She'd talk herself out of our relationship by morning. But I would take her back to her apartment if that's what she wanted.

I wanted her to come home with me, even if that wasn't the smart choice. But that felt selfish to say. We'd skirted some serious consequences tonight, and instead of scaring me off, I wanted to keep her more than ever.

"What if I don't want to be alone?" she asked quietly.

"Then we'll go back to my house, and we'll just sleep tonight. I just want to hold you. Do you want that?" I squeezed her hand, feeling the relief rush through my body.

"Yes. Please."

The drive home saw us both lost in our thoughts. The comfortable silence of earlier in the evening now had an edge to it. I hoped with a little distance from tonight's upset that Abbie would see that nothing bad would come of Ethan finding out about us.

Once we arrived back at my place, the quiet continued as we got ready for bed. It wasn't until we were under the bedcovers with my arms around her that Abbie broached the topic again.

"Do you think we need to do anything different at work?"

"I don't think so. I barely see you as it is. We can just be careful like we have been."

Since we had begun our relationship, I had been consciously monitoring how much time I spent out on the floor with the various teams. I'd been taking a lot more meetings in my office when it was possible.

"I'm not sure anyone will miss your 'daily rounds.'" A tiny smile appeared on her lips for the first time since we left the restaurant.

"I'm not really that bad, am I?"

I felt her press her nose into my shoulder, a place that had become her favorite place to shore up her thoughts. I tightened my arms around her as I felt a tremor move through her body.

"It's okay, you can tell me," I whispered, thinking she was nervous.

She lifted her head and met my gaze, and I realized the little brat was chuckling.

An adorable, tiny snort came from her nose before she completely lost it.

"Not that bad? Are you…"

She was laughing so hard she had the whole bed shaking. She rolled onto her back and covered her face with her hands to stem the laughter.

"It's not even that funny. It's just… So much stress tonight."

I was glad to see her body releasing that pent-up emotion. If she was teasing me, it meant that she wasn't totally bogged down with worry.

"Har, har. I get it. I might have a tendency to be a bit overbearing."

Wiping her eyes, she leaned back toward me and brought her lips to mine before nuzzling back as deeply into my neck as she could.

"Of course, Aiden. Only a bit," she said, trying to sound serious but failing when I felt her smile against my skin.

"Good night."

Two weeks later, I felt like we had gotten back to level ground again. True to his word, Ethan hadn't said anything to anyone, nor did he treat Abbie any differently now that he knew about our relationship, much to my relief.

Abbie was staying at my house for the weekend, like she had every weekend since we'd gotten together.

So when I was startled awake in the early hours of a Sunday morning by a sound coming from downstairs, it took me a minute to realize I was hearing the low ringing of my phone over and over. Shit, I'd always remembered to put it next to my bed as my alarm. Why had I left it downstairs?

I recalled the night before when we decided to head up to bed in a hurry after she teased me with tiny touches throughout the movie that neither of us was really watching. By the time the credits rolled, I was so desperate to have her that I'd practically dragged her upstairs to my bed and devoured her, saying, "Screw the dishes," when she mentioned tidying up first.

Gently extracting my arm from around Abbie's waist, I stood unsteadily, still half-asleep, to go down and find my phone.

I made it down the stairs, relying only on the railing, not bothering to turn on any lights.

My phone lit up the living room from its position on the coffee table. It wasn't until I'd picked it up and looked at the screen that I realized it was two a.m. Adrenaline shot through my system.

Unlocking my phone to see, I saw five missed calls from Claire. *Shit!* Something must have happened because my sister preferred text over all forms of communication. I could count the number of times she had called me on one hand since leaving for college.

I pressed her number and waited for her to pick up.

"Aiden…" Her voice was a broken whisper.

I heard her breath catch in her throat.

"Claire, what is it?"

Her hesitancy had me panicking. Was it Mom? Had something happened to her?

"Claire, I need you to tell me what's going on."

My words came out harsher than I intended. The tidal wave of fear inside me was taking away any patience I had to modulate my tone.

"Claire?" I tried again, speaking more softly this time.

The muffled sound of quiet voices was replaced by a low "Hello, Aiden?"

Who the fuck is this?

"It's Heath, man. I'm with Claire, and we're at the hospital."

"What the fuck is going on?" I couldn't keep the anger out of my voice that he was there with my sister, and I didn't have the slightest clue what was happening.

"Whoa, take it easy. I'm just trying to explain…" Heath's voice came out in a defensive growl.

For a guy who I had heard say about a dozen words to me in the decade my sister had been hanging out with him, the abruptness in his voice shocked me into momentary silence.

Heath took that as his opening to elaborate.

"Listen, man, Claire got a call from Isabel about two hours ago saying that Rennie was being rushed to the hospital by ambulance. Last time we hung out with them a week ago, she was a bit crabby, and Isabel thought she was coming down with something. Apparently, she's been sick all week with a fever and cough, but tonight, she acted listless while watching TV. She kept saying she was so tired and then stopped responding to Isabel at all."

My heart seized when I thought of what could be happening to my niece.

"Oh fuck!"

"Yeah, they're covering all the bases, apparently, checking her out. They've been waiting in the ER, and she's just being admitted now. They are going to run some tests, so we won't know what's going on for a while yet. We're at the children's hospital."

"I'm coming. Tell Isabel and Andreas that I'm taking the next flight out."

I heard more rustling, and it became clear that Claire had taken back her phone.

"Aiden… I'm scared. What if it's something awful?"

"I'm sure she will be okay." I wasn't sure of that at all. But Claire was my baby sister, and I needed to be strong for her at this moment.

I tried to inject more confidence in my voice than I felt. Internally, I was panicking as badly as Claire was, maybe even more.

I felt every mile of distance between my family and me at that moment. A sinking feeling of guilt started to build in my stomach. Why had I let myself be so distracted that I forgot my phone downstairs? How long had Claire been trying to reach me? The sick feeling grew layer by layer in my gut.

Since the age of fourteen when my stepfather died, I'd always made sure I was available to help my family at a moment's notice. Losing my stepfather to a drunk driver had shown me that nothing in life was guaranteed, and I needed to be ready to take care of my loved ones when they needed me.

And here I was, sitting in the dark hundreds of miles away, having failed to even answer the fucking phone in an emergency.

These were the actions of someone who made their family a priority.

"Hang in there. I'll see you soon. Make sure Heath stays with you, okay? Love you."

"Love you, Aiden."

I needed to do everything possible to never fail them like this again.

Thirty-One

ABBIE

I was woken by Aiden's urgent tone on talking to someone downstairs. Wasn't it the middle of the night? What was happening?

Confused and worried, I got out of bed and headed quietly to the stairwell. I heard him mention Claire's name. My anxiety increased. Turning on the hall light, I moved quietly down the stairs. I didn't want to startle Aiden with my presence.

With nearly silent footsteps, I made my way into the living room. Aiden was staring straight ahead, focusing on nothing. The side of his face was visible from the light in the hall. He looked frozen with worry.

"Aiden, what's happening?"

I went to sit beside him on the couch, but he stood up before I could reach for him. His abrupt motion took me by surprise.

"Aiden, baby?" I tried again to bring him out of whatever this state was. I noted absently that this was the first time I'd called him that endearment, never having been confident enough before, and I wasn't even sure he'd heard me.

Dragging his hands over his face, Aiden met my stare.

"I need to leave for LA right now. My niece is sick, and I need to be there for my family."

I gasped. I knew how much he adored his niece from our many hours of quiet conversations huddled under the covers of his bed. Not to mention that I'd never stayed over on a Sunday night because those nights were reserved for his weekly video calls with his family.

"What can I do to help?"

Aiden didn't reply. I racked my brain. He'd want to get to the hospital as soon as possible. I could book him a flight while he got ready.

"I'm just going to head to the airport and get on the first flight they have for LA." He paused for a minute, thinking. "Can you clear my calendar for the next couple of days? It'll be faster if you do it rather than worrying about getting Miles up to speed. And let Jack know I'll call him when I can to explain?"

The emotional distance between us increased when he gave me work tasks instead of answering what I could do to help *him*. I did everything I could not to let the hurt show on my face. He didn't need to deal with my issues right now.

I didn't follow him when he returned to the bedroom to throw on some clothes and chuck a few more into an overnight bag. Instead, I unlocked my phone, which I'd brought down with me, and began searching for a flight. Next, I went to the front door, where he usually dropped his wallet when we got home, grabbed his card, and booked the flight.

By the time he made it back downstairs, his flight was confirmed, and his wallet was beside his phone on the coffee table.

"There's a flight in two hours that I've just booked you a seat on. Hope you don't mind. I grabbed your wallet from the front table while you were upstairs. I forwarded the boarding pass to your work email."

"Thank you. You're a lifesaver. Go back to sleep. Are you going to be okay to call a cab or an Uber in the morning?"

I nodded, and he gave me a quick kiss on the cheek before he turned to walk to the front door.

"I'll let you know when I get there, okay?" His stare was outside as he opened the door.

Biting my bottom lip, I wanted to say something to get him to look at me. But I couldn't force out any words other than a goodbye.

"Okay, Aiden. Drive safely to the airport."

"I will. Thank you."

And he was gone.

Still in shock over Aiden's abrupt departure, I sat frozen on the couch, trying to process what had just happened. Not that he should have stayed, but it was unbelievable how quickly it felt like everything had just changed in ways I couldn't contemplate at 2:00 a.m.

I was tempted to call a cab to take me home at that very moment, but I didn't feel safe getting in a stranger's car in the middle of the night.

If I really needed to, I knew I could call Indie or Emery, but this wasn't an emergency. Neither of them had their own car. Even though my feelings were overwhelming, there was nothing they could do about it in the middle of the night. All they would be able to do was worry.

I pulled the throw blanket off the back of the sectional and covered myself with it. I decided I'd sleep on the couch until it was light in the morning and then call an Uber to get home.

Several worrisome thoughts crept to the forefront of my mind. There was worry about Aiden's niece and whether he'd make it to the airport in San Jose in time.

A small voice inside me echoed the worry about what it meant that he'd left without needing anything from me. Anyone could have booked him a flight, but it felt like he'd turned away from me after he'd hung up. At the same time, it felt wrong to think of myself when there was so much going on, which only brought on feelings of guilt.

My chest muscles tight with anxiety, I gave up on sleeping. I opened my web cartoon app to reread one of the more heartwarming webcomics I followed. Not even Nick and Charlie could hold my focus for long.

My inner voice was louder than the narrative on my screen.

Why would he just leave like that? I wished he would have asked me to go with him.

Well, you can't expect him to be thinking about you *when his niece is sick in another city, can you? That's pretty selfish on your part.*

Yeah, but we've been practically living together this last month, and he just… walked out.

Come on, give him a break. It's not his job to take care of you right now. He's thinking of his family.

Still, it hurts that he considers me such a satellite part of his life that he didn't even think that I'd want to go with him to support him. He didn't even touch me after getting the phone call! When something's really wrong, don't people need comfort?

Hey, don't forget he kissed your head.

You're being too dramatic and too needy right now. You're thinking of yourself and not what he's going through. What kind of person does that?

Round and round, the negative thoughts swirled in my head as I stared at the thick wooden beams that decorated Aiden's ceiling. The ability to shut my brain off would have been a blessing. I could take a sleeping pill, but I had to be up in a few hours, and I didn't want to have a cloudy head in the morning.

When 6:00 a.m. arrived, I forced my gritty eyes open with some major willpower. I must have caught a few hours of sleep if I felt this groggy.

The hours after midnight came right back to me. Aiden had gone to his niece.

Shit. Right.

Quickly getting Mew into his travel carrier, followed by gathering up my belongings from Aiden's bedroom, I ordered a cab to pick me up.

Being a Sunday, there was little I could do to change Aiden's schedule. I also didn't want to email Jack Blakley on his behalf. I'd confirm what I needed to later on, hopefully after an update from Aiden when he landed.

All I was going to do when I got home was feed Mew and then spend the day in bed catching up on sleep. The stress of the night and getting so little sleep had me feeling nauseous. I needed to sleep off everything I was feeling before I had to face work on Monday.

After Sunday passed quickly while I was in bed, I found myself exhausted before ten a.m. after meeting with Miles to update him after I'd rescheduled Aiden's whole week. To my relief, Aiden had contacted Jack and copied Miles, so I didn't have to look weird being the first one to know about his absence.

Sitting numbly at my desk, I wondered how I would get through the day. I didn't text Indie for our midday coffee infusion, still feeling queasy with anxiety. I didn't think adding caffeine to my already wired system was a good idea right now. I wasn't even sure I could swallow it at the moment. It didn't take long for Indie to notice my absence.

Indie: Where are you? Don't tell me you're skipping work to stay in bed with your boyfriend?

Any other day, I would have rolled my eyes at her antics. But today, thoughts of Aiden were a thousand prickling needles. My instinct was to avoid being a burden. But Indie would come upstairs if I didn't tell her something, so I gave in and explained.

Abbie

His niece is sick. He left for LA at 2 a.m. :(

Indie

What?!! Is she OK?

Abbie

I don't know. I haven't heard from him other than a text to say he'd arrived in LA.

Indie

Shit, girl. I'm sorry. There's more to this. I know it. Lunch?

Abbie

I don't think I'm up for anything.

Indie

I get it. I'm gonna text Emery to meet us after work at your place.

I knew just because I didn't feel up to seeing anyone now, I would feel better having Indie and Emery's support rather than letting my own thoughts get the best of her.

Abbie

OK. 6?

Indie

Yep. Don't make me find you, babe ;)

Indie's threat pulled the first semi-smile to my lips since Aiden had left.

The phone on my desk rang from Jack Blakley's extension. Picking up, I was surprised he was calling me. Shouldn't this call be directed to Miles?

"Mr. Blakley?"

"Abigail? Hello. I saw Aiden's email regarding his family emergency. What can you tell me?"

Oh, you know, I know shit-all, Mr. Blakley. Because the second he walked out of the house last night and told me nothing else since.

"Umm, I'm sorry, sir. I don't have any new information other than he's going to need the next few days or even a week? I just assisted Miles with rescheduling his entire week." Well, if by assisted I meant I did all the work, then yep, I'd definitely assisted him.

"I see."

I wasn't clear what exactly he "saw" at the moment. All I could hope for was that he didn't know I had a much more personal stake in this whole thing.

"Listen, Abigail. This is not ideal timing. I'd prefer to do this a different way, but can you be available for a meeting in my office at 3:00 p.m.?"

"Ugh, sure, sir. Is this about the BrownBag project? Because Ethan absolutely can oversee anything that comes up in Aiden's absence."

"I'd prefer to go over everything at three if you don't mind, Abigail."

That sounded like a "I don't have time for this now" or maybe a "You're wasting my time" kind of comment, so I agreed and hung up.

I spent the remaining hours before the meeting gathering everything we had on our newest campaign. The least I could do was show Mr. Blakley that things were under control in Aiden's absence.

Thirty-Two

AIDEN

I was going to explode if we didn't hear something soon. The cheerful walls of the waiting room seemed to mock me the longer I looked at them.

Claire was sitting with Heath in the seats across from my mom and me.

Mom's eyes stared blankly at nothing. She took turns between glancing worriedly at the doors to the unit, which held Rennie, Isabel, and Andreas, and back to their group in the waiting area. Every so often, she'd pretend to read the magazine in her hands before looking to the door again.

I had been too late to see Rennie before she was admitted. Isabel had texted that they'd gotten her on fluids for dehydration right away and some headache medicine. She was resting more quietly and showing more responsiveness than the early listlessness that had scared everyone so much.

I understood that we all couldn't be in there together, but I wished there was something more I could do than just sit here.

Mom covered my hand with hers, and I interlaced our fingers.

"Aiden, this is hard, but she's going to be okay."

"I should have been here for them. Isabel's hours are super long, and I know Andreas is working shifts on-site all the time. I could have helped somehow."

Sighing, Mom patted our joined hands with her free hand.

"Sweetheart, you've always done so much for us. Isabel and Andreas have all of us, including you, which you've proven by jumping on a plane. Sometimes things happen that we can't prevent." Her tone brokered no argument.

But I couldn't shake the feeling that this wouldn't have happened if I had been here.

"When we lost Patrick, it was a major hit to us all. I know having him as part of the family completed something we didn't know we needed so badly. It was your only chance to be a kid, and it was taken from you."

I dropped my head and let it hang forward as if the worry had a physical weight pushing down on my back. It was a weight I'd been carrying for over two decades. The responsibility I felt for my family knew no bounds.

I had been the one to pick up the slack when Mom got a weekend job to provide for us. I was the one who made sure my sisters were fed and taken care of. I kept them safe on their walk to school in our terrible neighborhood. I helped them with their homework and gave them pocket money for candy from odd jobs I picked up.

"He was your husband, Mom. It was the worst for you. And Claire too—she didn't get a chance to know him."

Yes, I loved him. But Patrick was the love of her life. I remembered overhearing her whisper that to someone at the funeral. And she'd lost my stepfather so quickly.

"You know, there is no quota on who gets affected when something happens in a family. It was just as bad for each of you kids in different ways. You grew up way too fast."

"Mom, I'm not up to talking about this right now. Rennie is all I can think about."

Turning her body to face me fully, she moved her hand to hold my cheek. She firmly guided my face toward her so that I had no choice but to look into her eyes.

"Aiden, I want you to hear me. You can't control everything. There was nothing any of us could have done to stop this. You can't avoid living your own life by spending your time worrying about us."

"I know..." I was lying. The guilt of not being enough was eating me alive.

Shaking her head sadly, "No, I don't think you do, love. But I hope you will. Claire mentioned there was a lovely young woman with you when she last saw you."

"Abbie. It's complicated. She works for me. And we've been seeing each other. It's going to be a mess. I'm her direct supervisor. It's an issue of ethics and professionalism."

A small smile graced her lips. "But have you felt happy when you've been with her?"

"Yes." I couldn't deny that I'd been happier than I could ever remember feeling. But even thinking about feeling something other than worry for Rennie right now had me swamped with remorse.

"That sounds like something worth fighting for to me. The best things are, you know. You have us behind you." She gestured around the waiting room.

"It doesn't matter right now, Mom. I need to think about Rennie."

"Whatever you say, love." Mercifully, she let the subject drop.

I glanced at my watch and saw it was nearly midday. When was the last time any of us had eaten? The need to do something useful overwhelmed me. I could get everyone something to eat, knowing we could use something else to focus on. Even if hunger was the last thing I was feeling, going through the motions would help my mom and Claire feel a bit better. It was something small in the face of all this powerlessness.

The wait was longer than we'd expected. It wasn't until after dinner time that we had a full picture of what was going on. We were finally allowed back to see Rennie, after basically clearing out the stuffed animals from the gift shop, of course.

My arms around two different stuffed animals, I followed Mom back to Rennie's room. When we pulled back the curtain that blocked her bed from the ward hallway, I had to cement my smile in place as my eyes stung.

Poor Rennie was hooked up to an IV and some other monitors. She looked tired but basically alert.

"Grammy! Uncle Aiden! You're here! Look at my cool bracelet. It has my name on it."

She held up her wrist, and I felt my heart shred into pieces. Leave it to this amazing little girl to look at the positive of a hospital bracelet. She looked so small in that hospital bed. What could have happened to her if she hadn't been taken to the hospital in time? Fear weighed heavily on my shoulders.

Walking over to the side of the bed, I set down my contribution to the menagerie of animals next to her. I nodded at Isabel and my mom to go out into the hallway so they could talk.

"I'm sorry, Rennie. I couldn't get you any new Pokémon this time.

There weren't any in the store here."

"That's okay, Uncle Aiden! I can just give them names." She held up a cat and scrunched up her little nose in concentration. "This can be… Firecat. He's a fire type. I'll teach him all he needs to know about being a Pokémon." She beamed at me.

Despite my exhaustion and frayed nerves, she was just too adorable not to chuckle at her dedication to her obsession.

It reminded me of all the moments at the Anime Expo, where Abbie had enjoyed geeking out over the various *Pokémon* merchandise.

Thinking of Abbie made something twist uncomfortably inside me. I couldn't handle the collision of worry for Rennie and the all-consuming thoughts of Abbie.

"Uncle Aiden, I wish we could go home already." Rennie sighed, her bottom lip popping out.

Jesus. They should make a warning system that came along with these kids. That was a weapons-grade pout, and it hit me right in the heart.

She pulled the cat into her chest. I saw the IV line and wires around her shifting with her movement. I grabbed my knee under the side of the bed so hard I was sure my fingers were bloodless. My other hand went to her little arm.

I wanted to pick her up and whisk her out of here. I'd do anything she wanted just to wipe that sad look off her face.

"I know, sweetheart. The doctors are going to help, right? We need to give them time to figure everything out."

"Yep, that's what they said to Mommy. But Mommy and Daddy seem sad." God, kids were so perceptive.

Careful not to jostle her IV, I leaned down to kiss her hand princess-style to make her smile.

"Grown-ups worry sometimes. It's kind of our job. But that

doesn't mean that they aren't okay. We're all so happy we can be here to visit with you. Let's do something while we wait for Grammy to finish talking to Mommy, okay?"

We agreed to watch a couple of episodes of *Pokémon* on her tablet. Abbie snuck into my thoughts again. I remembered how detailed the *Pokémon* universe was when Abbie had tried to make sense of it for me and how much she enjoyed it. Thinking Rennie might feel the same, I asked lots of questions that Rennie was happy to answer. It turned out she loved sharing her *Pokémon* knowledge.

After the second episode finished, I reached for my phone and opened my photos.

"Rennie, can you keep a secret?"

Her eyes went wide. At the prospect of knowing something the other adults didn't, she nodded quickly. I gave my phone to her. On the screen was a picture of Abbie and me from Anime Expo, Abbie's costume making it clear who we were dressed up as.

"Oh my gosh! Team Rocket! You dressed up as Giovanni? That's so much fun. It's not even Halloween! You even have a cat that looks like Persian!"

I was pleased that I'd asked Abbie for a copy of the photo for my phone. Seeing Rennie's excitement over our costumes made me grateful to have this memory to share with her.

I had Abbie to thank for pulling me out of my comfort zone. To think she'd unknowingly given me this gift to share with Rennie had my chest constricting. A rush of guilt hit me again, letting my thoughts drift to Abbie while I sat with Rennie in the hospital.

Pushing thoughts of Abbie away, I refocused on Rennie. She was still marveling at the picture on my phone.

"You're right. It was last month. But there are these big conventions where people dress up as all sorts of cartoon and game characters.

When you're old enough, I'll take you to one."

The gleam in Rennie's eyes intensified. I could see the strategizing going on in her brain.

"But you have to be a lot older, like twelve or something. And your parents have to say okay. In the meantime, Halloween is only a few months away. You can start coming up with costume ideas for that."

The truth was, all of us were likely to give her whatever she wanted after this hospital scare. I just hoped she wouldn't ask me for a pony. But I could at least tell Isabel I'd put parameters around my promise to Rennie.

The rest of the family came back into Rennie's room. My mom smiled at Rennie and then angled her head toward the hallway.

"Okay, Rennie. Mommy and Daddy are back, so I need to go for a bit."

"Aww, Uncle Aiden. Do you have to go?"

"Only for a little while, Rennie. I'll be back once I check in at the hotel. Grammy will be in soon."

I kissed her forehead and gave Isabel's shoulder a squeeze as I headed for the hallway, hoping my mom had an update on Rennie's condition.

We returned to our seats from earlier. Claire and Heath perked up to listen to the update.

"Okay, Mom, you need to tell us what's happening." I cut right to the chase.

We wait her out, giving her a moment to form the words.

"They are still doing a few more tests, but the doctors think Rennie was in diabetic shock, which was why she became so listless. She was sick last week, and it's tough keeping her insulin dose correct when that happens."

None of this sounded okay to me. That little six-year-old body in the hospital bed was at risk of serious complications from a simple flu virus. I knew logically it could have been so much worse, but I still didn't want this for Rennie. All I wanted was for her to live the carefree childhood that my sisters and I hadn't.

"Can this happen anytime she gets sick? How the hell are we going to protect her from this?" I felt panic rising in my throat.

"Aiden, look at me. It feels awful now, but this isn't the first time Rennie's been sick since her diagnosis, and she has been okay those other times. There's no reason to expect the worst. We're all here to help them along the way."

"Except I'm not here anymore, Mom. I'm up in Amado, too far to do anything practical."

"Aiden, you can't uproot your life again. This isn't yours to take on and fix. You can be a supportive, caring brother and uncle and still live your own life too. Neither Isabel nor Andreas would want you to give up so much when they can handle it."

Pushing my hair back from the sides of my head, I gripped it tightly. The slight pain helped give me something to focus on rather than the powerless churning in my gut.

I didn't agree, but I couldn't tell my mom that. There had to be something I could do. Not knowing what to say, I just nodded.

"Come on, let's take my car to the nearest bookstore and find her some *Pokémon* books and coloring books to keep her busy. She's still going to be here a few more days so they can monitor her."

Leaving Claire and Heath with a tired wave, we walked to the elevator together. I pushed the elevator button, wishing we were anywhere but here. Preferably, I would be in bed with Abbie. Just having her close to me was soothing.

But you wouldn't have missed Claire's calls if you hadn't been busy with Abbie.

The guilt of being unavailable when my family needed me was a lead weight in my stomach. I hadn't been thinking about anything other than Abbie for more than a month. We'd been so wrapped up in each other that I'd put my promise to myself, that I'd always be there for my mom, sisters, and Rennie, on the back burner. Hell, I'd even missed the last two Sunday dinner video calls, using the time to catch up on work so I could greedily spend more time with Abbie.

What if Rennie's diagnosis had been something so much worse? How would you deal with not being here to help? Can you risk that happening next time?

I couldn't.

My phone vibrated in my pocket, and I distractedly picked it up out of habit more than a conscious choice.

"Hello?"

"Aiden, it's Jack. Listen, I've just gotten out of a meeting with Abigail Summers. Apparently, you've been in a relationship with her, your direct employee, for weeks, and this is the first I'm hearing about it. Do you realize what a clusterfuck this is?"

My heart might actually have stopped for a moment. As if I wasn't already drowning in worry over Rennie, there was a shitstorm waiting for me back in Amado.

"I don't have any excuses, Jack. It was wrong, and I did it anyway. I want you to know that I'm 100 percent committed to Appeal. None of this will blow back on the company. I'll take care of it. I'll be back in the office within three days. I'll come see you first thing."

Just as Jack started to speak on the other end of the line, Mom came out of the ward's hallway.

"Jack, I need to go. There's a lot happening here. I'm sorry."

"Aiden…"

I didn't let him finish. "I'm sorry, Jack. Truly."

"All right. But I better see you in my office the second you're back."

I moved to Amado to secure a better financial future for my family, ensuring they had everything they needed. I wanted Rennie to have access to the best medical care. What if Isabel lost her job? Andreas worked contract jobs that didn't come with health insurance.

I'd already proven to be useless in protecting them from things like Rennie's illness. The least I could do was make sure they didn't have to worry about money.

Could I really risk everything I had worked for at Appeal in a relationship? Let my family's well-being hang in the balance of my irresponsible choices?

I knew what I had to do next, even if I had to cut out my heart to do it.

Thirty-Three

ABBIE

Walking into Jack Blakley's office was intimidating. I'd never had a reason to spend time on the top floor of the building. By rights, Aiden's office should have been up here, but he'd opted for a more hands-on approach with the senior teams.

As I walked down the nearly silent hallway to the CEO's office, I couldn't help but thank Aiden for that choice. It would have been like working in a fishbowl up here. All the glass offices with the admin staff in satellite offices. Shudder.

Mr. Blakley's EA assistant saw me coming and put a phone to her ear. Her face gave nothing away.

"He's waiting for you, Ms. Summers. Go on in."

I nodded and tried to push down my nerves. I didn't like the idea of being responsible for explaining things on Aiden's behalf. I wished Miles had more time under his belt so he could be the one in the hot seat today. It wasn't my finest moment to want someone else to deal with the details of a proposal that I had been involved in since the beginning, but worries were rarely logical. I didn't know how much to share or even what was expected. All I had with me was an update on each of the big projects the various teams were working on.

Stuck in my own head, I didn't notice until I stepped into the office that Mr. Blakley wasn't alone. Linda from HR was sitting in one of the two chairs in front of his desk. She gave me a gentle smile.

Oh shit. This was not an update meeting at all. That's why he had been so cagey and rushed on the phone earlier.

Mr. Blakley saw me hesitating by the door and waved me over to a chair.

"Abigail, please sit."

Some sort of social programming must have kicked in because I found my legs moving without my permission to the chair he'd indicated and sitting down.

I clutched the files that I now knew were irrelevant, just for something to hold on to. I needed some sort of life preserver to keep my head above water in this conversation. As if anything was going to save me from whatever sinking ship I'd just boarded.

I said nothing. Whatever was coming, they were going to bring it up, not me.

"Abigail, this wasn't the way I'd normally have this kind of meeting. But with Aiden's family emergency keeping him away from the office for an undetermined amount of time, this is where we are."

I hoped he knew where we were. I didn't have a clue. Was this a disciplinary meeting? A termination?

When I did nothing more than look at him with panicked eyes, he glanced over at Linda.

Linda faced me with a smile that I was sure another person without ruthless anxiety might have taken comfort in. Unfortunately, it didn't ease my nerves at all.

"So let me explain what's happened. There have been a few

rumors going around the office about an alleged relationship between you and Aiden Sullivan. Specifically, someone saw him speaking to you in such close proximity that it looked intimate. It was reported the body language of the encounter was inappropriate for the workplace."

Oh god, people know about us. I wracked my brain for when someone could have seen us. I thought we'd been careful at work.

What was I supposed to say here? Why were they doing this without Aiden here too? Were they trying to get me to say something that could harm him? Or myself?

"I'm not sure what you mean," I choked out.

"Nothing has been formally written up. Yet. But there have been enough whispers that the executive admin members on this floor have heard them, even with their limited interactions with the rest of the company."

Mr. Blakley felt he could jump back at this point, I guessed, after leaving the worst part to Linda.

"Each of us signed conduct clauses in our contract, Abigail. We are particularly concerned about the genesis of the relationship. Aiden is your boss. He has a direct influence over your career here at Appeal," he said.

My brain couldn't seem to process what he was saying.

"I'm sorry. Are you implying that I've been coerced into a romantic relationship with Aiden?" The ice in my tone was out of character for me, but to imply that Aiden would do such a thing was disgusting. He was a good man.

The bite in my tone hit as intended. Mr. Blakley put up his hands as if to tell me to calm myself. As if that was possible now.

"My concern here is the safety of my employees, Abigail. You haven't denied that there is a relationship. Any romantic or, uh, physically intimate advances made by Aiden would be considered an abuse of his position." His voice held no anger or overt disappointment. He seemed sincerely concerned as he watched me closely for my reaction.

I didn't know if he was a good actor or really meant what he said. I also didn't know him at all other than to say hello politely if I ever crossed his path in the building or at a company function. I was sure he'd never heard my name before this fiasco.

More likely, he was worried about a lawsuit.

"We just want to make sure we manage this situation correctly," Linda added. "Let's go over ways we can move forward, shall we?"

As Linda started listing my choices moving forward, my mind rebelled. I didn't want to talk about any of this with them. No matter what they said, I didn't want Aiden to be the one to pay for our mistakes.

With my racing thoughts, I only caught the gist of the next steps, which were about making the best choices for a conflict-free work environment. All of them involved an NDA. I needed Aiden. This wasn't the sort of decision I wanted to make on my own.

It took me an hour to get out of that office. A leave of absence hadn't initially been on the table, but Mr. Blakley and Linda readily agreed once they knew I had no issue with signing the NDA.

I returned to the digital arts pod in a haze. Gathering my stuff, I caught Ethan's gaze, and he came quietly over to my desk.

"Did you get pulled into a meeting with Jack Blakley?" He kept his pitch low to avoid attracting attention. "Because of the thing with Aiden?"

He didn't need to specify. I knew the "thing" was my relationship. I just nodded, defeated by the stress of the meeting.

"I swear. I haven't breathed a word to anyone. I'll do what I can to shut shit down when I hear it, okay?" Ethan's face shone with sympathy. It was the lifeline I needed in that moment, to have someone on my side inside the office.

I knew even before he said anything that it wasn't Ethan's fault. We should have known nothing stays secret forever.

"Thank you. I trust you. But I don't think I can face the rest of this day. Can I take my computer home, and I'll deal with everything from there?" I whispered.

"Absolutely. Take care of yourself. It's just shit timing with Aiden away. I'm sorry."

I quickly packed my things.

I had just made it out of the building when my phone rang. The display said it was Aiden calling, and I picked up, not ready to tell him anything about what was going on at Appeal.

"Aiden. Hi. Is Rennie okay? Are you okay?" Despite what had just happened, I knew if I could just talk it out with him, we could get through anything.

"Abbie." His tone was void of emotion. He didn't say anything else, silence ringing down the line.

"Aiden? What happened?"

"Abbie," he tried again, sighing. "I'm sorry. Jack just called me. This is not at all how I should be doing this. But what we have is over. My family needs me, and I can't afford to lose this job. I was wrong to start something with you, knowing I have bigger responsibilities."

"Aiden. Wait! Can we…" Panic bled into my voice. That was it? Had Jack told Aiden that he would be fired if he didn't end things with me?

My meeting had gone very differently. They had offered me their full support if I wanted to seek other opportunities.

"I'm sorry. I have to go. We'll figure out the work situation when I get back," he interrupted me before I could say anything more.

He hung up right after he finished speaking. I wanted to sit down on the sidewalk outside of the building and not move again. I had no idea how I was going to manage to get myself back to my apartment when my world had just exploded.

Barely managing to hold myself together, my mind wanted one thing.

To run.

Hours later in my apartment, Indie and Emery, wearing identical expressions of concern, sat on my bed watching me pack. I could just imagine what my haphazard shoving of random clothing into my backpack was doing to Indie's inner Marie Kondo.

To Indie's credit, other than a few eye twitches, she didn't mention it.

Mew sat between them, suspecting something was about to inconvenience his rule over the apartment. He deigned to allow Indie to give him gentle pats on the top of his head. Mew communicated his judgment silently, whereas my best friends looked torn as to whether or not telling me my plan was crazy.

"Are you sure this is what you really want to do?" Indie's tone was carefully controlled to weed out any hint of worry. "What happened in the last six hours to bring this on?"

I opened my mouth to explain, but Emery jumped in first.

"I mean, you don't even *like* going grocery shopping because it's too *peopley* out there," she said as she made air quotations with both hands. "And you're telling us that since texting at lunch, you've decided you're spending two weeks on a road trip down the coast alone, and you're leaving tonight?"

"Hey, at least she's letting us meet up with her for the last week of her trip," Indie pointed out. "We haven't gone away together since senior year of high school."

I understood Emery's skepticism, really. I was the consummate introvert (I had T-shirts that exclaimed this proudly, only worn at home, of course) and the overthinker. I always chose the path of least resistance to avoid conflict in absolutely every situation. Taking risks was not usually in my playbook.

Until Aiden. I'd taken a big risk with him, and it blew up in my face. What did it matter now if I stayed home and wallowed in my apartment or used my time to try to practice my photography as I'd always wanted to?

I watched their faces run the gamut of confused to panicked to outraged on my behalf as I explained the details of my meeting with Jack Blakley.

"So apparently, some rumor made it up to the top floor, and Jack Blakley heard about it. I guess he called reinforcements in the form of Linda and had her break the news to me. It was hard to tell what the motivation behind the meeting was, but regardless, they needed to cover the company's ass." I was able to deliver these details with a clinical tone that sounded like I was talking about someone else's situation, not my own.

I had a strange numbness inside me right now. There was a wall that was keeping out the most difficult realities I could be facing. My instincts were telling me to not be in Amado when Aiden got back to the city. I wasn't going to be ready to face him in just a few days.

I needed time to grieve our relationship and rebuild my armor if I was going to continue working at Appeal. I couldn't do that with Aiden knocking on the door of my apartment, trying to smooth things over for the sake of our jobs.

Watching him turn back into the inscrutable man I'd met on his first day in the office would absolutely crush me.

It was time to put my needs first. Aiden could deal with his desire to clear his conscience while I was away. I no longer had an obligation to make anything better for him. He'd made that bed when he'd broken my heart in a single phone call.

"That's awful." Emery grimaced. "I'm sorry you had to go through that by yourself."

"Yeah, it sucked." I agreed. "Then Linda basically said I had three choices: I could file a complaint against Aiden, be transferred to another department, or sign an NDA, quit, and take severance if I felt I didn't want to work there anymore."

The initial steadiness in my voice didn't last when I said Aiden's name.

"It was like one giant shitstorm. I'd just left work, and then Aiden called me. He just broke up with me like… like… it was these past months could be reduced to a single sentence. What we had was special. I was falling in love with him. I thought anyway. And he just ripped it to shreds over the phone." Tears ran down my cheeks as I spoke. "I wanted to say something, to convince… him to listen to me. Just anything other than ending it so fast."

Emery gently took my bag from my hands as I stood there sobbing while Indie got up to lead me to sit between them on the bed. They didn't say anything for who knows how long. They held me until my tears ran out, and my eyes felt gritty and swollen.

When I was ready to speak again, I tried to explain the work part. I wasn't ready to talk about Aiden at all. Even though I hated the way he broke things off, I couldn't even consider hurting his career. The guilt would eat me alive.

"I feel a call to my lawyer coming on," Indie muttered. "What did you choose?"

"I didn't. I asked to take leave, using up my sick days and vacation time. I need time to think about what I wanted to do. There was so much pressure in that room I couldn't think straight."

"Of all the patriarchal bullshit! What kind of nerve does this guy have to bring up your relationship with Aiden based on rumors and then to have an official meeting about it without talking to Aiden first? He's the one in the position of authority here, and if anyone is in the 'wrong,' it's him!" Emery was worked up now.

Once Emery got going, she was hard to rein back in. Holding my hands up in surrender, I tried to get her to understand.

"I know the optics of the whole thing suck. And absolutely, in many situations, this situation could be really bad news. I have to decide the right thing to do. Mostly, it's about what I can afford. But I don't want him to lose his job over this. That's why I offered to take the leave."

"But still… Does he even deserve your consideration after breaking up with you like that?" Emery looked like she was building up steam again.

"Wait, wait. This is his whole life. He's put every bit of himself into working for this opportunity for two decades. It's so important to him to be able to support his mom and sisters if they need him financially. I could never take that from him. Even though it's awful, I understand why his fear of being financially vulnerable would make him agree to anything Jack Blakley said."

Emery remained unconvinced.

"Fair point," Indie agreed. "You make your own decisions. If you want to do it this way, it's your right."

"I just can't stay here right now. Every single thing is going to remind me of Aiden, and I'll never be able to cope."

Emery had another suggestion. "Speaking of coping, I'm worried about you taking off when you aren't feeling okay. Would you consider talking to someone? You could do virtual appointments while you are away. I can give you the name of someone great. I know you tried talking to a couple of counselors in college, but maybe you just weren't ready then."

I hesitated before nodding. "You're right. I wasn't. And I know I'm in over my head here. If you give me the name, I'll set something up with the therapist. I have no idea how to untangle any of this. But I know I don't want to get so low that I can't function."

"Good. We don't want that for you either," Indie said.

Indie narrowed her eyes. Oh boy, that was the look that said she was about to say something I really wasn't going to like.

"Ohhhh no…" Emery groaned and fell back onto the bed, thankfully avoiding Mew.

"Why do you have to protect him now? He broke up with you, right? I think you need to be focusing on what's best for you." Indie ignored Emery's dramatics.

"You didn't hear him on the phone. Or see him the night he got the call from his sister. He loves his family more than anyone I've ever seen. For sure he's not going to change his mind. But even if he did, I don't want him to resent me later. I'd feel worse about that than making this choice for myself." I shook my head. It wasn't that simple.

Even if he'd hurt me so badly I wasn't sure how I was going to get over it, I didn't want to hurt him in return.

My relationship with Aiden had been so whirlwind that he had made decisions he never would have before in a short period of time. I loved him enough to not make him have to choose.

Indie was the queen of taking care of the few people she loved.

I knew Indie would identify with sacrificing what he wanted to protect his dream.

Emery's hand shot up in the air from her horizontal position on the bed.

"Yes, Prof. Yao, what do you wish to share with the class?" Indie channeled her British boarding schoolteacher voice, no doubt attempting to bring some lightness into our very heavy conversation.

"I just want to officially go on record that you should talk to Aiden before you go. Even if it's just to tell him what an asshole we think he is. He should hear that. But also, you know, the work thing."

Looking down at my lap, I whispered, "I can't talk to him after he ended things. It hurts too much. I need to get away from this for a while, and maybe with some time and distance, I'll be able to face him professionally again."

I felt Emery sit up and put her arm back around my shoulders.

"Okay, Abs, you're right. We fulfilled the friendship mandate of tough love. But now it's time to think just about you. There is nothing wrong with taking some time to travel and take amazing pictures. Just promise us you will be safe. And that you have all your medication," Emery said.

Indie chimed in, "The only thing that could make this more right is if you let me pay for it, and then you could stay in something nicer than two-star hotels." She visibly shuddered as if I'd find flesh-eating bacteria in my hotel sheets at night.

"Indieeeee…" I sniffed. "I'm going to be fine."

"You will with the spray can of Lysol and the emergency whistle I'm going to shove in your bag," she muttered.

Emery chuckled. "Always trying to take care of us, Indie." She directed her gaze to me, "You are going to have an adventure that'll probably turn out good and bad. Let's leave what's right for Aiden out of this completely. Is taking time away for yourself going to help clear your head?"

I nodded.

"Then that settles it. We're on board. Right, Indie?"

"Yeah, we are. Just please text us to let us know you're okay. And for the love of god, tell your mom you're working weird hours and weekends until you get back so you can just enjoy yourself without all her bullshit."

Indie and Emery had come to my rescue many times over the years. I was determined to do this next part on my own, just to know I could.

I'd already made some big choices lately. It was time to stop being so afraid to make mistakes and start living my life on my own terms. First and foremost, that meant determining whether I could pursue photography like I'd always wanted to.

"This is a good thing. I'll get time to think about everything without constantly being exhausted from working all day. I've gone nowhere with the specific purpose of taking photos. Everything looks so beautiful from the approximately five minutes of research I've done. I'm actually looking forward to that part. I'll have a great portfolio for my photography class by the time I get back."

I was also really nervous and really sad. But I didn't say that part out loud.

"Make sure to take lots of pictures of hot surfers all along the coast. We'll compare them when we meet you in LA, you know, for research." A blush crept over Emery's cheeks as she laughed.

I clung to the idea that a change of scenery would be distracting enough that I could lose myself in taking pictures and not spend all my time obsessing over a guy (er, man, whatever).

Even though I felt doubt simmering inside me, I wanted to do it.

Thirty-Four

AIDEN

I looked up to see Claire glaring at me from across the waiting room. Mom was still standing near the ward doorway, having stopped her movements when she heard me on the phone.

"What?" I wasn't in any mood to take any attitude from my sister.

Despite her fiery personality, Claire was conscious of this being a public space in a children's hospital, so she waited until she'd crossed the room and sat beside me to say anything.

"You're a fucking idiot." She didn't hold back.

"Excuse me?" Claire and I had always had a great relationship. We rarely fought, and she had certainly never called me a name since she was about four years old.

"Just what I said. You're a fucking idiot. You just broke up with the woman you love on the fucking phone. There was no way your boss gave you an ultimatum on that call. So what were you thinking?" If Claire scrunched her forehead any further in her anger, she was going to have permanent creases in her skin.

"First of all, you have no idea what you're talking about. I cannot fuck around with my job, and I was a *fucking idiot* to think I could keep my relationship away from the prying eyes at the office. I knew it was wrong, both professionally and ethically, but I gave in anyway." I shouldn't have to explain this to her.

I'd always told my sisters how important it was to make responsible choices. We didn't have the luxury of fucking up when we'd barely had enough money to make rent and feed ourselves. I'd been lucky to get out of a few run-ins with the wrong crowd unscathed as a teenager. I'd promised myself I'd do better for everyone after coming close to ending up in jail or worse.

"I'll give it to you that the optics suck. And yeah, maybe you should have told your boss. But we can't control who we fall in love with, Aiden. I saw the way you looked at her in the café that day. She could have personally hung the moon in the sky as far as you were concerned. Why would you give up a once-in-a-lifetime person like that for a fucking job?"

"Don't talk about things you don't understand, Claire. Who said anything about love?" I'd just hit the limit of my patience. First, Jack and then Abbie. I didn't have the capacity to take shit from anyone else today.

I felt Mom sit down beside me silently, but I was too wound up to acknowledge her.

"Explain it to me, then, big brother."

"Everything I've done for the past two decades has led me to this job. I'm finally making the kind of money that's going to ensure all our futures. We need this money. I can't risk my entire career on a relationship that probably wouldn't work out in the long run. Look at the start we've had. I insisted we keep things a secret, and now it's a disaster. Not to mention that Abbie is too young for me, which I knew from the start. She's going to want something different in a few years, and then where will that leave me?" Claire's frustration had my temper leaking into my voice.

Claire's shoulders had slumped as she listened, the fight now fully drained from her system. Her glare had softened into something like sympathy or pity, and I couldn't stand to look at it.

I turned to Mom for backup, only to find the twin expression on her face.

"What?" There was some sort of misunderstanding here.

"Aiden, honey. I'm so sorry." Mom's eyes had welled up at some point. "I failed you in so many ways. And now you're paying for it."

Failed me? That was impossible. What alternate universe had I suddenly been transported into?

"Come on, Mom. That's insane. You haven't failed me, ever." I didn't want her thinking she had.

"Honey, I did. I didn't see it at the time, but I leaned on you too much after Patrick died. You were just so mature beyond your years. And you loved your sisters so much. I let you take on so many adult responsibilities way too soon." She patted my arm.

"Of course I love Isabel and Claire. What are you talking about? It was my job to help you when you needed it." I was more confused by the moment.

"See, that's where you're wrong." I opened my mouth to disagree, but she squeezed my arm to stop me. "Your job was to be a fourteen-year-old young man who got to live your own life and make your own mistakes. Instead, you became a pseudo-parent to your sisters. And you've never let go of that massive burden." Tears fell down her cheeks as she spoke. I couldn't stand to see her hurting.

"You did everything you could for us, Mom. I wanted to help." I looked at Claire. "You were never a burden to me. You have to know that." A storm was brewing inside me, making me more desperate than ever to make sure they understood me.

Claire, who looked moments away from crying herself, jumped in.

"I know, Aiden. You are the best big brother I could ask for. I'm guilty of letting you take care of me for too long. I should have told you no years ago when you insisted on paying my tuition."

"Claire, why wouldn't I do that for you if I can afford it? I don't want you to start your career drowning in debt like I did, even with the help of scholarships."

"That's exactly it, Aiden. You feel like you need to take care of all of us just like you did after Dad died. Except we're all adults here. It's not your job to provide for all of us. We're more than capable." Claire wiped the tears that were now falling down her cheeks absently.

"There's nothing wrong with wanting to protect my family from hardship," I argued. They were insane if they thought I would just fuck off and not think about what they needed.

Mom had recovered enough to join back in the conversation.

"There isn't, honey. But you've done a lot more than that. You've sacrificed every part of yourself thinking that money was going to solve everything. You've worked yourself to the bone for years, given up any chance at a personal life."

She just didn't understand. To get to the top of my field, I had to put in the hours. There was no half-assing my way into a VP position.

"I want you all to be happy."

"I know you do. But why do we get to pursue the life we want and you don't?" Claire's words had made my gut sour.

I had no rebuttal for that one. I'd been obsessed with getting ahead for so many years I hadn't stopped to think about what I wanted. It didn't even register, I realized.

Except Abbie. You wanted her.

"You deserve to be happy too, Aiden. Don't let your fear of something bad happening, like it did with Dad's death, stop you from actually living. Can you honestly say that you don't love Abbie? That your age difference really matters all that much? That you'd rather spend your life alone, making piles of money, and working yourself into an early grave?"

Fuck, I couldn't deny that I loved Abbie. I don't know when it started. It could have been how adorable she'd been at Anime Expo or how sweet she was during lazy mornings in my bed, her insecurities melting away one by one. Hell, it could have been that first day at the park when I'd been drawn to her by a force like nothing I'd ever felt.

"Oh god. I've fucked up so badly." I brought my hands up to rub my face.

"Yeah, you did, big brother." I didn't need to see Claire to hear the smile in her voice. She couldn't resist a little bit of gloating when she was right.

A light tug on my sleeve had my hands falling back to my lap.

"Aiden, it matters what you do now. Are you going to let that young woman keep on thinking that you'd choose your job over her?" my mom asked.

Christ, I needed a drink. Or ten. Anything to ease the gut-wrenching shame and regret sinking into every cell in my body.

"I'm going to make it right. I have to."

I needed to get back to Amado and fix this disaster I'd created.

I prayed it wasn't too late.

I'd left LA on the red-eye once Rennie was discharged just hours later. In truth, I'd probably stayed longer than I needed to. I was kicking myself for my knee-jerk reaction to Jack's call.

Arriving home to my empty house only served to amplify the consequences of my decision. It had seemed simple while riding the waves of anxiety over Rennie, hooked up to fluids and wires, to make a snap decision when Jack had given me the news that my relationship with Abbie had become public knowledge.

I'd been so wrapped up in my own fears that I'd been paralyzed to make any decision other than robotically telling Jack that I'd end things with Abbie immediately.

Alone in my bedroom, I dumped my suitcase inside the door as I looked around the room, expecting to see my bed in disarray from the night I'd left Abbie standing beside it. Instead, it was freshly made, my cleaning service obviously having come sometime while I was away.

There was no evidence of Abbie anywhere. Her absence hit me that hard, coming face-to-face with the loss of her kind spirit and how much she lit up this too-big house.

She was really gone, and it was all my fault.

My gut clenched with guilt. I was a complete asshole.

Thank god for Claire and Mom.

With my thoughts clear from the panic I'd been drowning in for the past few days, I realized I had no idea what was going through Abbie's mind. I hated not knowing how she was doing or if she was okay. My phone had been strangely silent since Jack's call. The office hadn't contacted me all week. How was Miles, even with Abbie's help, fielding all the requests? If she felt anything like I did, I couldn't imagine how she was managing all that extra work on my behalf.

Stripping off my clothes in the en suite, I turned the shower water to just below scalding, and I tried to imagine what it was going to be like in the office now that we weren't together anymore. If I couldn't fix things, how could I pretend I wasn't hopelessly in love with her?

God. What if she left the company and I never saw her again? The idea of Abbie disappearing from my life made me physically ill.

There had to be a way to fix it.

Two hours later, I arrived at Appeal. I'd texted late last night that I'd be back in town for the start of the business day. Jack had sent me a meeting invite for 9:00 a.m.

I'd texted Abbie a few times, asking to talk later today, but she hadn't responded. Not that I could blame her.

My plan was to bypass our floor completely and head straight to Jack's office. If she hadn't texted me back by the time I was done with the meeting, I would seek her out at her desk.

Jack was on the phone when I entered his office, but something he saw on my face must have signaled that I wasn't prepared to wait.

"Listen, something just came up. Let me call you back shortly."

He hung up as I moved to stand in front of his desk.

"Aiden, sit." Jack gestured to one of his chairs. Not looking to start this conversation off on the wrong foot, I did as he asked.

"Jack, let's cut through any bullshit. Thank you for the no-questions-asked time off. I had a family emergency, and I'm very grateful to have been able to drop everything and get to LA. I know I've royally messed up, and I want to clear the air."

Jack sat back in his chair, resting his hands on the armrests.

Blowing out a breath, Jack began. "Aiden, I can accept your apology. Despite only being here a few months, your leadership is exemplary. This situation with Ms. Summer notwithstanding."

I nodded as he continued. There was a major "but" coming.

"But with the rumors that have made the rounds in the office, the board had to be made aware of the situation. The nature of the rumors was concerning because you've both signed conduct clauses in your contracts. I wish you had come to me first."

My fists clenched where they were resting on my thighs. Jack was right. I should have been transparent with him when I decided to pursue Abbie.

"I didn't want you to be blindsided by a summons from the board before talking with you. Before we plan for the fallout of your actions, I want to hear your side of things. When I hired you, I never thought you'd bring scandal to my doorstep."

The optics of the whole thing were shit, I knew.

Jack continued before I could respond. "Since we're just having an informal discussion, you'll need to excuse my language. But what the fuck were you thinking, Aiden? Do you know how bad that looks for you? For the company?"

The truth was, I wouldn't be able to defend my actions. They weren't logical. Despite my fears about my relationship with Abbie, I had no regrets about my decisions as an adult, except for my behavior in the last twenty-four hours.

My biggest mistake was ending things. Sitting in Jack's office, I wasn't worried about my own job or how much money I could lose. Abbie was all I could think about. And how I had destroyed my right to be there for her.

Abbie thinking I didn't love her sounded a whole hell of a lot worse than finding a new job. My mom's and sister's reckoning clarified my priorities. I knew I could make it through a rough patch in my career, but I wasn't going to make it without her by my side for the rest of my life.

"I don't know where I stand now, but I'm willing to accept the full consequences of my choices. Call a meeting. Let me speak to the board to make sure they understand my commitment to Abbie and Appeal. I believe this can work if they are willing to forgive my lapse in judgment. Please."

Jack narrowed his eyes, searching my expression for something. Hopefully, he saw my genuine remorse for putting the company in a bad position. I felt bad about that, just not enough to change the past or what I was planning to do next. A knowing look came into Jack's gaze.

"Okay, Aiden. I'll call an emergency meeting and let you make your case."

"Thank you." I had places to be and apologies to make. I wanted to wrap this up.

"Look, Aiden, Ms. Summers is on leave for the next two weeks. She had more than enough vacation time accrued to take some time for her decision."

"What decision?" This was all news to me. Abbie wasn't in the office? Then where was she?

Jack gave me a curious look. "There's no way she can return as your EA." Jack held up his hand, knowing that I would be pissed that they'd thought to fire her. "I didn't suggest she leave or that she firing was on the table, so calm down. But I will need to figure out the best way to manage the situation with her input upon her return. She didn't tell you?"

I shook my head no.

That news hit me harder than my own consequences. After witnessing how hard it had been for Abbie to deal with her family issues at the fundraiser, I understood why she was so fiercely determined to make it on her own. I hated the idea that she was in some sort of professional limbo where she had to worry about money more than she already did.

"Listen, Aiden, I don't like to speculate on the personal lives of my employees. But if you want the perspective of a man who's been damn lucky to be married to a very tolerant woman for forty-two years, that young woman loves you very much. She didn't say a single word that could harm you when Linda and I met with her. It could have been a very different type of meeting, and I still believe she would have done what she could to protect you. That type of selflessness doesn't come around more than once or twice in a lifetime. Don't you dare waste it."

Reeling from the revelations of everything I'd missed while away, I stood numbly and shook Jack's hand, leaving his office with a quiet "Thank you. Let me know the next steps with the board."

I didn't think I could feel worse than when I'd arrived home to my empty house. Missing Abbie was a physical pain at this point. But after hearing she'd been put through the wringer with Jack and Linda, the ache in my chest was building brick by brick, threatening to wall me in.

I'd been naïve to think they wouldn't meet with her too about the situation. I'd mistakenly thought that Jack would wait until I was back in the office to pursue the problem.

As I checked my phone yet again, there were still no notifications. Abbie was either ignoring my messages or not in the state to reply to me. I would be running through worst-case scenarios unless I found out where she was.

Before I headed to Abbie's apartment to plead with her to hear me out, there was one person who could help me: Indigo Layne. I'd bet all my money that Indigo knew everything about this. The only question was how generous she was feeling.

Thirty-Five

AIDEN

Upon arriving back on the main floor, I rounded the corner to face the reception desk, where my second dressing-down of the day awaited me.

Indigo looked up from her computer. No hint of shock was visible on her features.

Interesting, so she knew I was coming back today. But of course she did. She had access to our security passes, after all.

Her arms crossed as if to dare me to lay my grievances at her feet. I was sure she would stomp them out with great pleasure.

Once I was within hearing distance, one of her eyebrows rose in a "Really? We're about to do this here?" kind of expression. That was an impressive trick. Her take-no-shit attitude probably kept most unwanted attention at bay, but I was on a mission for answers this morning. Indigo wasn't going to stand in the way of that.

"Hey there, Daddy Aiden."

That nickname had me stopping abruptly and rocking back onto my heels as if I'd been struck. She had achieved what I thought was impossible in my current frame of mind: she'd shocked the shit out of me.

"Excuse me?"

"Oh, Abbie didn't tell you about my little nickname for you? Can't imagine why, DA. It fits, don't you think? You know, with your advanced age and all?"

Fuck. The attitude of this young woman. It was like getting blood from a stone.

"Jesus Christ, Indie. Can we just be serious for a minute? Where is she?"

She looked at me impassively.

"Pardon me, Indie. Jack told me Abbie took vacation time." I injected as much sarcasm into my enunciation of her name as I could. "Is she at her apartment?"

"Are we talking about my best friend, Abbie? The person you left standing alone in your living room in the middle of the night? Or the Abbie you broke up with her over the fucking phone? Wait! Those two Abbies are the same person."

My jaw clenched so hard I was surprised I didn't hear my molars cracking under the pressure. Fuck, I felt bad enough about the way I'd handled everything already. Now here was Indie, applying excruciating pressure to the already gaping wound.

Any other day, I'd give her credit for being such a good friend. Today, I was on the receiving end of her wrath, and it was keeping me the fuck away from my girl.

I took a deep breath to calm the raging inferno of impatience within me. The superior look on Indie's face said she knew exactly what she was doing and was enjoying my pain immensely.

"Yes," I ground out. Okay, not the calm and collected tone I was going for. "I just want to talk to her. I know I need to apologize, but

I can't do it if I can't find her!"

Indie chose that moment to sit back down primly in her chair and turn to face her computer. She didn't look at me as she spoke.

"Well, that's too bad. I'm sure you would like to apologize for all your fuckups. But I don't have any interest in making things easier for *you*. So no, I don't think I'll be telling you anything. Have a great day, *Mr. Sullivan*."

I'd been fully dismissed. However, if she thought that was enough to send me on my way, she was about to find out she was very wrong.

"Indie, of all the times to fuck with me, this is the one time in my life not to do it. I can personally guarantee to become a thorn in your side here at Appeal *if* you don't tell me where she is right now."

She didn't even reward my ill-advised threat with a reaction. She focused on her computer as if whatever she was working on was going to save the world from nuclear warfare.

When it became clear I wasn't leaving, she turned her head to make eye contact as she spoke.

"Bad move, DA. Threatening the best friend is not the way to Abbie's heart and certainly not to get me to cough up any information. Not to mention, I can't imagine you're in HR's good books at the moment, hmm?" Her smile was sickly sweet, knowing she had me there.

She swiveled in her chair to face me once more and clasped her hands on her desk as if she were a duchess. Who was this woman? She managed to look down her nose at me while I stood above her. It was a rare talent.

"Well, let me explain it to you in terms you will understand, DA. You fucked up big-time. I don't give a fuck about this job. I'm only here to piss off my parents. I have a big trust fund. That means I don't have to give a shit about anything you could possibly do. I could walk out the door right now without the slightest hesitation, so don't lower yourself to empty threats to get what you want. Abbie thinks you're a better man than that. Act like it."

Her voice was a hushed whisper, which I appreciated, even if her words were designed to take me apart, piece by piece.

Shit. She was right. I was better than this. I didn't treat others poorly. I'd had enough of that growing up. I felt as if I was simultaneously being chastised by my high school principal and the Queen of England. It was one of the oddest moments of my life.

"You're right, Indie. I am sorry. I'm just desperate to fix it. Please help me."

I matched the quiet tone of her voice. I didn't need anyone else to bear witness to my heart dangling out of my chest either.

She nodded as if I'd at least passed the first of many tests she'd cooked up.

"Thank you. That at least sounded genuine. I can appreciate you're sorry and feeling guilty. But after her meeting with the boss and HR, she's on her own timeline, doing her own thing for the next two weeks. I'm not going to be the one to help you sabotage her decisions."

I dropped my head between my shoulders and closed my eyes in defeat.

"What can I do to convince you to tell me where she is?" I wasn't above begging at this point.

"You can sure as fuck come up with a better idea than just apologizing for a start. You've got fourteen days to come up with the most epic gesture to prove to her that you are in this for the long haul. Only then can you come back to me, and maybe, just maybe, I'll help you. In the meantime, take the time to figure out what the hell you want, DA. If she's not the one for you, then you need to be kind and let her go."

"She is. Absolutely."

The eyebrow of skepticism made its return.

"Okay, well, you think on that for sure and get back to me. All right, DA? And it better be good."

I could tell I wasn't going to get anything more out of her today. She was right that I needed a plan. But I didn't need another millisecond to know if Abbie was the one for me. Every molecule of my being knew that for sure, and some part of me had since that very first day across the park.

"Yes, fine. I will. But when I come back to you, you'd better help me. And could we cool it with the 'DA' shit?"

"I'll be waiting with bated breath." Her tone indicated nothing of the sort. "And we can negotiate the DA title when I hear what you come up with."

"Fine."

She turned back to her computer before quickly spinning back with one more jab.

"Oh, before I forget, don't even think about bugging Emery at the college. I'm sure you could find her contact info quite easily. She's not going to tell you anything either. She's a sweetheart and doesn't need you bugging her. She has a bleeding heart. If you make her feel guilty with your sad, aggressive Eeyore routine, I'll shred you. And then I'll let her three brothers have a go at you. Get me?"

God, I was exhausted by this conversation. The government should seriously get this woman on their payroll. Good thing she hadn't decided to take over the company.

"Yep, got it. I'd say thank you, but this has been agony. I'll be in touch."

"Agony sounds just right, *DA*. Good talk. See ya!"

Now I had to figure out how to prove to Abbie she was everything to me.

The first thing I needed to do was put out the fires at work. Abbie had already dealt more than her share of stress from the fallout of our situation. Regardless of the problem, it never should have fallen on her shoulders to manage alone. As her boss, it was my responsibility to bear the consequences of our actions. It was a major source of heartache for me that things had blown up while I was away.

Feeling sufficiently ashamed after my trial-esque experience with Indie, I had to work to compartmentalize the hurt and pressure within me. I still had the entire workday to get through.

It seemed that the hits were going to keep on coming when I reached my office door to find a nervous Miles glancing between his work and Ethan, who was leaning against my office door and scowling.

Knowing Ethan was here to talk about Abbie, I didn't want to keep him waiting, but I needed to check in with Miles first. He'd had an awful lot on his plate too lately. More than he signed up for when he took this job.

That seemed to be the case for all of us. And it didn't sit right with me that I'd caused so much upheaval for my employees in addition to my personal failings.

"Miles. Everything going okay, considering?" I didn't need to elaborate on rumors I was referencing, nor would I say anything out in the open in the office.

Miles pushed his glasses up the bridge of his nose, his tell for the times he needed a moment to formulate his words.

"Hi, Aiden. Um. Glad to have you back. I have the morning updates for you when you are ready. But, um, Ethan wanted to meet with you first?"

Poor Miles. I had to let the guy off the hook.

"No problem. Let's ease back into things, okay? We can sit down after Ethan and I have a chance to talk, and then we'll make a plan to get me up to speed."

I made my way to my office door, where Ethan stepped out of my way so that I could open. Meanwhile, Miles's surprised expression was followed by his shoulders relaxing slightly.

I just didn't have it in me today to be my usual efficient self. I guess Abbie was right that I could be a little bit of a taskmaster when I was focused. I remembered her laughing in my bed about me having to control everything. My chest ached at the thought of never holding her again.

Shit. Are all the memories going to be this painful?

I gestured for Ethan to proceed with me into my office and shut the door behind us. Not bothering to take a seat, Ethan didn't pull any punches.

"I heard you met with Jack already. How much shit are you in?" He stood in front of my desk with his arms crossed. Clearly, this wasn't a pleasant social visit.

"Goddamn. How fast does gossip get around this place? They should have put that little fact in the job description when I interviewed. I might have reconsidered applying."

Ethan raised an eyebrow. "Are you kidding me? This building is worse than high school, Aiden. This is the biggest scandal that's ever happened at Appeal. You're lucky we don't have rows of chairs set up with the downstairs employees watching your every move like you're on an episode of *The Bachelor!*"

"Does everyone know?" I winced at the thought of my private life being fodder for the masses.

"Yes, everyone. Even the security guards have bets on whether you and Abbie are going to get back together or not." He gave me a pointed look that said he wasn't joking.

"They're *betting* on my personal life?! In what universe is that appropriate?" I aggressively scrubbed my face, hoping I could somehow wipe away this nightmare.

"Well, you'll be glad to know that no one on our floor is spreading it. They are all too scared of you giving us mountains of bids as punishment. No one wants to be the next Phillip. The smaller teams downstairs don't know you well enough to be frightened for their work/life balance. You should really get on that."

Seeing the stress I was surely radiating had somehow softened Ethan's wrath. The corners of his mouth curved upward as he delivered that piece of sage advice.

Too beaten down to continue this conversation while standing, I made my way around my desk and collapsed in my chair. Thankfully, Ethan took the hint and sat down across from me. He already had reasons to look down on me figuratively. I didn't need him to do it literally as well.

"My reign of tyranny aside. Did you come here to say I told you so?"

Leaning back in the chair, Ethan took further stock of my defeated posture. His features softened with what was probably pity, but I'd reached the point where sympathy was welcome.

"Oh, I don't need to say it. You're living it, boss. But as wild as the rumors going around the office are, I doubt there's much fact in any of them. They run the gamut from running off into the sunset to the more sinister theories of true crime fans among us. Things happen when a bunch of creatives get together. How is Abbie with all this?"

"Fuck. I don't know. I haven't spoken to her in days." I spoke through my hands, which were scrubbing my face with frustration and worry. "I fucked up big-time while I was in LA and ended things in a moment of panic when Jack called while I was waiting in the hospital with my niece."

After dropping my hands to my lap and leaning back in my chair, I could see Ethan's eyebrows shoot up in disbelief.

"Oh, shit. No wonder you look wrecked. No offense."

"Yeah. Thanks a lot. I'm well and truly fucked. I need to come up with a plan to get her back and get the pleasure of proving myself to Indie Layne before I can do that."

Ethan winced on my behalf. "Better you than me, man. That girl is scary. There's a rumor that she's a child prodigy trained in interrogation and has been planted in Amado by the FBI as an undercover operative."

Now it was my turn to be surprised. "Really? That's an actual theory someone in the office spoke aloud?"

Ethan waved away my naivety. "You clearly underestimate how starved everyone gets for benign entertainment. You should come to a digital arts dinner sometime. The person with the best rumor that can be verified gets their dinner courtesy of the group. But what are you going to do about Abbie?"

"Well, my plan this morning was to lock myself in this office until I figured it out. But you can see how well that's going." I raised an eyebrow to imply his derailment of my day before it even got started.

"Un-huh. Sorry not sorry and all that. You practically made me an accomplice to this relationship. And since I'd never seen Abbie so happy as the weeks you were together, can I give you some advice?"

I nodded. Maybe Ethan had a wealth of relationship experience in his back pocket.

"Just be honest."

"What?" That was his advice. I needed something spectacular, and this was his contribution?

"Yeah. You gotta start by being honest with yourself about what you're willing to do here. It's easy to make snap decisions in moments of stress, as you've already found out. Figure out what you want here. Then be honest with Jack…"

I interrupted him by mumbling. "I have to face the board in short order."

"Okay, fuck. Be honest with them too. Everyone makes mistakes. Even the infallible Aiden Sullivan. They fought pretty hard to get you here. If you come clean, they'll likely be more receptive than you think. Same goes for Abbie. That young woman is the sweetest person who likely would love to forgive you if you can be truly honest with her. She deserves an explanation and the chance to make decisions together. You're lucky she doesn't seem like the type to hold grudges. Not like that best friend of hers." He actually shuddered.

Begrudgingly, I had to admit that his advice was damn good. I'd been building up all the scenarios in my head when I just needed to face my actions head-on. One fuckup at a time and accept the consequences.

I stood and offered my hand in thanks. "You're right, Ethan. Thank you. I'm glad you strong-armed your way into my office this morning."

"You're welcome. And I'd hardly say I used any kind of intimidation. Abbie helped pick another sweetheart for your EA. Though he's loyal as fuck to you, so you're lucky there. I bribed him with a coffee from Dean's cart."

Nodding goodbye, Ethan made for the door and shut it behind him.

Sitting back down behind my desk, I sent a quick email to my "sweetheart" of an EA and told him to keep my day clear. I needed to figure out exactly what my next steps were and start damage control right away.

The next morning, I found myself in the company's largest conference room facing nine board members and a few of the highest-level executives in the company.

After opening the meeting, Jack wasted no time in directing everyone's attention my way.

"Aiden, we all know why I called this special meeting. Based on the informal conversations I had with several individuals around this table in the past few days, we have almost universally been impressed by your efforts these past few months. That's why we're giving you a chance to make your case here today. So if you would…" He trailed off and gestured for me to take it away.

Steeling myself in case this went downhill fast, I glanced around the room. I noted first and foremost that Indie had got herself an invite to my public reckoning. Truthfully, I would have been surprised not to see her in the room. Unfortunately, my eyes next landed on Phillip, looking smug as if he was about to see me get my comeuppance for daring to point out his legitimate errors as a leader.

Sitting next to him was Ethan, so I knew I had one ally in the room. But if what Jack had said was true, it was possible I could sway the board members my way.

Taking a deep breath, I stood from my seat.

"First, I need to convey my sincerest apologies to everyone in this room for having to take the time out of your busy day to be here. I take full responsibility for my wrongful actions."

Take that, Phillip. When you screw up, you admit it. I saw his smug smile slip slightly in surprise before I continued.

"I'm going to be completely honest with you. I should have gone to Jack right away when I realized my feelings for Abigail Summers. I have no excuse for that lapse in judgment. I can only hope that you will give me the opportunity to prove myself to the company in the future. From the beginning of my time here, I have demonstrated my total commitment to Appeal's success. I would also make the argument that we have seen my efforts, along with the senior teams, speak for themselves in the resulting revenue over the past months."

The next part was going to be the most difficult to say aloud. There was little I hated more than my private business out in the open, but I didn't want to walk out of this meeting without putting all my cards on the table.

"That being said, my poor choices when it came to my relationship with Abigail made me realize that I have neglected to apply one of my steadfast rules to myself in a way that I would never let any employee get away with. For too many years, I have allowed my workload to dictate my life. But these past months, during my relationship with Abigail, I have found myself more energized and inspired at work due to her presence in my life."

I looked to Jack briefly to see how my words were landing. He gave me the smallest of nods, which I hoped meant he approved of my slightly unorthodox approach.

"Maybe I should be standing here ready to tell you that I will end things with Abigail. But if I have learned anything lately, it is that it is better to be up-front and honest with my intentions. So here they are: I plan to continue my relationship with Abigail as long as she'll have me." That bit of self-deprecation got a few chuckles from around the table. "I will do anything the board wishes to rectify the ethical concerns and any conflicts of interest regarding Abigail's position in the company, if you allow me to keep my role. Further, I would work with HR to develop a transparent and detailed addition to employment contracts for inter-office relationships so that this conflict could be avoided in the future. I also understand if you need to make an example of my actions. If you see fit to ask for my resignation as the only way for me to continue my relationship with Abigail, I will offer it willingly."

It was time to wrap it up and throw myself, and my career, at their mercy.

"Ladies and gentlemen, we can't predict who we will fall in love with. But a wise man told me that when we do find that special person, we need to do everything necessary to hold on to them. So I hope in doing the right thing, you will give me a second chance. And if not, I only ask that Abigail not suffer any ramifications as a result of my choices as VP. Please place full accountability on my shoulders. Thank you."

Sitting back in my seat, I didn't hear a word that was spoken for the remaining several minutes to close out the meeting. I should have paid attention, considering my fate was on the line, but all I could think about was getting to Abbie.

Thirty-Six

ABBIE

Driving into the madness that was LA rush-hour traffic, I took a quick sip of my third iced coffee of the day. Navigating thousands of cars, all apparently wanting to be in a different lane than their current one, was not for the faint of heart or the undercaffeinated.

Two weeks of driving down the coast had been amazing and beautiful and sad and lonely, all at once. Having ample time meant I could spend a day or two at each stop instead of hours of driving every day. On one hand, I was proud of myself for actually navigating the conditions of all the misty roads along the Pacific. Driving down Highway 1, I'd learned that some areas of the coast didn't have reception, so I needed to make sure to keep my gas tank full and my caffeine intake up.

I had about two thousand photos to go through for all my efforts and more than one hundred release forms stowed safely in the back seat.

Needing permission to take pictures with people in them meant that I had to ask permission first. The first twenty… okay, forty times, I'd had to approach a person or group to ask if I could take their photo for my portfolio had made me want to vomit on the spot. I hated to admit that each time I asked, approaching the next group got a tiny bit easier.

Masking my sadness was easier with strangers. It still took a lot of energy, leaving me exhausted in the evenings, but it freed me from the worry that I would be scrutinized in any way. I was just some woman taking pictures on the coast. There was freedom in my anonymity.

It was enough to combat the sadness of missing Aiden until night fell. The heavy weight that hit the first few days felt like moving while wearing the lead blanket they put over a patient when taking X-rays. Each step was a siren's call to return to the warm covers in a quiet hotel room.

I caught a break when I got into my new therapist's schedule via a cancelation. Admittedly, I didn't know what to expect from the first appointment, but Sarah, my therapist, was someone who had the knack of immediately putting me at ease. Even just the thought of having someone who knew about anxiety and depression in my corner made me feel a little less overwhelmed by all my emotions. It was great to feel like I had an expert in my corner who would really be able to help.

By the second appointment, my sadness and worry were dragging me down to the point where I explained my breakup and job conflict. The simple act of describing the situation to my therapist helped start cracking the tightly constructed brick wall that had trapped me in the darkness.

It was going to be a lot of work to start to feel better. Maybe because I was in a different place in my life than when I'd first considered therapy, I found that my willingness to do whatever was necessary to help myself had fallen into place.

I'd received a few text messages from Aiden the day he'd gotten back to Amado. Guilt and regret had settled deep in my stomach when I'd decided not to reply to him. I didn't want him hurting, but I wasn't in a state where I could give concrete answers about any part of my life. His final text had been the hardest not to respond to.

Aiden

Abbie, I'm sorry. I've made so many mistakes. I'm going to make things right, sweetheart. I promise.

The term of endearment had cut sharply since I'd realized that I'd never hear him say those words to me again. I reasoned once he got over the guilt of the risks to my job, he would come back to his senses and remember the reasons he'd ended things between us.

I'd forced myself to stop revisiting our relationship through my photos. I had so few pictures of him and had gone over them incessantly the first few nights away from home. I had that first photo I'd taken while he was sitting with his sister in the little café, one of him dressed as Giovanni from Team Rocket at Anime Expo, plus a few cozy selfies I'd taken of us cuddled up in bed.

Obsessing over him hadn't made me feel any better. I didn't want to stay brokenhearted forever. Even if it felt like I would never get over him, I needed to find a way to move on.

When I'd left Amado, I had only wanted to run away from the pain of seeing Aiden again so soon after breaking up and from having to make a decision about my job.

Watching the rugged coastline, the rocks, beach, and sea play peekaboo with the heavy mist that took all day to clear. It was then I stopped running. With my therapist's help and beginner's mindfulness exercises, I was now stumbling toward something new and real.

I'd just need to keep taking it day by day.

Now, two weeks later, my heart lightened as I pulled into the maze of parking at LAX and thought about spending the next week on vacation with Indie and Emery. We'd never before collectively let go of our responsibilities to spend time together.

Dodging the never-ending stream of cars, buses, and shuttle buses, I found my way into the arrival area. I scanned the board for their flight's luggage carousel. From the look of it, the plane had landed about twenty minutes early. Hopefully, they hadn't been standing around waiting for me.

Even though my feelings were still a bit tender, the time to grieve and heal without the pressures of work had given me the strength to finish what I started with my photography project. It was to reward myself through time with my friends.

I walked toward the second to the last carousel, but I couldn't see them anywhere. I checked my phone for texts, but there were none. Odd.

Had they missed their flight? Surely, they would have let me know.

As bags continued to tumble down the chute and onto the conveyor belt, I kept my eyes peeled for my two friends. Did they think I was meeting them outside the terminal?

I ducked my head to shoot off a quick "Where are you?" text to Indie and Emery. I didn't realize I was in anyone's way until a rough voice was right behind me.

"Excuse me."

"Oh, I'm sorry!" I turned around to move, but a warm hand grasped my elbow. My soul momentarily left my body in shock.

"Aiden, I'm supposed to meet Indie and Emery? How are you here right now?"

Speechless, I took in every inch of Aiden that I could see. But he wasn't my Aiden. Oh no, he was dressed as Tuxedo Mask from *Sailor Moon*!

"Hi, sweetheart." There was that name again. Despite my efforts to be strong, I just melted as warmth surged through me with the affection in his voice.

He took a quick look over his shoulder before removing the mask portion of his costume.

"Sorry to ruin the effect. I just don't want to get arrested or taken into some interrogation room before I get a chance to say what I came to say to you."

He chuckled. "I finally convinced the MI6 operative you call one of your best friends to tell me where you were. Part of the plea deal I brokered with Indie was that you would call them right away when I arrived. Can you do that before she reneges on my clemency? I'd hate to see what she's like when someone crosses her on purpose."

Looking down at my phone, I pressed Indie's contact number.

"Hey Abs. You okay? Sorry not sorry to interrupt your reunion moment there, but I couldn't tell you this until I was sure he'd actually shown up. I'm just going to put you on speaker. Emery, say hi. I'm at her studio at the university while she organizes for next term."

"Hi," Emery's voice called in the background.

"I think I can handle it. Why did you want me to call you? Aiden's here."

"I know he is, Abs. Listen, as much as I wanted to unleash hellfire on him, he actually stepped up. For the sake of transparency and all the stuff about being a 'good person' or whatever, I need to tell you that he met with the Board at Appeal."

"What?" I watched Aiden as the horror of that idea sunk in.

"Yeah. I snuck into the meeting. The only thing important to him was that you were okay. And he told them they could fuck off if they didn't like it. Well, it went something like that anyway. Even though I'm allergic to romance, I have to admit, it was pretty amazing. Make sure he tells you about it, okay?"

"Wow. I don't know what to say." I kept staring at him as I listened.

"I just wanted you to have all the facts. We're behind you no matter what you decide to do after you hear him out, remember that. But he's made a pretty good case, so just listen, okay? Emery, say bye."

"Bye, Abs! See you in a week!" Emery called out.

"I don't know what's going on here. But okay, I will."

I ended the call and tucked my phone back in my bag.

He took my hand and brought it to his mouth, brushing his lips lightly across my knuckles.

"Just hear me out before you say anything, okay?"

I nodded, still in shock from Indie's revelation. Why would he have risked his job when he was the one to break up with me to save it in the first place?

"I made an unforgivable mistake. But I'm still going to beg you to forgive me, anyway. I want everything with you, Abbie. A whole life together. Until I met you, I'd only been half alive. I clung to the idea of moving up in my career because it was safe, and I was good at it. I'd prided myself on my ability to take care of problems for my mom and sisters, to protect them from all the terrible stuff we saw growing up. I believed that if I could just get to a point where I was financially secure enough, I wouldn't have to worry anymore."

His gaze swept over my face. The hopeful look in his eyes was heartbreakingly sweet. I couldn't remember a moment where I'd seen Aiden so unguarded.

Before I could figure out what to say in response, he continued.

"Then all of a sudden, I get that call from Claire about Rennie, who is fine, but it was as if some base part of my brain took over, and I stopped seeing anything clearly. I hadn't been that scared since we lost my stepfather to a drunk driver. Claire's call just brought all of those fears back, but this time about losing Rennie. Then, Jack's call about the rumors at the office lit up a blind panic in me. It turned me into the motherfucking moron that broke up with you."

He rubbed his thumb across the back of my hand absently as he chose his next words.

"I knew right away that I had fucked up so badly. But I couldn't stop myself from making the worst decisions possible in those moments. Since the second I was able to calm down, I've been miserable. I've never known real happiness until you came into my life, and parts of me just lit up in ways I didn't understand. Being around you was addictive, and it was like seeing the world in color for the first time. And I handled it poorly at first. Not that I regret anything we've ever shared, but I should have talked to Jack when I felt my resolve to stay away from you wavering."

"Aiden, it was all so new. That's too much pressure to put on yourself. We hardly knew each other."

The emotions that I'd been struggling to contain caused tears to run down my cheeks. The sense of relief I felt knowing he regretted his actions had unlocked the floodgates.

Yes, he had hurt me so badly by breaking things off. But could I really say I would have been able to make the best decisions if I'd been feeling the same level of overwhelming emotions as he had?

I knew a thing or two, or a thousand, about big emotions. Sometimes, they get the better of us, no matter how intelligent or in control we seem.

I could offer him the grace of making mistakes.

"It's true. I didn't know all of you then. But I already knew how special you were. You have been in my head since the very first moment I saw you. So you have to know that I am all in. I love you, Abbie. You were so incredibly selfless in protecting me from any backlash at work. I wish you hadn't felt the need to do that. You have to know that you are the most important person to me, okay? No more heroic gestures from either of us. I'll reign in the overprotective thing if you promise to talk to me. Deal?"

My heart burst with how deliriously happy his words made me. I pulled my hand from his to wrap both arms around his neck, bringing him closer.

Rising up on my tiptoes to reach him as best as I could. "Yes. Aiden. I promise. From here on out, we'll work things out together. I've been yours since that moment I embarrassed myself in your office on your first day. I love you too. Always."

"Always," he echoed. "That sounds just right to me."

Bringing our lips together, he kissed me like he was starving. I kissed him back with the same ferocity, drawing a groan out of him. God, I'd missed his open, unbound reactions to the passion between us. He never stifled his need for me.

I didn't know how long we stood there making out like teenagers. It could have been five minutes or an hour, but we were interrupted by a passerby calling out.

"Hey, man, I didn't know Comic-Con was in town this week. Nice costume."

Breaking the kiss to meet Aiden's eyes, I dissolved into giggles. Aiden didn't really have the best luck with cosplay.

"Oh, I see how it is. You think this is funny, huh? We'll see who gets the last laugh."

His fingers poked into the sensitive part of my rib cage, and he tickled me until I was bent in half.

"Okay, okay! You win. Let me breathe."

Gathering me in his arms, he whispered in my ear, "You're goddamn right I did, Abbie. I'm the luckiest motherfucker in the world right now."

"Oh, come on, now I'm going to cry. Again." I wiped furiously at my eyes as if I could stem the emotions threatening to pour out of me.

"I'm here for it, sweetheart. But if I don't get you into my bed in the next hour, I won't be responsible for my actions. I've had two weeks to come up with some very creative ways to show you how much I love you, none of which can happen in an airport."

"Aiden!" I looked around to see if anyone was eavesdropping.

Laughing with a lightness I'd never heard from him before, he tugged me toward the airport doors.

Before we could reach the exit, a voice called out behind us.

"Hey, man, wait! Do you think I could grab a selfie with you?"

"Oh god, not again," Aiden muttered. Despite his grumpy exterior, he wasn't one to disappoint. "Sure, but make it quick."

The young man walked over to us, handing me his phone. "Do you mind?"

"It would be my pleasure." I laughed. And it absolutely was.

Arranging his face into a grimace-smile hybrid, Aiden dutifully tolerated the photo. I handed the man back his phone.

"So, bruh, you're, like, dressed as Zorro or something? I remember my mom used to love those movies when I was a kid. I remember she kept her old VHS player to watch them."

"For the love of Christ!" Aiden couldn't catch a break.

"I'll get you out of here, I promise. Right after this nice guy takes our picture too." I smiled politely, trying not to laugh.

Aiden rolled his eyes as I pulled my camera out of its bag. This photo was going to be framed. I handed the camera to the man, and we posed for the picture.

"Only for you, baby. Only for you," he whispered in my ear as I wrapped my arms around his middle.

"Okay, Zorro. Say cheese!" the man called out.

Happiness bubbled inside me. I knew with every fiber of my being that he meant it. And that meant everything.

Thirty-Seven

AIDEN

I couldn't stop smiling. I knew for certain that I'd never felt so whole as we walked toward the parking garage and Abbie's rental car.

How could I have been so blind all these years thinking that climbing the corporate ladder was going to solve everything in my life? If I hadn't met Abbie, I wouldn't have realized that I'd been barely living, only existing to work long hours for money that I might never need.

She handed me the keys to the rental car. "I'm so sick of driving, Aiden. So many miles and so many hills along the coast. I'm done."

Even though a little bit of worry ran through me at the thought of all those hours on the road alone, I was proud of Abbie for going after something she wanted.

"Okay, I've been patient enough," she started once we'd buckled our seat belts, and I began navigating our way out of the parking area. "Tell me what happened with the board."

Right, of course she would be worried about my job. She'd tried to throw away her own livelihood to protect mine, after all.

"When I got back from seeing my family, Jack called me into his office and told me I'd have to face the board. Honestly, by that point, I was so consumed by getting you back that it felt like another hurdle before I could get back to what was important. That's you, if you hadn't figured it out by now." I glanced over at her in the passenger seat, quickly giving her a wink.

"You know, now that you mention it, I can see that." Her tone was teasing.

"Good. Glad we're on the same page." My tone was dry before a laugh escaped me. "I basically told the board that I would like to stay, but not if we couldn't be together. I mean, I said it more politely than that, but that was the gist."

"So you didn't tell them to fuck off?" she asked hesitantly.

"What? No! Is that what your menace of a best friend said I did?" I let out a shocked laugh.

"Yep. In those words. What did they say then? I'm nervous now."

I reached over the console to take her hand in mine.

"You are too sweet, Abbie. It's fine, though. No profanity was used in front of the board. They didn't torture me for too long while they decided my fate at Appeal. Basically, my former assistant did such a great job of making me look good to the company that they agreed I should stay on."

"Ha! Right, because I had so much influence over your work."

"Hey, don't doubt yourself. We worked great together. When I wasn't coming up with filthy fantasies about you, anyway."

"Aiden!" Winding her up was too much fun. "What happens next?"

"Well, Jack let me know that I couldn't be your boss anymore for obvious reasons. I'm sure they will have everything figured out by the time we get back next week."

Abbie was silent for a minute. I worried about what was running through her mind.

"Sweetheart, what is it?" I wanted to know what Jack had offered her.

"I don't think we have to wait. I was just thinking what you just told me was the reason Anne and Grace got in touch with me a couple of days ago. Apparently, Jack is starting a B Corp solely dedicated to marketing for nonprofits. They offered me a role on their super-small team. I've been too overwhelmed to really consider it. But now I see that it would be a perfect solution." Abbie's tone was enthusiastic.

I squeezed her hand gently. "But is that something you'd want to do? Because you know I'd absolutely support your going back to school for photography."

"I'm not ready to decide yet. But my favorite thing I've worked on at Appeal was the nonprofit stuff. So I think it would be a good fit."

"Whatever you choose, I will support you." Abbie had no idea the lengths I was willing to go to contribute to her happiness.

"I know, Aiden. Thank you." I looked over at her again to see her smiling. A real smile that met her eyes.

"I love you," I said again because I couldn't help it. Her smile widened further.

"Love you too." God, it felt good to hear her say it back.

I would have a hard time not saying it every time I looked at her now. She'd just have to get used to it.

I drove us to a tiny house near Long Beach, explaining on the way how Indie and Emery had canceled their flights so that I could spend the week with her.

After pulling into the driveway of the adorable little beach house, we walked hand in hand to the front door. By unspoken agreement, we opted to leave the luggage in the car.

Unlocking the door, I led her into the center of the house. Watching her take in the space, I grinned when she realized we were surrounded by bouquets of pastel purple roses, their heady scent permeating the space.

I watched her take in the beautiful display. Taking Abbie in my arms once more, I kissed her sweetly.

"To match your hair," was all I said, feeling bashful for the first time in my life. The shrug that accompanied my words was so unlike my usual formal posture that I'd perfected for the office. I was looking forward to the man I could be with Abbie.

I kissed her again.

"The thing I love most about you, other than your caring and tender heart, is your determination to be true to yourself. I have learned so much from you. You have reminded me of all the precious ways there are to find joy in life. All the teasing keeps me on my toes."

"Aiden, I think you need to say something snarky, or I'll be crying all week."

"The invading part comes next, sweetheart." I gave her a hungry grin, and she rolled her eyes at my terrible joke. "By the way, I want to see all your photos. From this trip and everything else you haven't shown me yet. But later. Much, much later."

"I don't even know if they are any good, Aiden." She ducked her head.

I put both hands on her cheeks to bring her gaze back to mine.

"Hey, now. If they are even one iota of the quality you took on our work trip, they are going to be brilliant. Sonia Martinez still sends me an email every time they use one of your photos."

"Fine. I'll show you some later. Right now, I need you to take me to bed. I missed you so much." She pressed herself against me.

"I missed you more, baby." I absolutely had. "Let me show you how much."

Leaning down to capture her mouth with mine, I picked Abbie up in my arms and carried her down the hallway to the master bedroom to make good on my word.

By the time I could think again, the sun had long set over the ocean. We'd missed it completely. I'd be sure to make it up to her over the coming days.

With Abbie on my chest, listening to my heartbeat, as she said she liked to do because it calmed her, I felt a deep sense of contentment that I had realized nearly too late.

"Abbie, I have something else I wanted to talk about."

In response, Abbie sat up, this time letting the sheets fall away from her torso. Her legs bent to press her bare shins against my side.

My gaze locked on her breasts. God, she had no idea how much power she wielded over me. Body and soul, everything about her seduced me. I continued staring at those luscious mounds and their tight pink nipples. I'd just made love to her, and I already wanted her again.

I loved that she felt safe enough to be comfortable in her own body like this. It showed me how far we'd come.

But how did she expect me to concentrate now?

"Hey, eyes up here, buddy. You wanted to say something, remember?"

My gaze darted to her briefly and then down to her chest again.

"Ah, what? Right. I did say that, but now…" I leaned toward her, determined to capture one of those tight buds in my mouth.

"Oh no! You talk. Then we can talk about how you are taking me to Disneyland this week." She squirmed backward slightly to keep me on track.

"Baby, I can't talk about Disneyland right now. My thoughts are as far from family-friendly as you can get."

"We can get back to those thoughts in a minute." She winked.

I reined in my baser urges, promising myself I only had to wait a few minutes and I could get back to worshiping her body.

"Actually, I have something important to tell you first. I've started seeing a therapist. Her name's Sarah. We've had two virtual sessions already and have set up an appointment in person for when I get back."

Her revelation caused me to sit up and gather her against me, hugging her tightly.

"I'll support you every way I can. But I'm really glad you have a professional you can trust that you can talk to." I sobered, pulling back enough that I could look into her eyes. "I'll never be able to make up for my part in all the hurt you experienced."

"Hey. I already forgave you." She brought her mouth to mine to kiss me gently. "It might be a complete disaster, but I'm learning how important it is to try. So I'm going to."

"Move in with me," I whispered against her lips.

Pulling back to see her face, she looked back at me with so much surprise and pleasure it took my breath away.

"What? That's what you were going to say just now?"

"Move in with me. I know it's too soon and crazy. I know we have a lot to figure out, and I'll understand if you say no. But I don't want to go another night without you in my arms. I want to live with you, Abbie." I was not above begging.

"But…" I didn't let her finish before rushing to continue.

"I don't care where we live. I can sell the house, and we can get a condo downtown or…"

"Yes, Aiden."

"I'll drink whatever coffee you make. And never complain again. Hell, I'll make the coffee for the rest of our lives just if you just say…"

She'd started giggling at my ridiculousness. It took a minute for me to realize that she'd agreed.

"Really?" I searched her face for any hint of doubt. I didn't want her feeling rushed, but I wanted us tangled up in each other like this every night.

"Yes, Aiden. I want to live with you too. My lease is up in a couple of months. We can start planning. We're both going to be busy, so I want all the time I can get with you." Her eyes were alight with happiness. "And yes, I'll take you up on your coffee offer."

"Me too, baby." Suddenly, a wave of emotion hit me. I felt pressure building behind my eyes. "We're really doing this. You're mine, and I'm yours."

"Yes, Aiden. We belong together, and I always want to do whatever it takes to make it work."

"We will, sweetheart. I'll always fight for us."

"I love you, Aiden." I'd never tire of hearing those words from her.

"I love you too, Abbie. And as someone who loves you so much, I'm always going to be looking out for your well-being. Right now, I'm worried you're getting cold."

"Really? Is that right?" She eyed me with faux skepticism.

"Absolutely. I think the situation requires attention." I looked down at her breasts once more, pulling her back under the covers. "They say the best way to warm up is through shared body heat. We'd better do that immediately."

"Well, if it's what 'they' say, then who are we to argue?"

Content Warnings

This book is intended for an 18+ audience only. It contains material that may not be suitable for some and is intended for a mature, adult audience. It contains adult situations and explicit sexual content.

The following topics are present in the book: an on-page character's experience with chronic anxiety, brief on-page emotional abuse by a parent, death of a parent and step-parent (off page), references to the effects of financial instability in childhood, Type 1 diabetes in a child, a medical emergency related to the Type 1 diabetes (only on-page representation occurs after the child is in stable condition) and brief mentions of body image.

Your well-being is so important to me. Please feel free to contact me at info@violetkavery.com if you are uncertain about the suitability of any of the subjects mentioned. I would be happy to provide additional information.

SNEAK PEAK:

Not a Chance

One

INDIE

"You will cease being an embarrassment to this family immediately."

My father's face was a mottled red now that he had been ranting for over twenty minutes. I sat in my usual chair in his study, enduring my quarterly "scolding" as Emery liked to call it. It was my parents' chance to review every detail of my life that didn't fit into their opulent and ruthlessly managed world.

Every four months like clockwork, I was summoned to the family home to hear what a disappointment or disgrace I was to the Layne name. The descriptors varied. Sometimes I was a disgrace. Occasionally, I got by with being a mere disappointment. My favorite variant came out last time I was in this seat when he called me a pariah. That was a new one.

I had been cataloging the contents of my father's study as he droned on. My mother had never been one for subtlety when it came to showcasing their wealth. I noted a change from the heavy maroon and gold wallpaper that had dominated until this past spring. Combined with the thick brocade drapes and their tasseled ties that she insisted every room have, she'd managed to make the 10,000 square foot mansion feel much smaller.

My mother was in her Marie Antionette Era. I wouldn't be surprised if she had brought in a designer straight from Paris and said, "Think Versailles and… Go!" Pre-revolutionary France circa 1788, was strong in her choices. I wondered if my father ever got a sunburn working in his office around all these gold accents.

"Indigo, are you listening to me?"

"Absolutely. I am a stain on the good name of Layne." Was I rhyming now? "I'm not fulfilling my obligation to this family by making a name for myself in this world. Or at the very least, using the considerable privilege that has been afforded to me my entire life, to contribute to the collection of companies that have supported the Layne name for so many generations."

I hadn't been listening to a single word other than a vague awareness of when he would finish talking. But we had all been through these motions so many times over the years that I had his Speech of Disappointment memorized by now.

"Well, er, yes."

I started to pull myself out of the deep cushions of the chair I was sitting in. It seemed urgent to make my exit as quickly as possible.

"I will strive to do better, Father. So if that is all…"

"Sit."

I sat. His tone had changed from the minor inconvenience of acknowledging he had a daughter at all to one he reserved for a corporate merger.

Maybe being labeled a pariah had more consequences than him picking up a thesaurus.

"You've had four years to do better and not a single thing has changed. That stops now."

"I'm sure I don't understand?" I peered at my mother scrolling intensely through what was no doubt a very urgent email from her legal practice partners. That or some juicy gossip from the country club their circle belonged to. Both happenings warranted the same level of concentration.

"Do not pretend that you there isn't at least a modicum of common sense in that brain of yours, Indigo. You did not earn a double degree on full scholarship by being an idiot. Stop being obtuse. It doesn't become you."

Ooookkay… We were on new territory here. A zing of trepidation had my spine straightening. Just when I thought Gerald Layne III couldn't surprise me anymore, he proved me very wrong.

He was good at pretending silence meant tacit agreement so he continued without regard to any answer I might have.

"Watching you insist on working a job outside our family's corporations with absolutely no advancement, despite being vastly overqualified, has shown me that I must take matters into my own hands. I refuse to allow you to embarrass our family any further."

"But, Father, I told you. I wanted to earn my way in the world, not have things handed to me."

"Oh yes, I am very aware of your well-practiced speech about 'pulling yourself up by your bootstraps.' That excuse has grown tired and flimsy, a mere veneer for the rebellious nature you seem to think we have forgotten wreaked havoc on our lives in your teenage years."

I stared at him, no rehearsed reply at the ready this time. Had he seen through me so easily all these years? I'd believed my anti-nepotism speech had appealed to his sense of work ethic. Had I been wrong?

"Here is what is going to happen next. You will resign from your current position at that second rate advertising company. We have shares in a large sports media company. I know the CEO from my Yale days. He is going to do me the favor of taking you onboard as a communications team assistant."

"Wait, wait. I'm trying to catch up here. What do you mean quit my job? I can't just quit."

"You can and you will. Unless you want me to put the full weight of the legal resources I have at my disposal to challenge your grandmother's will? I know you haven't touched the money she left you at eighteen, but I have the ability to drag this out for years. Do you think you can win if I take you to court?"

As much as I'd like to think that he would be more afraid for the reputation of the family, there is a part of me that believes he would actually do this. He could probably get the courts to seal the proceedings and figure out how to come out on top somehow.

I hadn't played this game with them for this many years to walk away with nothing. I wanted to make a real difference with this money. I was only eleven months away from properly getting started.

It galled me to admit he'd won this round. The consolation prize can be that I would be free of their control this time next year; a heartening thought.

"Fine. I understand. Where am I going?"

Acknowledgements

I can't believe *Not As Advertised* is out in the world. My first little book baby. I'm amazed at what it takes to write and publish a book. I have learned so much. It's been quite a ride and I'm grateful for all the support I've had along the way.

Firstly, to the experts that taught me many things about the writing and revising process:

To Dakota Nyght, for your developmental editing. Thank you for taking my baby-author fever-dream and helping me shape it into a narrative that I can be proud of. You are so thorough, and I learned a ton. Thank you for keeping me accountable to my characters and helping me grow as a writer. Without Dakota, there would have been a heck of a lot more "smirks" in this book. She helped cut the smirking down to an acceptable range.

To Jennifer Herrington, for your feedback in my second round of developmental editing (as a former high school English teacher, I'm a huge believer in feedback), copy editing and proofreading. I so appreciated your thoughtful feedback and helping me refine my ideas. Your encouragement kept me going through the revision stage.

To Sandra Dee of One Love Editing, thank you for going above and beyond in your proofreading to make my manuscript ready to publish.

To my Alpha Readers, Hollie B., Danielle G., and Julianne H., thank you for liking this book in its original state and encouraging me during all the stages along the way. Your comments helped shape this book and I am truly grateful. I hope you are ready for Indie's story next because you are all mine forever!

To my son, who taught me everything I know about Pokémon. You brought the Pokémon universe into our lives six years ago but your enthusiasm made it come to life. I love how you pursue your interests with your whole heart.

To my daughter, the inspiration for Indie's character. I can't wait to see you take on the world, missy!

My biggest thank-you has to go to my husband, who didn't blink when I said, "Er, by the way, I kind of wrote a whole book and want to indie publish it." Your support and encouragement through each stage of this process helped me so much when I'm deep in the throes of imposter syndrome or struggling with revisions. You never doubted I could make this happen. I wouldn't have made it to the finish line without you.

And finally, to you, my readers. Thank you for taking a chance on my debut novel. I hope you fell in love with Abbie and Aiden's story as they fell in love with each other. I'm so grateful to you for reading!

About the Author

VIOLET K. AVERY has been a fan of all genres of romance since she picked up her very first romance novel at the age of sixteen. It was like a whole world opened up before her and she hasn't looked back since. While her professional background is in education, writing a novel has been a lifelong dream.

Her characters deal with real issues and difficult emotions. Their HEAs are a celebration of how far they've come as individuals and as partners.

When Violet's not writing, she's spending time with her family and cleaning up the latest chaos created by their two adorable rescue dogs.

Let's Connect!

Want to talk about all the bookish things?
I'D LOVE TO HEAR FROM YOU!

EMAIL: info@violetkavery.com

WEBSITE: www.violetkavery.com

INSTAGRAM: www.instagram.com/violetkavery.author

TIKTOK: www.tiktok.com/@violetkavery.auth

FACEBOOK: www.facebook.com/profile.
php?id=61560409499379

www.ingramcontent.com/pod-product-compliance
Lightning Source LLC
Chambersburg PA
CBHW030935120726
47906CB00002B/574